The Scrivener

The Third Cragg and Fidelis Mystery

ROBIN BLAKE

Constable • London

CONSTABLE

First published in Great Britain in 2015 by Constable
This paperback edition published in Great Britain in 2016 by Constable

Copyright © Robin Blake, 2015
1 3 5 7 9 8 6 4 2

A CIP catalogue record for this book
is available from the British Library.

ISBN 978-1-47211-601-7 (paperback)
IBSN 978-1-47211-602-4 (ebook)

Typeset in Sabon by Initial Typesetting Services
Printed and bound in Great Britain by CPI Group (UK) Ltd, Croydon CR0 4YY
Papers used by Constable are from well-managed forests and other
responsible sources

MIX
Paper from
responsible sources
FSC
www.fsc.org   FSC® C104740

Constable
is an imprint of
Little, Brown Book Group
Carmelite House
50 Victoria Embankment
London EC4Y 0DZ

An Hachette UK Company
www.hachette.co.uk

www.littlebrown.co.uk

In memory of my mother

Beryl Mary Blake née Murphy

1918–2012

She is foremost of those that I would hear praised.

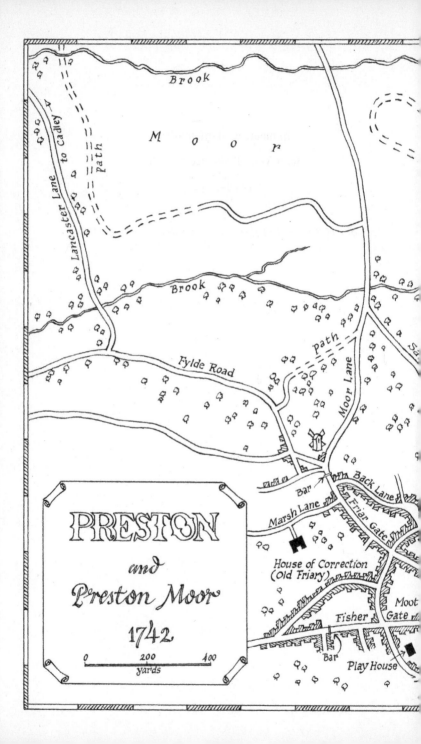

PRESTON
and
Preston Moor
1742

0   200   400
yards

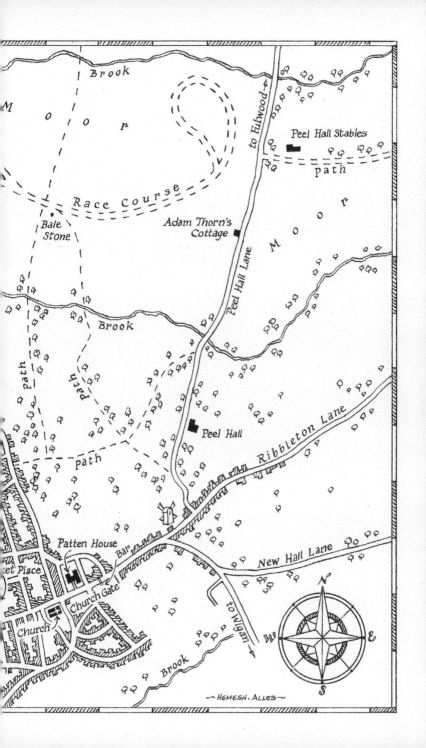

Brook

M o o r

to Fulwood →

Peel Hall Stables

Race Course

Bale Stone

Adam Thorn's Cottage

Peel Hall Lane

M o o r

Brook

path

path

Peel Hall

Ribbleton Lane

path

Patten House

Bar

New Hall Lane

...et Place

Church Gate

to Wigan

Church

N

W   E

S

Brook

~HEMESH·ALLES~

Chapter One

∞

STANDING IN THE doorway, with medical bag in hand, Luke Fidelis peered into the shadowed room until its main features had resolved themselves: the outline of the low pallet bed; the man's gaunt, ghostly face looking steadily upwards; the pale hand resting motionless outside the covering blanket. The doctor went to the window and pulled aside its rough curtain to admit more light but, in doing so, let in a damp gust of air from off the Moor. Picking up a stool beneath the window he placed it beside the bed and sat, depositing his bag on the hard mud floor. The prostrate man's breath was shallow but absolutely regular, as if he reposed with not a single care. Fidelis spoke in a low voice, his mouth close to his patient's ear.

'Adam. Adam Thorn. I am Dr Fidelis come from Preston at your wife's request to attend you. Do not fret about the fee – there won't be one.'

Fidelis touched Adam's brow and found no fever. He felt his wrist. The pulse was even, and so was the heart, which he checked by pressing a silver listening-trumpet to the chest, and placing his ear on the earpiece at the narrow end. Next he felt with soft fingers around the contours of the skull. Finally he drew a candle end and tinderbox from his bag, lit the wick and leaned across to peer with the help of its light upon Thorn's face. His skin was dry, his lips cracked, his eyes staring in his head. Fidelis shielded the light from those eyes for a moment with his hand, then revealed it again, and noted how the pupils contracted in response. By this he determined that the automatic processes of the body were continuing as normal. But was the man conscious? Was he aware?

Standing, he returned to the window and dropped the curtain again, then crossed back to the door and ducked his head as he passed into the main room. Here a child of three sat playing on the ground and a baby grizzled in its cot, while another sucked at the breast of its mother who sat on a rough bench beside the cheerless fireplace. This was the month of June, in the year 1742: far from cold enough to make a fire essential for warmth, though this had not been much of a summer in the north country, and the doctor knew that Dot Lorris, his landlady, would have a log burning back at his own room in Preston, and glad he'd be of its comfort when he returned home on this damp day.

'You have no fire, Amity,' he observed. 'Do you not cook?'

Amity Thorn unplugged the child from the nipple, and let it loll back against her shoulder, dreamy with milk. With her free hand she pulled up her dress to cover the breast.

'I'll cook tomorrow. There's not the fuel for a fire every day. I have to learn thrift, with him the way he is . . .'

She cocked her head towards the inner room.

Fidelis sat down at the worm-eaten table on one of the room's two chairs. To learn thrift, you first had to have something to be thrifty with, he thought, looking around the bare room.

'Well,' he said, 'I've had a look at him, and now I want to know more about how it happened.'

'I wasn't there. I didn't see.'

'But you found him, didn't you?'

'No, it was John Barton that found him and brought him home.'

'Barton the horse-coper up at Peel Hall Stables?'

'That's him.'

Barton's yard had been part of a dismantled estate that centred on Peel Hall, now more or less of a ruin on the edge of the Town Moor, to the north-east of Preston.

'Where did John Barton find him, then?'

'Out on the Moor, lying on the ground. It were near the Bale Stone. John Barton saw him and heard him moaning.'

'When was this?'

'A week ago now.'

'A week? Has he been lying like that for a week?'

'Yes, except the once, he's neither moved nor talked, just sort of twitched sometimes. He gave over the moaning after we'd got him to bed.'

'What about food and drink?'

She nodded to the table where a spoon and porringer lay.

'He's been taking soup and milk off the spoon. I have to pull open his mouth, mind, but he's been taking it.'

'Did you not think to send for me or another doctor before this?'

'I had old Mother Greenshaw in to look at him – the wise woman. She told me what to do – if he'd take it, give him the soup and milk and porridge and maybe a beaten egg and some brandy, and just wait, and he might come round. Was that all right, what she said?'

'It's not bad advice. My own would not have been very different. Did you follow it?'

'As well as I could, only he's not come round, has he? He just lies there staring, staring. It frightens me.'

'You said he was like that "except the once". What do you mean by that?'

'After he'd been in bed a bit, he seemed to revive, like. He started groaning again, then I could make out some words. Babbling he was, and I saw he was moving one of his arms.'

'What was he saying? Did he give any indication of what happened to him out there?'

'No, he was only thinking about how he felt. I came to feed him and he kept on lifting his hand and trying to bat away the spoon, saying "rich, rich" meaning the food was too thick for him, or too flavoured, I guessed. The same way, he couldn't stand too much light, or noise.'

'As if all his senses were heightened? It's a possibility.'

'Well he were grateful to me. He kept saying I was precious to him. It were touching.'

'So how long was it before he lapsed into the state I have just seen?'

'He went on with his babbling for an hour or more. Then when I went back in to him he was lying still again, just breathing quietly. I talked to him but it seemed he never heard. When the baby screamed, he never flinched and he made no more fuss about the food I gave him. He's been like that since. If he doesn't come round, what am I to do? There's no one here but me and the little ones.'

'Have you no family anywhere – someone who can come and help?'

'There's nobody, only Peg.'

'Peg?'

'His eleven-year-old niece that he's had charge of since her ma's died.'

'Does Peg live here?'

'Not now. She's gone into service as a housemaid. He thought the world of her, him. But we couldn't afford another mouth to feed even before this. Now I don't know what I'll do.'

'Can you make any money on your own account?'

'There's the little I get from selling my eggs at market. We have a few birds. But most of our money came from bits of work he did, for farmers and gardeners and such. He got some good pay at harvesting, which we put aside to help us through winter. But I had to pay the wise woman, and then there was the brandy to get. So I've had to spend.'

'If you're very short you can go to the parish. You'll be allowed something until your husband recovers. I'll put in a good word with the church warden. In the meantime, I'm afraid there is nothing more to be done except to care for him with warmth, food and drink, as best you can.'

'What is the matter with him, doctor?'

'He has suffered a seizure of the brain. There is also an injury to his skull, a lump from a bang on the head. It's difficult to know which came first. The head injury could have caused the seizure but just as likely he got the lump by falling down after the seizure. They very often do happen over their own accord, seizures. They make the sufferer insensible so that he falls to the ground.'

'But Adam will get better? If not, I don't know what I'll do.'

'I regret it's impossible to be sure, Mrs Thorn. He might come round at any time, or stay the same indefinitely. Or thirdly, I am sorry to say, he might suddenly be taken from us, without any warning whatsoever.'

She rose and deposited the child in the cot beside the baby, and went to a side table. There she took a scoop of cold gruel from a pot and poured it into the wooden porringer. After placing this on the table she picked up the eldest child from the floor and balanced it upon her knee to feed it. The somewhat battered and dented spoon carried the gruel inefficiently, but by working fast she managed to force a high proportion of the thin liquid into the mouth, though the child pulled faces and wriggled with dislike of its dinner.

'It will be terrible to live with such uncertainty – if we can live at all.'

Suddenly the child on her knee twisted around and one of its hands grabbed at the spoon. In surprise Amity let go and it fell, clattering off the edge of the table and bouncing to the floor. Immediately Fidelis stooped to retrieve it.

Before he returned the implement to her he glanced at it. Though damaged, pitted and discoloured, it had once been a fine piece of spoonery – the shank heavy and with the remains of chasing along its length, and a nobbled end, as of some figure now unrecognizable. He turned it over: there were four black pits on the shank, square in shape and black where dirt had compacted in them. Amity held out her hand.

'Give it back, doctor, if you please. I must feed him quick or he won't take it at all.'

'Of course. Here.'

He gave her back the spoon and, for the time being, thought no more about it, while they talked of Amity Thorn's hard life, and of what she could do to alleviate it.

'Remember to go to the church warden as soon as you can,' he said firmly, thinking at last it was time to leave. Then his eye caught sight again of the spoon, which lay in the now empty porringer on the table.

'And there is one more thing I should mention,' he said, pointing at the bowl. 'That spoon of yours looks silver. I fancy, if you clean it up, that it will raise a sum of ready cash in town.'

She picked up the spoon and turned it in her hand.

'This dirty old thing? Adam brought it back a month ago, off the Moor. You don't mean it's worth something?'

'It might be. Where did he get it?'

She shook her head.

'As I say, I reckoned he must have picked it up off the Moor, or somewhere about. It were all muddy and stained: just an old spoon, as I thought, though he did say different.'

'What did he say?'

She gave a short, melancholy laugh.

'That it was treasure. "Treasure trove, is that," he said. He's done it before – come home with some brass farthing he'd found on the Moor and said it was treasure trove. He was bitten with this idea that some old soldier had buried a big lot of silver up there a hundred year ago. But he'd got himself killed and the secret died with him, so the silver was never found. Adam even told me he'd gone to Preston to talk to the Recorder to prove it were true.'

'The Recorder? Mr Thorneley?'

'I don't know his name. Adam kept on about looking for it but I just said if poor folk ever do find such things they get them taken off them, as sure as the Gospel, so what's the use? He shut up about it after that but I'll give you a warrant that he never gave over looking for it. That was his way.'

Fidelis looked carefully at the underside of the spoon's shaft, and showed it to her.

'Well, I don't know about any treasure, but I am saying that, if these pits on the underside of the handle are hallmarks, then it really is made of silver – assayed silver. Maybe that's what Adam was trying to tell you when he was saying "rich" and "precious". He was talking about the spoon you were feeding him his gruel with.'

Her face fell. She had imagined she was the precious one. The doctor gave her back the spoon.

'So you can exchange it for some silver coin. Do it, Amity. Buy some wholesome food for the little ones, and for Adam too. Marrowbone broth is always recommendable.'

Fidelis got to his feet and returned for a last look into the darkness of Adam Thorn's room. As before nothing there moved, only two tiny winking sparks of light from Adam's eyes, which every few moments were extinguished and immediately reappeared.

Then he returned to where Amity was, bade her good day and

ducked out into the drizzle. He put his hat on his head, turned up the collar of his coat and strode off towards town.

You, the reader, might very well suppose, in order to recount all this to you, that I, Titus Cragg, must have been loitering about under the dripping eaves of the Thorn house, peering in through chinks in the window sacking, listening at the door, committing the conversations I heard to memory. In reality, I was not: all that afternoon I was in Preston town, more than a mile distant from the Thorn house, seeing to my practice as an attorney-at-law and my work, which I hold to be equally important, as the town Coroner.

But how, you must ask, can words describing an event in the world seem so convincing – so real – when their author never him-self observed the event? It is a question that often bedevils a law court. It doesn't matter how many times witnesses are warned to tell only what they directly saw and heard, they will run on with the gossip of chair-carriers, and chambermaids' tittle-tattle, taking the jury with their story-telling into the realm of speculation, and soon into a state of firm belief. Many poor innocents have gone to the gallows in those realms and states of fantasy, but their necks were not the less truly broken for it. Stories and lies are so knitted together with facts and experience that they can never easily be disentangled – not in a law court, and not in life.

In a book, then? That, you may suppose, is my aim. The events I have just described were long ago and nobody's neck depends on whether or not you believe my writing. Nevertheless, let me reassure you: every word of what I have written about Dr Fidelis's visit to the Thorns is true, for I had it on the following evening detail by detail from the lips of the doctor himself, and assiduously committed it to my journal before going to bed.

And the reason I set it down here will be clear in due course.

Chapter Two

∽

ARLIER IN THE same day I had been in my lawyer's office, adjoining my house on Cheapside at the very heart of Preston, when a note arrived by hand of a messenger. It came from the merchant Phillip Pimbo of Fisher Gate, one of Preston's leading sellers of gold and silver, and was written in the hand of Pimbo himself.

'*Dear Cragg*,' he wrote, '*I would be extremely obliged if you would attend me tomorrow morning at your earliest convenience. A matter of wrong-doing has arisen which taxes my understanding, and I am very much hoping you can provide me with some legal assistance in the matter. I am &c. Phillip Pimbo.*'

Pimbo was a bachelor who lived with his mother at Cadley, and was noted for large ears that stood at right angles to his head. I had last spoken with him at any length about three or four months earlier, when we had met at the postal office in the Shambles. We were waiting to take our turn at the clerk's window, and he was talking volubly about his partnership with a scrivener from Liverpool called Zadok Moon, and of their plans to provide Preston, for the first time, with something like a bank.

Looking back across the span of more than thirty years, it seems incredible that we in the country had managed affairs for so long without our own local banks. We still relied on strongboxes to keep our money safe, if not on secret holes in the ground, or sliding panels in the wainscot. Goldsmiths had long accepted plate and other valuables on pawn, and some also took in cash on account for safe keeping, or on security, which they could then use to finance their pawnbroking advances. In my grandfather's day it was done by the age old tallystick method: the amount of the deposit would be marked by a certain number of notches on the stick, which would be split along its length, one half to be kept by each side of the bargain.

Beside these moneylending goldsmiths, here and there a scrivening lawyer could also be found (Moon of Liverpool was, I assumed, one of them) whose specialty was the investment of money on behalf of clients in interest-bearing Exchequer Bills and Debentures, or in the profits from voyages, toll-roads or waterways. But so far no one in the County had taken the next step. No one had put these two services together and formed a bank that took in deposits at interest and issued notes to the public.

Pimbo had brought with him to the post office a brown and white spaniel pup, and as he talked – which he did a great deal – he repeatedly called it to attention – 'Suez! Sit! Good boy!' – in order to treat it to little balls of bacon fat, of which he kept a supply in the pocket of his coat. Between treats Suez persistently attacked the buckle of my shoe making it hard to concentrate on what its master was saying.

But his burden was the tale of how he, Pimbo, had persuaded the Corporation, a couple of years back, to place in his keeping the entire fund of money built up and laid aside to pay for the Preston Guild, the grand civic celebrations which were held every twenty years, and which as he spoke would be coming round again in six months. Pimbo puffed out his chest like a cock pigeon.

'It is a great amount, very great, for the Guild is no cheap undertaking.'

'I hope your strong room is safe, then,' I said in a jocular tone.

'Safe?' he boomed. 'Yes, my friend, it is indeed safe. Imagine the Bastille of Paris lodged inside the Tower of London. That would not be safer. My strong room's door has inside it a gate made from thick bars of iron, closed by a pair of strong locks of the latest design. Safe? I should just like to see the man who can dig or break his way into there. But no matter, because the large part of a bank's money is not in the strong room.'

'Oh? Where is it?' I asked, shaking the dog off by waggling my foot.

'Circulating, Titus. Money is like blood, the town's blood, and if it does not circulate, corruption and death must follow. So we cannot let it rot in some locked hutch in the Moot Hall, or even in my strong room, merely waiting to be expended. We must put it to work and let it engender more of itself.'

'You told the Corporation this?'

'Certainly, and they were so well convinced, you might say they were converted. They saw the light.'

'And agreed to your proposal?'

'Yes. It was an excellent stroke of business, was that.'

'So what do you do with this money?'

'That is my partner's concern. He places it at a profit in money-making enterprises – the importing of sugar, spices, or tea from China.'

At this point a stranger waiting just ahead of us, a prosperous looking farmer from somewhere towards Clitheroe, turned and tapped Pimbo on the shoulder to get his attention.

'And what, Sir, if the enterprise breaks and the town wants its money?' he wanted to know.

Pimbo looked flustered for a moment, but quickly recovered his confidence.

'No, no, that cannot be, not at all,' he said wagging his finger. 'You would sooner break the Rock of Gibraltar. At all events, we furnish promissory notes. Each is redeemable by the depositors on demand for a particular sum of money. The total of promissory notes is the total of money they have entrusted to us – which in this case, as I say, is a tidy amount. They shall also, of course, be in receipt of interest at 4 per cent.'

The farmer leaned back a little, with eyes half closed, assessing the proposition as he might a ram at market.

'I'll allow it's a clever scheme, to use another man's money for your own profit. But I won't say I approve it. Suppose you send me fifty head of sheep for pasturing out, like. Well, you may allow me the shearing but you'll want the animals still picking grass in my field when you come back for 'em. You'll have a good deal to say to me if I've sent 'em off to breed in Yorkshire, never mind China.'

Pimbo's upper body deflated, as boasting gave way to earnestness. He appealed to me.

'Our friend doesn't understand. Money is not sheep. What a banker does is to follow the Bank of England in London: takes in money – *nota bene*, not sheep – pays interest and meanwhile puts the money to work by lending it at a greater rate of interest. If he can get the better rate, there's nothing wrong in that.'

'But,' I replied, 'is not the Bank of England something of a special case? Firstly it lends to the government, which is rather a safe transaction, and secondly it issues notes payable on the spot "to bearer". To call yourself a bank you will have to lend your money to general enterprises and issue notes on the same basis. Can you stand the risk?'

'Oh! Of course, of course! I have no doubt.'

Pimbo puffed out his chest and protruded his lips.

'If there be a Bank of England in London, and a Bank of Scotland in Edinburgh, I can see no reason why not a Bank of Lancashire, you know, or even a Bank of Preston. Moon, for one, believes we can safely issue bank notes redeemable by the bearer.'

He turned back to the farmer, who was puzzled.

'When the notes are payable "to bearer", Sir, it means anyone who happens to have such a note in his hand can go to the bank, you see, and on presenting it receive full value in gold and silver there and then. In that way, paper can be used in place of coin.'

The farmer considered this proposition for a moment, then said:

'And why would any man want to do such a thing?'

'Because the note is so much lighter on the pocket, man, so much easier to transport than the coin.' Pimbo rubbed his hands with glee. 'It is a very safe scheme, depending on the issuer's confidence, and Mr Moon is very strong in confidence. Very strong indeed. There is demand for this, I am certain of it, and the day is coming when my partner and I shall establish Preston's first dedicated banking office.'

His remarkable ears, the twin beacons of his fervour, had begun to glow red. The farmer, however, shook his head in grizzled scepticism.

'No,' he declared with emphasis. 'Folk like their gold and silver too much. Change it for paper? They'll like as change a clog for a cloud.'

I recalled this conversation on the morning of our appointment as I walked the short distance to Pimbo's Fisher Gate premises. These were yet far from resembling what we now think of as a bank: in fact, the place was still a working goldsmith's shop, with two counters, running away from the door to the right and left – the left hand counter being reserved for valuing, buying and pawning, while the right was for selling items in precious metals. At the far end of the shop, facing the street door, there was a cashier's desk protected by bars. Here sat Robert Hazelbury, the Chief Cashier, with writing stand, cash box and brass scales on the desk before him. In the wall at his back, a bookcase sagged under a load of thick ledgers, and there were doors to the right and left, one of which led to the smithing workshop and the other to Phillip Pimbo's private business room.

I walked up between the two counters to the cashier's cage, where I passed the time of day.

'How do, Mr Cragg?' he replied.

'Mr Pimbo asked me to call,' I said. 'A legal matter.'

Hazelbury jerked his thumb up and over his right shoulder at Pimbo's door. The words *Phillip Pimbo Esq.* were painted on it in a plate-engraver's script, below which hung a sign, written on pasteboard in block capitals: *ENGAGED AND NOT TO BE DISTURBED*.

'He's been closeted behind that sign since before we opened, before I had even arrived myself.'

'He is alone?'

Hazelbury shrugged his shoulders.

'I hear no voices. Happen he's writing.'

He rose from his stool, stretched, and stepped up to the door. He gave it three firm knocks with his knuckles, then waited with an ear cocked. There was no answer from within.

'Mr Pimbo?' he called with his lips close to the door panel, 'I have Mr Titus Cragg here to see you.'

There was still no reply and he gave a second knock, twice as loudly. Hearing nothing, he took a step back.

'Strange. Perhaps he's dropped asleep.'

'Or is taken ill,' I ventured. 'You had better disregard that notice and go in, Mr Hazelbury.'

Hazelbury turned the door's brass knob and pushed on the door. It did not move. Hazelbury turned to me with an impotent look.

'It's locked. What should I do, Mr Cragg?'

'Unlock it,' I replied. 'And with dispatch.'

But unlocking could not be done with dispatch. After a search for a duplicate key had failed, a boy was sent into the alley that ran along the side of the shop. He climbed onto the sill of the barred window that lit the room but, as he reported half a minute later, the window was shuttered and he could see nothing inside.

Next, Arthur Benn the locksmith was fetched to come and pick the lock. He made sure that we onlookers admired the mystery of his craft as, with much muttering to himself, he assessed the thickness of the door and then, removing his hat, put his eye analytically to the keyhole. He had with him a leather roll containing, as we saw when he now unrolled it, a range of instruments shaped like miniature hayrakes. He meditated on these for a few moments before selecting one, which he introduced into the lock. With eyes shut, he twisted it this way and that, blindly seeking the position that would turn the lock. After a minute or so of failure he picked out another hayrake, which also failed, as did the third, fourth and fifth hayrakes. Finally he stood back, uttered a curse, and rolled his lock-picks up again.

'Key's in lock on t'other side. There's your obstruction, and I can't push it out. If you'll have my advice, you'll break the door.'

Watched by a craning audience of shop customers and passers-by, it took two men, a crowbar and a mallet to break in. They were recruited from a house-building crew at work a few doors along the street. With Hazelbury visibly wincing at the damage, they drove the crowbar between the door and the lintel, then levered it until the wood creaked and gave out a few sharp cracks. An instant later, with the sound like a gunshot, the frame splintered and the door was freed. One of the workmen pushed at it and the door swung open. There was a momentary pause in activity as two dozen eyes focused on the interior room, then the workmen and their mob of attendants surged through the doorway. But as soon as they had done so they stopped again, letting out a collective cry.

'Oh!'

It was a spacious room, with a large sash window on the side wall to the left. In the wall facing us, behind Phillip Pimbo's writing table, was a fire grate with a handsome marble surround, in which lay a heap of cold ashes. A second door stood between the window and the fireplace while, hung on the walls, were two suites of engravings: one showing a waterside city, perhaps Venice, and the other a set of Hogarth's *A Harlot's Progress*. But it was the writing table – or rather what lay across it – that had brought the crowd up short: a man's body face down and motionless.

He had pitched forward from a position on the other side of the table, for his head lay towards the door. Two things could be seen immediately: he wore an expensive silk coat, edged with golden braid, and he displayed a black blood-caked hole in the top of his bald head. The great quantity of blood that had flowed from the wound had swamped the desk and dripped to the floor. Although his face was downward and turned to the side, I could clearly see that it was Phillip Pimbo: his visible wing-like ear betrayed him instantly.

By now the room was crowded with a rabble of people. Few, in my experience, can resist the breaking down of a locked door, and those who had gathered around the breakers-in – customers of the shop, and others drawn in from the street – were pressing through the doorway now, to see what was inside.

'We must get these people out of here,' I called to the Chief Cashier, hurrying to the window and opening the shutters.

It could not be done in less than two or three minutes, and not without barging and pushing, as everyone present took the chance to get a good look: even if they lacked the curiosity themselves, a man would be flayed by his wife, and a woman by her neighbours, for coming home without a full account of the corpse.

At last all had gone but one: a young woman dressed in the plainest clothes, without even a hat, who had fallen to the floor. I knelt beside her and found that she was bleeding from the head.

'We must have the doctor,' I said, rising and closing the damaged door as best I could. 'Hazelbury, will you send out to fetch Dr Fidelis?'

But Hazelbury had not even seen the injured woman. He stood staring, his face chalk-white, at the corpse across the writing table.

'There is nothing a doctor can do, Sir,' he said in awed tones. 'I perceive Mr Pimbo cannot be alive.'

I took him by the arm, turned him and pointed to where the woman lay.

'It's for her, Hazelbury. She was hurt in the crush. Will you send the boy? Running, mind! We should see to the living before the dead.'

I put my hand to his back and gave it a push to hurry him on his way. Then, while I waited for Fidelis to arrive, I crouched beside the woman and tried to talk to her. But I hardly knew what I was saying, so extraordinary were the circumstances of the room: Pimbo with a hole in his head and his blood and brains spilling out, all behind a locked door. Meanwhile the woman was groaning gently but saying nothing.

After a few minutes, Luke Fidelis bustled in, having been found by the messenger at home. He seemed not in any way affected by the presence of a corpse across the table, merely glancing in its direction, before kneeling beside the injured woman and inspecting her face. As soon as he did he uttered a cry of surprise.

'Well, well, it is Amity Thorn, that I saw at home only yesterday. Amity? Can you hear me?'

His patient had begun to recover herself. From her clothes she was evidently very poor but her poverty did not conceal the other notable fact about her: she was extremely pretty. Carefully Fidelis helped her to a chair and, loosening the ribbon of her bonnet, took it off and examined her shapely head. She had a cut about the temple, and the beginning of a swelling on her cheek.

'It wouldn't do to have you falling into the same condition as your husband, Amity. But I think you have escaped lightly.'

He brought a piece of clean lint from his bag which he folded and pressed against the temple, securing it with a few turns of a cloth bandage around her head and brow.

'There. That will serve. So, how is it with you now, Amity? Can you speak? Can you say what happened?'

Her voice was faint but her meaning was not confused in any way.

'Well, I followed the crowd into the room but there was such elbow banging that I was off my balance when a gentleman violently crashed into me, and down I went to the floor. I knocked my head that hard I think I fainted.'

'And now?'

'My head, it does ache a little, but my thoughts are clear.'

Fidelis briefly held up three fingers before her eyes.

'How many fingers did you see?'

'Three.'

'Good. Did you come into the shop today about that spoon I wonder?'

Grasping both hands he helped her to her feet.

'Yes, doctor, to pawn it.'

'Well, perhaps it had better wait for another day, after what's happened here. Can you sit quietly for a few minutes in the shop? I shall willingly take you home, but first the Coroner and I have a little business to conduct.'

He inclined his head towards the corpse across the desk. Amity Thorn took the point and nodded, though a little gingerly.

'Well, I'd be glad of a few minutes' rest before I get off home, doctor, for I am right dazed.'

When she had carefully replaced her bonnet, Fidelis opened the door, guided her out and settled her securely in the cashier's chair.

He rejoined me with Hazelbury himself and for a few moments the three of us jointly and in silence surveyed the fatal room. Then Fidelis approached the body and began a superficial examination, bending to peer at it from various angles, laying a hand on the cheek and lifting the shirt to feel the flesh of his back.

Pimbo was lying, as I say, in such a way as to indicate that he had been standing at the table before falling forward onto it. His feet were still in contact with the ground, his arms were up and lay on the table's surface with the hands resting one on each side of the shattered head. The hands were empty but on the floor, a few feet from the desk, lay a pistol.

'Well, his brains appear to have been blown out by a pistol shot,' Fidelis said casually, as if remarking on a change in the weather. 'It will have been an instantaneous death.'

He stooped to pick up the pistol and looked it over as I turned to the Chief Cashier.

'Do you know of this pistol, Mr Hazelbury?'

'No, Sir,' said Hazelbury, his voice slowed by shock. He was still trying to grasp the implication of what had happened. I went on,

'Mr Pimbo had asked me to come here this morning for a consultation, urgent he implied, about some legal worry. Can you help in any way with that?'

'A bad do, is this,' was the best Hazelbury could manage by way of reply, still shaking his head slowly from side to side. 'A very bad do.'

'Well, that is certainly an accurate statement,' I agreed. 'But the harder question is not what it is, but why? Was Mr Pimbo in some trouble?'

But Hazelbury's mind was elsewhere. His mouth hung slightly open and his eyes were glassy with tears. I took him by the elbow, steered him towards a chair and sat him down. When I returned to the corpse, Fidelis had placed the pistol on the surface of the desk beside a powder flask that lay there, and was examining the floor around and under it.

'What do *you* make of it, Luke?' I asked. 'One must suppose he shot himself by accident whilst loading the pistol.'

My friend was staring upwards, with particular attention to the ceiling.

'But I wonder why he would happen to be loading a pistol in his office before breakfast.'

His eyes darted down again, and cast about on the floor in the area of the table.

'Well then, he meant to do it,' I persisted. 'Such is not unknown in a man that suffers great reverses – in his business, for instance.'

'It is better,' said my friend, 'to consider what we can find out by looking.'

He stooped and looked once under the table, then returned to the dead man's side and began to examine him closely around the head. After a minute or two of this, he straightened and began to walk around the room with his gaze fixed on the floor.

'Where the devil is it?'

'Is what, Luke?' I asked.

He looked at me as if surprised that I was not able to share his thoughts.

'The wig, of course. What's happened to his wig?'

'Perhaps he left it at home.'

'I doubt it. Just look.'

He was standing at the door now, pointing to the floor at his feet.

'Here's a smear of blood and it is, what? Eight feet from the corpse. I noticed it as soon as I came into the room. How do you think it got here?'

'The injured woman, Amity, was bleeding.'

Luke gestured to his right.

'Yes, but she was lying over there. You can see where she bled. This here is not her blood, it isn't fresh.'

'Who's blood is it?'

'Pimbo's, naturally. You are not very sharp today. I have an idea it was smeared on the floor from his bloodstained wig, which is why I want to know what happened to the wig.'

'Why must the blood be from the wig?'

Luke tipped his chin in impatience at my evident stupidity.

'Because he was wearing his wig when he died, Titus. Obviously.'

In three strides he was back beside the goldsmith's corpse. He beckoned me to his side and seized Pimbo's head in both hands.

'See here?' He tilted the head. 'The pistol was fired upwards into the jaw. The bullet passed through his mouth and brain before coming out at the top of his head.'

From the two wounds he indicated to me – one about an inch and a half from the point of the chin, the other in the dome of the cranium – this indeed looked a likely case.

'So he held the pistol like this, and pulled the trigger,' I said.

Jutting my chin, I held a forefinger pointing upwards at a spot immediately in front of my Adam's apple.

'He might, if it really was him that pulled the trigger,' agreed Fidelis. 'But I think there's a counter indication. Look here, on the cranium, where the ball came out. Blood has spread or spattered over the skin. I would think that would be the effect of his head being covered with a wig. Had there been no wig, the blood would have flown entirely away from the head.'

'I see that. But why does it cast doubt on this death being by his own hand?'

'Because of the wig, Titus. We do not have it. The wig is missing.'

Before I had time to fully consider this point, another voice had joined the argument.

'And so is his dog missing,' said Hazelbury.

Turning in surprise, for I had quite forgotten Hazelbury was there, I saw that the Chief Cashier was revived, and looking considerably more alert.

'What dog, Mr Hazelbury?' I asked.

'Mr Pimbo's terrier, Sir, Suez. It came to the office with him every day, without fail. It must have been here today, though I do not see it.'

The remembrance of Pimbo's bothersome dog came back to me, snuffling and yelping around my shoes at the post office. I turned, intending to relate this to Fidelis, and saw that he had again begun to prowl around the room and was now standing in contemplation before the oak door beside the fireplace, which I now noticed was very slightly ajar. Before I could speak he had pulled it open.

'What's in here? Ah! The strong room.'

The open door revealed a second very different sort of door immediately behind it – an iron-barred gate, such as is commonly used at Newgate and other prisons to prevent escape. In this case the purpose was a contrary one: to bar entry to any that did not have a key or, in this case, two keys. The gate was secured by a pair of formidable locks, above and below an equally large ring-handled latch.

'Aye, it's the strong room, is that,' confirmed Hazelbury.

'So I see,' said Fidelis. 'And what does it contain?'

A voice booming behind us forestalled the Chief Cashier's response.

'Our treasure, Sir! Or so it better. I mean the Corporation's treasure.'

We all turned and saw the resplendent figure of Mayor Grimshaw filling the doorway.

'To be even more specific,' Grimshaw went on, advancing into the room, 'I expect it to, and trust it will, contain our finances for the coming Guild.'

Despite this confident assertion the Mayor's lips were rigidly pursed, as if braced against unwelcome news. He advanced into the room and looked over the corpse of Phillip Pimbo, like a man happening upon the remains of a dead horse beside the highway. He wrinkled his nose.

'We have just had word of this at the Moot Hall. Shot himself, has he?'

'It seems possible,' I replied, 'though from a Coroner's point of view we will need to know why he—'

Grimshaw sharply interrupted me.

'I don't much care about your point of view, Cragg. You may rummage around looking for your causes and motives, if you have to. *I* must think only of the safety of that money, which is *my* duty. When a man does away with himself, it stinks of one thing – his failure in business. In the case of this goldsmith, such a thing makes me sorely and severely uneasy. Sorely and severely.'

The Mayor went to the strong room gate and peered through its bars. The room was windowless and dark, and he could see nothing more than some shelving and the presence of a number of stout chests. Pointing his finger through the thick bars he addressed Hazelbury.

'I want your reassurance that the town's money is safe inside one of those chests? Is it? Is it?'

'Well, Sir, that is not quite such a simple matter as you may suppose—'

'SIMPLE?' roared the Mayor. 'This is not a matter of simple! It is one of very grave consequences. Will you please get the gate open, so that we may look for our money?'

Hazelbury bowed his head, in a mourning way.

'That isn't a simple matter either, Mr Grimshaw,' he said almost in a whisper. 'For I do not have the sole power to open this gate. It has, as you see, two locks. Here at the office we have but one key, and Mr Pimbo keeps the other.'

Chapter Three

∞

ROBERT HAZELBURY DARTED out of the room and came back a moment later with a brass key at least four inches long. He went to the strong room door, fitted the key into the lower of the two locks and turned it. The mechanism made a sound like a plop and the lock was released.

'So where's Pimbo's?' barked the Mayor. 'Fetch it and we can get this door open.'

'That would be irregular, Sir. Without Mr Pimbo the strong room cannot be opened. That is our strict rule here.'

Grimshaw was quick to propose a way around this problem.

'As Mayor, I shall take the responsibility upon myself. Fetch the other key, Hazelbury, and I shall act Pimbo's part.'

Hazelbury shook his head, and stood his ground.

'Even if I had both keys I am not authorized to act by myself. It must be Mr Pimbo who turns the upper lock.'

'He's right in law,' I put in. 'Pimbo's key must only be turned by Pimbo.'

Grimshaw swung towards me and pointed at the corpse on the desk.

'Has it escaped your attention that the man is *dead*, Cragg?'

'Then you will need a magistrate's sanction, at the very least, to overturn the rule.'

'That is easy. I am a magistrate, Cragg. I am Chief Magistrate. I hereby give myself permission.'

'I do not think you can, with any legal propriety. Mr Pimbo's locked property is now under the protection of his executors, and at this stage we do not even know who they are.'

But Grimshaw was not prepared to let legal nicety get in his way.

'Be damned to that. I must find that key. Hazelbury – help me!'

We all began to search the room. The key was not in the dead man's pockets. It was not on his writing table. It was not in any of the drawers of the pieces of furniture in the room. After a few minutes we admitted defeat.

'Pimbo has spoken to me of a business partner,' I said, as we now stood uncertainly around the body, which still lay where it had been found. 'One Moon, whom I believe to be a money-scrivener. Might he have the right of access to the strong room? Might he have a key?'

'Moon, you say?' growled Grimshaw, turning to Hazelbury. 'I remember Pimbo mentioning him when we talked about our investment. Said he was a very sound man. He must be sent for immediately, Hazelbury.'

Hazelbury flapped his hands to indicate a negative.

'Like yourself, Sir, we in the shop have heard of Scrivener Moon, but we have never seen him. I don't believe he has ever been in Preston, and I'm sure he could never have had a key to Mr Pimbo's strong room. Never.'

Grimshaw persisted.

'I must speak with him nevertheless. Where does he live? Not in Liverpool I hope.'

'I understand he does. Mr Pimbo sometimes goes there – I'm sorry once again, *went* there – to hold discussions.'

Deliberately the Mayor paced up to the wall, where he found himself face-to-face with a scene from Hogarth's *Harlot's Progress*.

'Liverpool is a cesspit of vice and double-dealing,' he said, more declaratively than ever. 'I detest the place.'

I said, 'It's strange, is it not, that Moon, so often and so publicly spoken of by Pimbo as his business partner, should not have been known here in Preston.'

Grimshaw was still looking at the engraving, his eyeballs moving from side to side to take in every detail. He produced a silk handkerchief and began mopping his brow.

'I don't call that strange, I call it suspicious,' he said. 'Pimbo lies shot dead by his own hand and we can't get into the strong room. There is cause for suspicion in that, even before we begin looking where it may fall. But when we do, I suggest that our suspicion will fall naturally upon Moon.'

He turned and began walking up and down, still sorely agitated. I noticed that he trod unheeding in the pool of blood left by Amity Thorn. This reminded me of her presence in the shop and, catching Fidelis's attention, I mouthed her name. He nodded and moved towards the door. I followed as the Mayor talked on.

'We must learn more of this fellow,' he was saying. 'Who knows of Mr Pimbo's affairs? We must speak with his mother, his lawyer.'

'His dog would help us too,' murmured Fidelis as we escaped out of Pimbo's business room and into the shop. 'If only we could find it.'

I took this to be a facetious remark and was surprised when Fidelis asked in the shop if anyone had seen the dog. None had.

'But where is Amity?' I asked, not seeing her in the chair where she had been resting.

'She's gone,' said a fair, well-made young man in an apron who stood leaning against one of the door-cheeks of the workshop. This was the shop's journeyman goldsmith, Michael Ambler. 'She felt better and is walking herself home, or so she told us.'

'I should fetch my horse and catch her up,' said Fidelis, making for the door.

'So you should, Luke.'

I followed him into the street where, to tease him, I added,

'Amity is certainly too pretty to be allowed to walk home without assistance.'

Fidelis was good-natured enough to laugh.

'True. But also a blow to the head can have a delayed effect and there is nothing more I can do to help you here, not for the time being. We will talk of Pimbo's death later. I must take a proper look at the body, but not while the Mayor holds the field. And you should take some interest in what his mother has to say about the soundness of his business. You will be speaking with her?'

'Yes, and searching his home for the strong room key too, if I can.'

'Therefore let us meet at nine at Plumtree's.'

I returned to the shop where Ambler was beckoning me. I crossed the shop and went into the room where he worked all sorts of metal, from gold to pewter, beating, bending and casting it to make anything from a snuffbox or a watch-case to a punchbowl. The bench at which he worked stood under a window giving light from the ginnel. On either side of this window were clipped his tools in a stratified array: both soft and hard mallets, planishing tools, shears, stamps, rasps, files, and many that I didn't know the name or function of. On the bench itself he was working a circular piece of silver, hammering it with infinite patience to raise it from flatness to the shape of a bowl.

The apprentice clerk to whom I'd nodded as I walked through the shop had looked fearful – pale-faced and with wide eyes – at the thought of the chill shadow that Pimbo's death had suddenly cast over his future. But Ambler's handsome face expressed neither surprise nor sorrow. Such is the effect of shock, too, sometimes.

'How is it with master?' he asked, as he picked up his mallet and began once again to work the metal. 'What said the doctor?'

'That he is dead, Michael.'

'Ah.'

Ambler swivelled around and stared at me, his eyes bright, and said with a lift in his voice as he returned to his work,

'She's a bonny one all right, is Amity Thorn.'

I could only agree, while thinking Ambler spoke like a simpleton, though I knew that he wasn't one.

'And she's got a bonny silver spoon, an' all. She was showing it around, saying she'd come to ask master its worth. He won't be telling you today, says I, not if what we hear is right.'

He was talking rapidly, though his voice was confidential, almost a murmur, so that I had to strain to hear him over the popping of his mallet.

'So, says she, will *you* tell us? So she gets it out and I looks at it close, and it's a nice old spoon. I mean, proper silver, no question to it, and so-called an apostle spoon because the knob, which we more politely term the finial, is the cast figure of an apostle. Worth a good shilling or more is that, says I, and it's aged, too, such as some old antiquary would pay good money for. Where'd a poor girl like you get such a valuable? says I. She won't tell me. Just says she'll be back when we open again for business.'

'Her husband's had an accident and can't work,' I put in. 'She is looking to pawn it to raise some money, I believe.'

'Oh, aye, likely she will. If the owner doesn't come forward and do her for larceny.'

'Larceny?' I was taken by surprise. 'What do you know of larceny?'

Ambler stopped tapping.

'There is fair play and foul play, Mr Cragg, and I know what it is when a somewhat costly object is in the hands of a pauper.'

I waved my finger.

'Now, young man, you know no such thing. It is presupposition.'

'Well she was not born with it in her mouth, that's certain. So where *did* she get it?'

I shrugged.

'What concern is that of mine, Michael? Or of yours, since she has not yet offered it for pawn. Leave these suspicions until she does, if she does. You have more pressing concerns here, I would have thought.'

We heard the Mayor's voice as he and Hazelbury emerged into the shop from the inner room.

'If the key's neither in his desk nor his cabinet nor his clothing,' I heard Grimshaw saying, 'and if you, Mr Hazelbury, do not have it, it must be at Pimbo's house. I shall send Mallender there immediately to conduct a search.'

I excused myself and went out to join them. The thought of our sergeant-constable, as clumsy in manner as he was in speech, turning the Pimbo house upside down, was not a congenial one. He would have little regard for the distressed mother, and even less for her servants.

'Mr Grimshaw,' I put in, 'we may spare Mr Mallender the trouble. I must go out to Cadley myself today. Allow me to enquire about the strong room key and if necessary have a look for it. It may be that a thoroughgoing search by the constabulary will be unnecessary.'

Grimshaw shot me with what he may have thought a penetrating glance, then grunted.

'Very well, Cragg, I'll leave it to you. But I shall require your immediate report.'

He swept from the shop and I returned to the inner room, bringing Hazelbury and Ambler with me. We found every drawer and cupboard open and its contents hastily emptied onto the floor after the Mayor's attempts to find the missing key. The body too had been lifted up and deposited on the floor. I asked Ambler to send the apprentice out for a dust-sheet which, when it came, we draped over the late Phillip Pimbo. I then instructed the Chief Cashier to get the apprentice to wash away the blood and to have the door of the business room repaired so that it could be securely locked. Finally I picked up the pistol and powder flask, which still lay on the writing table.

It was a small weapon, fit for a coat pocket or a bedside drawer, with a curling somewhat bulbous grip and a stumpy barrel. I thumbed the hammer so that, in an easy, silken movement, it came into the cocked position. Then with a bare touch to the trigger I released the hammer. Its flint flashed against the frizzle, there was an instantaneous faint crack as it hit the pan, and the gloomy business room was charged with a scintillating flicker of lightning from the sparking flint.

'This would be better locked up at my office,' I told Hazelbury. I slipped it into my pocket with the flask and stepping out of the shop turned homewards – and dinnerwards.

Fortified after a meal of mutton stew with dumplings, and gratified by half an hour's conversation with my dear wife Elizabeth, I rode out to see old Mrs Pimbo at Cadley. The villa, Cadley Place, that her son had built some eight or nine years before, stood a little way back from the road, and had two gates, with the legends 'In' and 'Out' painted on them. The drive was in the shape of a shallow horseshoe, at the top of which stood the residence. It was a house of some pretension to the latest architectural fashion, though by no means so big as to support more than three servants living under its slate roof. It boasted four high sash windows in its front, two on either side of a porch supported by elegant columns, a further floor above and an attic floor with three dormer windows for the servants.

One of these, a scrawny maid hardly older than a child, opened the door to me in a markedly timid way. I asked for the mother of Mr Pimbo.

'Mrs Pimbo, she's in the salon,' she told me.

'Then will you tell her I am here to see her?'

The girl looked flustered. She hesitated, glancing over her shoulder into the hall behind, so I added by way of encouragement,

'This is Coroner's business. I would be obliged if you would announce me without delay. It is a matter of importance.'

She bobbed and blushed and opened the door wide for me to enter.

'I'll show you the way, if you please, Sir.'

I was conducted into one of the front sash-windowed rooms. It was a parlour, though it was easy to see why a man like Pimbo would want it referred to as a 'salon', for it was papered all over, and furnished according to the mode – that is, more sparsely than Elizabeth and I would consider homelike. A pair of settees was ranged facing each other on either side of the fireplace with a low tea-table of walnut wood between them; an escritoire of the most fashionable design stood between the windows; and a brass-faced clock in a tall inlaid case was mounted against the wall opposite the fire, giving out a sonorous tock.

By the time I had taken all this in, the maid had silently made herself scarce. Alone in the room, old Mrs Pimbo stood before the clock and was examining it intently with her eyes. Not having previously met this evidently retiring lady, I found her to be small and stout, and dressed in the fashion of two reigns ago. I put her age at about sixty-five.

I announced myself.

'Good day, Mrs Pimbo. I am Titus Cragg, Coroner of Preston.'

Though she heard my words, Mrs Pimbo did not turn to greet me. Her attention remained fixed on the clock.

'I cannot imagine who has brought this in here, this ... machine?' she asked in a faint, wondering tone. 'Was it you?'

I moved a little way into the room.

'No, madam. Your son, perhaps. Is it newly bought? It is certainly handsome.'

'You say it is handsome? I do not. I don't like it. I don't understand it. What did you say it is for?'

'Surely you know that it is a clock!' I said.

'A clock? Is that what you call it? A clock. A clock.'

She was musing over the word, as if testing its soundness.

'Yes,' I said, 'for telling you the time, you know.'

I at once realized my mistake in persisting with this. Someone who does not know a clock when she sees it is unlikely to benefit from having the matter explained.

'For telling me the time?' she repeated.

'Yes.'

At last she turned and acknowledged my presence.

'So you! Who are you? What's your name?'

'It's Titus Cragg, madam,' I repeated. 'I am the Coroner.'

'And have you come to tell *me* the time?'

'Not exactly. I—'

'Fiddlesticks! What's the use of telling the time, if not exactly?'

The transition from remoteness to sharpness in her tone disconcerted me.

'What I meant was—'

'No, Sir! No! Don't excuse yourself! I do not like the time. I do not like being told it, either exactly or, or . . . or not. So kindly be off with you!'

She raised her arms and showed me the flat of her hands, as if to ward off an evil spirit. Then she spun around and went towards the fire, where she perched on one of the settees and sat silent for several seconds with her gaze resting on her knees, seeming to compose herself. When she raised her eyes again, she took in my presence anew, as if I had just entered the room.

'Oh! A stranger! And who are you?'

'Cragg, Titus Cragg,' I told her for the third time, moving now to sit on the facing settee. I thought that I may as well broach my business, however unexpected the result may be. 'I have come about your son.'

She shook her head.

'My son. He's dead.'

'Yes. I am very sorry.'

'Don't be. It was the smallpox, you see, but so long ago and he was only a young man, unmarried as yet.'

'No, madam, I mean Phillip Pimbo, the goldsmith.'

'Oh! Ha! The goldsmith, you say? I suppose that is right. My husband is certainly a merchant in gold, jewels and such stuff. All trinkets and trumpery! I wanted a gentleman to marry but I only got a bauble-monger.'

'Forgive me once more, I am referring to your *son* Phillip.'

'The boy, is it?'

Her voice became peevish, as of one overburdened with cares.

'What do you mean by referring to the boy? What do you *mean*? Scrapes is it? Scamping off again? Rolling his hoop under horses? Stealing apples? Such a boy for mischief! What's he done now?'

'No. I, er, well, I am sorry to say that he—'

The door catch snapped and a woman, whose age I put at a little above thirty, bustled in. She wore a plain dress and cap, and a wide belt around her waist to which was hooked a ring holding several keys. The two most noticeable things about her, however, were first that her face and figure were strikingly beautiful, with a strong nose, deep black hair, dark eyes and wide, full mouth; and second that she wore her left arm bandaged and in a sling of soft leather.

'I'm sorry, I was detained at the kitchen door,' she said. 'I'm Miss Peel. I keep the house. You should not have been shown in here, you know. I cannot imagine what possessed that girl. She's new to us, but it is no excuse.'

I rose and bowed first to Miss Peel, then to Mrs Pimbo, and turned back to Miss Peel.

'I'm afraid I specifically asked to see Mrs Pimbo. Perhaps I intimidated the girl – unintentionally, of course. I am the Coroner, you know.'

I took a sideways step towards her and continued in a lower voice.

'Might I have a private word with you instead, Miss Peel?'

Compressing her lips together, the housekeeper stood aside to let me out. I bowed again to Mrs Pimbo, who was now looking placidly puzzled, and so left her. Miss Peel followed, locking the door behind us.

'You shut your mistress in?' I asked.

'For her own good. She goes a-wandering else.'

Miss Peel led me across the hall, along a short passage and into a smaller and more old-fashioned stone-flagged room.

'I am fortunate enough to have my own parlour in this house,' she explained. 'Please sit.'

The parlour was furnished in plain style with a beechwood work-table and two upright chairs tucked under, a dresser and a couple of high-backed fireside armchairs. She gestured towards one of these and hanging my hat over its arm I settled myself there. She sat opposite me.

'You have seen the condition of Mrs Pimbo,' she said. 'It is quite impossible to speak sensibly with her, so I am afraid you will have to explain your business to me.'

'Do you not already know why I've come?'

'I have not the slightest idea.'

'So you have not heard the terrible news from town?'

The muscles of her face tightened fractionally, and the eyebrows arched.

'No. What news is that?'

So I told her gently that Pimbo had been found dead in his

business room. I said nothing about the pistol, or his wounded head, which made her response very singular: she emitted an involuntary cry, something like a mirthless laugh, then clapped her free hand to her mouth.

'Oh! Did he murder himself?'

'What makes you ask that, Miss Peel?'

Her eyes flashed this way and that and then looked down. She withdrew the question.

'I . . . well, I don't know. I suppose he didn't. I suppose he was taken ill.'

'Forgive me, but it so happens that he was not. It pains me to tell you, but I must. Mr Pimbo died violently, from a gunshot – a pistol.'

'Oh,' was her only reply.

There was a silence while the clock on her mantel ticked nine or ten times. I studied her face. It betrayed nothing. Whatever that sudden explosive sound had been – a laugh or a cry – she had subdued the emotion behind it.

'For how long have you kept house for Mr Pimbo?' I asked at last.

She got hold of a spring of her hair and pulled it down the length of her cheek.

'Five years. Ever since his mother began to be . . . as she is.'

'I wonder: had Mr Pimbo been particularly given to melancholy in recent days? Had he given any indication that he might try to end his life?'

She shook her head, as she wound the hair around her forefinger.

'Not that I observed, or heard.'

'Had he been worried or anxious? Melancholy? Had his manner shown any change?'

She let go of the hair and straightened her back a fraction.

'Not towards me, Mr Cragg. Not towards me.'

In repeating the phrase her voice sounded a new expressive note – with just the slightest hint of bitterness. I leaned towards her, shamelessly performing a familiar lawyer's courtroom trick to indicate my friendly concern.

'Go on, Miss Peel.'

My trick did not work. She stiffened again, then rose from her chair.

'All this is a great shock, Sir, and I am quite nonplussed.'

'Of course you are,' I said, also standing up. 'This is not the time. I'll leave you now, and return tomorrow when I hope you will have composed yourself. Will that be convenient?'

'I suppose you must. I shall expect you.'

'I just need to know one more thing now, if you can help me. Did Mr Pimbo spend last night here?'

'He supped here and was still here late in the evening when I retired.'

'When did he leave this morning?'

'I did not see him. I expect he left at daybreak. He often did in summer, with the early sunrise.'

'He would walk to Preston?'

'He would.'

'And was his dog with him?'

'Suez was always with him.'

'Thank you.'

I stooped to pick up my hat, which had fallen to the floor, and involuntarily brushed against her injured arm, causing her to give a sharp cry of pain. I began to apologize, until she asked me not to.

'As you can see, I have hurt my arm, but it is nothing really.'

'How long have you been in pain?'

'For two weeks, no more. A burn.'

'That is long enough for a burn to heal, in the normal way. It should not still be hurting you. What does your physician say?'

'Oh, I haven't seen one. It will heal in time.'

'It may, but you should consult a doctor.'

Without further mention of the injury she conducted me to the front hall and I stepped out under the porch. As I turned to give her goodbye, she stayed me, her lips forming into something, but not exactly, like a smile.

'Mr Cragg, your profession makes you experienced in these things. What must be done with my employer? With his body, I mean. If I do not make the necessary arrangements, whatever they may be, I don't know who will.'

'Only the funeral arrangements need concern you, Miss Peel. I suggest you speak to your vicar, but you will not be able to bury Mr Pimbo until I have held an inquest.'

'And in the meantime, what of the body?'

'Under most normal circumstances it would come to lie in his own house, but in this case it must remain in Preston until the inquest.'

'When will that be, Mr Cragg?'

'In a few days, no more.'

I settled my hat on my head.

'Until tomorrow, Miss Peel. And, if I may, I shall bring my friend Dr Fidelis to look at that arm.'

As I reached Town Moor I reflected on the several things about Pimbo and his family that I had learned. Mr Phillip Pimbo had held quite advanced ideas about housebuilding and decoration. Mrs Pimbo had lost her mind. The little maid was new. But the housekeeper, even superficially, was less easy to read. Miss Peel's first words on hearing of the death of the master of the house were to ask if he had killed himself. Then she had sharply given up the thought when I did not immediately confirm it. And her reply to my question about a possible change to his behaviour: 'not towards me!' That surely meant something too.

I had reached the Town Moor and was half way across it when I remembered the strong room key. I had quite forgotten to search for it.

Chapter Four

∞

Before going home I called again at Pimbo's shop, not only to ask if the body was securely locked up but also to see if any word had come from Zadok Moon. None had. I told Hazelbury that, should Mr Moon appear, he was to be directed without delay towards me.

Back in chambers I asked my clerk Robert Furzey if he knew the name of Pimbo's attorney. His answer surprised me.

'That would be *you*, Sir.'

'Me? No, I don't recall ever—'

'Oh yes, Sir. A fortnight ago Mr Pimbo came, you might say, back into the sheepfold. Old Phillip Pimbo, the father, was a client of your father's, you see. But not the son, until – as I say – just recently.'

'What happened?'

'Well, his family papers just turned up in this office sent from Rudgewick's and packed up with a note reappointing you his family's attorney. I reckoned Mr Pimbo had fallen out there, so I simply accepted them and filed the documents downstairs together with the Pimbo papers of old.'

'Why did you not tell me, Furzey?'

He shrugged.

'It slipped out of my mind. Would have slipped back in one day soon, no doubt.'

I sighed to overcome my exasperation.

'Oh, well, it's convenient as it happens. Would you look and see if there's a will among the papers?'

Furzey, already half way back to his desk in the outer room, stopped with exaggerated reluctance.

'I have a power of writing to do, and yet you want me to go down there immediately and scour out a piece of paper?'

This time I laughed.

'That is your job, Furzey. You put the papers there, and you must be able to find them quickly enough.'

He frowned at me.

'A slave I am, and this no better than a sugar plantation.'

Whenever I was out of the office, or so I suspected, my clerk worked at the pace of a slow worm taking the morning sun. At the sound of my footfall or voice, however, he would appear always in a froth, and dart about as quick as a lizard. Now he disappeared into the basement at a run and, less than five minutes later, returned to slap a folded paper onto my desk. I saw inscribed on it the words *The Last Will and Testament of Phillip Pimbo Esq.*

'Tell me, what sort of client was old Pimbo, the father?' I asked, picking it up.

'He was a very solid merchant. His count-books balanced. And he knew enough to think twice on a good bargain.'

'The son was not so cautious I expect.'

Furzey gave a sardonic smile.

'He was not. His head was inflated by windy dreams, that strain the skull and split the seams – as the poet says. Now, may I get back to my desk?'

The fact that Pimbo had reappointed me his family attorney would explain the letter summoning a meeting between us at the Goldsmith's shop. But I still did not know what business 'of wrong-doing' he had summoned me about.

I unfolded Pimbo's testament. It was dated Lady Day of the present year and was a document of four pages. I went straight to the meat of it, to see how Pimbo had disposed his estate. With neither wife nor offspring to provide for, all his worldly effects went to his aged mother for the length of her life, and then to a distant cousin in Shropshire.

Of specific bequests there were just two. One was a small sum to Robert Hazelbury, while the other was very curious: 'To my housekeeper Ruth Peel I leave my four-acre orchard at Cadley, including all its beehives, that she shall maintain it and them ever in the production of fruit and honey, and so provide for herself, on the sole condition that she never give herself in marriage, and that if she should do so the said orchard and beehives shall be forfeit and revert to the property of my aforementioned cousin and his heirs.'

The last two pages took the form of an inventory of the contents of Pimbo's home, which I glanced through before looking back at the preamble, and to the clause in which Pimbo's executors were named. Here I read that, 'I hereby appoint Mr Zadok Moon of Liverpool and Mr Titus Cragg of Preston to be my executors.'

'What would you think of this case?' I asked Elizabeth as we sat at our supper of cold meats and buttered cauliflower. 'A testator leaves a bequest to his spinster housekeeper, on the sole condition that she does not marry. Is it that he thinks, if she *were* married, she'd have no need of the bequest and it would be better employed elsewhere?'

Elizabeth considered the matter, chewing prettily and dabbing her shapely lips with a napkin.

'That's possible, I suppose. But Titus, my heart, how like you only to see the more benign case! That would not be *my* first thought at all.'

'Am I naive, my dear?'

'Sometimes. But I do honour it in you.'

'Then what is your first thought?'

'That he wants to bind her to spinsterdom. That he wants dominion over her, even from the grave.'

'Why would he want that?'

Elizabeth laughed.

'Really Titus – that you are a lawyer and can ask such a question!'

'What is the answer, though?' I said, with lawyerly persistence.

'Because she was his mistress, of course, and he was passionately jealous, even from the grave, at the thought of another man touching her. Happen we're speaking of the will of poor Phillip Pimbo, Titus.'

I conceded that we were and went on,

'And I asked Miss Peel, who is the housekeeper in question, whether Phillip Pimbo's manner had recently changed, hoping it might explain his unexpected death, and she answered in an oddly personal way: not towards *her*, she said.'

'Tell me how did she say it, Titus. In regret? In anger, or bitterness?'

I chewed the last of my meat for a few moments, as I recalled the conversation with Miss Peel more sharply.

'She spoke it with spirit, I would say. Almost in defiance.'

'Against what?'

'Let's say Fortune.'

Elizabeth rose and went to the dresser, where there lay a cold asparagus tart to finish off our meal.

'In that case there may be another explanation, I think.'

She cut me a slice of tart, placed it in front of me, and watched while I ate it.

'You are not having any tart?' I said.

Evidently not, for she stuck to her theme.

'I mean that the case may have been the perfect opposite: not love, but animosity that led him to bind her.'

'Does not animosity sunder, rather than bind?'

'Delilah wanted Samson bound, because he had rejected her – so she hated him. That could be the case here.'

That was my Elizabeth – clever and to the point. She stretched down and picked the last piece of tart from my plate and put it in her mouth. She took up my empty plate, laid it with her own on a tray, and carried them towards the door on her way to the scullery. I followed her.

'That is very possible,' I said. 'But how can I tell which it is, love or hate?'

'Ask Miss Peel.'

'She may not choose to say. She can be a very – imperious woman.'

'What precisely was Mr Pimbo's bequest?'

'His four-acre orchard, and beehives.'

And now Elizabeth was laughing as she clattered the plates into the stone sink.

'Why are you laughing?'

'Don't you see?'

'Not I.'

'She was being made to play the part of Eve, Titus. He's given her a garden to be hers alone, just so long as she does not sin against him. But if she should sin – well, then she is cast out for ever and ever, Amen.'

'He was playing God?'

'Yes, the God of the Pentateuch. The God who devises tests. The Jealous God. There was something between them, Titus, and it seems to me you will have to find out what it was.'

After supper Luke Fidelis came to my house and we walked together to our favourite coffee house, the Turk's Head. As we went along he told how he had fared taking Amity Thorn home.

'I found her on the road and took her up to ride rump. We got on very well but compared to yesterday, when I first met her, she didn't say much.'

'What happened yesterday? You had better give me every detail. If Thorn dies he will have to be inquested.'

So Fidelis gave me the exact course of his previous day's bedside visit to Adam Thorn, of the man's state and of the silver apostle spoon that he'd advised Amity to get valued, all of which I've related in my first chapter.

'She didn't get much luck with the spoon this morning, though,' I said. 'The pawnshop's closed for business and who knows when it will reopen?'

'After she left this morning she was showing it around town hoping for a buyer. She has it polished up since yesterday and very handsome it looks too with its saint perched on the end. But people she showed it to were wary and there were no takers, yet it looks to be very good genuine silver, even though it's old.'

'People might be right to be suspicious. Pimbo's journeyman Ambler, for one, thinks one of the Thorns stole it.'

'Well, from the state of it I'd say it had been lying some time in the open, which would argue that it was just found. But we will see if an owner comes forward.'

We entered the Turk's Head, an establishment well kept by Noah Plumtree. As Plumtree's own character was marked above all by geniality, so was his coffee house and, this being a Friday night, the room was even more than usually full of coffee drinkers and wine bibbers standing and sitting in groups, their voices raised in toasts and laughter. In one part of the room a pleasant argument was in progress; in another, a boisterous card game; and in a third a good tenor voice had launched into a ballad. Every now and then a group of men would fall into attentive silence while one related a story, the climax of which they greeted with an explosion of hilarity and back-slapping.

I ordered wine and pipes and, finding a table bay empty, we settled there in a fair measure of seclusion.

'The death of Pimbo has occupied me all afternoon,' I told my friend, 'though I'm no nearer to knowing why he is dead. And now I am in double duty, having been appointed his executor. This means that if as Coroner I find the man murdered himself, I must as executor surrender all his worldly goods to the Crown.'

'You may rest easy on that point. I do not believe that he murdered himself.'

'Every circumstance of that room says that he did. You had better explain.'

Fidelis took a long draught of wine and replaced his glass carefully on the table before him.

'Very well. It's quite true that there was just the one way to leave that fatal room, and that it was found locked on the inside. And yet I feel someone else was in the room when Pimbo died.'

'You are not reverting to this business of his wig, Luke. Surely it's a minor detail.'

'In the case of inexplicable death, no detail can be said to be minor. There is also the dog. That dog was reputedly always with him.'

'That is so. His housekeeper confirmed it to me only this morning.'

'So why not at the hour of his death?'

I put a flaming spill to my pipe-bowl.

'Here's why not,' I retorted, when I had set the tobacco nicely smouldering. 'Having determined to shoot himself, Pimbo himself put the dog out of doors, to spare him the sight of it.'

'That would be too delicate. If he really shot himself he'd have shot the dog first. The man that kills himself, first kills his dog – that's a proverb in Ireland.'

'I am not sure that bears the same interpretation as—'

'Yes it does. Pimbo's dog was not found shot in the room; consequently, I say, Pimbo did not kill himself.'

I laughed at Fidelis's obduracy.

'He might have killed the dog elsewhere, and that's why we haven't found it.'

Fidelis shook his head.

'No, he would have done it in the room. He would have killed the dog, and then himself, in immediate succession.'

'Do you know William of Ockham?' I asked.

Fidelis shrugged.

'A wrestler?'

As so often, I was astonished at Fidelis's ignorance of the literary and the philosophical.

'He was a philosopher who denounced those that cloud an argument with over-complication. He recommended the use of a razor to cut away obfuscations.'

'And?'

'I propose we employ the razor and state the case simply: Phillip Pimbo was alone when he shot himself behind the locked door of his business room. It is perverse to look for ways for the case to be different.'

Fidelis put his two elbows on the table between us and pressed his hands together, almost in an attitude of prayer.

'Indulge me a little longer, Titus. Tell me again exactly what happened when you had the door of the room forced open and you went inside.'

So I filled our glasses and indulged him. When I had finished he sat as if meditating, his wine untouched, and himself oblivious to the cheerful noise of the surrounding coffee house. I rose and went to the jakes.

On my return, he snapped out of his reverie.

'And you are certain the dog was not alive in the room?'

'Certain. I knew that dog. It was a busybody dog. Had it been in the room, we would have had it chewing our shoe buckles.'

'But your eyes were fixed upon the corpse lying across the desk. So were those of Hazelbury and the others who crushed into the room. Under such circumstances the dog might just have run out through the crowd all unnoticed. Is that not possible?'

With a sigh I indulged him once more.

'Very well. That might have happened. It's possible.'

'And, if a dog could escape in that way, then tell me why not a man? Why not a man, concealed inside the room, who simply mingled with the insurgent crowd, and made his escape unnoticed? As unnoticed as the dog. What was its name?'

'Suez. But a man is much larger, Luke. A man would be seen.'

'It was a large crowd of men that came in, all together. This hidden man left in their midst. And *that* man, I warrant you, was Phillip Pimbo's killer.'

'And who was this hidden man?'

'Ah! That is the question, is it not?'

He paused again for a moment of reflection, and then said, 'Suez. It's the perfect name for a dog. It makes me like Pimbo all the more, that he would think of it.'

'Things in themselves have, peradventure, their weight, measures and conditions; but *when once we take them into us* the soul forms them as she pleases.'

I came across these words of Montaigne while reading later that same evening in my library. Having written up the events of the past week in my journal, as I did every Friday, I had turned to the French Seigneur for some light philosophical amusement. Indeed he had been my almost constant companion ever since the day, a few weeks earlier, when I'd stood in Sweeting's Church Gate bookshop, leafing through an edition of the *Essays* in a translation (so the good bookseller told me) by Charles Cotton, a literary gentleman of the last century.

'I do assure you the sense is much easier to get than in old Florio's fantastical language,' Sweeting was saying. 'Cotton turned Montaigne's plain French into plain English, which is the reason that Cotton is preferred to Florio almost everywhere nowadays. Futhermore this is a new and much improved edition.'

Although I had heard of Montaigne, I had never until that day read him. I turned a few pages, and at once noticed the extreme variety of subjects that came under his eye – 'Of Sorrow' . . . 'Of Cannibals' . . . 'Of Smells'. Sweeting, who was notoriously cunning in matching a customer with a book, said:

'If you've not read him before, I suspect you'll find he suits you rather well, Titus. You and Michael de Montaigne might even be made for each other.'

Still I leafed through the pages: 'Of Books' . . . 'Of Cruelty' . . . 'Of Thumbs' . . . Of *Thumbs*? I closed the book and handed it to Sweeting.

'I'll try it,' I said.

'If it doesn't suit, bring it back.'

'I think it will. If a man can entertain a reader on thumbs, what great heights might he reach on sorrow, or cruelty?'

As so often before, the bookseller had hit the mark. I found that Montaigne wrote as much good sense as any of my favourite English essay writers – those of the *Spectator* being highest in my esteem – but there was another quality in the Frenchman that I relished even more: a candour, and a sort of bluff courage in the face of his own human failings. This quite disarmed me. There are few that will address in print their own ignorance and fearfulness as bravely as Montaigne does. So, while he was an excellent guide and authority for thinking about difficult questions, I enjoyed him principally because he made me feel I was sitting in company with a witty, resourceful and admirable old uncle.

On this night, reading Montaigne's sentence about how facts are modified within each of us to suit our predilections, it struck me, with the force of a hammer on a nail, that Fidelis's interpretation of Phillip Pimbo's death was just the same case. My young friend's knowledge of literature may have been faint, but he had a most analytical mind, and this, compounded with his medical knowledge, had many times been of help to my work as Coroner.

On the other hand he had to be watched, with a view to taking a strop to Ockham's razor. My friend rated the finding and solving of puzzles high among all life's pleasures and this frequently led him to take normal sequences of fact and twist them quite perversely into Anglo-Saxon riddles or Euclidean equations. With Pimbo he was determined to make it a case of murder, but was faced with the seeming impossibility of it having been committed inside the locked room, and yet the murderer had escaped. So he arranged the facts in his head until he'd made such a murder possible, and the hypothesis of the hidden man was the result. It may have been ingenious, but it was wholly speculative, and I had no more need to believe it than in the cat and the fiddle.

I had frequently observed Fidelis as he approached a dubious death from, as I considered it, the wrong direction. Physicians I suppose must always look for practical solutions, for ways to reverse a malady. They ask, how best must I proceed against it? But as a Coroner I know that I am concerned with not the causes but the consequences of evil and death – matters that cannot be so proceeded against, and certainly not reversed. In this work there is nothing to be gained by at once running off like a hare-hound in pursuit of ways, means and possible culprits. Thinking again of Montaigne's remark, I understood that my own soul's predilection, in contrast to Fidelis's, was not to ask who killed, and how. It sought to explain the deeper causes of the death by examining what followed from it.

It was late. I yawned, shut the book and placed the guard before the embers of the fire. It was time to go upstairs.

I found Elizabeth in bed, but still awake and with a book of her own. It was Mr Richardson's *Pamela*, the craze that had arrived in Preston like an epidemic and was now at its peak, raging among the ladies with such intensity that it seemed they spoke of little else. I had bought my wife the novel at Sweeting's only a few days before, but she was already more than half way to the end.

'I am thinking I am on the wrong path with the Pimbo business,' I mentioned to her, as I slipped off my shoes and began to unroll my stockings.

I could not see Elizabeth's face behind the book. She lay slightly curled, as if wrapped around it, her eyes held on a tight rein by the lines of print.

'Fidelis is fixed like a fish on a hook by the idea that Pimbo was somehow murdered. Can you believe it?'

There was still no response as Elizabeth read on. I unbuttoned my breeches, stepped out of them and, turning to the glass, addressed my stock. As I did so, she spoke.

'I doubt that Pamela's master would untie his stock with his legs bare.'

I saw that she was peeping at me over the top of *Pamela* but, before I could reply, she gave a giggle and immersed herself again in the story. I tried twice more to interest her in my difficulties over Pimbo, to be ignored the first time and then be told:

'Titus, dearest, I am *reading*!'

Nightshirted by now, I rolled into bed and lay still. The only sounds were those of passers-by outside our window on Cheapside, of Elizabeth's fingers turning Mr Richardson's pages, and of her mouth giving out an occasional 'Oh! Ha!' of surprise or pleasure at some twist in the tale. After five minutes of this, I blew out the candle on my side of the bed and composed myself to sleep.

Chapter Five

∞

SHORTLY AFTER NINE on the next morning, Luke Fidelis and I stood at the door of Cadley Place.

'The patient you come to see this morning will interest you, Luke,' I had told him as we rode across the Moor. 'Miss Peel has brains and striking beauty, yet she hasn't married. I wonder why.'

'Many men would rather eat thistles than marry an intelligent wife.'

'Would you?'

'Oh no, Titus. I run the other way. I would favour rank ugliness over gross stupidity.'

'While hoping to avoid either.'

'Naturally. Anyway I am in no position to marry. I must establish myself first. There are still four medical men in Preston with bigger practices than me. I shall marry when I have the largest.'

'But do you not feel the want of being with a woman?'

He looked at me with a faint smile.

'As much as any man. But I know how to supply the want, Titus – though naturally not in this town of gossips.'

Don't imagine from this exchange that Luke Fidelis had an adamantine heart, indifferent to sentiment. There had been a time not long ago when his heart had been much battered, if not quite broken, by a girl who'd come to Preston but had proved beyond his reach.

'Did I mention I shall be in Liverpool tomorrow night?' he said carelessly, after our horses had taken a few more paces. 'It occurs to me that you must wish to communicate with the Liverpool scrivener that Pimbo talked about, Zadok Moon. May I be of service in that respect?'

I did not ask for details of what he would be doing in Mayor Grimshaw's cesspit of vice. I said instead that, yes, I would be obliged it he would carry a letter to Moon.

Our ring on the door was answered by the same little maid as I had met before. This time she took us straight to the housekeeper's parlour, where Miss Peel stood at her table shortening the stems of some crimson roses. Having just the one working arm she could not use scissors, and so had laid the stems on a board and was hacking off the ends with a knife.

I introduced the doctor who asked if she permitted him to examine her arm. With that half smile of hers she nodded her head, at which point it was my part to withdraw. I suggested I might be allowed access to the contents of Mr Pimbo's desk during her conference with the doctor. She rang a handbell and the little servant appeared.

'Peggy will show you to the master's study. The desk is unlocked. I do not know what's in it.'

The study into which the maid showed me was on the ground floor, and stood next to the salon in which I had met old Mrs Pimbo. Its window looked out of the side of the house over a dusty path, a lawn and a clump of bushes, or what the up-to-date Mr Pimbo would have called a shrubbery.

'This is sad news about your master, Peggy,' I remarked as she showed me in.

'Yes, Sir. We are shocked, Sir.'

'Had the servants noticed anything that might explain it? I wonder if Mr Pimbo had recently changed in his manner.'

She shrugged her thin shoulders.

'There's only one thing they're saying in kitchen, Sir. That he'd gone off his food. In two days he'd not ate a proper meal but only piddled it round his plate. That's what cook said, not me, Sir. I never saw it. I'm only three weeks here, and I'm not let in to wait table just yet.'

'Have you been told anything of how you are all situated? About what the future may now bring?'

'No, Sir. Nothing. But if I am going home I shall not mind.'

'You have not been happy here?'

'I didn't say that, Sir.'

But I could tell it was true. I felt the whole household to be locked in unhappiness, but without a key to the secret it was not possible to know why.

This thought reminded me that one of my tasks this day was to find a more tangible key. I dismissed Peggy, and made a quick survey of the room to see where a man might keep one – a large brass key to match that which I had yesterday seen in Hazelbury's hand. There was no hook-board of the kind on which keys are hung. Two small vases stood at each end of the mantel, both empty, and a flat matching dish between them on which lay a clay pipe and nothing more. On a side table there was a snuff barrel, half full, from which I took a pinch and enjoyed a sneeze.

I looked through the bookcase. Pimbo had not been a very interesting reader. There were the usual volumes: sets of sermons by forgotten divines, a copy of *The Pilgrim's Progress*, another of *Robinson Crusoe*. There was no poetry, no plays. I pulled down one tattered book whose title on the spine I could not read. It was an old account of El Dorado, 'written by one that hath been there and beheld its golden glories'. He had it no doubt for professional reasons.

Next I addressed myself to the desk. It was in the form of a large and solid inlaid escritoire, with a lid that hinged down to form a writing surface. The interior, considerably deeper and more spacious than the lady's writing desk I had seen the day before in the salon, was subdivided into small square compartments and narrow drawers, for ordering documents and stationery.

I went through the little drawers first. They were reserved for the accoutrements of writing: quills, pen-knife, sealing-wafers, wax, tapers, a tinderbox. There was no key. Then I turned to the open compartments, each of which was stuffed with paper.

I settled myself into an armchair and began to glance through the contents of these in turn, and found that the papers had been more or less rationally organized. There were many mundane household letters, all of which had been stuffed into the compartments towards the left hand side of the desk – estimates tendered, accounts rendered, demands submitted and receipts remitted – mostly in connection with repair works or domestic supplies and services. I noticed that many of these were of quite an old date and not many had been countersigned as 'paid', while there were a number of increasingly exasperated duns from the grocer and the butcher, and one stonemason's account in the sum of four guineas that had remained unpaid for seven months.

Putting these on one side, I was left with items from the right hand side, which were all papers connected with Pimbo's business. One compartment was devoted to letters signed 'Zadok Moon', with an address at Pinchbeck's Coffee House, Liverpool. In one, Moon provided Pimbo with costings for a range of purchases which had nothing to do with goldsmithing: hogsheads of Wigan nails and china beads, numerous bales of cotton cloth, firearms, gunpowder, spirituous liquors and a range of ironwork. In another paper, headed *The Fortunate Isle*, there was a schedule of chandlery such as chain, cordage, sailcloth, caulking, brass fittings and hammocks, as well as such provisions as raisins, dried meat and biscuit. A third had a list of men's names, who seemed to be prospective crew members. *The Fortunate Isle* was evidently a vessel being fitted out for a voyage.

There were considerably more letters to inspect but I had hardly looked at these before Peg knocked at the door and said that Dr Fidelis and Miss Peel had finished, and would I like to return to the parlour? I quit the chair and took one last hasty look inside the escritoire, thrusting my hands deeper into the compartments or slots to find anything lodged at the back I might have missed. I found nothing significant but, as I withdrew my hand from one of them, my knuckle caught the leading edge at the top of the cavity, and something moved. I put my fingers under it and pulled. A shallow drawer slid out. Looking more carefully I saw it had been made outwardly to appear part of the desk's construction. So completely was it concealed that merely looking would not tell you it was there.

With some excitement I slid it fully out. It contained a single sheet letter, folded and covered with writing. Hurriedly I slipped it in with the other papers, which I had decided to take away with me for further study. I had only time to notice that the hand was that of Pimbo himself.

Fidelis seemed to have put Ruth Peel more at her ease than I had yet seen her. They were talking together about trifles. The lady, still wearing her left arm in its leather sling, now sat in the second fireside armchair rather than the removed upright one on which she had perched during our previous day's conference. If this was indeed a sign that awkwardness had left them, I feared that I was about to reintroduce it.

I brought the upright chair from the wall and placed it in between the two of them, opposite the fire, but angled towards Ruth Peel. I sat down.

'Miss Peel, I still have a few questions in the case of Mr Pimbo which I fear only you can help me with. Would you object if Dr

Fidelis remained in the room while we discuss them? He is my trusted friend, but his advice as a medical man is also most valuable to me as Coroner.'

She inclined her head to say she had no objection.

'Very well. Now, did Mr Pimbo talk to you about his business?'

'No, never.'

'Did you form any impression about how his business stood? Was it flourishing?'

'He was always very bluff about it, very confident. That is all I can say.'

'But from the contents of his desk it would seem that in the household accounts there were numerous unpaid bills – grocery, meat and the like. And at least one long-standing mason's debt.'

'I know nothing about the mason. As for the household, I myself manage the weekly accounts, settling with what money I am given. Only when I could not pay some larger bill did I refer the tradesman to Mr Pimbo. They've let me know that he was lately a very bad payer, but I don't know any details. He did not let me into the privacy of his accounts.'

'You say you were given money.'

'To run the household weekly, yes.'

'And it wasn't sufficient?'

'It was adequate for the matters of day-to-day – when he gave it.'

'What do you mean by that?'

'There have been occasions recently when he has not given me the full amount. It should be ten shillings out of which come all wages, and all provisions. Some weeks lately he has only given me five shillings. One week it was as little as three and sixpence, which barely covers the servants' pay. Myself, I haven't had any surplus for myself for two months.'

'Is that how he did it – let you keep any surplus from the ten shillings for your own wage?'

'Yes – he said it encouraged thrift in me. It sufficed, so long as he gave me the full ten shillings.'

'So would you say his failure to do that recently means that his business affairs have been running into difficulties?'

'I couldn't say. As I told you, I really know nothing about Mr Pimbo's business.'

'Did you know Mr Zadok Moon, Mr Pimbo's business associate? Did he visit this house?'

'Yes. He was here, but only once to my knowledge. It was some time ago.'

'Why did he come?'

She shrugged.

'On business, I suppose. He went into Mr Pimbo's library and stayed a hour or two. Then he left.'

'Can you describe him?'

'A small dark-haired man, bearded, wearing riding habit and a wide-brimmed hat.'

'That is all?'

'I only saw him briefly, when I answered the door. It was after dark. Mr Pimbo came immediately, sent me to my quarters and brought Mr Moon inside himself.'

'Would you know the man again?'

'I am not sure that I would. I am sorry.'

'Would you say Mr Pimbo had been in any way melancholy, low in spirits or unusually irritable in recent weeks?'

She shrugged and her mouth tightened.

'I don't know. Perhaps.'

'Peg happened to mention that he had been off his food?'

'That's true. But he said he was poorly in the stomach.'

'Were there any other symptoms of this? Was he in pain, for instance?'

'I don't know. But let me say something. Mr Pimbo was a man whose habit was to talk big and bold – you understand?'

She was talking more urgently now, and patches of colour had spread on her upper neck and cheeks. She went on,

'So even when I had suspicions about his not paying the full amount of the housekeeping, even when I heard from the tradesmen that he still owed them. Or *even* when he lost his appetite for food and said he was poorly, this big-talk, this – what d'you call it?'

'Bombast?' I supplied.

She thumped her fist on the chair's arm.

'Exactly! This *bombast* of his hardly diminished. He was going to be the great banker, the great merchant, the great man! So it was difficult, you see, to tell what more quiet feelings, if any, lay beneath.'

'Thank you, Miss Peel. I understand what you are saying perfectly, but I do have a slight difficulty with it. When we met yesterday, as soon as I gave you the news that Mr Pimbo was dead, your first reaction was to ask if he had done away with himself. Why, if you couldn't tell his state of mind, did that of all questions drop first into your head? It suggests to me that you had been half expecting such news.'

For a long moment Miss Peel said nothing, but I noticed that the high colour of her complexion was still deepening.

'I asked that for— I mean, I was prompted to ask it for another reason. A private reason. I must ask you to respect that privacy.'

'I'm afraid it may be rather material to the inquest, Miss Peel. But let's put it aside for now. May I ask you instead about Mr Pimbo's will? I wonder if you know what's in it?'

'His will? No, of course not! I know nothing about it.'

'I can inform you of this because, as well as Coroner, I happen to be one of Mr Pimbo's executors. He has left you a legacy, Miss Peel.'

She started.

'He has? What legacy?'

'It is his four-acre orchard and his beehives. Do you have any idea why he picked that particular property for you?'

'The orchard lies across the lane from here,' she said. 'He knew that in my leisure time I like to walk in it and, if the weather's fine, sit there; and it was I who supervise the annual fruit and honey harvests. Those must be his reasons.'

'That seems very likely. But I must add something more. Mr Pimbo attached a condition to the bequest and I'd like, if possible, to know his reason. He said you must forfeit the bequest should you ever marry.'

'Oh!'

Her eyes widened in outright shock and her mouth dropped momentarily open before she covered it with her hand. She was looking directly into my eyes, a woman transfixed by surprise.

'I don't know, Mr Cragg. I can't think. I'm . . . at a loss.'

'Miss Peel, this is difficult but I am charged with finding the cause of Mr Pimbo's death. So I must ask. Was there any matter between you and Mr Pimbo that I should know about? Was there any understanding, perhaps?'

By now she had flushed a deep crimson, and was breathing deeply, but she continued to stare at me.

I prompted her.

'Such testamentary conditions are not unknown. Sometimes a husband does not wish his wife to remarry out of jealousy or even – I am sorry to say – spite.'

'Mr Pimbo and I were not secretly married, if that is what you suggest.'

'No, I am wondering, were you engaged to be married?'

During the marked pause following my question I could see she was thinking, and suspected her of calculating how much to tell me of what she was thinking. I waited and slowly she composed herself. Her furious blush had largely faded, and her breath become more measured, when at last she decided to speak.

'No, we were not engaged to be married. There was no understanding between us and nor was I . . . I mean, I was not dishonoured. But, but . . .'

'Yes, Miss Peel?'

She turned her large black eyes full on mine once again.

'He wanted to, Mr Cragg. He pressed me, pressed me *so* hard, that there came a time when I was afraid I would submit. Yet I did not. I did not!'

Her free hand was clenched now and she held her whole body in tension.

'What did he say to you, when he was pressing you in that way? I mean, what was his tone? Wheedling? Threatening?'

She shook her head. The colour in her face and neck had completely drained away, and the complexion was again white as paper.

'I don't know . . . I mean, I would deliberately distract myself, try not to listen. It is a jumble. I really cannot tell you any one thing in particular that he said to me.'

'And when was all this? Recently?'

'Last year.'

'So he had more recently stopped pestering you?'

'Some months ago, when he knew at last that he could not persuade me. After that he always treated me abruptly.'

'And the condition in his will that you never marry: what do you make of that? Do you think it came from resentment that you would not, as you put it, submit?'

As our conversation proceeded I saw that she had begun to relax her posture, as she regained control over her feelings.

'I don't know what his thoughts were. I could never comprehend him. So how, I ask you, could I love such a man? How could I debase myself with such a man?'

'Would it have been debasement to marry him?'

'Marriage, Sir, was not his prime object.'

'I see. Yet he must have loved you, for all that.'

At this she rose from the chair and stepped past me towards the door. I went on, quickly, with my last remaining question.

'Wasn't that the personal reason why you asked me yesterday if Mr Pimbo had done away with himself? That he loved you, and you couldn't love him back?'

She turned around and I could see that the young woman, who had so tremblingly heard the news of the conditional bequest, had now become again the imperious housekeeper of Cadley Place.

'Loved me? I think not, Sir. A man like him does not *love* a woman such as me . . . as me – the way I am.'

Before I could say more she held up her good hand, its palm towards us.

'Mr Cragg, doctor, if you please! I have tasks to complete.'

She gestured towards the rose stems lying on the table. Out of water the petals had already begun to lose their tone and crispness.

'I am sure these must appear very trivial to professional men, but they are my duties, and I have to attend to them. Allow me to show you out.'

'What do you make of her, Luke?' I said, when the door had closed and we were mounting our horses.

'She is not easy to decipher,' he replied.

'Certainly there's more to know about her and Pimbo – more than what she's told us.'

'Yes, if she did not lie, she did speak selectively, I think. Would the mother help to fill in the gaps?'

'She is half-crazy.'

'Sometimes half-craziness has much to tell.'

'I have met the old woman: nothing she says would be admissible in law.'

We rode through the gate marked 'out' and started along the lane. I looked over the wall opposite the house into a well-planted apple grove, in full leaf, and with the unripe fruit hanging in clusters.

'The orchard in question,' I said. 'See the beehives?'

But Fidelis had already kicked his horse into a trot and was soon hacking on ahead of me. I did not catch up with him until we reached the brow of Town Moor, where he was resting his horse. The spot had a wide view of the roofs and smoking chimneys of Preston, though Fidelis was looking in a different direction, towards a lone ruined house visible away to our left, on the far side of the Moor and standing bleakly on raised ground: Peel Hall. It had been built in the time of Henry the Eighth, of brick and stone, with a tower and tall chimneys. Only the remains of these could still be seen, for the main house was now broken down and uninhabitable, though there was a cluster of usable out-buildings not far from it.

'I wonder if she is from the family,' he said.

'I doubt it. She is a stranger here. And how is her arm, by the way? You and she were getting along well while I was in Pimbo's study.'

'She'd burnt herself on a hot lamp glass. The burn was not very well dressed and had suppurated slightly but in my judgement it is already recovering so I covered it with a soothing honey-balm and redressed it. But to tell the truth, the burn is not what is really wrong with the arm; it is not the reason why she carries it in a sling – which she only does in the company of strangers.'

'What *is* the matter with it then?'

'The limb is deformed, Titus. It is, I confess, somewhat disconcerting to look at.'

'In what way?'

'In its distortion, stiffness and uselessness. The skin is mottled, with the overall colours associated with a thorough bruising. The elbow and wrist don't flex, and the fingers are curled into a rigid fist. The whole limb, while it is sensitive to touch and to pain, cannot move of itself, but only swing uselessly from the shoulder.'

I was filled with a mixture of horror and compassion.

'What an unfortunate young woman! How did this happen to her?'

'She was born with it. But let us not dwell upon the matter.'

My friend swung around and gestured towards a mean hovel with an untidy straw roof which stood at another point on the edge of the Moor.

'I shall leave you here and call on Adam Thorn, as I am passing. I shall see if there's any progress in him, but also I want to make sure his wife has been to the church warden for poor relief.'

So we parted, and I made my way back to town, my thoughts filled with the melancholy fate of Ruth Peel, a woman with such beauty marred from birth.

Chapter Six

∞

ELIZABETH'S MOTHER AND father were in town from Broughton for Saturday market and were dining with us at midday.

'Can they not catch up with the age, and dine at the proper hour?' I had asked at breakfast.

'They are old-style people, Titus; country people. To dine at two is much too late for them. They will have been up and doing since dawn. I'm roasting a nice piece of beef I've had hanging the past few days in the larder. Don't be late for the carving.'

I arrived with minutes to spare, just as deaf old Charles George was tucking his napkin into his shirt, and his wife was fussing around tasting the boiled cabbage for saltiness and the horseradish sauce for vinegar. My Elizabeth had the patience of a saint in regard to her mother, in which virtue I tried and sometimes failed to match her.

Yet dinner with the Georges was to provide me with some intelligence of real interest. We started in a way I had expected, with Elizabeth reverting to the little girl that the old ones still thought she was. This performance, which was of special delight to my mother-in-law, did not exclude the embarrassment of baby-talk and nicknames, of childhood reminiscences, and arguments about which kitten drowned in the porridge pot on New Year's Eve. And so on, and on, while I tried to show interest.

I had carved their second and third platefuls, I had fetched more ale, I had amiably endured sly asides from her mother ('And when are we going to hear from you two of that Fortunate Event that we pray for every day?'; 'A woman can die truly happy only when she is a Gammer'; etc. etc.) and more direct allusions to the same, shouted jocularly by old Charles ('I hope tha don't lack the vigour, young man, that tha's not got brats! Eh? Eh?'). Finally, having enough of all this I turned the subject to that of my visit to Cadley Place that morning.

'Poor little Ruth Peel!' said Mrs George, when I had done. 'I remember her birth at Peel Hall so well, and the shock of it.'

'She is a Peel of Peel Hall?'

This came as a surprise to me. I'd thought, as I'd said to Fidelis, that she must be a native of some distant county.

'Oh yes, she was born there, like I said.'

'You knew her?'

'Not knew her, but I saw her as a babby. I used to milk at the Hall. It's where I met Mr George, you know. He was one of the dairymen – eh, Charley? Before we went to Broughton and took over your dad's cobbling shop.'

She repeated this at twice the loudness, and Charles chuckled obligingly.

'Oh aye,' he said, 'tha were my little milkmaid.'

I asked for more details about Ruth.

'She was the daughter they wouldn't own to, that ashamed they were of her, with her stunted arm. All sorts of daft things were said – that she'd been touched by Beelzebub, that her mother had lain with a fish, that sort of nonsense – so to end the talk they sent her away after a few months to the mother's brother in Lincolnshire to be brought up and forgotten about. She had good schooling there in time, I'm told.'

'So she was the daughter of old Benjamin Peel, was she?'

'The last of them. He had several, but no sons. Ruth must be the only one left of them now, any road, because the rest's dead as far as I know.'

'Happen that's why she's come back,' put in Elizabeth. 'She's inherited.'

'It's precious little if she did! Just the house, which is a ruin since the roof caved in. The land and farms are long since sold off. How fallen the mighty! Time was when the Peels ruled for miles around this town.'

Like many that are deaf when surrounded by conversation, Old Charles spent much of his time removed or abstracted, as if thinking inwardly. But from time to time he would stir and be jolted into speech that showed he was following some of the talk.

'Forty year afore I were born,' he announced loudly, 'Benjamin Peel's grandad were Mayor, am I right? He were another Benjamin Peel – the Great Benjamin Peel, he were called actually. But then he took on Cromwell, and the family went downhill after. Slowly, mind. But Preston never glorified the Peels again, and they lost all their money – I forget how. Any road, that's it. That's what happened.'

'What happened to Benjamin?' I asked.

'Don't know. But he was never seen here no more.'

He took a large swallow of ale and lapsed back into silence, while the conversation between mother and daughter moved on to the variable prices in the day's market. I was thinking that I knew now where Ruth Peel had got her patrician manner, and her education; also that I understood her feelings about her poverty, and that she might feel it was unjust. She seemed to have much ill-fortune to complain of, not only in how she had been treated by Pimbo, but by her own family.

After we finished eating, Elizabeth and her mother retired to drink tea in the parlour, and I was left sitting with Charles over a bottle of Madeira wine. After five minutes, with the old man sound asleep in his chair, our girl Matty came in to clear the dishes. I asked her to keep an eye on him, and slipped away into the office, which I reached through a communicating door off the hall.

On Saturdays, Furzey worked only in the morning, so I had the place to myself. I arranged the papers from Pimbo's escritoire on my desk and began looking through them – each pile representing documents from a single slot in the escritoire.

I looked first through the large stack of bills and correspondence with tradesmen. One or two were receipts for payments made, and these I kept together. The others were almost all requests, and increasingly demands for payment: 7s. 8d. to the currier; a couple of guineas for a horse; £1. 6s. 8d. at the wine merchants; 9s. 10d. for shoes. One letter was asking for sixteen shillings on account, towards payment of a bill of more than three times as much. 'We conclude that you take advantage in every way of us and we request immediate payment of a sum on account, which we think not unreasonable. R. Pilkington.' Taking a pen I noted down every sum that still appeared owed by Pimbo and added them together, from which I learned that on this evidence alone he was domestically indebted to the extent of £36. 15s. 9d. None of these debts, I should make clear, were those of the goldsmithing business, whose financial records I would have to look at with the help of Hazelbury at his office. These were the transactions of his home where, so the proverb has it, charity begins.

Having carried out this small audit of Pimbo's household debts, I turned at the first bundle of correspondence with Zadok Moon and at once the sense of gloom and indebtedness was quite dispelled. On this evidence, Moon was a man with a preternaturally sunny and optimistic view of life – and more particularly of business. The letters continually emphasized 'zealous backers', 'the most willing buyers', 'accommodating traders', 'highly excellent merchandise',

'the best ship and crew money can obtain' and, several times underlined, 'tip-top compound profits'.

When I had read this entire packet of papers together, the
upshot was clear: Phillip Pimbo had joined with Moon as the prin-
ciple investor, or so Moon's letters repeatedly stressed, in a joint
enterprise for buying and fitting out a ship – *The Fortunate Isle*
of Liverpool, Edward Doubleday Captain – for a Guinea voyage.
The way in which it worked, and most particularly the notion of
'compound profit', was explained in an enthusiastic summary by
Moon. This was in a letter dated eighteen months previously, when
the scheme was just under way:

*The hold of the ship being filled with such goods as are
monstrously desired by the natives of the Guinea coast,
but very cheaply obtained at home viz. simple metal
manufactures, coloured cloth, beads, spirituous liquor
(they are exceeding drunkards there), gunpowder etc;
these goods are exchanged after sailing to Benin for a
full cargo of prime slaves, which are in a matter of weeks
ferried comfortably across to the West Indies and traded
in exchange for sugar, rum, tobacco and cotton. The ship
then cruises back to Liverpool on the bosom of the trade
winds, to complete a year's voyage. Her final cargo is then
sold, believe me, Sir, at a prodigious return on the sum of
money originally placed with the venture. For every guinea
they have invested in such enterprises, it is not unknown for
gentlemen to receive a hundred back! A more usual return
would be of about ten times the principal. You have been
bold enough to invest such an amount as to make you the
Prime Investor and, at the conclusion of the voyage, give you
much profit, Mr. Pimbo, as befits a man of your wealth and
station. I will make a more modest profit myself but it will*

*suffice to give me a good stake in a second similar venture in
the future.*

Another set of letters, seemingly in reply to expressions of anxiety from Pimbo, were devoted to reassuring him of the safety of
the enterprise. *The Fortunate Isle*, said Moon, was a thoroughly
new vessel of the 'snow' variety. She was captained and crewed
by expert seamen, and she would be fully insured, both in herself and in respect of any cargo she would carry, against all risks
whatsoever. So, while there was no expectation at all that anything
could go amiss, in that unlikely case his capital was fully covered.
Pinned to this letter was another, in which Pimbo was asked to send
immediately, as his share of the insurance premium, the sum of one
thousand five hundred pounds.

A third, smaller sheaf of correspondence was of an earlier
date – a full six months previous to those concerning the Guinea
venture. It helped me much in understanding Pimbo's motives in
joining it – his ambition to move into the novel business of private
banking in Preston.

'*I have had obliging letters from Lord Oswaldene and Sir
Henry Amplesides*', wrote Moon. '*Both of these gentlemen are
intimates of the First Lord of the Treasury and they assure me that
the administration smiles upon your idea of establishing a local
bank in Preston, as it does on similar projects by gentlemen in other
cities and towns of the realm. However both my correspondents
emphasize the need for such ventures to be established on a very
secure basis, with an initial working capital of at least £20,000. I
would add that in my own opinion even more might be required,
since these by law must be private businesses whose partners must
accept unlimited liability for any losses.*'

This letter placed in relation to the other later correspondence
revealed the progression of Pimbo's thoughts. More than twenty

thousand pounds? He must have wondered where in all creation he was going to find such an amount, until the notion of a trading venture came into his head, combined with . . . Of course! Grimshaw's Corporation money! The Guild savings!

My thoughts were interrupted by a ring on the street door: Luke Fidelis, holding in his hand a shiny silver spoon seven or eight inches long.

'Here is a spoon transformed,' he said coming in. 'The mysterious apostle spoon. I have just bought it from Amity Thorn.'

'As a medicine spoon?'

'Don't be daft. I have no need of a spoon. I did it to help the Thorns. Amity's found it impossible to raise any money in Preston by it, and the church warden – silly man – says her entitlement to relief is doubtful so he must put the case to the parish council. Here.'

He handed the spoon to me and I looked at it more closely. It was indeed a fine piece of work. The bowl, which was cracked at the edge in two places, was circular and the slender shaft tapered and then at the end enlarged to form a platform on which stood the robed figure of the saint. I could see that he had in his hand a cup, or chalice.

'It's a pity she showed this around. People suspect she stole it, which will count against her with the council. Have you changed your mind about that?'

'No, I think Adam Thorn found it on the Moor, or somewhere out in the open. It was in a filthy state. But just look at it now, will you? She's cleaned it in a vinegar bath and it's come up bright. I gave her three shillings and sixpence for it. Did I overpay?'

I swivelled the shaft and inspected the little square dents on the underside. The immersion in vinegar had made these much clearer. They were undoubtedly hallmarks: a crown certainly, a capital letter C, and two with shapes that I could not make out.

I had on my desk a letter knife in silver that had a very clear set of marks, and which I knew to have been made in the reign of King James the First. I fetched it and we made a comparison: one of the marks was the same on both pieces – the crown – but the others were all quite different. What that meant neither of us could say.

'These marks will authenticate the piece,' I said. 'We need a silversmith to tell us more, however – and we haven't got one!'

'We will consult the nearest thing to it,' announced Fidelis. 'Come on!'

A minute later we had left the office and he was leading me, with a certain difficulty, along the edge of Market Place towards Friar Gate. Trading was now almost at an end, so that we had to thread our way through a disorder of barrels, baskets, sacks and coops as traders, impatient to get home, dismantled their stalls and tossed boards, trestles and unsold produce onto their carts.

Nicholas Oldswick, watchmaker, was established some half way down, and on the right hand side of Preston's third principal street. Broader at its Market Place end than either Fisher Gate or Church Gate, Friar Gate gradually tapers as it dips down, and then rises again, towards the moorside bar. The buildings that line it, most of them shops and workshops, become less imposing the further they lie beyond the dip and Oldswick's, being just at the point where the street begins to rise, was of medium size. A sign saying 'CLOSED' was displayed in the window glass from which we inferred that Oldswick had not yet reopened after his dinner.

His ancient servant Parsonage came puffing to the door, a sour expression on his face.

'If it's a watch that's stopped, you've to come back later,' he told us. 'If you've got news that he's won the lottery, you've to come in.'

'It is neither,' said Fidelis. 'It's Coroner's business.'

He stepped past him and into the shop, where I followed.

'He's asleep in his dining chair, doctor. Or was, until that accursed doorbell rang.'

'Will you be so kind as to fetch him out?'

As the old man shuffled away into the back, I touched Fidelis's arm.

'Coroner's business?' I whispered. 'How is that?'

'I'll tell you later.'

Nick Oldswick did not keep us long.

'How do, Titus? Doctor? What can I do for you?'

Fidelis produced the spoon.

'Would you have a glance at this?' he asked.

Oldswick took the spoon and beamed at us in turn. He showed no ill effects from having been awoken from his nap and was in jocular mood. He turned the spoon over and over like a curiosity, as if he had never seen such a thing before.

'Well, as a watchmaker, I am at a loss, doctor. Where is its mechanism? How does it tell the time?'

Fidelis reached across and turned the spoon over in Oldswick's fingers to show him the hallmarks.

'As you mention it, Sir, it does tell the time in one way, though without mechanism. It tells its own age – and that is why we are here. We hope you can interpret the hallmarks for us, since you work much in silver.'

Oldswick shrugged and smiled apologetically.

'I handle silver from time to time, doctor, but I regret I am not an assayer and know nothing of old hallmarks.'

He turned to me.

'What of it, Titus? Is the spoon evidence in one of your investigations?'

'It may be,' I said. 'If you cannot tell us its age, can you at least estimate its value – the value of the metal, that is, assuming it is indeed silver?'

'I can, if I weigh it.'

From a shelf he fetched a brass balance set on a wooden base and worked it by placing the silver spoon on one side, then adding small weights incrementally to the other.

'One ounce and five eighths,' he said. 'Let me see: assuming the metal is of sterling standard, I reckon it would be worth something like four shillings at today's prices.'

'It seems I did not overpay,' said Fidelis drily, taking the spoon back.

We thanked Oldswick and leaving him, if he liked, to resume his after-dinner nap, stepped into the street.

'Why was that Coroner's business, Luke? This is just an old spoon.'

'Follow me,' he said, 'and you may find out. It's not far and it's best to deal with this matter now.'

He strode off ahead of me up the sloping street, in the direction of the bar. Though it was undoubtedly true that I had more important matters to attend to, this business of the spoon was beginning to interest me and I followed eagerly.

It was a small house on Marsh Lane and very old, its beams twisted and roof uneven, as if they had been squeezed out of shape by the taller premises on either side. A shiny-faced woman of about fifty answered our knock.

'Good day, Mrs Farrowby,' said Luke with a slight bow.

A smile swept the care from her face.

'Doctor. This is a pleasure. Is it to see grandfather you've come?'

'Yes, though be assured this is not any medical matter. I have brought Mr Cragg along. Is Mr Feather well, by the way?'

'Never better than middling, but he says that's all anybody can hope for at ninety years old. And as you know he likes a visitor. Come in both of you, please.'

Wilfrid Feather was known universally by a different name: Methuselah. He was the oldest man in town – and, in all likelihood, the oldest inhabitant Preston had ever known, and his visitors came in expectation of being treated to stories and episodes from life three generations back. Upon superannuation, after serving many years as Town Clerk in the reigns of King William and Queen Anne, he devoted himself to antiquarianism. No one knew the history of Preston better, or remembered more of it by direct experience, than Methuselah did.

In the old style, the house had no kitchen and Susan Farrowby did her cooking on the range in the main parlour. Coming in, they found the old man sitting beside it now, nodding half asleep into his abundant white beard. His granddaughter pinched and shook his ear.

'It's Dr Fidelis to see you, Grandad. And he's brought Mr Titus Cragg.'

'Who?'

'You know. The young doctor – the good-looking one that saw to that old boil of yours last year – remember?'

Nodding benignly, Feather held out a palsied hand for his visitors to shake. He looked up and squinted but I knew that he didn't see much any more, just blurred shapes with voices.

Tea was offered and accepted and, while we waited for the kettle, Mrs Farrowby said, 'I'm sure the gentlemen would be interested to know the secret of your longevity, Grandad.' And then, in a whisper to us, 'He does love to tell, that's all.'

The old man roused himself. He lifted his inefficient eyes.

'Oh, aye. It's simple, is that. The secret of my surpassing longevity is the avoidance of cheese, Sir. All my life – no cheese!'

His voice was thin and sibilant, but clear.

'But we have such tasty cheese here in Lancashire, Mr Feather,' said Fidelis. 'Do you not like it?'

'Oh yes, I like it.'

'Then why have you forsworn it?'

'Are you not listening to me, young man? I say, if I'd eaten it, I wouldn't be here talking to you now, would I? I'd be long dead.'

'Ah! Yes, I do see that.'

Fidelis and I exchanged a glance and he moved on to the business that had brought us there.

'We have something to ask you, Sir. It's about a point that's cropped up in Mr Cragg's legal work. Ancient history, but I thought you with your knowledge might be able to help me.'

'If it's history, I'm your man. Spit out your question.'

'A little before your time, of course. But during Cromwell's war against the King, Preston was in some danger from Cromwell's men, isn't that so?'

'From Cromwell himself. My daddy was there. They were coming from the east and there was an attempt to stop them at Ribbleton Moor, Red Scar, that way. But the King's forces were out-fought, and a few of them were slaughtered, and not only that they were out-manoeuvred, outwitted if you like, and before you knew it Cromwell's men had got through to Gamull, and they were in Deepdale and they'd killed a few and taken the bridge at Walton. They were swarming all over the eastern end of town. Then he sent word into Preston, did Cromwell, in the midst of all this chaos, that he'd take the town's surrender in Market Place at such-and-such a time.'

'Was there fear?'

Old Feather gave a high-pitched laugh.

'Not fear, Sir: panic. This town's indefensible. There's no walls, no ditch around it. It is as open as the Queen of Egypt's legs. If Cromwell came in fighting there would be fire and rape and God knows what – the town in ruins, Corporation members hanging from gibbets and not a virgin left between the Moor and the Ribble.'

He paused, looking down at his beard and smoothing it with the palms of his hands as you do a bedspread.

'So what was to be done?'

'Why, treat with him. Pay him off. But then they remembered, did the Mayor and Corporation, that three or four days earlier they had divided the town's treasury between three of their number, three of the Burgesses that had been sometime Mayors. This had been on the understanding that each of these worthy men would remove his portion secretly at night to a place of safety, telling no one where, to keep it out of Cromwell's greedy hands. And that they did.'

'What had been in the treasury?' asked Fidelis.

'Coin, bits of plate, or that sort of thing. The town's entire portable wealth, more or less, at that time. Well *now*, of course, they wanted that coin and plate back, or else how could they pay Cromwell? And you know what?'

We waited, and so did Feather. The man was enjoying himself. Finally I broke out.

'What? Tell us.'

'They got it back from the first man, and they got it back from the second man, but as for the last chap, they couldn't find him, nor the money he'd taken charge of. Not a shilling of it turned up. It had disappeared, and so had he.'

'How did they pay Cromwell?'

'Had to make up the money with their own personal coins and plate. They had no choice. Every one of them went home and came back with a sack of his own money. But angry? You can hardly imagine it! They would have willingly strung up that old colleague of theirs, only for one thing. It turned out he were dead already. Killed in the battle, along with three of his estate workers. It was reckoned that he had buried the chest with the help of those men and then gone off to fight, without telling anyone where it was.'

With the help of his granddaughter holding the cup to his trembling lips he took a sip of tea.

'What was his name, this unfortunate man?'

'It was Benjamin Peel, of Peel Hall.'

I expect my mouth fell open at the coincidence.

'How very singular! That name was mentioned at my dinner table, not three hours since!'

Old Methuselah was shaking his head in the bemused fashion common to the very old.

'Not many remember him now. They blackened his name, see? Stead of telling the truth that he died bravely in battle, it was put about that he ran from the enemy. The family never recovered. Never served on the Corporation again, lost their money, lost their estate. Very sad that, and unjust too.'

'And has the money not been found since?'

Feather looked at me, his eyes twisted in a rheumy squint.

'You know what me dad said when he told me the story: that Peel had sent the silver away across the sea to the Isle of Man for its safety, and the boat foundered with all hands drowned before they got there. So it's lost forever, is that silver.'

And giving a sigh he closed his eyes, dropped his chin and reverted to the state we had found him in.

'Of course I now see why you think this is Coroner's business Luke. You have treasure trove on your mind.'

We were strolling back towards Friar Gate. Fidelis smiled.

'It isn't me alone. Adam Thorn has it on his mind – or rather he did. Remember what his wife told me when I first spoke to her about the spoon? It's evident he was much occupied with Peel's lost hoard, and wanted to find it. Of course, one spoon does not a treasure make. But if any more of the same should turn up, it would become your sworn duty to hold an inquest, would it not?'

Before we parted outside my house, I fetched the letters to Pimbo from Moon that I had been reading, and planted them in his hand.

'Cast your eye over them, Luke. I would be interested in your opinion. Oh, and will you lend me that spoon, just for a few days? I promise to look after it.'

Chapter Seven

∽

I ENTERED MY HOUSE, and found Matty waiting. She was jigging up and down in a state of some anxiety.

'The Mayor's been here this past half hour, and calling for you most impatiently,' she told me.

The tall, thick-necked figure of Grimshaw, as splendidly accoutred as ever, was planted on the hearth rug with his back to the fire. Elizabeth was sitting and sewing to his left while her parents sat quietly to his right, cowed by the air of pent-up anger that so often surrounded Grimshaw.

'Cragg, what time d'you call this?' he cried. 'I have been looking all over for you. Where the devil have you been?'

'Making various calls, Mr Mayor. Of course, if I had known you required me . . .'

Leaving a sentence unfinished is a useful rhetorical device in which lawyers and government servants are adept. I ushered him towards the parlour door.

'Would you like to come through to the office, where we can be more private?'

Even in my office he would not sit, but paced from wall to wall.

'Have you been to Cadley Place, Cragg?'

'This morning.'

'I trust you found the key to Pimbo's strong room there.'

'No. I searched his bureau and around his study. There was no key.'

'Where else did you look?'

'There was nowhere else, short of tearing the whole house apart.'

'Did anyone know about the key? The mother?'

'She has no memory.'

'Oh yes? We have heard stories of that sort before, usually on the Bench.'

'You misunderstand. She suffers from loss of memory. She is not mentally competent.'

'Was there no one else you could speak to?'

'A housekeeper. She knew nothing of Mr Pimbo's business affairs.'

'This is intolerable, Cragg! Pimbo had creditors. It must now be agreed that the key is irretrievable and steps taken accordingly. The strong room gate must be blown apart with a charge of gunpowder.'

If Grimshaw's remedy seemed extreme – and it did to me at the time – his urgency was understandable. In the autumn of the previous year he had assumed the mayoralty, much as Nero ascended the Quirinal Hill, as if by his own divine right. His grandiosity allowed for no doubts, and certainly for no future thwarts and reverses. He had vowed publicly and loudly that his hegemony would present the most golden Guild Year ever known.

The Preston Guild, as the world knows, is a two-week-long festival that occurs every twenty years. Its original ancient ceremonies – the renewal of by-laws, civic freedoms and title to parcels of town land known as burgages – were still performed, but had become almost incidental to what accompanied them – the rout of parades, balls, assemblies, plays, concerts, horse races and other sports, staged more lavishly with every renewal. The eating and drinking would commonly go on throughout the night, laying waste to almost the entire male population and a good part of the female.

Grimshaw well knew that the Guild draws fine society to Preston, and in return for its own expense of money, fine society expects these entertainments to be extravagant. So it's the duty of every Guild Mayor to make his Guild outshine all previous ones. The outlay in money in that endeavour is prodigious.

However, I had little time, now, for Grimshaw's petulance, and I had divided feelings about his dilemma. A disastrous Guild would be uncomfortable for our town. On the other hand it would draw a line under Ephraim Grimshaw's long baleful influence over us, as surely as Great Benjamin Peel had fallen from grace more than a hundred years before. In a trading town like this, to lose the Burgesses' money on such a scale can only lead to disgrace. Grimshaw may try to deflect the blame to others, but the decision to place the Guild fund into Pimbo's hands for investment had been, if not his alone, then driven through the Corporation by the strength of his persuasion. If he fell now, it would only be because of his own foolishness, ambition and greed, and I would not be sorry.

I took a deep breath, and inwardly steeled myself to withstand the blast that would inevitably come my way after I had said what I meant to say.

'Mayor Grimshaw,' I began. I knew he preferred 'Your Worship', but was damned if I would worship him. 'Have you consulted Recorder Thorneley about such a course of action?'

'I have.'

Matthew Thorneley acted as the Corporation's chief legal officer. He was a scheming, self-serving ferret who, as Recorder, was mostly required to ride along in his master's coat pocket, and to scurry down rat-holes at Grimshaw's bidding. On the other hand – and this was the reason he was valuable to Grimshaw – he knew the law.

'Then I am sure he has told you that for you, or any creditor, to blow open the door of a dead man's private vault before his estate has cleared probate would be illegal.'

Grimshaw snorted a mirthless laugh.

'You do understand, Cragg, that I am not talking in any personal capacity? It is the great Corporation of this borough that is owed money. It is Preston, Sir! And Preston wants answers to three questions. Is Pimbo's business sound? What is in his strong room? And most important what has happened to its money?'

'That is very well but, as you and the Recorder both know, the Corporation stands in relation to the deceased Mr Pimbo's estate just as any other individual creditor. Until the condition of the estate has been fully determined by the executors, nothing can be paid.'

'The executors will surely need to inform themselves of what is in the strong room.'

He was of course right. If no key were found, some form of forced entry would be needed. But all in good time.

'That might be months, even years away,' I said, then watched as a surge of fury empurpled Grimshaw's face.

'Years? Have you taken leave of your senses, man? We do not have years. The Guild opens in thirteen weeks' time. I shall have these damned slow-footed executors brought before me and give them a kick in their arses. Who are they?'

'They are two, of whom one is Pimbo's partner Mr Zadok Moon of Liverpool.'

'Who has not seen fit to appear as yet. And the other? I'll have his guts if he doesn't get that vault open fast.'

I took a certain immodest pleasure in replying:

'The other executor is myself, Mr Grimshaw.'

Having this power over Grimshaw was something to be relished, and the glow of it had me in silly spirits all evening, humming tunes about the house, joking for half an hour in the kitchen with Matty and being every way disinclined to return to those papers. Even by bedtime, I was still skittish, and tried to bring Elizabeth along with my mood. But she was again immersed in *Pamela* and hardly heard me as I lay beside her, embellishing certain details, which I had already told at supper, of my interview with the Mayor and how I had bested him and left him floundering.

'You are very proud and triumphant tonight, Titus,' murmured Elizabeth, turning a page.

'Yes, but the number of times that man has tried to do me down—'

'And you do know what inevitably follows all attacks of pride? A nasty fall.'

'A fall will be worth it!'

'Just don't break your neck, Titus.'

'Pride is not only or always bad, I think.'

She read on and, I suppose, half-listened to me as I began to describe the proud Ruth Peel, and what I had learned of the relations between herself and her employer.

'She's a proud one all right,' I was saying. 'You know you said last night that she was probably Pimbo's mistress? You had good reason to think so, as I agreed, but I now know that we were wrong.'

The grip of Mr Richardson's fiction began to loosen as the events of actual life exerted their spell on her.

'Why were we wrong?' she asked.

'Oh, he did try, you know – he pressed and he pressed, she told me, but she would not yield. I think it was actually her pride that saved her.'

'Good heavens!' Elizabeth exclaimed. 'It is like *Pamela* in reality. The master consumed by lust for the beautiful innocent servant girl, who clings ever more precariously to her virtue.'

'Although Miss Peel is not a girl. She is the housekeeper.'

'That is an important difference, Titus, I grant you. Tell me more. I want details.'

I looked into my wife's eyes. I loved them most when they were like this, bright with concentration and feeling.

'What troubles me in this, dearest, is that in order to believe Pimbo did indeed want Miss Peel for himself, and also to believe in this virtuous pride of hers, we have to accommodate one difficulty.'

'What is it?'

'In every other way she is rather handsome, you see. But when I saw her yesterday she carried her left arm in a sling. On my asking why, she said she had suffered a burn, so I took Fidelis to her today, in case the arm required treatment. Of course I left the room for their consultation, but Fidelis's later description of the arm was extraordinary. Your mother described the arm as stunted: it is far worse than that. It is hideously deformed, even repulsive. It dangles useless from her shoulder. It's the reason for the sling, which she always wears in company.'

Elizabeth gave a little gasp.

'Oh! The poor unfortunate! And otherwise good-looking, you say?'

'In every other way, Ruth Peel is a positive beauty.'

Elizabeth was openly curious now. She closed *Pamela* and put it aside for the night.

'So you are asking, could Pimbo really feel lust for her to that degree, knowing of her gross deformity?'

She turned to me and I took her in my arms.

'He left her the orchard in his will,' I murmured into the hair covering her ear. 'He bound her to celibacy. These are not the actions of indifference. But still, I wonder.'

Then I kissed her tenderly and for the time being we ceased to exchange any more words.

*

The next day was Sunday, which the town ideally gave up to religious observance in the morning, roast meat at midday – or a little after – and the continuance of sober, tract-reading domesticity until nightfall. In practice church attendance by all could not be enforced, meat for all could not be afforded and, as for sobriety at home, attempts to have Preston's more than thirty taverns and alehouses closed up on the Sabbath had always failed.

Not every Prestonian planning an evening of indulgence had to spend it in Preston, however: Luke Fidelis, for one, would take himself off quietly to Liverpool from time to time and this was one of those times. It was about half past ten in the morning that he called at Cheapside in full riding habit, with the bundle of Moon's letters to Pimbo in his hand.

'I look forward to discussing them on my return,' he said, passing them over. 'They are remarkably full of interest.'

I had a letter to give him that I had written myself. It was addressed to Zadok Moon at Pinchbeck's Coffee House, Liverpool.

'It informs him of his appointment as co-executor with me of the estate of Phillip Pimbo,' I explained, 'and asks him to communicate with me at his earliest convenience. I took the opportunity to enclose a summons requiring his presence at Pimbo's inquest. Will you be my post-rider, Luke?'

He took the letter and tucked it into a saddlebag. I said:

'Give it to the keeper of Pinchbeck's Coffee House of Paradise Street. But keep an eye open for Zadok Moon yourself. He may actually be there when you call. You have read Moon's letters to Pimbo?'

'Yes.'

'Then you know about the scheme for a Guinea voyage, in which he and Moon were investors. Pimbo was the principal investor, it seems. I would like to know how the voyage has prospered. Moon writes of it as if it cannot fail. Will you find out more?'

Fidelis, having promised that he would try to do so, rode away.

I would have been glad to spend the afternoon in my library but after a week of relative cold the weather had begun to warm, and as Midsummer approached, it promised warmer still. So, anticipating complaints from neighbours in Fisher Gate, I decided to remove Pimbo's body, from where it was still lodged in his former business room, to a cooler and more remote place.

Hazelbury met me there with the key of the goldsmith's shop. He was disappointed that I had not yet flushed out the missing strong room key, and was concerned about the safety of the shop's stock.

'There's a quantity of gold and silver items from the shop that I would prefer to put in the strong room. They are in a cupboard in his office for now, and have been protected by the body being in the same room. But after Mr Pimbo's body's gone to some other place, and with Midsummer so near, there's those that might take a drink, lose the fear that they had of the corpse and come for it. Where can I put it for safety?'

'There is Oldswick's shop, he's got a strong press with an iron door. Go and ask him if he's got the space and will take the things that most concern you. They'll be safe enough with him.'

But Hazelbury had not finished.

'There's another thing, Sir. Me and the lads had no wages Friday, and what about this coming week? What'll we do? We'd like to open up Monday and keep trading. We've met together – me, Michael and the lad – and we're all ready and willing.'

I shook my head.

'No, Hazelbury. The business was Mr Pimbo's. You are his employees not his partners. You cannot continue business however much it is second nature to you. Trading must remain suspended until such time as there is a new owner.'

'There's this Mr Moon, Sir. If he were a confidential partner in the shop—'

'That would be different, but don't raise your hopes too high. I know Pimbo spoke of him as his partner, but he seems to have had little to do with Preston and I am confident the supposed partnership was about a different business altogether. I am actively looking for Moon, you may be sure of it, and soon as I find him we'll know the truth.'

Poor Hazelbury looked utterly crestfallen, and I imagined what his wife would have to say at the prospect of a second week's wages lost.

'Cheer up, man,' I said. 'You must have something put away. Don't tell me you have nothing under the floorboards!'

We were waiting for John Oatseed the coffin-maker with his cart, bringing a rough box from his stock to shift the corpse in. When he came at last we all three carried the box into the inner office, where Pimbo had died, and placed it beside his prone body. Oatseed removed the coffin lid.

The corpse lay on the floor, covered by a blanket which I removed. It was still clothed as before but the flesh, where I could see it, was grey and seemed damp as if – impossibly – it had been sweating.

'I'll take the head end, Mr Oatseed, if you will take the feet,' I said, leaning forward to grasp beneath the late Pimbo's armpits.

Hazelbury left us but I walked all the way alongside the cart. With little traffic on a Sunday we covered the distance quickly – down Lune Lane, wheeling left into Friar Gate, and from there into Marsh Lane. As we passed Methuselah's house I saw the pale face of his granddaughter glancing out, and the movement of her hand as she crossed herself at the sight of the coffin.

A few hundred feet further along we turned into the House of Correction, a squarely built stone building formerly part of the living quarters of the Old Friary, amidst whose ruins it stood at the end of a rutted track. The building had served over the years as a Lazar House and hospital before being adapted to meet the present time's growing need for incarceration.

I had arranged with the Keeper, Arnold Limb, for the use of one of his cells, the coolest he could provide, in return for a fee I hoped would be allowed from civic funds. Limb had allotted me what he described as his 'isolation cell', as it was in a small building separate from the other prisoner accommodation. He showed it to me and I told him this would suit my purposes very well.

'Well this'll be one guest I shan't have to feed or water,' he said jovially.

'Or find employment in the workshop,' I added. 'But do ensure he will be locked up tight when we have finished, if you please, Mr Limb.'

'I will indeed, Mr Cragg. I don't want him walking abroad, do I?'

Oatseed had, at my request, summoned the corpse-washers Mary Maitland and Dolly Chapman to attend us there. Mary and Dolly received eight pence for every corpse that passed through their hands. They were familiar figures to every house in town on this most dreaded business, and had seen every family at its most distressed. It made them women worth listening to and, after a few minutes' conversation with Limb outside, I went in to join them. They had already stripped off his clothes and packed them away in a linen sack.

'He were a strange one, Mr Cragg,' said Mary, contemplating Pimbo's remains stretched out on the trestle table provided.

'I'm afraid to say I did not know him well,' I admitted.

'Nowt to be afraid about. Not many did, eh Mary?'

'Not many Dolly. He were one of those, was Mr Pimbo, that slapped every man on the back, and winked at every woman, but were a real friend to nobody.'

'And a moneylender, mind. No amount of backslapping and winking's going to make folk cherish a moneylender.'

'That's right. "Lend to an idiot, borrow from a rogue."'

'I liked his dog, though.'

'Me too. Mischief on four legs.'

Dolly went to fetch a tub of soapy water and they each took a soft brush which they dipped in the water tub and carefully washed him, giving special attention, with coos and cries of dismay, to his head wounds. After that he was sluiced down and dried with linen towels, and Dolly combed the fringe of hair around what was left of his bald head. With a tender last touch she ran the comb a couple of times through the tangle of his pubic hair.

'There, Mr Pimbo,' she said, standing back and crossing herself. 'You'll do.'

Finally, just like two chambermaids working together to make a bed, the corpse-washers each took an end of a white sheet. They spread and stretched it in the air like a canopy, then let it float down to drape and cover the body completely.

'I'll see to the return of his clobber to his house, shall I, Mr Cragg?' said Mary when they had done. I knew that this task, and the perquisite to follow, was part of her franchise. I had already gone through Pimbo's pockets, so I agreed and they left with the clothing bag. As I locked the cell door, I realized that, in all the time they were working, neither woman had commented or asked a question about just how, or why, Phillip Pimbo had died.

Back at the office I worked as fast as I could through the rest of the dead man's correspondence that I had taken from Cadley Place. This continued to fall into groups. One related to shop business:

notes tracking fluctuations in the price of gold and silver, letters of
account from the assay offices of York and Chester, and dealings
with Liverpool ship-owners for the purchase of pearls and precious stones. Another concerned Pimbo's pawnbroking activities,
including many letters from pledgers requesting him to extend
their agreed loan terms. I presumed these could be tallied with the
books that would have been kept at the shop, but there were no
copies here of Pimbo's replies, and the amounts of the loans were
without exception trivial. Nothing here seemed to shed any light on
his death.

I was collecting and tying up the piles of paper with legal ribbon
when I remembered the tightly folded paper I had found in the
secret drawer. It had to be of some importance, or Pimbo would
not have concealed it in the writing desk. Remembering that I had
slid it among the other papers, I thought it must have fallen out
during my arrangement of the documents and got down on my
knees to search the floor.

I found it under one of the pedestals of my writing table.
Reaching it out I unfolded and read it while still kneeling on the
floor. Having gone through all those pages of business paper, I was
completely unprepared for the nature of this one. It was neatly laid
out in best handwriting.

MEMORANDUM and RESOLUTIONS for 1741:

- *THAT I do love Miss Ruth Peel, my housekeeper, in the
  very deeps of my heart;*

- *THAT likewise I do lust after her body and would join
  it with mine;*

- *THAT on Christmas Day, 1740 I laid before her all my
  desires, and proposed that she come into my bed;*

- *THAT on Boxing Day, 1740 I received notice from Miss Peel that she rejected it as dishonourable, and would resign from my service;*

- *THAT on the same day I persuaded her to stay, promising that I would not repeat the said proposal until the disposition of my life makes our MARRIAGE possible;*

- *THAT to change the said disposition will be exceedingly costly;*

- *THAT I shall make myself sufficiently rich and, within two years, shall make all right.*

(signed) Phillip Pimbo 1st January 1741

I turned the page over, where I read the following:

MEMORANDUM and RESOLUTIONS for 1742:

- *THAT my circumstances, and those in my household, are as they were this day twelve months since;*

- *THAT the resolutions I made on that date are this day renewed;*

- *THAT the said resolutions shall this year be fulfilled in all particulars, so help me God.*

(signed) Phillip Pimbo 1st January 1742

Laying this astonishing paper down again, I saw that I had, after all, found a key – not to Pimbo's strong room, but to his soul.

Chapter Eight

∞

SUNDAY NIGHT HAD been the warmest and clearest of the year and, given the choice of a sober early bed in preparation for next week's work, or sitting in the garden of a public house under the stars, many Prestonians preferred to sing and drink until dawn. In the morning, with splitting heads, most could not face the light of day and so stayed at home and called it the Feast of Saint Monday.

Consequently there were fewer on the street than usual at nine o'clock in the morning when I walked the short distance to the Moot Hall. I had two pieces of separate business to do. One was connected to the Thorns' spoon, still tucked into my waistcoat pocket. The other was more ticklish. Following our confrontation the previous day, I had received a letter from the Mayor, in which he expressed his amazement that I 'presumed' to act as executor to the will of Phillip Pimbo, while at the same time having the duty as Coroner to conduct an inquest into his death. There was, he wrote, a clear conflict of interest in this, and 'it is the Corporation's view, informed by the Recorder's advice, that you should therefore cede the Coroner's role in this case to the one who is by tradition emergently deputed to that role, viz. the lawfully elected Mayor'.

This was certainly a bold stroke. It was quite true that the Preston Coroner had no permanent deputy and that during his sickness, or absence, his inquisitorial role could be taken over by the Mayor acting *pro tempore*. At the same time, the ploy was not going to work. There was simply no precedent for the Mayor to displace a sitting able-bodied Coroner, and I doubted very much if it would be legal for him to try to do so. My opinion was backed up by Furzey, who possessed formidable legal knowledge of the Coroner's jurisdiction. The whole point of Preston's Coroner, he said, was to balance a Mayor's power, and to stand up for the interests of the Crown, as the very name 'Coroner' implies. Or, to put this as Furzey himself did, 'you can tell Grimshaw he must stuff it, and the King will say aye'.

So I was on my way to tell him to stuff it. I knew what was in Grimshaw's mind. Given the amount of money that he urgently wanted to reclaim from Pimbo's estate, the verdict of suicide in this case would be disastrous. The worldly goods of self-murderers, like those belonging to the murderers of another, were the property of the Crown, meaning if the Guild fund invested with Pimbo should indeed be lost there would be no hope of even part of it being paid back to the Corporation by his estate. On the other hand if murder, manslaughter or fatal accident were the verdict Grimshaw might hope for some restitution and, should he wangle himself into the Coroner's chair, he would be in a position to steer the jury to such a conclusion.

I caught the Mayor descending the main staircase, with Recorder Thorneley following one step behind. They could not avoid facing me so I waited at the stair foot. I was determined, despite Furzey's recommendation, to adopt a conciliatory tone.

'Ah, Mr Mayor!' I said. 'I have your letter. Its suggestion that you should take over as Coroner to Pimbo's inquest is most considerate.'

'It's a bad business, is that,' Grimshaw said lightly. 'I expect you are glad to be relieved of it.'

'That is as may be, but I fear your proposal can't be allowed.'

94

His face changed from geniality to the assumed puzzlement of a politician girding to debate.

'Not allowed? How so, if I allow it? If the Mayor himself allows it?'

'There's no pretext, for I am perfectly well, and I am here present. Therefore the inquest must be done by me, whether you or I like it, or not.'

Grimshaw's tone became a shade harder as he raised his finger.

'I warn you, Cragg. You will find that you have no choice but to give way.'

He made to brush past me. I stepped sideways into his path, still speaking softly.

'I *do* have no choice, as I cannot give way. I must do my duty on behalf of His Majesty the King.'

Grimshaw's face was set in a pouting glower as he pointed to the man beside him.

'Mr Thorneley has assured me, Cragg, that there is conflict of interest in this case, and that you are disqualified. That satisfies me.'

'But it is pure nonsense. There is no conflict. I am not a beneficiary of Mr Pimbo's will and there is no verdict that my court might deliver that can either benefit me or prevent my executing the will.'

I turned to Thorneley.

'Surely you agree, Mr Recorder, knowing the law as you do.'

Thorneley looked startled, like one who found himself standing at the point of his own weapon. He knew I could not be argued into submission with jargon and half-baked legal arguments, as others could.

'I, er, don't know, Cragg. We would have to see if there were precedents, and that sort of thing. We are looking into it.'

This less than assured response earned the Recorder a savage look from his master. I said:

'You will waste your time, I fear.'

Now I stepped aside and as the two men walked past me, I heard Grimshaw mutter,

'That is not what you told me, Thorneley!'

I did not yet leave the Moot Hall. Instead I skirted the grand stair and penetrated the building as far as the office of Tom Atherton, the Clerk of the Records. We were old friends.

'How do, Titus?' he said warmly.

I shook his hand and we exchanged family news for a few minutes, until Tom said,

'So, what brings you today? Consulting burgage rolls?'

'No, Tom. I want to go back to 1648 and the battle. Will there be records?'

'There's records of almost everything in here.'

'I've been talking to old Methuselah, and he's spun me a yarn that I want to verify. There was a former Mayor in it, Benjamin Peel of Peel Hall.'

'He was a big man then, in the early part of the King's war.'

'And a King's man, I think.'

Atherton shrugged.

'I couldn't say. The Corporation had been for the King, more or less. Until it happened that Parliament was winning, of course.'

'Well, this is what Methuselah told me: they were fearing that Parliament was not only after the Scotch invaders but eyeing the town's treasure, and that Oliver Cromwell was on his way to get it. So Benjamin Peel and two others were deputed to remove the money and plate to safety. Then Cromwell gave a beating to the royal forces on Ribbleton Moor, and the Corporation fell into terror. They sent word to Cromwell offering to pay him off, in return for not putting the town to the sword, for which they needed the town's money and plate. They got two-thirds of it back but when they sought out Benjamin Peel to know where his share of the treasure was that he'd taken to safety, they found he had gone to the battle and been killed. He had told no one where he'd put it.'

Atherton laughed.

'That's good! They were stuck on the sharp end of their own cunning.'

'And they had to raise the lost money amongst themselves, Tom. That would have hurt.'

'So what sort of record are you hoping to find?'

'I am interested in precisely what Peel took away for safety.'

Atherton stood up and beckoned me down into the archives, a set of dusty, low-ceilinged rooms tightly packed with shelves on which were piled rolls, parchments and ledgers. As he led me through this labyrinth he gestured around with pride.

'This is not just a warehouse full of old paper. It's our memory is this – the town's, I mean. There's hundreds of years of town life preserved here. Imperfectly, of course.'

'No memory is perfect, Tom, but think what we would lose if we could recall nothing.'

The Clerk of the Records rubbed his hands with pleasure as he proceeded between the stacks, checking shelf labels as he went.

'We would not be human, Titus. We would not feel alive.'

I thought of old Mrs Pimbo, locked in her own salon, taking her long slow leave of memory and sentient life.

Atherton brought me to a shelf of leather-bound folios, with dates in the 1640s marked on their spines. He took one down, opened it briefly, then led the way back towards the door.

'If any of these books contain what you want to know, this one's your most likely.'

The volume contained the memoranda of the Corporation between the years 1646 and 1651, either written into the book directly by a scribe, or on sheets pasted in place. Atherton turned the pages, many recording the unfolding events of the war, as reflected by a town anxious to end on the winning side.

'Feast to celebrate the King's victory . . . feast for the Parliament's victory . . . celebration of the Parliament's triumph again . . . of the King's escape . . . of his capture . . . No, I've gone too far. Turn back . . .'

After much turning and turning back, we came at last to a run of pages dealing with minuted meetings of the Burgesses in the summer of 1648 as they trembled in increasing anxiety. The King was in prison by this time but his man, the Scotch Duke of Hamilton, had descended on Preston while he set his Scotch army running around the county to plunder the farms. In the meantime word began to come through that Cromwell was bearing down from the east. No civic feasts appeared on the roster now, but hasty attempts to improvise defences, to barn up grain, to requisition horses and pack wives and children off into the country. Preston, so long known for its pride, was faltering on the edge of a nasty fall.

On the fourteenth of August, Preston's Burgesses had '*report that the forces of Parliament are at Clitheroe, and mean next to bear down as fast as may be possible on Preston, and that the Duke's scattered force will scarcely have time to prepare*'. Terrified, they resolved to '*entrust unto three faithful friends, and former Mayors of the Corporation, the bulk of the town's exchequer, to be divided between them, that they remove each privily for the duration of the present emergency to a safe place, whereof no man save them will know the whereabouts.*'

This memorandum confirmed the triple division of the treasure Methuselah had told of. I looked where the names of the three hand-picked trustees were given: Jonathan Greenwood, Francis Harty and, yes, Benjamin Peel. I said,

'According to Methuselah's account, the Burgesses had to pay Cromwell out of their own pockets. Did it happen like that, Tom?'

Atherton was still reading and concentrating hard, frowning and protruding his lips.

'What happened was that none of the treasure could be retrieved in time. The Burgesses' contributions from their own pockets were to be treated as loans, repayable when the three chests of money were dug up and returned.'

'And . . . ?'

Atherton turned a couple of leaves and put his finger on a line of scribal writing.

'Well, look here! Methuselah was right.'

He read out, against a date some three months after the battle of Preston, a resolution *'that Sergeant Wilkinson be paid three shillings per diem to search for that part of the town's treasure entrusted during the late emergency to Benjamin Peel Esq., and hid by him before his death in the battle.'*

'Three shillings a day? It's a sizeable outlay. Did the sergeant find the hoard?'

'Let's see.' Atherton turned another page. 'No, he didn't. There's another resolution by the Burgesses a week later, *'That the three shillings paid daily to the Sergeant shall cease, him being unable to find the treasure hid by Ben: Peel; and, further, That a bounty be offered of five pounds to any man that shall give information leading to the return of the same to the Corporation treasury'*. I think we can assume that two-thirds of the hidden money – Harty's and Greenwood's portions – were safely recovered long before this, but that Peel's allocation could not be found.'

'All because, as it confirms here, poor Peel was killed in the battle.'

'And the treasure entrusted to him is still there – wherever he hid it. A tantalizing thought, is it not?'

'Do we have an indication of what the treasure consisted of?'

'Yes, look, it is all clearly laid out here.'

He showed me, opposite the last resolution to offer a reward, a sheet had been glued onto the page. It was headed '*SCHEDULE: GOLD AND SILVER BELONGING TO THE CORPN THAT JON: GREENWOOD, FRAN: HARTY AND BEN: PEEL TOOK TO HIDE IT*'. The Moot Hall clock began striking ten as I glanced through, but five had not sounded before I'd stopped reading and asked Tom Atherton for a scribal copy.

Walking back to the office I reached out the spoon from my waistcoat. It glinted as I spun it between my fingers and I wondered. There had been two unhelpful things about the schedule Atherton had showed me. There was no indication of how the treasure had been divided between Greenwood, Harty and Peel. And there had been no mention of any apostle spoon. Most of it had been money – gold coins, silver crowns and a few of smaller denomination. Various items of plate were also listed: a gold chafing dish; sauce boats; a candelabrum; and a pair of silver lamb and flag figures, emblems of the town. However, there was a compendium item at the bottom of the list: '*such sundry silver items as forks, spoons, rings, buttons, etc. value fifty shillings*'.

Could what I held in my hand have been one of these sundry items? Obviously it might have been, but the schedule document could not be used to prove that it actually was. And to consider the matter more broadly, we did not even have a hoard. Was this whole suspicion a mare's nest?

Behind my desk once more I resolutely put seductive thoughts of buried treasure out of my mind. There was work to do on Pimbo's inquest which, wanting to get it over before Midsummer's Day, I had decided to hold on the day before, the coming Wednesday. I first sent Furzey to secure an inquest room at the Friary Bar Inn, as being close to where Pimbo lay, and on his return I put him to work raising a jury. Meanwhile I drew up summonses for the principal witnesses. I wrote them out for Robert Hazelbury, Michael Ambler, and the young apprentice Roger Waterton. I turned out two other speculative summonses, one for Ruth Peel, though I had not definitely decided to call her, and another for Zadok Moon, though he might not be found in time to be called.

What to do about Miss Peel was a question that turned on another – what use should I make of Phillip Pimbo's New Year Resolutions? On the previous night I had showed them to Elizabeth, and she had made me see them in a different light.

'Well, I was half right, Titus,' she said. 'Miss Peel was not his mistress, but he wanted her to be just as she told you.'

'And, perhaps reluctantly, his wife. She forced a marriage proposal out of him.'

'Did she?'

'That's what he says.'

'No he doesn't. He says nothing of whether she wants marriage. He assumes she wants to be his wife, because she refuses to be his mistress. That is typical of a man.'

'Well, looking at this as possible evidence, the main thing is the point about making himself rich very quickly in order to marry her.'

She wanted to interrupt but I stopped her.

'No. Let me first think this out aloud. Phillip Pimbo knew that he would need much money – twenty thousand pounds, he had been told – to establish his bank. But this document gives, does it not, the urgent reason behind this ambition? His desire for Ruth Peel led him to gamble through Zadok Moon for very high stakes in a Guinea voyage. That, it seems to me, is like putting all your money on the turn of a card. If the voyage went wrong he would get no other chance to keep his resolve within the limit of time he set himself. So now. Let's say it *did* go wrong. Would he not despair? And despairing, might he not end his life? If that is what happened then this document is a vital piece of evidence.'

'Have you thought it through now, Titus? May I speak?'

'If you please, my heart.'

'This document may be what you say, but it is also much else. It is eloquent. It speaks of Pimbo's tender heart, of his love as well as his lust, of his *character*. Granted, he doesn't let Miss Peel think for herself – men rarely do with women, though you are a great exception, my love! But Mr Pimbo does not force himself upon Miss Peel, does not attack or bear down on her. In short, he is not at all like Mr B. in *Pamela*. That man is a cunning, stalking beast of the desert until Pamela tames him at the last. Pimbo is more like a confused and worried farm animal.'

'On Saturday you said he was playing God. Does a farm animal play God?'

'Not face to face, but he might in his will.'

The picture of this in our minds made us both laugh out loud.

'How does what you said help to explain his death, though?' I asked, a little ashamed that we had made sport of the dead.

'It does, supposing that all along he *wanted* to be a beast of the desert; if he meant to prove to this imperious woman – that was the word you used of her – that he was her equal in firmness of character. So suppose then that he concocted a fantastic, far-fetched, all-or-nothing solution for his woes: to win her with one enormous manly stroke of profit. And finally, suppose that he failed. Would his life not then be ashes?'

I realised that I could not after all spare Ruth Peel. She must give evidence and be confronted with Phillip Pimbo's sheet of resolutions. So next morning, having sent for one of the Parkin brothers who, as constables, I could use to convey summonses, I thought further that the court might benefit if it heard also from a disinterested witness in the Pimbo household. So I wrote a second summons addressed to the young maid Peg and, within the hour, I had dispatched both documents to Cadley Place by hand of Esau Parkin.

While I was sending these out, an item of post came in. It was from Luke Fidelis, written earlier in the morning from the Mermaid Inn, Liverpool.

Dear Cragg,

I have been on the scent but the quarry still eludes me. I know Zadok Moon is in this city but he lies low – I cannot tell why, but I have the name of one that knows him, and I think knows more. Indeed I suspect this whole business runs deeper than we had apprehended and I intend to alter my plans and stay here today to look into the matter further. Please let my appointed patients (listed below) know that I shall call not this afternoon but tomorrow instead. None is seriously ill (let us hope).

I am etc. LF

I glanced through the list of seven patients. Three were lady residents of Preston, for whom the doctor's visit might perhaps be more social than medical. Two of the other four were Burgesses – a wine merchant and a shoemaker – and two were servants in wealthy houses, one of them Lord Derby's. Fidelis's practice, I reflected, was growing, and becoming more fashionable.

The fact that he was prepared to give up a day of appointments, and fees, only to satisfy his curiosity over Pimbo's death suggested to me that there was a limit to his worldly ambition, and his desire to be Preston's largest doctor. He was not my personal officer, and these were not official inquiries, yet he wanted to pursue them, though he had nothing to gain by it unless it was the fun of testing himself against the puzzle.

I thought also about Moon. Was he in hiding, or did 'lying low' only represent Fidelis's colourful figure of speech? I tried to imagine Zadok Moon, and saw before my mind's eye an intense, wiry figure with a thin nose and black hair, added to the beard that Ruth Peel had mentioned. This Moon of my thoughts had fierce eyes and was a demon of quicksilver energy, doing terrific bouts of work followed by thorough indulgence – wine, women, horses and the card table. He was in all things confident and capable, but never too serious. I rather liked him.

When I told Elizabeth at dinner how I had constructed this character she laughed and said I happened to have made a man very much opposite to his partner Phillip Pimbo.

'So, they were complementary,' I said. 'It makes their partnership something that Mr Philosopher Plato would have been quite delighted with.'

'And I shall be quite delighted if Mr Moon turns out to be fat, stupid and very dull.'

Stealing half an hour in my library before the afternoon's work, I picked up Montaigne and made a start on the essay 'Of the Power of Imagination', thinking it might illuminate the puzzling process by which the mind always feels compelled, in Shakespeare's good words, to give to airy nothing a local habitation, as I had done in imagining Zadok Moon. I found the Frenchman's thinking, however, running along different paths. The imagining he deals with is not an airy nothing, but a force capable of making real things happen outside the bounds of the head: for example, that we may catch a disease by thinking too much about it. I wondered how Luke Fidelis would regard that.

Reading on I came to a curious sentence: *'Tis a common*

proverb in Italy that he knows not Venus in her sweet perfectness who has never lain with a lame Mistress.'

The words naturally brought Pimbo back into my mind, and his feelings towards Miss Ruth Peel. Nothing, says Montaigne, is straightforward in physical love, and nothing should less surprise us than that the thought of a bodily imperfection might throw someone into amorous longing. But as Montaigne might also say, the word that counts here is *thought*. So was Pimbo's erotic mind excited by Miss Peel's deformity? And was that the mainspring of all his other decisions?

Chapter Nine

∽

LUKE FIDELIS KNEW Liverpool, but few at Liverpool knew Fidelis. In Preston a man's life was open to scrutiny wherever he went, but in Liverpool your actions might go unremarked by anyone for several hours, or even days, for the great seaport had a thousand times more strangers in it than it had acquaintances. Its business was conducted not by single men but by companies of them, competing with other companies, in affairs which are bound I think to be habitually as secretive as possible.

This was not – at least it was not in those days – a town that enjoyed refined amusements, though there was no shortage of rough entertainment for the sailors, as in a theatre, cockpits, gaming houses, fight booths, freak-shows and brothels. But, for the class of men engaged in business, economic activity took the place of fun. The port was always in a ferment of business; it bubbled with news. Men talked of ships into and out of the river, of privateers, and pirates, and of ship-loads lost at sea; of the prices and tariffs on this or that cargo; and always of profit, and loss. Discourse of this kind was conducted at coffee houses in and around Pool Lane and Castle Street, which stretched between the Exchange and the enclosed dock. Here they drew up bills of lading and exchange, made lists of crew and chandlery, pored over maps and charts. They told each other tales of Spanish prizes counted in doubloons, of fabulous cargoes lost in storms, of slave revolts and plagues.

Pinchbeck's Coffee House in Paradise Street was buzzing with just such conversation as Fidelis sat down. He had waited several minutes for a vacant table and was hungry and thirsty after his ride from Preston. He ordered food and drink before asking the serving girl for an interview with Mr Pinchbeck himself.

The man made Fidelis wait a little longer, as must be expected of one that regards himself as a person of importance. Pinchbeck, who had formerly been a Sergeant-Major in the Grenadiers, had begun to affect in middle life a weary manner that, while still being recognizably that of a non-commissioned officer, suggested one that bore the burden of social importance.

'Zadok Moon, you say?' he asked, tapping his chin with a crook-finger. He had graciously acceded to Fidelis's invitation to sit down, but refused refreshment. 'Yes, I know the name. There's been mail for him posted to and collected from here, I can say that.'

'What does he look like?'

'An ordinary fellow. Wears a seaman's beard, but that's not remarkable here.'

'So he may have been to sea?'

'I couldn't say.'

'What is his dress?'

'Ordinary – but not shabby.'

'And what is his age?'

'Middling. Closer to thirty than forty.'

They were no further on when Fidelis's meal arrived. As Pinchbeck was telling next to nothing about Moon, Fidelis abandoned the interrogation. He picked up his knife and Pinchbeck left his customer to enjoy his plate of boiled ham and pickles.

After satisfying his appetite Fidelis ventured out again. Going from coffee house to tavern to coffee house, he asked after Moon and, receiving no satisfactory answer, began to wonder why the man was so elusive. He also, as he progressed, started to suspect that there was someone following behind him. He pretended to look with consuming interest into the window of a print-seller, in the hope of noting someone conspicuously idling in the street behind him. There was no such thing. At another moment he saw a blind beggar crouching in a doorway across the street who, after a few moments' observation, he found to be just as blind and destitute as he appeared.

Fidelis walked on, past the theatre which appeared to be closed, and on to Castle Square, where he joined the audience for another kind of show, but one that required no ticket: an acrobat was tying his body into knots. Fidelis took a certain medical interest in such performances, and stayed to watch, though he glanced around from time to time. Somewhere near the theatre a few minutes earlier he'd noticed a woman dodging along in his wake, and he was keeping a sidelong eye out for her. But he was momentarily distracted by an extreme of bodily contortion and did not notice the woman was by his side until he felt her tugging at his sleeve.

'Only a bit of silver will have me, kind Sir,' she wheedled. 'Just a couple of shillings is all I ask and you can have my company for half an hour, you can.'

She leaned forward so that her broken-toothed mouth was beside his ear.

'I've got a place to meself, and with a bed in it too,' she whispered.

Fidelis looked at her. She was not young, and nor was she pretty. Her face needed a wash with soap, and the ragged hem of her dress trailed on the ground. He sent her briskly on her way, for her approach had reminded him to look at his watch. He had another engagement, and in a politer part of town.

He left the Castle behind him and walked up Castle Street, past the Exchange and into a district whose streets were recently built, and whose inhabitants prided themselves in sobriety and respectability – at least in public. He turned into Edmund Street and approached the door of a well-kept house, the brasses on the door brightly polished, the windows clean. It was opened discreetly by a woman.

Without saying a word she led him into the parlour where the drapes were closed, and candles had been lit. A bass viol lay on the floor beside an upright chair and a stand with a sheet of music open. On a table was a salver with two glasses and a bottle of port, from which she poured. They touched glasses and drank, and then she poured again for him alone.

While he sipped the wine she sat in the chair, took up the viol, placed it between her legs and began to play a slow, beguiling, amorous tune. All through it her eyes remained fixed on his and a teasing smile drifted across her lips.

Coming to the end she lifted the bow from the strings and waited. Luke drained the wine glass and moved to her side, from where he could see the sheet open on the music stand. This was something jauntier, a sea shanty. Among Fidelis's attributes was the possession of a more than serviceable baritone voice and after a few opening notes from Mrs Butler's viol he ran through the song. I have heard my friend sing on a number of occasions and, though I cannot say he puts great feeling into it, he sings with energy and accuracy.

When he had finished, his accompanist rose and stood facing him.

'The servants are out,' she murmured, and putting her hands on his shoulders, she raised herself on her tiptoes and kissed his mouth.

Her name was Mrs Belinda Butler, a fair-haired, nicely proportioned woman of thirty-five whose husband, Captain Butler, had been lost at sea five years earlier, leaving to her the house and a sum of money from his life insurance. Luke had known Mrs Butler since the autumn, and had become a regular visitor. I do not think he had fallen in love with her in the dreamy, impractical, boyish way that I had known him fall before; but he and Mrs Butler had a firm and fond understanding that rested on the base of their mutual needs and desires.

So, as a matter of course, he took her up to bed and they gave themselves over to the conversation of the body. Then, as was their custom afterwards, they lay side by side, talking and often laughing together about odd things they had seen and done since their last meeting. But what she broached with him this evening was less of a laughing matter.

'I have something to tell you,' she said, 'which I fear you will not like, but I must. A gentleman has been calling on me and he has asked me to be his wife.'

I imagine Fidelis lay still for some moments, before making any reply. Then:

'Shall you accept?'

And I imagine Mrs Butler waiting for this inevitable question, and having her answer ready.

'I believe I shall. I have lived a good enough life since Captain Butler was lost, but my portion from his insurance shrinks by the year.'

'Who is the man? What's his name?'

'Mr Moreton Canavan. A merchant, a most genial gentleman and very well-dressed.'

'I do not like him already. How long have you known him?'

'Since last month.'

'Then you hardly *do* know him.'

Her husky laugh pleased his ear.

'Yes I do! He declares he has a great love of music, and also the theatre, which he attends constantly.'

'But how can you tell he is sincere? He loves you, I hope?'

'He has assured me that he does.'

'And he has competent means? He can keep you fitly?'

'I do believe so. He tells me he has his own carriage and horses, and a horse for the races too, and good land in West Derby. He plans to build a house there and hunt, and one day hopes to become Master of the Hunt.'

'A sportsman as well as a drama-loving merchant! Who do you know that can attest to his character?'

'He was brought to this house by the Captain's cousin William.'

'You told me William is a halfwit.'

She sighed.

'So he is, I fear.'

'Does no one else know this Canavan? I am concerned that he don't abuse you.'

'I can hardly think that he will.'

'You must be sure. I shall make enquiries myself. Do you know anyone in his circle?'

'I only know of a Mr Pimbo. He is a business associate of some sort.'

Fidelis looked at his mistress in extreme surprise. 'Pimbo? You cannot mean Phillip Pimbo, the Preston goldsmith?'

'I don't know about his being a goldsmith, but that was certainly his silly name.'

'Well, this is extraordinary!'

'Why? Do you know him?'

'He is, or was, Preston's largest goldsmith. He has died. I have just left a letter concerning him at Pinchbeck's Coffee House. What do you know about Pimbo and your Mr Canavan?'

'Very little. Mr Canavan wrote him a memorandum at my writing desk which after making a fair copy he crumpled into my waste paper basket.'

'When was this?'

'Last Sunday afternoon.'

'And you read the rough copy of the memorandum?'

He heard that bewitching laugh again.

'Of course I read it. I am a woman, a mere spectator of affairs, but I lose no opportunity to spectate.'

'Do you have it still?'

'I put it back in the basket. It is long gone now.'

'What did it say?'

'Oh, it was conveying bad news. A ship had been reported lost at sea, with all hands presumed drowned. That is why I read it – I was put sadly in mind of poor Captain Butler.'

'What ship was it? Did he name her?'

'No – he just called her "the ship", I think. The memorandum told that Canavan was not sure if these reports were true, or fabricated by someone called Moon for his own gain, but at all events Pimbo ought to steel himself for some bad news about his investment.'

I imagine at this point Fidelis was quiet for a time, thinking over what Mrs Butler had told him. And, at some time after that, she would have risen from the bed and perhaps pulled on a shift, saying,

'The servants will be home soon. It would be better not to embarrass them, doctor.'

Quickly Fidelis dressed and they went downstairs where Mrs Butler drew him by the hand into the parlour.

'Just one more tune before you go,' she said and sat down again to her bass-viol. This time it was a jaunty, optimistic air she played, and she smiled all the while, even laughing at one point when she caught his pensive eyes fixed on her face. When she had dragged her bow across the strings in the last chord she laid the instrument carefully aside.

'Dear doctor,' she said in a soft voice. 'I hardly need say that my marriage to Mr Moreton Canavan would necessarily bring an end to . . . this.'

She gestured not very precisely at the space between them. He nodded his head.

'Of course. Yes. I understand.'

'Shall you mind?'

'I am a grown man and will live. You shall always be in my memory as a true and treasured friend and an accomplice in pleasure.'

With these eloquent words – which I cannot swear to, but only hope he spoke, or words very like them – he kissed her one more time and left without glancing back. For her part I am sure she stood at the door looking after him as he made his way along the street.

Fidelis's sense that he had been followed earlier in the day was immediately rekindled as he walked away from Mrs Butler's house along Edmund Street. While she had been so pleasantly entertaining him indoors, a sharp shower of rain had fallen and the dampness now made footsteps crunch audibly on the ground. This was what he heard behind his back as he turned the corner into Old Hall Street. Determined to discover his pursuer he stationed himself with his back to the wall immediately around the corner. The footsteps approached. At the very moment that the one making them would turn the corner Fidelis raised his leg. The fellow was caught at shin height and went sprawling down.

'Good God! Jacob Parkin – is it you?'

The fallen man lay for a moment with his nose in a puddle, immobilized by the embarrassment of his situation. Then he placed both palms on the ground and pushed himself up. Back on his feet he smiled nervously at Fidelis, shook the water off his hands, and wiped his muddy nose dry.

'Yes, doctor, it's me.'

Jacob Parkin who, with his brother Esau, was one of the two constables appointed at Preston to assist Sergeant Mallender in his duties, looked like a boy expecting the birch from his governor.

'So, you must explain yourself,' demanded Fidelis. 'Why are you dogging my steps?'

'Mr Mallender asked me to keep an eye on you. In case you came to harm, so he said.'

Fidelis roared with laughter.

'What harm would that be? I wonder. That I might fall into the dock and drown? Come, come. He sent you to spy on me, admit it.'

Jacob's hands let each other go and dropped to his side. He straightened himself and his voice acquired a measure of defiance.

'He was concerned for your safety, doctor.'

Briefly Fidelis's face darkened with anger but then, without warning, his manner changed. He smiled, took a gentle hold on Jacob's arm and began to steer him along the road. At this stage kindness was more potent than curses.

'Come across to my inn, Jacob. We need to have a talk, you and I.'

The Mermaid Inn stood nearby, on the other side of the street. It was a comfortable but by no means palatial house where, a few hours earlier, Fidelis had engaged a bedroom. The two men found a table in the dining room and Fidelis ordered wine, cold meats and pickles. Jacob would not be used to wine and it would be sure to loosen his tongue.

'Having you follow me all the way to Liverpool cannot have been Oswald Mallender's idea, Jacob,' he said after a few draughts had gone down. 'Who gave him the order? Was it the Mayor?'

Jacob again drained his glass.

'Happen so, doctor, happen so. Sergeant gets his orders from no one but the Corporation, and Mayor's at the top of that. In Preston, as we know, it is the Mayor rules all, and so it must be.'

I have noted it in men that, as the drink goes down, they tend to load mundane remarks with the weight of philosophical truth. Now, having pondered his own wisdom for a moment, Jacob held out his empty glass like a child for more. Fidelis obliged.

'And did Mallender mention a man called Zadok Moon at all?' he asked.

'Oh, aye. Zadok Moon. He is wanted in Preston. We want him. The Mayor wants him.'

'So it is not my safety you are most concerned with, after all. It is the whereabouts of this Moon. You lied to me, Jacob.'

Jacob's admission was sheepish.

'I know. But I do what I'm told. See, the Sergeant said most particular, I was not to let you discover me.'

'But what did he say to you about Zadok Moon? What does he want him for?'

'He's a witness in Mr Pimbo the goldsmith's death.'

'That's true,' confirmed Fidelis. 'As I know because I myself have been enquiring after him on behalf of the Coroner. But that is not the business of the Sergeant, or the Mayor.'

'The way I see it, doctor, is what isn't their business is nobody's business. D'you follow me? They wanted me to take particular note of where you would meet Moon. And then most particular to find out Moon's residence, by trailing him there.'

His cup was drained again and so, more significantly, was the bottle. But instead of ordering a new one, Fidelis stood up and spoke sharply to the constable.

'It's time to give this up, Jacob. Your mission is revealed to me and you are unmasked. You are miles from your own parish and have no conceivable authority here. Take a bed for the night and trot back to Preston first thing. You may report to your masters that I have not found Zadok Moon, and they must be satisfied with that.'

Jacob turned his watery eyes towards the empty wine bottle, beside which Fidelis now laid some money.

'Pay for what we've had out of that, and get yourself another drink with what's left. I wish you good-night.'

Chapter Ten

∞

R ISING EARLY IN the morning Fidelis wrote the letter to me that I have already transcribed. He asked about the postal service between Liverpool and Preston, and the landlord, taking possession of the letter, engaged to put it on the seven o'clock post-chaise, which would get it to its destination by ten-thirty.

There was no sign of Jacob Parkin, whom he presumed to be sleeping off the effects of the previous night's wine. Happy enough to leave the constable snoring, Fidelis went out, meaning to break his fast at Pinchbeck's Coffee House. But first he strolled to the bottom of Pool Lane to have a look at the celebrated Dock.

I have seen this remarkable feat of engineering for myself: a rectangular basin of deep water constructed in stone and invested by wharves and warehouses on three sides, with the Customs House on the fourth and a cleverly conceived floodgate, or rather lock, to allow ships to pass in from the estuary to discharge their cargoes, and out again to sea. Standing on the wharf, the dense array of uplifted masts and spars, with their webs of cordage and netting, made an impression like a ghostly leafless forest rising from the water through the morning mist. Ships were tied up alongside each other in twos and threes, and the business of loading and unloading was going on in a cacophony of rolling barrels, screeching blocks and the shouts and curses of the dock men.

A one-armed old seafarer sat on a bollard. As he puffed at his pipe, his eyes darting this way and that, he was taking in every activity on the dock. Fidelis approached and, seeing an opportunity, fell into conversation. Had there been a vessel called *The Fortunate Isle* here, he asked. The old man narrowed his eyes.

'Oh aye, that one. She sailed last year – September, October. Guinea voyage they said. Not likely, I thought. I never saw an old ship so badly set for it.'

'You mean she was not seaworthy?'

'I'll not say that. Depends on the sea. But I will say that to my eye she wouldn't stand long in the deep ocean. No, Sir! I didn't like the look of her planks. The seas out there are murderous. The Guinea Trade is murderous, which no one in Liverpool knows better than me. Thirty years on snows and brigantines I was. For ten years I was pressed into the Navy. I was on a ship once when—'

'That is an impressive career,' Fidelis interrupted, holding up his hand. He did not have the patience to listen to a string of yarns. 'It is this particular ship that I want to know about, however – *The Fortunate Isle*. Did you see her loaded? What cargo did she carry?'

Denied the chance to tell his life's history, the sailor shrugged and pouted.

'I dunno that I saw her loaded.'

He knocked out his pipe against his knee, scattered the ash into the water, sent a gob of spit after it and said,

'You'll spare an old man a fill of 'bacco, I suppose.'

Fidelis drew out his tobacco pouch, handed it over and, while the old man stuffed his pipe one-handed, asked as if by the way.

'Would you as an old sea hand be so kind as to settle a matter that I have been arguing about? In which direction, pray, do the trade winds blow?'

Returning to Pinchbeck's Fidelis ordered coffee and toast and looked around him. The coffee house was even livelier than it had been on the previous evening. Men of business sat together with ship's officers at almost every table eating their breakfasts and poring over papers, charts and newspaper reports. At the other end of Fidelis's table three men were arguing amiably about the future price of tallow. A fourth man sat directly opposite him with creased brow, spectacles on his nose and an abacus and a bundle of papers before him. He was running his index finger down a column of figures while mouthing the numbers and pausing occasionally to flick the abacus beads across. Fidelis noticed that the base of the abacus bore a paper label with the name of Pinchbeck's on it. Every possible convenience of business, it seemed, was provided in this place.

During the time it took Fidelis to eat his toast, his counting neighbour completed and noted down the totals of figures on three sheets of paper. He had just picked up a fourth and was tilting it towards the light and peering at it when Fidelis leaned across and made a noisy clearance of his throat.

'I am looking,' he said, 'for the merchant Moreton Canavan. Is he present here and, if so, will you kindly point him out?'

With a degree of deliberation, the stranger laid down the paper, reset the abacus and, bending a little back in his chair, swivelled his head whilst peering over the rims of the spectacles.

'Moreton Canavan,' he said returning to the perpendicular, and with a sigh of indifference, 'is at the table beside the fireplace. He is the plumpest member of the company.'

Upon which his brow creased again and he returned to his calculations.

Looking across the room Fidelis saw that Mrs Butler's suitor was a florid, thickset fellow of about fifty, and that he was doing a good deal of laughing, and his companions were laughing, with a certain obsequiousness, along. Fidelis observed them carefully as he refilled and sipped from his coffee cup. Canavan did much of the talking, and appeared to be entertaining the others with tales, and also with opinions, for he heard the occasional shout of 'Odds on it!' and 'No word of a lie!'

Fidelis drained his cup. Rising and approaching the table, he coughed into his fist.

'Do I have the honour of addressing Mr Moreton Canavan?' he asked.

Interrupted in his flow the older man darted a look upwards.

'You do,' he replied. 'Who are you?'

'Fidelis, Doctor Fidelis.'

'Clergyman or physician?'

'The latter.'

'I don't believe I've seen you in this Coffee House before, Sir.'

'I came in here for the first time yesterday.'

'That would explain it, for I rarely come here on the Sabbath.'

He gave a hearty laugh, as if he had said something funny, and lifted his cup of coffee to his mouth.

'I wonder, do you know a gentleman named Moon – Zadok Moon?'

Canavan gave a kind of hiccup as he drank, as if the hot coffee had scalded his throat. As he slowly reunited the cup and the saucer, Fidelis watched his face change from vast good humour to sober seriousness.

'I might know him,' he said cautiously. 'Why do you ask?'

'I would like him pointed out to me, if he is present. I have a letter for him.'

Canavan dabbed his lips with a napkin and seemed to make up his mind to something. He looked around.

'He is over there, Sir.'

He pointed towards the most crowded part of the room, so that it was impossible to decide which individual Canavan had indicated. In a bustling way, the merchant jumped to his feet. He was tall and, though his coat was that of a gentleman, there was much of the boxing booth about his manner.

'Allow me to fetch him to you here, Sir.'

He marched across the room and into the noisy throng, pushing between those that were standing until he reached a slight, dark-haired and bearded man who sat with a noisy company of breakfasters. At first Moon looked quite put-out, as if he did not want to break off from those he was with, even for a moment. But Canavan leaned down and spoke into his ear, whereupon Moon got up and consented to be guided across the room to where Fidelis was waiting, with my letter in his hand.

'Mr Zadok Moon?' Fidelis asked.

'Yes.'

Moon's eyes were evasive, glancing at Canavan but meeting Fidelis's glance only briefly.

'I have the honour of delivering this letter to you from Preston.'

Moon took the letter and immediately, without so much as a glance, slipped it into the pocket of his coat.

'Shall you not read it?'

Moon took a deep breath, as if gathering himself. Then he spoke in a more decided way.

'I am obliged to you, Sir. But I am having my breakfast. I shall read it at my leisure.'

He gave a flourish with his hand and a bow.

'Good day to you,' he said.

Moon turned and strode purposefully back towards his table. Fidelis followed his progress with his eyes, expecting to see him resume his seat at the breakfast table. It was a surprise therefore when Moon dodged past the table and, with a rapid glance over his shoulder, disappeared through a door beyond. My friend turned back to Canavan, but found that he, too, was nowhere to be seen.

*

Fidelis would have liked to stay a little longer in Liverpool. The identity of Moon, the coincidence of Canavan's engagement to Mrs Butler and now the appearance – at last! – of Zadok Moon had whetted his interest. He was like a fisherman studying the concentric ripple patterns made by rising fish. But the pond was still too muddy and, besides, there were patients in Preston to see. Leaving Pinchbeck's he walked thoughtfully back towards the inn where he had stabled his horse overnight.

He had strolled no more than a hundred yards in the direction of the Mermaid when the feeling grew on him that yet again there was someone behind him, tracking his footsteps. He quickened his pace. Had that foolish Jacob not heeded his advice? Was he still playing his game of shadows? He turned left towards the water, and then right along Old Hall Street. It was quieter here. He swung suddenly around and saw not Jacob, but a stout man of about his own age, puffing as he waddled along. He stood directly in the man's path and challenged him.

'As far as I know, Sir,' he said, 'you and I are strangers and yet you are following me.'

His stalker looked flustered. He produced a handkerchief, mopped his broad face and said:

'I wanted a word. I am sorry to alarm you. I saw you conversing with Mr Moreton Canavan at Pinchbeck's, and then with another gentleman, you see, and it made me curious.'

'Curious?'

'To know you.'

'Your name, Sir?'

'I am Tybalt Jackson. And you, Sir?'

Fidelis did not answer but, looking Jackson over, went on with his own interrogation.

'You are an associate of Mr Canavan?'

'No. However, I have an interest in the other gentleman, if he is who I think he is.'

'Who do you think he is?'

'Someone with whom you do business.'

'That is not how I would put it. But is my reason for speaking to this man any business of yours?'

'If you were touching on his business then it is, for his business is very much my business. Were you doing so?'

'We were not. However, I fail to see how it would be your business in any event.'

'It would be my business, I do assure you.'

They were fencing with their questions, probing for advantage without conceding any. Both seemed to understand this at the same moment for each man now stood in silence staring at the other. Suddenly, changing his mind, Jackson touched his hat and said,

'I regret that I have made a mistake, Sir. I bid you good day.'

He turned around and strode off. Fidelis watched him for a short time, then went on towards the Mermaid Inn, where he collected his bag and his horse and headed up the northern road, across what Liverpool people call the Dale, and northward to Preston.

Whether this Tybalt Jackson had executed a feint, and had in fact continued to shadow Luke Fidelis, is a debatable question. But there is no doubting that he would turn up in Preston a short time later, where his presence considerably complicated my investigation into the death of Phillip Pimbo. But that is to be told later.

Chapter Eleven

∞

ON THE MONDAY afternoon I rode out again across the Preston Moor, intent on questioning John Barton at his stables at Peel Hall about Adam Thorn's seizure. Thorn, as far as I knew, was still lying on his bed silenced by paralysis, and there was nothing that could be learned from him. The horse-coper, on the other hand, had come across him in the throes of his seizure, and must have something more to tell of the circumstances. He might throw a glimmer of light on the mystery of the silver apostle spoon, and the whereabouts of any similar findings. But of more importance to me was that his testimony would be needed if Thorn should die.

The establishment where Barton plied his trade had been the old house's stable yard which, in the reign of Elizabeth, and on the whim of a Mrs Peel in whom proximity to straw provoked palpitations and asthma, had been removed half a mile away to the north of her dwelling. Barton had taken it over some years ago, firstly to buy and sell horses and, more latterly, to keep and train them for racing. There was a cottage in which Barton was accommodated but most of the premises consisted of two rows of horse boxes arranged opposite each other like a truncated street. A boy carrying a pitchfork of hay told me where I could find his master.

John Barton was down on his knees in one of the horse boxes, feeling the legs of an imposing mare. He was a small, skinny, slightly hunched figure whose complexion looked oddly pasty on a countryman in the business of exercising high-mettled racers day after day in the open air. His mouth was thin, and twisted sardonically beneath a narrow, bent nose.

As I approached the horse box my shadow fell across the mare's eyes and she snorted, her feet skittering.

'Be careful, man,' warned Barton, immediately springing to his feet and going to the head of the horse. 'This animal here's the Flanders Mare, or Molly we call her in the stable. She spooks easy, *and* she belongs to the Mayor of Preston, Mr Ephraim Grimshaw. He'll not thank you or me if she rears and hurts herself before the Guild races.'

The way in which he stroked the mare's nose to calm her reminded me of a magician making passes over a crystal ball, and Barton's gesture certainly worked a kind of magic. As his hand floated down and across her nose, which displayed a startling white flash, Molly immediately became placid.

Barton came out of the box, then carefully closed and bolted the lower half of the door before turning to me.

'I'm talking to Mr Cragg from town, am I not? What brings you up to Peel Hall Stables?'

'It was you that brought in Adam Thorn after his brain seizure. I just wanted a word about that.'

Barton turned his head sharply towards me, his pallid green eyes narrowing.

'Adam Thorn is dead, then?'

'Why do you assume that?'

'Last time I heard your name being spoken, you were Coroner. You deal in death.'

'Thorn isn't dead,' I said. 'However, he may die at any time. In that event, I shall need to convene an inquest and I make it my business to be properly prepared.'

'Ah!'

With a gesture he indicated that we move away from the Flanders Mare's box and into the centre of the space between the rows of horse boxes. As we walked I noticed that his eyes strayed to the roof of the stable block opposite, or perhaps to the sky. They did not at any time look at me.

'So, what d'you want to know?' he asked.

John Barton's tone hesitated on the edge of sneering supercili-ousness. I always try not to leap into judgement of any man, but I found myself instinctively disliking him.

'Will you tell me, please, the precise circumstances of how you found Adam?'

'I was riding out on the Moor on King Alfred, one of Lord Strange's string that I keep for him. He's a five year old that His Lordship thinks in his wisdom will make a big success down south. Well it's true he is fast, though if you ask me he's as mad a scrub as I ever saw, which will go all against him at Newmarket and Epsom.'

'Were you alone when you rode out?'

'That's what I'm saying. King Alfred won't work with other horses. He only wants to fight them.'

'So what did you find during the ride?'

'It wasn't a ride. I was not out for a hack. It was what we call a brushing gallop – that means a fast one.'

'And?'

'Well, I was passing the Bale Stone at speed when I saw him – you understand where I mean?'

I nodded.

'I didn't know him right away. We were flying past and I just got a glimpse – that is all I'd call it – of a man on his knees beside the Stone groaning. I just thought it was some religious fanatic that was praying. But when I pulled the beast up after another furlong, and was trotting back towards the place, he had lurched sideways and fallen to the ground. So I rode up and dismounted, and it was Adam Thorn. He was thrashing about, exactly as a horse will when it's cast in its box, and also he was crying out all the time. I spoke to him but he didn't seem to hear. I touched him but he took no notice. Then all of a sudden he convulsed, like, and after that he just lay still. He was insensible, but staring, like a man I once saw lightning-struck. And his head was pouring blood. He must have hit on a stone in his fit.'

'What did you do?'

'Slung him over the withers of the horse and rode him home to that ever so pretty young wife of his.'

His smile was mirthless, but not meaningless. His tongue slipped out furtively, not just to wet his lips but, as I thought, to give point to his estimation of Mrs Thorn.

'It took all my powers to get that bloody horse not to throw us off.'

'Were you acquainted, you and the Thorns? Before these events?'

'Yes. Adam and me – we knew each other.'

'Was Adam ever a guest in your house?'

'A few times.'

'And you took a jar of ale at the Thorn place sometimes?'

Barton shook his head, still smiling, but the smile had grown openly insincere, almost threatening.

'No. He never had the money for ale. But I bought eggs off her – the wife.'

'Were you on good terms?'

'What d'you want to know for?'

'I am just trying to establish—'

Cutting me off with a laugh, but such a laugh as you hear from a man growing inwardly angry, and outwardly defensive.

'No. Don't excuse yourself, there's no need.'

The voice was even and the emphasis light, but I was left in no doubt from the look in his eyes of Barton's hostility. He went on in the same way:

'I see the truth in your eyes, Mr Coroner Cragg. You were just looking for a way to plant the seed of an accusation. You think maybe Thorn and me fell out, and maybe had a fight, and maybe I knocked him down – yes?'

I did not reply, although I might have said that I had indeed been entertaining all of those maybes.

'Well, let me make it plain,' he went on without a pause. 'We were on friendly terms, too friendly to have a fight. So anyone saying otherwise – well, they'll soon learn that John Barton does not only know how the law works – he knows how to work the law.'

He stepped a pace back from me. The false merriment was gone from his face, which now displayed the kind of icy satisfaction of one that has fired a gun, and hit the middle of the target.

'Now I have work to finish,' he added. 'Will you very kindly be off with you?'

So I had little option but to leave him.

I rode up to the Moor, a rolling wind-scoured tract of houseless semi-scrub, almost a mile across, which wrapped itself around the northern boundary of the town. Once the area had been thickly wooded, but all the trees save a few thorns and coarse bushes had long ago been cut down. Now the place was good for nothing but casual activities like rabbit-snaring, grazing animals, courting and the Preston races.

Half way to the Bale Stone itself my horse entered onto the race-course, along which John Barton had been riding on Lord Strange's racer at the time that, according to him, he'd played the Good Samaritan. The track was a strip, ten-yards wide and laid with tufty turf, that undulated around the Moor in a course of about two miles. I stayed on it until the Stone came into sight, on a small hillock or vantage point to my left. This sizeable mass of granite, irregular in shape but with a broad, flat upper surface, seemed to preside over the Moor with a certain dismal menace. Some said it was the remnant of a cromlech or standing stone; others an altar set up by our ancestors for sacrificial killings, whether animal or – as some would relate with a theatrical shudder – human. This had given it a certain superstitious notoriety, and in the main the people of Preston steered clear of the Stone.

Even though I have no truck with such nonsense, I will admit that my heart was thudding a little fearfully as I tethered my horse. I approached the Stone and put my hand on it, seeming to feel some sort of warmth, though this must have been my fancy for a cool breeze was blowing and there had been no sun all day.

I paced around it, looking down at the ground. Here and there I crouched or went down on one knee to peer beneath the Stone's overhang. There was a good deal of thick furzy undergrowth, and here and there the bones of small creatures, but nothing notable. I then climbed up – not without difficulty – and stood on the Stone itself where I turned through a full revolution. For a spot only a short distance from habitation it felt bleak and lonely, I thought, as I took in the line of Preston's roofs and smoking chimneys to the south, the distant fells to the east, the northern villages and settlements, with Cadley among them, and the flat cultivated Fylde stretching away to the sea in the west.

I looked in particular towards Peel Hall, and the stables I had just left, and then swung my eyes to the right. There, by the hollow-way known as Peel Hall Lane, was the Thorns' hovel. I decided to make my way down there and see if I could further my double enquiry – into his seizure, as well as the possible treasure he may have found.

*

As the door lay open I knocked on the door-post and Amity Thorn appeared. She carried a child on her hip.

'How do, Mr Cragg?' she said, without much enthusiasm.

'I was passing your house, Amity, and thought I should call and see how you were faring after your fall.'

'I'm well enough.'

'And Adam?' I asked.

'Oh, he's just the same. I don't know what to do nor think. Sometimes I am convinced he has no more wit than a carrot; others, I get the feeling he's still himself inside: concealed, but there, thinking and listening, though not able to move a muscle or say a word.'

'May I see him?'

She showed me through to the darkened room where her man lay. I bent over him and whispered.

'Adam! Can you hear me? This is Titus Cragg, the Coroner. I've come up here on the business of the silver spoon you found. Let me be plain. If you have found more silver like it, then you cannot keep it, you know. It must be given up to an inquest, that I shall conduct, with the purpose of determining whether the silver have an owner, or be treasure trove and the property of the King.'

I studied his face. It did not move. Was his wife right in her suspicions? Was Adam Thorn somehow awake and aware inside a cruelly pinioned body? Or was he no more sensible than a vegetable, alive but devoid of thought, of sense, of feelings, dreams, language?

On returning to the other room it was clear that Amity had been listening carefully at the door.

'I heard you speak of treasure to him, Mr Cragg,' she said. 'The doctor said something of the kind too, and Adam did himself, more than once.'

'Did he? What led him to be interested in that?'

'He'd been talking to some men in a tavern, that's all. I thought there were nowt in it, only talk. But, Mr Cragg, if Adam did find treasure would the King give him a reward?'

'Yes, I think he would, if Adam truly has unearthed some treasure trove.'

'What does that mean, Sir? Not everything you find is the King's, I'm sure, or we'd never have an end to giving him things.'

'Treasure trove is valuables that have been hidden long ago. By ancient law they belong to the Crown, but the King is always grateful to a person that makes such a find, and likes to reward him, you know. However, I see obstacles to such a happy outcome.'

'What are those?'

'As Coroner, my task would be to summon a jury to decide the matter by an inquest. But first there must be a treasure. One spoon which may or may not be a part of a treasure will not be enough on its own. Until we do have a quantity of things there is nothing the Coroner can do at all. But even if we do find the treasure, we still must have evidence how it was placed when found, for which the only witness would seem to be Adam. And if he is to be a witness, of course, he needs his wits, which I am sorry to see he has not got.'

I was a little pleased with this touch of word play, though it seemed wasted on Amity, who was chewing her lip.

'If I could waken him up, I would, Mr Cragg. But he won't come around.'

'Then I cannot see how he can tell us what he found, and where it is now.'

It occurred to me that having no actual treasure, but only the rumour of one, might be thought by the Thorns to be an advantage, a bargaining point. Amity had already told Fidelis how Adam had run on about an 'old soldier' who'd buried a fortune in silver. Perhaps she knew more than she had cared to reveal. Perhaps she knew all about Benjamin Peel and the Corporation's silver. If so, she would know, too, that Grimshaw was not the type to reward poor cottagers who brought in Corporation property that they had merely happened upon. But he would surely pay for something he wanted, if this were the only way he could have it.

'You don't by any chance know where it is, do you, Amity? You haven't taken charge of what your husband found, and hidden it again?'

Her eyes widened in surprise at my suspicion.

'No Sir! I'd have told you. I've not seen owt like that.'

I watched her face, looking for signs of concealment. There were none.

'That's a pity,' I said. 'It would be good to know if this so-called treasure even exists.'

Riding back to town, along the edge of the Moor and coming in by Tithebarn Street, I was thinking my expedition had achieved little. I did not believe Amity was hiding anything from me and, though I had no doubt that John Barton was capable of doing so, I had no evidence of that either. My inspection of the Bale Stone had yielded nothing and now I noticed that the mare was increasingly favouring her nearside forefoot. I cursed. It seemed the outcome of my afternoon would be nothing but a lame horse.

After dismounting and leading the animal the last half mile, I handed the mare over at Lawson's Livery, where the animal was stabled, and where a stone lodged in the hoof was the resident farrier's diagnosis. I left the man to deal with it and walked home to Cheapside, where I found Elizabeth counting linen for the laundry. Immediately our talk made me see that I had made more progress with investigating Benjamin Peel's hidden treasure than I realized. I had been telling her how much I had disliked John Barton – the way he laughed, and the way that his slithery tongue had betrayed a lascivious thought of Amity Thorn.

'You must beware of John Barton, Titus,' she said. 'He has a bad character and may not be so innocent in this matter as he claims.'

'I agree. And now I am wondering if he could have the silver himself; if he knocked Adam down and took it.'

'Whether or not, he likes his chances with pretty Amity Thorn, now that her husband looks out of the game. He'll be haunting the Thorns' cottage, Titus, possibly not now, but soon. He'll be after her, you can depend on it.'

I went into the office to catch Furzey before he went home. My clerk was working at his writing desk.

'Has there been word from Dr Fidelis?' I asked.

By way of reply he sighed, picked up a piece of paper and held it high for me to take, then returned silently to his writing.

'*Titus*', I read in Fidelis's handwriting, '*I believe I have set eyes on Zadok Moon & there is much to tell. Will await you at the T.H. at 7 this evng?*'

Chapter Twelve

∞

L UKE FIDELIS WAS hungry, having eaten no dinner but only bread and cheese by the wayside during his journey from Liverpool. So when the serving man came to our table that evening he ordered a steak and kidney pudding, while I confined myself to the cold pinions of a duck and a plate of pickles.

While we waited for the food, Luke told me the full story of his visit to Liverpool. In order to explain his sighting of Zadok Moon, he had to tell how he'd heard the name Moreton Canavan; and to do that he could not avoid making mention of his visit to the house of Mrs Belinda Butler. He made out, as he had done to Jacob Parkin, that it was merely a question of musical recreation: I was vastly entertained by the transparency of this pretence, but did not let my friend know it.

By the time he had finished his tale, and I had put in questions of my own to clarify the detail, I knew enough of his twenty-four hours in Liverpool to write the account of it that I have already set out, even if I have fleshed it out here and there. But a narrative of events is one thing; their analysis is another, and I picked out one of the points that seemed most salient to the Pimbo case.

'Jacob Parkin was sent after you by the Mayor, because he hoped you would lead him straight to Moon. Grimshaw trusts no one in his desperation for the return of the money that *he* entrusted to Pimbo and Moon.'

'If Parkin hadn't been such a blockhead and allowed me to catch him out, I would indeed have led him to Moon.'

Our meal was brought and Fidelis immediately dug a fork into his pudding, splitting it open and lowering his head to peer at it. Then he began to investigate, stirring the reservoir of meat-clogged gravy with the fork, separating the kidneys from the cubes of beef, shreds of onion and lumps of turnip. He pronged a piece of offal and held it up, the better to inspect it.

'The question is . . .'

He kept his eye on the offal.

'Would it have made Grimshaw any the wiser?'

'What do you mean?'

'I mean that I formed a suspicion of Zadok Moon.'

He popped the morsel of food into his mouth.

'Hmm,' he said as he chewed. 'Tangy!'

'What are you saying, Luke? That Moon is not what he seems?'

'Well, for a seasoned Guinea trader, he knows even less of the sea than I do.'

'Go on.'

'"Sailing back to Liverpool on the bosom of the trade winds". Remember that?'

'I do – from one of Moon's letters. Colourful language indeed.'

'Colourful, yes, and complete nonsense. I have it on the authority of an old salt in Liverpool that the trade winds will do many things, including speed you to the Azores and beyond. But blowing as they do from north to south, they cannot assist a ship on its passage from Barbados to Liverpool. Of course, such a mistake would hardly signify to Pimbo, as he himself knew little or nothing about the sea, or sea trade.'

'He knew about money, though, and he manifestly thought highly of Moon as a money scrivener.'

'He did. I wonder if Pimbo knows Canavan well. He had a

letter from him warning about a possible shipwreck, but there was not a trace of correspondence between them in Pimbo's desk at Cadley Place. So whether they were personally acquainted does not appear.'

'What about this other fellow, Jackson, that you stopped in the street? Who is he, and what is his interest in all this? Another investor grown concerned of the enterprise?'

'He assured me he was no associate of Canavan.'

'Perhaps Jackson is not himself an investor, but represents someone who is. We shall have to wait upon Moon, on Wednesday, I suppose. We shall know more then.'

'Wednesday?'

'You forget the letter you carried to Zadok Moon, Luke, summoning him to the inquest. It is clear that he received the letter and so we must hope he travels to Preston and gives evidence.'

Throughout this conversation Fidelis had been eating the pudding in his usual, peculiarly analytical way. First he found the kidneys and forked them one by one into his mouth. Then he proceeded systematically through the ingredients of the dish – the beef, turnip, carrot, celery and finally onion, turning each piece on his fork and examining it before eating it and starting on the next. Finally he painstakingly cut the suet case into neat mouthfuls and used these to mop up the remaining gravy. At last, his plate was clean.

I was used to seeing him do this, and made no comment. Instead I offered him my tobacco pouch and we stuffed pipes while I turned to the subject of Benjamin Peel's treasure. I told him of my activities during the day: the encounter with the horse-coper at Peel Hall stables, the visit to the Bale Stone and my later talk with Amity Thorn. Fidelis attended to my words carefully.

'Elizabeth thinks John Barton is merely a lecher,' I said, 'who sees this as an opportunity for an easy seduction. But I have been wondering if he knows something about the Peel silver, and even if he may have it in his possession. Suppose he and Thorn found it together, and then Barton attacked Thorn so that he could keep it for himself. It would not be the first time such a thing had happened. There is a tale in Chaucer . . .'

I lit my pipe from the now guttering candle between us and settled back again.

'It's "The Pardoner's Tale",' I continued, 'and in it—'

But Fidelis interrupted me, suddenly animated.

'This interests me, Titus! The idea is worth pursuing.'

I allowed Fidelis's interruption without comment. He often cut me short when I began to speak of literature.

'Go on,' I said.

'It would be no surprise to me if John Barton had indeed attacked Adam Thorn. I have met the man, and he's shifty. He cannot look you straight in the eye.'

'I came away from him with the same opinion,' I said. '"Shifty" is the correct word, at least in his dealings with people. Not with horses: he is remarkably straightforward with a horse.'

Fidelis laughed.

'My father used to say only a fool will try to fool a horse; a wise man knows he can't.'

'Which argues that Barton is a very wise man. If so he is not a temperate one. He passionately refuted any suggestion of a feud between himself and Adam Thorn, and angrily maintained that they were friends.'

Fidelis was lighting his pipe.

'I think his anger betrays him,' he said between puffs. 'I would wager a good sum that the two men really were at war. I wonder what it was about.'

'It might have been about Amity Thorn, or this supposed treasure. When two men fall out it is generally over money, or a woman.'

A girl came to snuff our dying candle and collect the crockery. It was time to go home. I pointed with my pipe stem to Fidelis's empty plate as she took it away.

'You enjoyed the pudding?'

'Oh yes, very much, though there was a piece of turnip more than there should have been, and it was short by two cubes of beef.'

In my office the next morning, Tuesday, Furzey and I ran through the lists of jurors and witnesses for Wednesday's inquest.

'That's the names, and they've all been served,' said Furzey, his finger tapping the two lists as they lay before us on my desk. 'You had better be content, for I will not go rooting out any new ones.'

I assured him that I was perfectly content and, changing the subject, put to him a different question.

'Furzey, remind me of the definition of treasure trove, would you? It has been a few years since we last dealt with a case.'

Furzey half closed his eyes and recited as follows.

'Treasure trove is what comes to light of coin, precious metal or gems that has been deliberately concealed by a person unknown, with the intention of returning to collect at a later date, the which was prevented by reason of the said person's presumed intervening death.'

'A person *unknown* – you are sure of that? Even if it be a matter of many generations, or centuries ago?'

But my question remained unresolved because now we were interrupted by Robert Hazelbury, who came running in with some urgent news.

'Mr Cragg, Sir! You'd better come down to the shop. Mr Mayor's there and he's fetched the locksmith back to open up the strong room. I can't do owt to stop him.'

I hurried out with him and arrived at the goldsmith's shop to find Arthur Benn at work once again, this time sitting astride a stool in front of the locked gate of the strong room, his roll of tools laid out on the floor in between. With back bent and face set close to his hands in a rictus of concentration, he was working with a much larger picklock than I had seen before, for this was a much greater and more formidable lock than on the outer door of the business room. Standing at Benn's side was the Mayor, urging him on and making snatching motions with his hands as if itching to seize the picklock himself and try his luck with it.

'Well, Mr Grimshaw!' I exclaimed. 'I hope you are prepared to accept any consequences of these actions. As I have already mentioned to you the legality of this is highly questionable.'

He turned to me four square, hands on hips and legs straddled to ensure that, whatever I might say, I understood he was immovable. His words were fired through angrily flared lips.

'Here is what I say to you, Sir: fiddlesticks! I am in pursuit of Corporation property. I am looking for our rightful money, and shall not be gainsaid on the matter, or denied entry to wheresoever it may be found, on any piddling pretext you may come up with.'

He snapped his fingers. 'So fiddlesticks to your questionable and fiddlesticks to your legality.'

He had set out this morning to intimidate the world with all the force and depth of his mayoral authority. He was dressed to that end with full formality: long-bottomed wig, heavy golden chain of office, lace shirt and silken coat and breeches. The brocaded waistcoat shone with silver embroidery and embossed buttons across his bulging belly. But I, for one, had known Ephraim Grimshaw for too long to be intimidated by his cock-feathered display.

'I will make one more point, Mr Mayor, if I may. This procedure is very likely a waste of time. I spoke about this strong room with Pimbo quite recently, and he stressed that moneys deposited with him were never kept in it for any length of time. They were, he said, taken on by his partner Moon to be invested, lent out at interest or in some other way put out to work – that was Pimbo's own curious expression. He insisted that any money entrusted to him would never lie idle in a strong room chest.'

Grimshaw reached into his pocket and drew out a folded fools-cap sheet, which he opened and shook before my nose.

'This is Pimbo's promissory note, Sir. This is his assurance that our money would be repaid, with profit. And what does a man have a strong room for, if not for the keeping of money and valu-ables with which to pay his debts to another man?'

He coughed.

'Or in this case, I mean of course, to a Corporation.'

Grimshaw did not seem to have a very strong grasp of the principles of investment. I did not belabour my point but turned to see how Benn's endeavours were coming along. He must have been at work for some time already, since he was now beginning to mutter strings of frustrated curses, and to change implements with increasing frequency. Then, after another five minutes, just as in the case of the outer door of Pimbo's business room a few days earlier, the locksmith suddenly abandoned the attempt. He leaped to his feet and cursed one final time, upsetting the stool beneath him with a clatter.

'Be damned to it! I can't get the fucker open, Mr Grimshaw! Some fiend devised that lock and only another fiend will ever pick it.'

Galled, and worse, at having been bested by two locks on the same premises, and in a single week, Arthur Benn withdrew. But Grimshaw's campaign against the obdurate lock had reserves wait-ing to enter the fray – reserves of force. A pair of labourers, both heavily muscled, stood by with rolled sleeves to apply a vast file to the iron bars that held the lock in place. As the filing operation was set to take some time, I wandered back into the shop with the air behind me resounding to the regular sing-song of the file. No business had been done here in the shop for five days now. The cashier's position was shuttered and the glass-topped counters were covered with lengths of baize.

I crossed to the door that opened onto Fisher Gate and looked out through the glass towards the premises directly opposite – those of Aloysius Hutton, the tobacconist. I could see through his open door Goody Hutton, the wife, stooping to place a bowl in the middle of the floor and then, as she took up her broom, giving a high-pitched shriek to alert her pet that it was time to eat. The animal, a big-eared puppy parti-coloured in brown and white, immediately darted forward and began to devour the food with considerable voracity. There was something about that puppy . . . I moved nearer to the glass, just to make sure. Then I pulled open the door and strode across the street.

'How d'you do, Mrs Hutton?' I enquired as I entered the dusky, aromatic space of her shop. The woman, a spindly figure of roughly an age with myself, looked up from her brushing.

'Oh! Mr Cragg, it's you! Will it be your usual ounce of 'bacco?'

'Yes indeed. And a packet of snuff if you please – the Number 3.'

She reached down a jar and weighed out an ounce of the tobacco mixture, which she twisted inside a doubled sheet of oiled paper. Then she fetched a tray labelled Number 3, and loaded with plain paper cones, each tightly filled with snuff. I flipped open my snuffbox and laid it on the counter.

'That's a spirited little dog you have there,' I remarked, watching her carefully open the cone and pour the snuff into the snuffbox. 'What d'you call him?'

'That's Suez is that. He was Mr Pimbo's you know, from across the road.'

'Suez! Of course. I thought I recognized him.'

'Funny name for a dog, but there you are – Mr Pimbo had his peculiarities.'

'How come he is here?'

'The poor little tyke turned up on the day it happened, whimpering and shivering he was like he'd caught a chill.'

'The dog was upset?'

'Of course he was upset, and from what he'd seen over there, I'm sure. Well, we found an old basket for him and he went fast asleep, unnaturally fast I thought, like a body that's been badly shocked. When he woke up he seemed better and I gave him some warm milk. Hutton said we would have him with us till we heard what to do, but there's been never a word, so we've kept him on, though he's driven me distracted with his behaviour. He does shit everywhere, and he's that badly spoiled, and Hutton says he'll never be trained to obedience or the gun, not now, though he's still a young'un. Up to all sorts of tricks, he is, and terribly fussy about his food. Always wants his treats of bacon fat, just like Mr Pimbo used to give him, though it makes his bowels even looser, that's my opinion.'

'When did he come to you?'

'Oh, on Thursday morning. I reckon it was about the time Mr Pimbo was found, because we shut up the shop for a few minutes, not having an apprentice here just now, to go over and have a look at what the fuss was about. It were dreadful, Mr Cragg. Of course, you know that, as you were there yourself. Well we stayed, me and Hutton, long enough to get a look at the corpse, and then we came back and, by heck, there was the little dog actually inside the shop! He's that cunning, you see, and quick as a whip when he wants to be. He must have run across the street and slipped in past us, just as we were going out. We never noticed a thing, and that's how he got in here.'

'Are you absolutely sure about that? About the timing, I mean.'

I must have altered my tone. I had been customer and suddenly I was inquisitor, and she was too sharp to miss the change. I received a quick look of anxious surprise.

'Of course I am. But we've done nowt wrong, Mr Cragg! Just an act of charity till the little thing were claimed back. We've not *stolen* the dog, I hope. And anyway, if you really want to know, I've had my fill of cleaning up after him, and I'll be glad to get rid, the sooner the better.'

I hurried to reassure her that she was not about to be arraigned as a dog thief, merely that as well as being Pimbo's executor, I was also Coroner, and so interested in everything that had occurred in Phillip Pimbo's business room on the morning he died.

She seemed reassured as I pocketed my purchases and, after declining the offer of a dozen clay pipes at a specially reduced price, withdrew from the shop. Out in the street I could just hear the two notes of the file as it travelled along its groove back and forth, cutting into the iron of Phillip Pimbo's strong room gate. But before going back inside to see how the work progressed, I walked along the street to Fidelis's lodging and left word with Mrs Lorris that her lodger could do worse than join me as soon as possible at the goldsmith's premises. He would learn, I said, what had happened to Pimbo's puppy. I was fairly confident that such a message would bring him in a hurry.

Chapter Thirteen

∞

IN PIMBO'S BUSINESS room they worked furiously by turns, doing a minute of filing, then taking a minute of rest. In this way, after little more than a half hour, the two burly workmen had completed three of the four cuts necessary to remove the iron casing that contained the lock's mechanism. When I returned from Fisher Gate they were half way through the fourth, though by now they were growing tired, and accompanying the music of the file with bestial grunts of effort. Yet, nearing the completion of the task, the men's rate of work seemed, if anything, to increase: Grimshaw must have promised them a good fee for their work.

The Mayor stood like a hungry dog with his bulging eyes fixed upon the reciprocating motion of the file, ready to spring forward as soon as it broke through. The moment came with a clatter five minutes later, as the lock fell inwards from its position and onto the stone floor of the strong room. In a moment Grimshaw had pushed the gate open and disappeared inside. We all waited and within fifteen seconds he had reappeared.

'Well, don't be idle, you men. Bring us a light. It's pitch dark in here.'

Hazelbury fetched two candles from Pimbo's mantelpiece and fumbled with a flint box to light them. Grimshaw snapped his fingers impatiently, and growled.

'Get on with it, man! I'm waiting.'

At last the lights were ready. Grimshaw seized them, one in each hand, and went back inside. I could see the interior of the room clearly now, as he placed the lights in vacant spaces at either end of a broad shelf, one of the half dozen with which the strong room was furnished from its ceiling almost to the floor. The whole space was ten feet wide, no more, and only perhaps eight feet deep. The shelves were ranged along the length of the opposite wall, and two of these were reserved for trays of items held under pawn. Grimshaw picked through these, greedily examining each in turn – watches, pewter tableware, snuffboxes, ivory combs, a pair of crystal decanters, some scent bottles, a lute and a few items of jewellery. These were not, I thought, the chattels of true poverty, but the pledges of reduced gentility – of solitary ladies struggling to live off a shrinking portion, and of young gentlemen gambling above their means. Each pledge had a paper label attached, inscribed with a number that would correspond to an entry in the loans ledger.

The shelves above were devoted to records, held in case-bound volumes and bundles of paper tied with ribbon. Grimshaw spent a further few moments sampling these before he glanced to his right and noticed something else: a stack of leather-covered deed boxes standing by the wall. After trying the top one and finding it locked he came out of the strong room and ordered the two labourers to bring out the deed boxes, and get them open without delay.

Over the next ten minutes the boxes were wrenched or cut open, and their contents tipped onto the floor. It was all paper, most of it stamped and sealed. The Mayor was disconcerted.

'Those things inside, on the trays, are mostly trash,' he complained, 'and this is nothing but old paper. Hazelbury! Is there nothing in all this rubbish of monetary value?'

The Chief Cashier looked dutifully through a few of the documents, though he knew quite well what they were.

'I fear none of it will be directly pecuniary, Your Worship,' he said.

'This is intolerable!' Grimshaw moaned, picking up an armful of paper. He began thumbing pages off the top and letting them fall back to the floor, like a dealer at cards, but half way through gave up and hurled the bundle to the ground.

'Christ! Is there no money here at all? Get back inside the strong room, Hazelbury, and look again.'

'There's nothing left to look at now, Sir, but the ledgers.'

'Do as I say!'

The pawnbroker's cashier returned to his late master's strong room with an impassive face, though from the set of his shoulders I could read his resentment at the Mayor and his hectoring.

As we waited Grimshaw glowered at me.

'This inquest is tomorrow?'

'It is.'

'Do you expect to find out what's happened to my money?'

'Your money, Mayor? I did not know that you had made personal deposits with Pimbo.'

Grimshaw drew in breath slowly through his nose, controlling himself.

'Obviously, I speak for the town, Cragg, and I mean the *town's* money. The cash we saved over two decades to pay for the next Guild which, as if I need to remind you, is twelve weeks away. If we don't discover the money, the Guild will be a farce – with the joke against me.'

For a moment his bull-face softened to that of one making a pathetic appeal.

'I shall be a laughing-stock. I did not promise a golden Guild only to be remembered for a leaden one.'

'Look here, gentlemen!'

The raised voice was that of Robert Hazelbury, emerging from the strong room carrying a polished wooden case, slim enough for a man to carry tucked under his arm.

'This was on the floor, pushed back under the lowest shelf,' he said. 'That's why we missed it.'

'Well, get on, open it! It may contain cash, or something valuable. Open it!' cried Grimshaw.

The case had a lock in which reposed a small brass key. We gathered round as Hazelbury placed the case on Pimbo's desk, turned the key, released the catches and opened the lid. The case was lined with velvet and divided into cavities, each sculpted to enclose a particular object. Most of these were small tools; one was for a powder flask, which was missing; the largest cavity was in the shape of a pistol and this, too, was missing.

Grimshaw cursed. Hazelbury placed a couple of fingers into the pistol-cavity and looked up at me.

'This would be where the weapon that killed him came from, Mr Cragg.'

'Did you know that it was there, in the strong room?'

He shook his head vehemently.

'No, Sir. As I told you, Mr Pimbo controlled the strong room – what was in there, what went in and out. But I can tell you one thing about this: it is a pledge against a loan. See this?'

Attached to the brass handle of the pistol case was a label, and on that label a number written in an ornate hand.

'I should be able to check this number against the Pledges Book,' added Hazelbury, 'and find out the particulars.'

'Thank you,' I said. 'That would be helpful.'

'Helpful be damned!' said Grimshaw. 'This is not helpful. This is a waste of my time. I'm leaving.'

Upon which the Mayor turned and jerked his head at his two men. As he led them out he gave a savage kick to a pile of documents in his path on the floor, sending an eruption of paper into the air.

With a sigh of helplessness Hazelbury followed him out. I went down on one knee to look more closely at the heaps of paper, and saw what a farrago it was: redeemed exchequer bills, receipts, old cheques, counterfoils, certificates, deeds, schedules, pedigrees and land surveys – all the records of the Pimbo family's personal and business dealings over the past hundred years. I groaned inwardly. This was a jungle of detail for the conscientious legal executor to hack his way through.

'Titus! So it's true: the strong room is opened!'

This was Fidelis bursting into the room.

'What was found inside it? The body of the dog, I hope.'

'No, it contained no dog,' I said.

'Good! I was worried you would find that dog dead inside.'

'As I said in my note, I do have news of the dog, but it is not what you supposed. As for the strong room, it contained assorted items pledged against loans, and all these papers, which it will be a job to go through.'

In a broad gesture I indicated what lay all around on the floor.

'So you found nothing immediately enlightening?'

'Just one thing – but a good one: we know where Pimbo obtained the weapon that killed him. Hazelbury found this inside.'

I showed him the pistol case lying open on Pimbo's desk. While we talked, the Chief Cashier had returned from showing the Mayor out. Now he knelt and began trying to bring some order to the chaos of paper and deed boxes that had been scattered across the floor by Grimshaw – re-filling the deed boxes, sorting the papers into bundles as best he could, and re-tying the ribbons that had held them together.

'So tell me, Titus,' said Fidelis, as we watched Hazelbury's endeavours. 'What *have* you found about Pimbo's dog? Is the mutt dead or alive?'

'Oh, it is living, Luke, and all the time just across the road.'

Hazelbury looked up from his ribbon tying.

'Mercy, Mr Cragg,' he exclaimed. 'Did I hear right? You've found Mr Pimbo's Suez?'

So I told them everything Goody Hutton had told me: how she and her husband had crossed the street to see what the fuss was about at Pimbo's; and how, when they returned not half an hour later, they found the animal waiting for them inside their premises.

'There it was,' I said, 'shitting and pissing all over the floor. They've been looking after him ever since. The animal was much shocked, apparently.'

'So do you now believe what I have been saying from the beginning?' challenged Fidelis. 'That the dog was inside the room all along, with the corpse of its master?'

'Yes, that does seem to have been the case.'

'It was certainly the case.'

Suddenly Fidelis was in the best of humours.

'Mr Hazelbury,' he said briskly, 'would you be so kind as to come with me into the strong room?'

Hazelbury looked up, then got up wearily from his knees and followed the doctor, with me at his heels, into the now almost stripped-out strong room.

'Please explain,' said Fidelis, 'exactly how you discovered this box, for I believe it was you?'

'It was pushed into that corner, see?' said Hazelbury, 'Under the lower shelf. It's that dark down there, I only found it by going down on one knee and feeling for it.'

'Just so, but it makes me wonder,' said Fidelis, murmuring more to himself than to me or Hazelbury.

Fidelis took one of the candles and put it on the floor near the shadowed corner space. Then he stooped to peer into it, before working his way along the length of the shelf, bringing the candle along in one hand while holding the shelf's edge with the other. In this way he searched the space under the shelf from one end to the other.

'Aha!' he exclaimed suddenly, when he was almost finished. 'So there it is!'

He reached down and brought something out, which at first I could not properly see.

'What have you got, Luke?'

Instead of replying Fidelis pushed past us out of the strong room, and examined his find by the light of the window. I joined him there.

'You see?' he said. 'Here it is!'

And I did see: he held in his hand a gentleman's wig, whose underside was stained with quantities of encrusted blood.

For some moments I was dumbstruck, and then exclaimed,

'Good God, Fidelis, you are a wonder!'

I rubbed my chin and considered the wig, a quite ordinary type such as one sees scores of times in the course of a day. This one, however, was in a sorry state, not only bloodstained but with its side curls unravelled and its tails torn.

'Hazelbury, can you confirm this was Mr Pimbo's wig?'

Hazelbury said he would not swear to it, but it was of the type that Pimbo customarily wore.

'But doctor,' he added, 'how on earth did it get into this state? I understand the blood, if he was wearing it when he . . . you know. But it's been attacked as well. It's been deliberately torn and damaged. Did Mr Pimbo do that himself?'

Fidelis found the suggestion amusing. He smiled.

'And put it back on his head before blowing his brains out? I think not.'

'Who then, Luke?' I asked. 'His murderer? I cannot see that this entirely proves your case for murder by another party.'

But Fidelis was laughing now.

'No, gentlemen. It was no murderer that did this.'

'Who, then?' asked Hazelbury.

'It was Suez, of course. I may have no recent experience of raising a puppy, but I can recall their enthusiasm for chewing things. But there is one more thing.'

He went back into the strong room, where Hazelbury and I followed him. Fidelis went down on his hands and knees as he had before, and began feeling around on the floor, and in particular in the shadowed space underneath the stack of shelving.

'Ah!' he exclaimed at last.

'What is it, Luke? What have you found?'

He held up his hand, with his finger and thumb closed around what looked in the gloom like a pea. He jumped to his feet and stepped past us into the office once more. There, by the light of the window, he laid it in the palm of his hand and showed it to us.

'The ball, Titus. The bullet that killed poor Pimbo.'

'How did you know it would be there?'

'Because it lodged in the wig, of course, which Suez took to the strong room where he shook and worried it. So the ball fell out. Here – keep it safe.'

I took the ball and dropped it into my waistcoat pocket.

It was growing dark and I was at home. I had worked all afternoon on the arrangements for tomorrow's inquest, and everything was in place. I was in the mood to read something but, just as I was hesitating between taking a turn with Montaigne or refreshing my memory of Chaucer's 'Pardoner's Tale', I was interrupted by a rap on the front door. I went myself to answer it. Hutton the tobacconist stood on the step, holding in his arms what looked like a leather tool bag.

'Mr Cragg, no I won't come in, only I wanted to make sure Mrs Hutton was right when she told me you are Mr Phillip Pimbo's will's lawful executor, and have the duty of tidying up the poor man's affairs.'

I told him that was quite right.

'Then you'd best tidy up this.'

He thrust the bag into my hands. At the moment of the exchange, the mouth of the bag gaped a little and the head of the puppy, Suez, appeared. He looked at me with a mixture of surprise and – unless I flatter myself – recognition.

Before I could protest, Hutton went on, his voice hard and implacable.

'He's pissed all over a parcel of new tobacco cake that just arrived from Virginia; he's been sick on one of my best customer's feet; and now he's shat under my fireside chair. We've exhausted our patience at home for him and his tricks, Mr Cragg. We've done our Christian duty by him, and now it's time for you to take charge. Good-night to you, Mr Cragg, and be assured I shall always be gratified to serve you in my shop . . .'

Hutton was backing down the front door steps now, while keeping a wary eye out in case I should decide without warning to foist the bag, with its cargo of dog, back on him. He relaxed a little as he reached the street without this happening.

'I refer,' he went, raising his hat as he took a couple more backward steps up Cheapside, 'to the next time you should need a supply, at which time you may perhaps be so kind as to return the bag. Good-night, Mr Cragg.'

Chapter Fourteen

∞

Z ADOK MOON'S TESTIMONY, though desirable, was not in my mind strictly necessary at the inquest. I was reasonably sure a just verdict on Pimbo could still be reached without him. In spite of Fidelis's fervent advocacy of the mysterious hidden man – the murderer lurking within the business room and escaping along with Suez under cover of the surging crowd – I could not believe it. We had discovered much about Pimbo and his affairs in the course of our investigations, but we had turned up no one that might have wished him dead – unless it was himself.

Nevertheless I was on tenterhooks of curiosity about whether Pimbo's business partner would after all show his face. There was a ragged orphan, Barty, who scratched his way through life doing odd jobs around the market, but was willing and intelligent, and so got employment sometimes from me to do errands. On this morning of the inquest I sent him very early to go around the inns to ask if the man had arrived from Liverpool and taken a room in town. The boy came back after an hour, panting and hot from running.

'I've not heard tell of your Mr Moon, Sir. But there's another I'm thinking you want to know about. He's called Mr Tibble Jackson, *and* he's gottun with him a boy who's black as coals. They've put up at the Lamb and Flag and been asking about where inquest is on at.'

The Lamb and Flag was a shabby tavern off St John Street that let a few bug-ridden rooms to our poorer visitors. Having heard about his encounter in Liverpool with my friend, I had supposed Tybalt Jackson must be some rival to Moon in business, and commensurately prosperous with him. Jackson's present address showed him in a more penurious light than this. I already knew that he sought an interview with Zadok Moon: the question was, had he actually pursued his man to Preston, or come merely in the hope of finding him? I could not guess. Nor, more importantly, did I know why he was interested in the inquest.

Fidelis came in and we ran through the evidence he would give later, and the timing of my prompting questions. I told him in severe terms that I would not tolerate any excursions into the wilder shores of conjecture.

'By which you mean?' he said.

'That Pimbo was murdered. We must speak only of what we know, from direct observation. Nothing fanciful – is that agreed?'

'All right,' said Fidelis, a little gloomily.

'And by the way,' I went on, 'you will be interested that your friend Mr Tybalt Jackson has turned up in town. And he's accompanied by a negro – his servant, I suppose. They're put up at the Lamb and Flag.'

'I am not surprised that he's come,' said Fidelis. 'There was much about that man of the terrier that won't let go its grip.'

'But is it a terrier or a bloodhound? Has he followed Moon's scent here, nose to the ground?'

'That is the question. Perhaps Moon is here at this moment preparing to give you his evidence.'

Anticipating a large attendance I had sent Furzey ahead of me to open up the inquest room in good time. When I got there the crowd was already in, jostling and bargaining over sitting space and, when they could find none, occupying the standing room at the back. The jurors stood around in a single group at the front with Furzey, who was instructing them in their proper behaviour.

We lost no time in getting the business under way, swearing the jury, and then taking them off to view the body at the House of Correction, a walk of a few minutes. As we stood around the stretched-out corpse I pointed to the two terrible wounds sustained by the dead man's head.

'Can you all see that the ball from a gun passed upwards through his jaw, through the roof of his mouth and his brain and came out here, at the top of his head?'

They all craned to look. One of them, the baker Thomas Proctor, said drily, 'I see two holes in his head, all right. I see no ball.'

'You will see it later, Thomas.'

'What I mean is, what's to say it didn't go t'other way – top to bottom?'

Their chosen foreman, James Purvis, gave him a pitying look.

'Don't be soft, Tommy. How could he shoot his'self through the top of his head?'

'I'm not saying he did,' persisted Proctor. 'What if he hasn't shot his'self? What if another's shot him?'

'That's what we are here to determine, Thomas,' I said. 'But we do know, at least, that the ball was shot upwards through the bottom of his chin.'

'How could we know it? Was any of us there?'

'You will hear how in the court, Thomas.'

Back in the inquest room we arranged ourselves around the long table. I took the middle place with Furzey at my right hand as clerk of the inquest, and the jurors along the table's length on both sides. Chairs had been placed in rows facing us for the townspeople, and these were almost all occupied. I quietened their chatter and wasted no time in calling Robert Hazelbury. He had been first through the broken down door of Pimbo's office, which qualified him as the first finder – and so, by tradition, the first witness.

Furzey had placed the witness chair at a right angle to our table, so that both we and the public in attendance could see the speaker's face. The Chief Cashier looked pale and apprehensive, and took the oath with such a shaking voice that it seemed he might even begin to weep. Gently I took him through the events of that shocking morning – the time of day, the locked inner office, Mr Benn's attempts to pick the lock and finally the intervention of the labourers with their crowbar. By this time Hazelbury seemed to have mastered himself.

'We found him lying athwart the writing table, Sir, as you yourself saw. The blood, it had burst out of his brains and was all around him and dripping on the floor. A terrible sight, it was, terrible.'

'Tell the court how he lay.'

'Like he'd fallen forward from t'other side of the table. His head was turned, so that he rested on his cheek.'

'How was he wounded?'

'At top of his head. That's all I saw at first. His skull had a horrid big hole in it.'

'Did you form any opinion as to how he might have sustained this terrible wound?'

'From the shot of a pistol, Sir, so it seemed. We found one lying on the floor near his table.'

I had brought the pistol to court, now restored to its place in the wooden case. I took the case and laid it flat, then opened it and withdrew the weapon. There was a collective gasp from the audience. I handed the pistol down the table until it reached the witness.

'Is this the weapon?'

Hazelbury held the piece with grave uncertainty, as if any moment it may fire itself spontaneously in his hand.

'Yes Sir, I would say it is.'

He hurriedly passed the pistol back to the juror nearest his seat and I indicated that it go hand-to-hand around the table for the rest of them to examine, which they did each in a different fashion: one with a knowing smile, another with startled reverence, a third weighing it in his upturned palms. This was Peter Lofthouse, who was a gunsmith and anxious to convey to us his interest not just as a juror but as a professional man.

'Mr Lofthouse,' I said, 'while you have it in your hands, would you help the court with your estimation of the piece?'

'Aye,' he said. 'It's an old'un, thirty year or more. What we call a Toby and a dagg – small, you see, to go in the pocket.'

'Might it be a military weapon?'

Lofthouse shook his head.

'You couldn't use this in a battle, if that's what you mean, Mr Cragg. See, you've to load it by unscrewing the barrel right off. You've to put the charge and the ball in, screw it back again and pour the priming. Takes too long when you're fighting, you see, and you might drop the barrel, being hot an' all. This is more a one-shot gun for personal safety – or for murder if you'd a mind to it.'

At the mention of murder a kind of audible shiver went round the room.

'Thank you, Mr Lofthouse, that is very helpful. Now, Mr Hazelbury, had you ever seen this pistol before you found it in Mr Pimbo's business room on the fatal day?'

'No, Sir.'

'Were you even aware that Mr Pimbo kept a pistol at the office?'

'It wasn't that he kept it on purpose, Sir. That pistol was pledged against an advance.'

'Can you tell the court about that transaction?'

'Yes Sir, I found it in the book. It's a very old one, Sir. The pistol was pledged long ago, in old Mr Pimbo's time. It was never redeemed and so it lay unnoticed, almost hidden it was, in the strong room.'

'Is that likely? Were there other pledges as old as that still in the younger Mr Pimbo's possession?'

'Very likely, Sir. Not all unredeemed pledges were or could be sold. Sometimes the term of the loan was very long – even the length of a lifetime. Those could never be sold on until the owner was known to be dead.'

'So who originally pledged this pistol, and when was it?'

'Our records say it was twenty-two years ago, by a Captain Avery, Sir. He was with the militia, I believe, and has long ago moved away.'

'And was it one of the lifetime pledges to which you have just referred?'

'Yes, Sir.'

'And is Captain Avery alive?'

'I don't know, Sir.'

'And if he were – or if there were uncertainty about the matter – that would explain the continuing presence of the pistol in the strong room, I suppose. Now, Mr Hazelbury, I would like you to tell us about the state of Mr Pimbo's affairs? I mean, the shop. Was it solvent?'

'Oh, yes Sir. Insofar as the shop itself went, I have no reason to doubt that it was quite sound.'

'Mr Pimbo had invited me as his legal adviser to attend him on the morning of his death. Do you know on what business this was?'

'No, Sir. I cannot think.'

'What was your employer's state of mind in the days before he died? Would you say he was troubled in any way?'

Hazelbury considered.

'He might have been. He might not. You didn't know with Mr

Pimbo. He was all jokes and hail-me-good-fellow on top, but there was much underneath that you couldn't see.'

'He was a difficult man to discern?'

Hazelbury nodded his head and I thanked him, then called Michael Ambler. He came to the witness chair with easy grace, a good-looking young man but with a self-pleasing smile that looked out of place in the circumstances.

'You are Mr Pimbo's journeyman goldsmith?'

'Yes.'

'And you worked under Mr Pimbo and Mr Hazelbury?'

'I worked under Pimbo, not Hazelbury. Though I don't know about "under". I understand my work. I know gold and silver and how to work it. The workshop, it's mine, really.'

'You mean you run it?'

'Yes Sir. I direct it, you might say.'

'Do you have anything to do with money-handling in the business?'

'No, Sir. That's Hazelbury's job. He knows about money, I know about precious metal. There's a difference that folk don't always appreciate.'

'Notwithstanding that, can you give me your estimation of the state of Mr Pimbo's business – of your side of it, I mean?'

'It seemed all right. Business came in every day, near enough.'

'What of Mr Pimbo himself? His state?'

Ambler glanced down and drew a deep breath.

'In my opinion he was a man in pain, Sir,' he said at last, looking up again. 'Much of his usual old bluster had gone. I saw it on his face every day recently.'

'You say "a man in pain". Do you mean physical pain? Was he ill?'

'No Sir, I mean mental pain. It was as if there were something gone sideways in his life, and he didn't know how to set it right again.'

'And how long had this been going on?'

'He was always noisy in company, he was. But, close to, he was close himself, and didn't confide, like Robert Hazelbury just said. But in my opinion he had got much closer over the last weeks.'

'Thank you Mr Ambler. You may leave the chair.'

Next, I called Luke Fidelis.

'Would you give the court your purely medical opinion of this unfortunate death?' I opened.

Fidelis raised an eyebrow – a way he had of indicating that he sensed some mild subterfuge in my words.

'Very well. In my *purely* medical opinion the man died by a pistol ball passing upwards into the centre of the jaw, cutting through the root of the tongue just a little in advance of the epiglottis. It continued on its way, boring through the roof of the mouth and the nasal sinuses before entering in turn the brain stem, the *medulla oblongata* and the *pons* from where it proceeded into the *cerebrum* and burst out through the parietal bone, where it left a jagged hole. The brain being awash with blood, as it always is, much of it flowed or splashed out through this hole, all over the desk and onto the floor.'

'Would Mr Pimbo have died instantly?'

'Oh, yes. As fast as I can snap my fingers.'

In the corner of my eye I noticed a hand movement by one of the jury. It was Thomas Proctor, with a question of his own.

'But what I want to know is, why not the other way, doctor?' he asked. 'How do you know the bullet did not go downwards?'

'Quite easily,' said Fidelis. 'It cannot have done.'

He looked at me and touched his wig. I took the hint, pulling the dead man's own bloodstained peruke from the bag and passing it along, as I had previously passed the pistol. When the wig reached him, Fidelis held it up so that the jurors could see the hemispherical inside.

'This is his wig,' he said, now addressing Proctor directly. 'The lining is as you see caked and stiffened with dried blood, with some pieces of the brain intermixed. And here in the centre is a declivity just the size of a pistol ball.'

He looked back at me for an instant and mouthed the word 'bullet', but this time I was ready with the item which I had taken, wrapped in a handkerchief, from the evidence bag. When it reached him, Fidelis held the pellet of lead up between finger and thumb for all to see and then showed how it fitted exactly into the little cavity in the wig's lining.

'The bullet lodged itself here after it had blown a hole through the cranium,' he went on in a ringing, dramatic voice, which was now receiving the audience's rapt attention, just as an actor's would in a play. 'Its momentum carried the wig up into the air and through an arc of flight before landing some feet away on the floor. There, it was picked up by Mr Pimbo's pet dog, who took it into the nearby strong room, where he chewed and shook it until the bullet dropped out and rolled away. It was there that we found both items on the floor, detached from each other. Does that satisfy you, Mr Proctor, or will you be Doubting Tommy still?'

The audience loosened the strain of the moment by laughing heartily. Proctor flushed red and cried out,

'Dog? What dog? I've heard nowt about a dog.'

He jerked his head this way and that, his mouth pouting angrily.

'Ah yes, I should explain,' I said, and did so, finishing by saying that the dog was now *pro tempore* in my own possession. Proctor was not mollified. He had taken great umbrage at Fidelis's gibe.

I asked Fidelis, as a matter of form, to be on hand in case the court needed to hear from him again, and I then called Ruth Peel to give her evidence. She had been found a seat at the extreme end of one of the rows and now she stood and walked with a firm step to the chair.

Miss Peel took the oath, confirmed her name and place of residence, and settled herself to answer my questions. She did so throughout in a steady, unwavering voice, with little inflection and no overt emotion.

'You are housekeeper at Cadley Place, the late Mr Pimbo's home?'

'I am.'

'Do you remember the morning of Friday last week?'

'I do.'

'Did you see Mr Pimbo that morning?'

'No. He'd gone to business before anyone else had risen.'

'At what time did he leave?'

'He would have left the house at five-thirty. It was his custom to rise at dawn, whatever the time of year, and to go to Preston half an hour after that. He liked to get started early on the business of the day.'

'I assume you can shed little light on what business he had that day, so I shall move on to your own—'

'Wait!'

It was Miss Peel that interrupted me. Being about to raise the difficult matter of her relationship to the dead man, I was a little put out.

'You have something to add?'

'Yes, Sir, I have. Quite by chance, although he did not discuss it with me in any way, I *do* happen to know something about the business he had that day. It was something important.'

'How do you know this?'

'It was because his clothes came back, brought by one of the women who washed him and laid him out.'

'Yes? What about them?'

'Well, amongst them I found this.'

With her good right hand she took from the bosom of her dress a paper, which she held up for all to see.

'What is it, Miss Peel?'

'If you like, I can read it to you. It is a note addressed to the Mayor; it is dated on the day Mr Pimbo died; and it is in his hand.'

I told her please to lose no time in doing so.

'*Your Worship*', she read, holding the paper up before her eyes. '*Please be advised that I intend to bring before you this day under arrest a man, Moon, whom I believed I could trust in business but whom I now know to be a villain, and to have been so from the first moment of our partnership. For your consideration, as Chief Magistrate, I intend to prefer charges of fraud and embezzlement against him. Subject to his presenting himself as I have asked him to do at my shop, I shall bring him before you at about ten in the morning. I beg you to be ready for us. The matter bears not only upon my own losses but on the good economy of the town. I shall in this business have the assistance of my attorney and a pistol, which I have ready, and shall not need the Constable's attendance to ensure the arrest.*'

She lowered the letter.

'That is all it says.'

The entire courtroom had fallen silent at this revelation and I myself was astounded. I knew we had searched Pimbo's pockets. How had we failed to discover this?

'Was this letter a finished copy? Was it sealed?'

'Yes Sir. It had been sealed ready for delivery, but the seal had cracked open.'

'Where was this found? Was it in one of his pockets?'

'No. I asked the woman the same question, because she had stopped for a cup of tea in the kitchen. She said she had found it tucked in between his waistcoat and his shirt.'

'Had she read it?'

'No Sir, she said she was not able to. She had just stuffed it back amongst his clothes.'

'Had Mr Pimbo spoken or dropped any hint about being defrauded?'

'Not to me.'

I took a few moments to absorb the information, then said:

'We have heard from Mr Hazelbury that he knew of nothing amiss in Mr Pimbo's business affairs. Can you yourself enlighten the court in any way on this matter?'

The witness was pale but steady.

'I cannot think of anything.'

'Is it true that Mr Pimbo had become erratic recently in his settlement of household accounts? That he had been making a smaller amount of money available to you, for instance, for household expenses?'

'Yes, that is true. But I do not know why.'

'In that case, may I ask you to stand down for the moment, but to remain in the courtroom, as I may have further questions?'

As she left the witness chair I glanced to left and right along the table, to gather the attention of the jury, and then addressed the public ranged in front of us.

'Among the witnesses called to this hearing I have summoned a Mr Zadok Moon, who appears to have been the late Mr Pimbo's business partner in a certain venture, and who is the subject of the surprising letter to the Mayor which we have just heard the contents of. So now I ask, has Mr Moon answered the summons? Is he here present?'

No voice was raised.

'Is there anyone here, then, who can cast light on the matter we have just heard about, or indeed on the venture in which this Moon and Mr Pimbo were colluding?'

No one stirred.

'I see the Mayor is present,' I went on. 'Did you, Mr Grimshaw, have any prior knowledge of this charge that Mr Pimbo intended to bring before you?'

From the centre of the audience Ephraim Grimshaw hoisted himself into sight, ready no doubt to deliver a substantial address to the court.

'None whatsoever, Cragg. But if I may say a few words—'

Grimshaw's speech got no further, for now a man pushed himself out of the standing group of spectators at the back.

'Mr Coroner!' he called out in a rich, sonorous voice. 'I believe I can help the court.'

Every head turned to see the interruptor, though from the whispered questions they exchanged none, it seemed, knew who he was.

I motioned the Mayor back into his chair.

'Thank you, Mayor. And you, Sir, pray come forward. Take the witness chair, if you please.'

And as the newcomer ambled down the side aisle towards the front I believed that I knew who he must be. I glanced at Fidelis across the room for confirmation of the man's identity. He nodded, and his mouth framed the name:

'*Tybalt Jackson.*'

Chapter Fifteen

∞

T HE STRANGER WAS a bulky young man unwigged and dressed
in clean but drab clothing such as a clerk or a shop assistant
might wear. Every eye in the room followed his progress to the
chair. Every bottom rose six inches from its seat to see him settling
into the witness chair. Every tongue whispered an opinion to its
neighbour, before every breath bated itself to hear him speak. The
speculation continued as I took him through the witness's oath,
which he gave in an accent not of the North country but of somewhere to the south and west of England, I guessed. When we had
finished the swearing I called for silence.

'What is your name, Sir?' I asked.

'Tybalt Jackson.'

'From?'

'From Bristol, Sir.'

'And your occupation?'

'I am the agent for a company in London.'

'In what business?'

'Marine insurance.'

'Well now, Mr Jackson, I presume you are aware we are putting
to inquest the sudden death of Phillip Pimbo, goldsmith of this
town. Did you know Mr Pimbo?'

'No Sir, in person I did not.'

'You did not do business with him?'

'Not directly.'

'Indirectly, then?'

'I recently discovered him as the backer of one with whom my company has business.'

'And that person is?'

'Mr Zadok Moon.'

A new ripple of interest agitated the room.

'The court is delighted to hear that name, Sir,' I said with feeling. 'At last we've found someone with knowledge of the mysterious Mr Moon.'

Jackson had been sitting with his hands clasped in his lap, and I saw that I could measure, by the tightness of the clasp, the tautness of his nerves. But now he partially loosened a forefinger from the clasp and raised it.

'I do not say I know him, Sir. I have never met him, although what I do know of him is not much to his credit.'

'Ah! Perhaps now we are getting to the point. You have said you can help the court in this matter of the allegation of fraud by the late Mr Pimbo against Mr Moon. How can you do that?'

The witness's voice had a tendency to hoarseness. He cleared his throat before answering.

'Mr Moon was engaged in a venture in the Guinea Trade. He had undertaken insurance of a vessel, *The Fortunate Isle*, and paid the premium accordingly. But then a few weeks ago Mr Moon sent in notice of claim for the loss of the vessel, along with a large and valuable cargo. The company believes that this claim, before it is paid out, should be enquired into further.'

'Can you be precise? How much did Mr Moon claim?'

'An indemnity of fifteen thousand pounds – a very large sum for a loss that had not even been entered in the Casualty Book at Lloyds.'

'Which means?'

'A casualty is a ship totally lost with all its cargo. There is a book at the Coffee House in London where the underwriters meet, and every confirmed casualty is entered there.'

'And this particular casualty has not been so confirmed.'

'Not to my knowledge.'

Amidst a buzz of comment from the audience, I glanced along the table and saw that one or two of the jury were finding the evidence hard to follow.

'Well, I understand why your company feels it must investigate. The sum in question is, as you say, an enormous one. How much was the premium they had to pay for this amount of cover?'

'One thousand five hundred pounds.'

'Was it a single payment?'

'Yes.'

'And paid by Mr Moon himself?'

'I don't know. It was forwarded by Moon, but it was in the form of bills or notes payable to bearer.'

'And these notes were good for cash?'

'Oh yes, they were legitimate.'

'So there is no question of fraud in respect of the premiums?'

'No – the policy was sound and properly paid. The suspected fraud was in relation to Mr Moon's claim.'

'Very well. Let us turn to that claim, which, you have told us, was for fifteen thousand pounds. Shall we examine that figure? What was the approximate value of the ship, in round numbers?'

'Five thousand pounds.'

'And what was its cargo?'

'Slaves.'

'How many?'

'About one hundred and fifty.'

'Male and female?'

'Yes.'

'So, according to Mr Moon, if his complement of negroes was worth ten thousand pounds, they must sell for about sixty-five pounds apiece.'

But Jackson shook his head violently.

'Oh no! Nothing so high. At market an adult slave fetches between ten and, for a really good specimen, twenty pounds. A child is of course less.'

'So let us say the mean is fifteen pounds: a hundred and fifty might then be sold for two thousand two hundred and fifty pounds?'

'Yes.'

'Why then was Mr Moon's cargo insured so high?'

'Because the price of a slave in the West Indies can buy sugar that will be worth three or four times as much when it is brought home.'

'I see. Three or four times. Is that right? So converted into sugar, the real value of the 150 slaves might indeed be uplifted to ten thousand pounds?'

'Just so.'

Someone in the audience whistled at the increment.

'Very well. Now, what did Mr Moon say in his claim?'

'That the ship was lost at sea. All souls on board were drowned except for one. The claim came accompanied by the survivor's statement.'

'Who was that happy person?'

'His name is Edward Doubleday.'

'And Mr Doubleday was?'

'He was Captain Doubleday, the master of *The Fortunate Isle*.'

'Have you the Captain's statement?'

'Not here, no.'

'Will you summarize it for us?'

'It related that the ship had gone without incident to the Guinea coast where manufactures were traded for the 150 negroes, who were brought on board. The ship then commenced the Middle Passage, at the end of which the disaster happened.'

I interrupted.

'The Middle Passage: what was that?'

'The Guinea Trade is a triangular voyage, Sir, and a clever contrivance for multiplying profit. The first passage is to the Guinea coast to get negroes; the second is across the ocean to the West Indies where those negroes are sold for cash which is then exchanged for sugar, spices, coffee or tobacco; and the last is the passage home. As I have just demonstrated, the ship-owner expects to make a multiplied profit on each of these exchanges.'

'But the profits are earned only at considerable risk, I understand,' I said. 'Tell us more about those risks, would you?'

'The risks are from disease among the negroes, a negro insurrection, an attack by pirates or by the Spanish, and finally a storm or accident to the ship.'

Jackson was speaking fast, and on a single level, as one stating matters of fact with neither forethought nor reflection.

'I do not suppose we know how many ships are lost by these means,' I said.

'Of course we do. My company's business is to know, as it calculates premiums according to the level of risk. It is known at Lloyd's that one in a dozen ships undertaking this voyage is lost.'

'And what of the other eleven? Are they reliably profitable?'

'Prodigiously profitable, if the voyage is carried out with the necessary rigour. All costs must be kept as low as they can be. A few metal trinkets, barrels of rum or bales of cloth will secure negroes from the baracoons.'

'Baracoons?'

'Slave compounds at the entrepots, or slave-markets, on the

coast. The negroes are brought there from the interior of the continent to be sold. Seasoned Guineamen then say that, once you have them aboard, the secret is to keep them alive while feeding them as little as possible during the Middle Passage.'

'How long does that last?'

'It is considered to have gone well if it is done in fourteen weeks. But the captain must get his navigation right, and avoid attacks and bad weather.'

'I see that many factors are in play. So continue, please, with Captain Doubleday's account of events.'

'Well, according to her captain, *The Fortunate Isle* had sailed for a hundred days and was a day or two away from landfall at Barbados when the negroes rose up and attempted to gain their freedom. In the course of the struggle the ship was fired and as she blazed the captain and three other white men got away in the cutter.'

'The cutter?'

'Every ship carries one. It is a small open boat which can be rowed or sailed.'

'And what of the others – the crew and the human cargo?'

'All burned alive, or drowned as the ship was consumed. The captain could do nothing to help because of the danger from the slaves and the intense heat.'

At this point the jury foreman, James Purvis, had a question.

'There were three others in the boat with Doubleday? You said before he was the only survivor.'

'His statement is that his companions in the boat died while the boat was at sea. They succumbed to their wounds, or burns, so that he was alone by the time he reached the coast of Barbados two days later.'

Now Thomas Proctor butted in with a query of his own.

'All this happened a long way from here, Sir. Have you met

this Doubleday fellow? How do you know that what he says is true?'

'His statement came in the form of a letter from Barbados. He has not yet returned from there, and he has not been examined.'

'You said you doubted this claim, didn't you? You thought he was lying.'

Proctor's challenge made Tybalt Jackson, all of a sudden, uncomfortable. It was as if having volunteered to give evidence he suddenly saw the extent to which he was exposed. He answered cautiously.

'I said the company, not me, has deemed it necessary to enquire into the claim before it could be paid. I am merely charged with that duty. I travelled from Bristol to Liverpool to speak to Mr Moon on the matter, but could not find him. Not being able to find him perturbs me, naturally.'

As Proctor lapsed back into silence, I picked up the interrogation again, for Doubting Thomas's question had been very pertinent.

'Is there anything inherently unlikely about Doubleday's account of the events at sea? This revolt of the slaves?'

'Everything is done to prevent such a thing, but sometimes it happens.'

'So the very element that rose up and fired the ship was also – how shall I put it? – the element that made it valuable.'

'Yes, she was destroyed by the very commodity and cargo that she was intended to carry.'

I reflected for a moment, then burst out, unable to prevent myself:

'By God, Jackson, I find it uncomfortable to hear and use such language. You speak of commodity and cargo, but they were human beings were they not?'

As soon as we had started to speak in detail of the slaves there had been a slight but audible disturbance in the room. Now a few voices were being lifted above the level of a whisper, so much that Jackson was obliged to raise his own voice to be heard himself.

'I merely use the common language of the Trade.'

'Which treats such individuals only as commodities, not as members of humanity?'

'Yes.'

'What do you yourself think, Mr Jackson?'

'I am not . . . qualified to judge. I do not engage in the Trade myself.'

I could not let this pass.

'But you do! Your business is to insure the value of men whom their fellow men presume to own.'

'Some do say that the negro is not human at all, and therefore—'

'And so he isn't!' called someone in the room.

To which another answered:

'Yes he is! For shame!'

I rang my handbell.

'Quiet, if you please. No interrupting. We must hear the evidence.'

As the noise began to subside I hastened it down by speaking more urgently.

'Mr Jackson! You were about to say?'

Jackson had grown red in the face, and he was rapidly blinking his eyes. His voice was hoarser now and, for a moment, he almost coughed over his words.

'We cannot approve of, we cannot judge, every activity of those we engage with. Business would become impossible.'

The room was quiet again, all agog, except for one voice which growled out,

'Judge, or be ye judged!'

'No! Listen!' Jackson cried, his voice still cracking but clearly heard. 'My employers believe that the business we speak of is a good and profitable one, conducted for the righteous welfare of our nation, but also as a means whereby the negro is brought to civilization, and to true religion. The continent he comes from is full of darkness, tyrants, terrors and diseases, while the place he goes to offers useful employment and safety. My employers believe that everyone should be happy about this; they see it as their vindication. I do not say—'

The noise in the hall had grown considerable once more. Some of the audience were crying 'Aye!', while others shouted out in hot denial.

'I don't say that I myself *agree* with them,' went on Jackson, redder and redder in the face and with his voice cracking, 'I merely state their position.'

I was feeling heated myself. I wished I knew more and would have liked to continue my questioning about these rights and wrongs. But it was the court's purpose to listen to the facts, not fall to moral wrangling. I quietened the audience, then said,

'Well, Mr Jackson, that is a debate for another time and place. If we may return to matters here in hand, you volunteered some information that might help us with our difficulty over Mr Pimbo's allegation of fraud against Zadok Moon. Is it not the case, then, that you do suspect Mr Moon for fraud?'

Jackson's cheeks had previously indicated some emotional arousal, but their glow now faded and his complexion was inclined to the chalky, though not as white as his knuckles in their handclasp. Was he beginning to regret his impulsive decision to give evidence?

'I may have gone too far,' he said. 'I make no accusation at this stage. But I do say that there is no corroboration of the loss of the ship so, while I do not say there has been fraud, I say there is no proof that the loss was suffered. No insurance company in the land would pay out a claim so large without being certain of the facts. I have nothing more to add to that. I . . . I really cannot say more.'

'Cannot, Mr Jackson, or will not?'

It seemed to me he was like the man that has lifted the roof off a hive for the honey but forgotten about the bee-stings. And some of those stings would be inflicted by his employers should he speak out of his turn.

'I have given my evidence,' he stated. 'May I please go now?'

I heard the decision in his voice and yielded. It was past dinner-time and if I did not feed the jury soon they would become truculent.

'Mr Jackson, I thank you,' I said. 'You have helped us a great deal.'

'What I want to know,' said Fidelis, 'is what happened to the bodies.'

Juries prefer the Coroner not to dine with them in the middle of an Inquest, as it cramps their enjoyment of the meat and ale. So I had left them to mount the stairs to the room reserved for them at the Friary Bar Inn and gone with Fidelis a few score of yards back down Friar Gate to the Black Horse, where we had been served with roasted salmon.

'What bodies?'

'The three men from *The Fortunate Isle* who died in the open boat. Much depends on whether Doubleday brought them ashore or not.'

'Please explain.'

Fidelis was dissecting his collop of salmon carefully, to remove the bone with as little disturbance as possible. He did not reply until he had completed the operation.

'Without the bodies in the open boat, there is not the slightest evidence that anything bad has happened to *The Fortunate Isle*. Now it is clear that Jackson, whatever he says, is investigating the supposition that the ship was never burned, and never sank: she is even now bobbing about on the ocean wave, as happy and seaworthy as a cork. If that is the case, an insurance claim of fifteen thousand pounds for her loss is a clear case of embezzlement. Not only is it not payable, it is prosecutable.'

I had almost cleared my plate, but he now engaged in separating and picking up single flakes of the fish, one by one, with the broad part of his knife. Each flake was examined for a moment, then slid into his mouth and swallowed before another was taken up.

'I agree, of course. But how does it help us with Pimbo?'

'A man would surely hang for dishonestly trying to obtain such a sum. No pardon for him, I think.'

'I agree with that, too.'

'It's a thing that a man, to escape from it, might risk committing great crimes.'

'You mean firing the ship and escaping in the cutter?'

'No, no, no, Titus, keep up with me! On this hypothesis the fire never happened. I am talking about the killing of Pimbo.'

I sighed.

'You are returning to your idea of the Hidden Man, Luke! You know I don't credit that. You really must resign yourself to the fact that Pimbo killed himself.'

Fidelis sighed.

'But at least not deliberately, I hope. Because, you know, if he did not kill the dog—'

I held up my hand to stop him.

'The possibility of suicide has shrunk to a speck of insignificance. On the morning he died Pimbo was waiting for Moon, and he was waiting for me. He wrote in his letter to the Mayor that he had a pistol ready and was intent on arresting Moon. It was no time to be killing himself on purpose. It must have been by chance.'

'Compared to murder it is a dull conclusion. Oh well – will you sum up after dinner and send the jury to deliberate?'

'I expect so. Miss Peel's discovery of that letter has changed my whole plan, but I am not sorry. Not to call Miss Peel back will spare the airing of Pimbo's love for her and, on account of that, his desire to make himself rich very quickly. Those were all matters pertaining to a possible self-murder, while now that is discounted they are altogether nugatory as far as this inquiry is concerned.'

I don't know if Fidelis had heard me out, for he had now directed his attention back to the plate of salmon, eating it flake by flake.

'Oh! Don't mind me, Cragg, if you want to get away,' he said abstractly.

But before I left he had one request.

'May I take another look at Pimbo's pistol, Titus? I am not sure it has yielded up all its secrets yet. I should like to make sure.'

Seeing no harm in this, and having the linen bag with me, I passed it to him, asking him only to bring it back to court within the hour.

Chapter Sixteen

∞

I BEGAN MY SUMMARY by reminding the jury of everything we had heard about the events within Pimbo's business room in the early morning of the fourth of June. I went on to speak of the health of Pimbo's business, and of his home life.

'Mr Pimbo showed signs of lacking money – he deferred payment of bills and he kept his housekeeper chronically short. Yet his business here in Preston, as we have heard, was going along nicely. The source of difficulty therefore lay, I believe, not in Preston, but in his connection with Mr Zadok Moon, with whom Mr Pimbo hoped to establish a banking house. From letters I have with me, and which I shall provide for the jury's consideration, it is clear that the connection had involved Mr Pimbo in a heavy burden of personal expense and that this caused him anxiety.'

From the bundle of papers in front of me I held up a sample of the letters found in the desk at Cadley Place, all pertaining to the voyage of *The Fortunate Isle*. I read out those parts proving that Pimbo had undertaken to buy a ship and largely to fit it out for a Guinea voyage, and that the bills found with the letters were all for the sort of items needed on such a voyage. I also showed the letter where insurance is mentioned, and Pimbo is asked urgently to provide the sum of fifteen hundred pounds sterling to pay the premium.

'The voyage itself evidently began more than a year ago, and such ventures usually take this length of time to be completed. But there has been no sign of *The Fortunate Isle* returning to Liverpool and, as we have heard, Mr Moon has now put in a claim for insurance compensation and produced a letter from the ship's captain detailing the ship's loss. Yet his letters to the deceased prior to the voyage and during its early stages were full of optimism. Let me read to you from another of them.'

I gave them the letter in which Moon dangled the prospect in front of Pimbo's eyes of a hundred-fold profit, after the ship had bounced home 'on the bosom of the trade winds'.

'The profits from the Guinea Trade are very large, as we have heard, but not as incomprehensibly vast as Moon says here. That gross exaggeration is deeply suspicious. Furthermore, as some of those present must already know, the trade winds blow from north to south, so that to descant about a homecoming on the trade wind's bosom is to promise something impossible. Unfortunately Mr Moon, just as he did not appear on Friday when sent for by Pimbo, has not answered our letters or summonses to attend this inquest. Therefore we cannot question him about these oddities, but we have heard instead that the same man has fallen under suspicion of dishonesty in another quarter – the insurance company.

'So let me then draw all the threads of this together. Picture Mr Pimbo arriving early, as is his habit, on the morning of last Friday, locking his door and preparing to confront Mr Zadok Moon with an accusation of fraud. He took out the pistol that, as we have heard, he intended to use if necessary to enforce Moon's arrest. Would not he have then loaded it? And may not this action have accidental consequences – consequences that the deceased could not have foreseen, and that might have been fatal to him?'

As if as an afterthought – though in fact by design – I ended by telling the jury that they should also consider whether Pimbo slew himself, in a moment of despair at the loss of his, and the Corporation's, money. I would leave the final decision to them, of course, but they must be swayed by the most likely, not the most colourful, explanation. Then, just as I was about to send them back upstairs to deliberate, Luke Fidelis returned to the court and sent a note up to me.

'*I have changed* volte-face. *Let me take the witness chair again. I have something of the highest importance to convey to the inquest.*'

Many say I allow that young Mercury too much latitude, and perhaps I do. Perhaps I did that day, but still I called him back to the chair.

Fidelis took the witness chair and I reminded him he remained under oath.

'You wished to give us another piece of evidence, before the jury retires. Is it something relating to the pistol, by any chance?'

'Yes, it is.'

'What have you to say?'

'I have nothing to say – but something to show. Will you allow me?'

Fidelis had with him a roll of cloth. As I nodded my assent he extracted from this roll, with considerable care, the pistol. He held it high to confirm that it was the same one which had been seen earlier, and which was Pimbo's gun, then rose to his feet. Holding the gun by its barrel with the butt down, he approached the long table at which we sat. He looked along the row of jurors' faces, catching the eye of each of them in turn, making sure they were paying attention. Then without any further warning he dropped the pistol from a height of two feet, so that its butt struck the tabletop.

The report that accompanied the impact was extraordinarily loud. Simultaneously the bright flash lit the room and acrid smoke puffed from the gun barrel, which was still smoking after the gun had bounced and clattered to the floor. Everyone save Fidelis himself flinched and most cried out at the suddenness and shock of the demonstration, and there was a moment of profound silence following the explosion, as everyone in the room except Fidelis looked aghast.

Fidelis of course was smiling. He bent and retrieved the pistol and returned to the witness chair.

'Are there any questions?' he asked.

The public did not melt away while the jury deliberated. A few left with business to do, but most stayed on, walking out for some fresh air, or around the room to stretch their legs and exchange views with neighbours. To leave before the result would be, to them, like letting a novel go unfinished, or a netted fish uneaten. So they waited, as I waited, for the jury's verdict on the death of Phillip Pimbo.

Grimshaw came bustling up to me.

'I will say to you now, Cragg, what I was rudely cut off from saying in open court. That this supposed fraud on Pimbo by Moon confirms the strong opinion I gave on the day of the shooting: that when he died Pimbo was ruined and had lost the Corporation's money.'

'Did you have any previous knowledge of this supposed fraud?' I asked.

'No idea of it. Pimbo had said not a word. He was always sunny when I saw him. But at least we may hope to rescue something from the wreckage. There's no chance now, I assume, of a self-murder verdict?'

'Yes, I think that danger has passed, Mayor. Fidelis's demonstration, that the gun would fire itself spontaneously if dropped on its butt, has made sure of it.'

'Thank heaven for that. There'll be no forfeiture of his goods, and we may hope that some of our cash at least can be scooped out of the estate.'

'I should not count on there being very much there,' I warned. 'Perhaps the Corporation should consider alternative means of funding the Guild.'

He gave a brief horse-like snort – in derision presumably at my suggestion – and moved away. I now noticed the little servant from Cadley Hall, who had received a summons to appear but had not, in the event, been called. Wearing a bonnet, she had sat throughout the hearing between two other summoned witnesses, Ruth Peel and Michael Ambler. Now she was alone, as if not knowing what to do. I went and sat beside her.

'How do, Peggy? Where is Miss Peel?'

'She has gone out for some air. She told me to stay here.'

'I hope you don't mind that I never called for your evidence.'

'No. If you want to know, I was scared to do it.'

'Were you frightened when Dr Fidelis let off the gun?'

'A little.'

'That was needless: there was no bullet, you know, only the powder charge.'

She smiled at me in the way older children do when an adult explains something already obvious to them.

'I like Dr Fidelis, though,' she said.

'So do I. So do many hereabouts. He is a skilled doctor.'

'Well I like him specially because he is kind to my uncle.'

I did not follow her, immediately, though I ought to have.

'Your uncle?'

'Yes. He had an accident, and is very poorly. Dr Fidelis looks after him without fee, my auntie says, because they have no money.'

And then I remembered some of the details of Fidelis's first visit to the Thorns.

'Of course, of course! You are Adam Thorn's niece who went into service. I never made the connection.'

'I hope my uncle wakens up.'

'So do I, Peg.'

And so I did, for it would make my task with the so-called hoard of Benjamin Peel a good deal easier.

At that moment I noticed the people filing once again into their seats, and those who had gone outside returning. One of these was Ruth Peel and so I rose to allow her to resume her chair. She did it with a bleak smile for me but no word and, a moment later, Michael Ambler took the seat on the child-servant's other side. I thanked them both for their evidence and, looking as it did that the jury were coming back, I returned to my own place.

They duly came back, each man breathing out the fumes of the ale that had been provided for their refreshment. Fidelis's demonstration of the unsoundness of the pistol's mechanism, informed by the special knowledge of juror Peter Lofthouse, had made it all too easy for them. A brief whispered discussion with Foreman Purvis afterwards gave me to understand that there had been a sticking point over Proctor's suggestion that Pimbo did kill himself and merely wrote the letter to the Mayor as a ruse to avoid the inquest's verdict of self-murder. Once that was argued out of the way, and the breaker of ale companionably finished, they came to their decision and trooped back into the courtroom. It took no time for Purvis to report the verdict: the pistol had slipped from Pimbo's fingers just after he had loaded it, perhaps in too much haste. The butt of the gun had struck the desktop and the action of the gun being very loose and easy, the impact had discharged it even though it may have been only in the half-cock position – a possibility that juryman Lofthouse confirmed for us. Thus the ball was fired upwards into the goldsmith's jaw and brain, killing him instantly. This, in short, was a case of accidental death by the shot of a pistol worth two guineas, that was formerly the property of a Captain Avery.

Elizabeth always attended my inquests and I relied on her to let me know with candour where I had made my worst mistakes. But this time I already knew where I had been at fault.

'I am very disappointed with myself,' I told her that night as we lay in bed. She had just closed *Pamela* and snuffed her candle.

'How so, my dearest? Not about the inquest?'

'Yes, I allowed my feelings about the trade in Africans to get the better of me. I should not have let the discussion go into the moral sphere. It was bad practice and to make it worse the public were joining in most disorderly. My father would never have permitted such a thing to happen in the conduct of an inquest.'

'Well, I for one am proud of your words, husband, and I wish you had pressed the matter more. We know so little of this Guinea Trade, because no one is talking about it openly. It appears to be a mightily secret process, though one that makes a great deal of money. But people ought to be powerfully interested in the philosophical question that you put to the court – the question of the negroes' humanity?'

'And what do *you* say to the Trade, Lizzie?'

'I am with those in the audience that called out against it. I say that the negroes are people, and have immortal souls. And I say too that I don't understand how in conscience one can buy and sell such beings.'

'Mr Jackson says these traders are righteous men, who are bringing the negro to Christianity.'

Charmingly, she laughed.

'I doubt it. Their purpose is to make money, not Christians! And our Lord would not endorse that purpose, or their methods, I think. The camel and the needle's eye – remember?'

'Yet if there are indeed men among them who wish to bring the Africans to Christianity, perhaps they at least should be applauded. It is hard to judge right and wrong in a cloud of ignorance.'

'Tybalt Jackson is not a man of means anyway – not from his appearance. I suppose he is a lowly clerk in the service of rich masters. He does their bidding.'

'Did he do that today, though? When he first came forward to speak, I thought that he was spurred on by the warmth of his blood; and that when he sat down he became increasingly guarded, and afraid of what he was revealing.'

'I saw the same, my love. Mr Jackson started his evidence as a bull and finished it as an owl.'

I was seized with sleeplessness that night. I had confronted during the day, for the first time, the question of slavery and the traffic of people as if they were cattle. Of course I knew this had existed in the ancient times, and never been opposed by great men. Pericles, Alexander, Hannibal, Caesar all had been the owners of slaves. But in our own modern world we had begun to prize the liberty of men.

People say the African has a black skin and a thick skull and wears no clothes, and so cannot be the same as ourselves. I thought about this. In his essay on cannibals Montaigne advises not to take things on trust from vulgar opinion, but to look at them with the eye of reason. Reason says the negroes are not the equal of us in many things: they cannot build great warships, great cathedrals or engines of great power. They hold perhaps to a rudimentary philosophy of life, and to religions of blood sacrifice, fire-worship and the like. But in these things, they are not so different from our own ancestors, as may be learned from the scholarly writings of Sir Thomas Browne in the last century – and we do not call our ancestors anything but our family. Clothing and a fair skin are not tokens of humanity, but of living in a cold climate, out of the sun. Even cannibals, Montaigne finds, are very sensible people and, though different from ourselves, are not in everything inferior. In some ways they are better than we are.

There is another side of this, I told myself. Some people cannot be trusted with freedom and to enslave them is best, while they learn how to be free. That is what we do with children. They are beneficially the property of their parents until they reach the age of freedom. Might that not also be the case with the negro when he comes to the civilized world?

I had decided I must seek out Jackson tomorrow and question him further. I burned to know for my own satisfaction the condition of the slaves and whether they can be civilized. But now I was becoming drowsy, and my mind began drifting on to disparate things – the coat that I would wear tomorrow, the lovely blue of the sky, the beauty of my wife sleeping beside me, how I must pay the roofer that patched the hole in our thatch, the worn cover of my copy of Hobbes's *Leviathan*, that took such a pitiless look at the savage beneath the skin of the civil man. Yes, I thought, I might get that book down and see what it says on the matter that had been occupying me.

A furious thunder shattered these peaceful thoughts, and all peace throughout the house. I started up, and so did Elizabeth.

'What's that?'

It took me a moment to realize that someone was hammering at the front door, which lay immediately below one of our bedroom windows. I eased from the bed and slid the window open.

'Who's there? And what do you want?'

There was a small group of men gathered round the door, one or two of them holding lanterns, others with poles and one, I saw, with a musket. They all started shouting up at me.

'Send down the Coroner, if you please.'

'Urgently wanted.'

'Are you Mr Cragg? We need to speak to Mr Cragg.'

'They've found a dead man.'
'They've got a corpus.'
'Dead he is, up on Moor.'

Chapter Seventeen

∞

THERE HAD BEEN no time to fetch a horse, and so we walked it. The dawn was breaking over to our right, where the hills made a dark barrier of the horizon. Morning birds darted along the hedgerows and, as the light crept out across the land, rabbits hopped here and there and a hare moved with its limping, wary walk alongside a ditch. Most of the night creatures were fast in their nests and burrows: I did see one late fox slinking guiltily away from us as we entered upon the Moor, and there was the slightest smudge of white on the edge of a copse as a badger went home to bed. Above all, the night's cloud had moved away to the north and the sky was clearing. It promised to be a warm day.

The men with me were an assorted group that had been out all night after game. They were excited, and a little overawed by the discovery they had made and, as we walked, I tried to get a clearer idea of how exactly it had happened.

'It were a man, Mr Cragg, lying flat out on the Bale Stone. I saw him but I didn't know him. No, his face were battered so bad we couldn't recognize him, not from ground. So Michael got up to shine lamplight on his face – I got up on the Stone, see, and they handed me up the light and, as I stood over him, I brought the light across and I saw the terrible thing right below me. We could all see it from where we stood. There were this great stake right through his heart, a terrible rough stake of wood driven deep into the chest. No chance that he was alive. No chance. We left him as he was with Leo Porter and two others to look after him and so we came down, and we decided amongst ourselves it should be you, Mr Cragg, we should knock up, and that you would know what to do.'

I assured them they had done the right thing.

'Did anyone find him first?' I asked, 'Or were you all in a group?'

'Not one group. Different groups. It were me and Simon here and John Bailey that's stayed up there with the corpus that saw it first. The rest came up later.'

The speaker was a man called Edward Etherington, a carpenter, whom I knew to be literate and fairly sensible on the whole. I marked him out in my mind as the first finder.

We reached the Stone after a stiff walk of less than twenty minutes. Now morning sunlight was bathing the Moor, making dew and cuckoo-spit glisten and picking out the green of the trees, the yellow of gorse and the velvet purple of the heather. The combination of silvery early light and receding dark made my senses dance, heightened as they were by sleeplessness.

Three men emerged from the Stone's shadow to greet us. One of them, Porter, hailed me and cheerfully volunteered the latest news.

'He hasn't stirred, Sir. He hasn't uttered.'

'Have you seen anyone else about?'

'No. No one's been near.'

I could see the outline of a man's bulk lying on top of the Stone.

'Here, Sir, you should get on top for a look.'

Porter, a man built like a bear, laced his hands to make a stirrup. I planted my foot on it and he heaved me easily up until I stood on the Stone beside the corpse, which lay on its back, splayed and empty of life.

The sun was high enough now and there was no need for a lamp.

I could see how grievously the fellow's face had been assaulted. It was glazed in blood and there was little left of its original features, an ear half torn off, the nose and cheekbones smashed, and the jaw taken right out its hinges by what must have been a scything sideways blow. The eyeballs caught a ray of the sun, but nothing could animate their rigid stare.

The Stone was large enough to enable me to walk all round the body. I did so, noting that the coat, breeches, shirt and stockings were of very ordinary cloth and that the one visible shoe – the other being absent – was of sturdy manufacture. And, although I could never have sworn to the identity of the man from what was left of his face, I knew who he was. I had seen all of these pieces of clothing in my courtroom on the previous day, when they had been worn by Tybalt Jackson, insurance agent of Bristol. Now they covered Mr Jackson's mortal remains.

I knelt, pulled out the tail of his shirt and pushed my hand under it, up as far as the armpit. Fidelis had taught me that I should do this on every occasion that I came across a body, to test the temperature. In this instance the flesh felt cool by comparison with my own body heat and I turned my attention to the object jutting, some way out of the vertical, from Jackson's chest, with about three inches of it showing. The men's enthusiastic evocation of a 'great stake' driven into his heart had made me visualize something the thickness of a fencing post, sharpened and malletted with mighty blows through the body. It was nothing like that, but thinner and unshaped, like a piece of wood split for kindling. I grasped it and pulled upwards. It must have penetrated between two ribs, for it was wedged quite firmly. I left it in place.

I took out my watch. A quarter past five. The sooner Fidelis got out here the better for we could not leave the body long exposed to the June sun. I vaulted down from the Stone and asked which of the men could stay and assist. I really did need help: a messenger to convey a summons to Dr Fidelis in Fisher Gate and then, unfortunately but inescapably, to Sergeant Mallender at his house in Tithe Barn Street; and I required some of them to fashion an awning for the body, and then a litter, in order to be ready, when the time came, to carry it back to town. But I also wanted to detain as many of these men as I could, to delay by a little the spread of the news. In truth, I had little real hope of this. The word would be carried with the baker's boy and the dairyman, so that by breakfast-time it would be in every house and hovel in town. But I did not relish the lot of gawpers that would be trailing out here as a consequence.

Two or three of the men nevertheless insisted that business called them away, though the greater part were so much enjoying the dramatic moment that they did not want it to end. While Etherington got a group of them to work on the awning – saying they would improvise a screen for the body from the long-nets they had with them, which would later form the bed of a litter to carry it – I set to work speaking to each of the men, starting with those wanting to leave us.

The picture that I formed from these discussions was inconclusive. The men divided into three groups. Each had been out on the Moor, or ranged further off into the Fulwood or over the fields beyond Cadley, and had come together around the dead body after Etherington, with his brother Simon and brother-in-law Bailey, had first found it. Etherington's own group had only just come out from town. They had set the Stone as their meeting place, being intent on erecting long nets nearby in which to drive the morning's crop of rabbits as they ventured out of their burrows. A second group, that came up shortly after, were five fellows with a pair of lurcher dogs. They had been up all night beating the edge of the woods, hoping for a deer but now bringing home only a brace of hare. Finally there had been Leo and his son, a lad of sixteen built along similar lines to his father's massive frame, who were on their way back after a night's fishing on the little Savage River above Cottam Mill.

None of these ten men reported seeing or hearing anything suspicious on the Moor. I had made sure to take each one apart from his fellows to question him, but separately no man had anything to disclose that contradicted what another had said – except that both Leo and young Alan Porter claimed to have caught the fine pike that lay in their fish bag.

A drumming of hooves was heard coming from the north of us, and I recalled that was where the path of the racecourse passed the Stone. I looked and saw John Barton with a stable boy, each of them riding a strapping courser heavily rugged and bonneted.

Barton pulled up his mount and called out when he saw me.

'Cragg!'

I walked towards him and down the shallow bank until I stood on the track itself.

'Someone was fatally attacked here last night,' I said. 'Have you seen anything? Heard anything?'

Barton shook his head.

'No. This is our first string to come out. I was dreaming in bed until twenty minutes ago, all night undisturbed since ten o'clock.'

He looked at the boy.

'Seen anything suspicious last night, Bobby?'

Bobby shook his head.

'So who's dead?' Barton went on, turning back to me. 'Anyone I know?'

'A stranger.'

'Probably a stranger who did it, then.'

I let that go without reply and waved goodbye to the horse exercisers, who set off again at a steady canter.

Three of the hunters were now ready to leave. The two dogs they had with them were alert to this and were suddenly nosing the wind, barking and pulling at their leashes, all straining in the one direction towards the east of the Bale Stone. The owner of one of them said:

'Well, us'll have some sport before we go home after all, eh lads? It's likely a deer that's strayed too close.'

He slipped his dog's leash and he tore off, followed by the other, and by their owners with their guns, galloping through the brush in increasingly distant pursuit. No deer was sprung, however, and at a hundred and fifty yards from the Stone the dogs found their prey exactly where they had scented it. I could hear growling and yipping as they worried at it, but soon they were roughly called off. I saw the men kneel to look at whatever creature their lurchers had caught, and then one of them leapt up, waving and shouting towards the Stone, his words blown away from us by the breeze. They began hauling whatever creature it was towards us, and we soon realized it was not an animal, but a young person with the appearance of a boy, in cap, shirt and breeches (though no shoes). He was being both pushed and dragged along, his eyes wide from fear and holding with one hand the wrist of the other, in the place where one of the dogs had seized it. I was struck by his crying – it was silent. The other notable thing about him was his skin: he was as black as a cottage kettle.

At this point a heavily puffing Sergeant Oswald Mallender arrived at the spot. He had received the message of a dead body at the Bale Stone and hastened out without even waiting for his courtiers, the two Parkin brothers. The Sergeant took one look at the dead body, and another at the unfortunate prisoner, who had now been brought to stand with his back to the Stone. Mallender acknowledged my presence with little more than a grunt before he turned his attention fully towards the prisoner.

'What have we here, lads? A dead body – and a suspicious person in custody, by the look of it. What, men? Was this wretch caught running away?'

The owner of the dog that had caught the boy explained the circumstances.

'Well, boy, speak English do you?' growled Mallender, gesturing towards the body. 'What do you say to all this? You've been caught lurking near the scene of a death – no! A murder! Did you do it? Did you?'

He took the boy by his ear and twisted it, but could wring no sound from him except for the snuffles of his streaming nose.

'No answer? You young savage, of course you did! Who's the corpus? Does anyone know him?'

'His name is Tybalt Jackson,' I said, 'and yesterday he gave evidence at the inquest into the death of goldsmith Pimbo at the Friary Bar Inn. This boy I believe to have been Jackson's servant. I also believe he may be a mute, which would explain why he does not answer your questions.'

'I have a readier explanation, Cragg. Guilt!'

Mallender seemed quite uninterested in looking over the body, and I noticed he kept himself at an uneasy distance at all times from the Stone on which it lay. When I suggested he take a closer look at Jackson, he hastened to decline with a wave of his hand.

'Time enough for that, Cragg, when you get it to town. Meanwhile I shall personally escort this Devil-child of Satan to Moot Hall where his judgement awaits, shall I?'

Mallender's behaviour had so far been entirely consistent with his usual procedure. He liked, when called to a crime, to convey the impression of a man of decision, a man of action, able in an instant to penetrate to the heart of a mystery and point his finger at the villain. He must have been delighted at what he found by the Bale Stone, nervous though he was of the Stone itself. A killed man, and an already-made murderer of that man fallen without effort into his hands. I knew it would be useless but still I warned him.

'I really do not think we should hurry to judgement on him,

Mallender. He may be a witness; I very much doubt he is the murderer.'

Mallender looked astonished that I should contradict his own instinctual grasp of criminal truth.

'But what we have here is a black savage, Mr Cragg. Kill without a second's thought, they will. We must take him before the Mayor without delay for, in my opinion which I am sure Mr Grimshaw will share, the piccaninny must be kept in gaol until he comes to the Assizes. So I'll be happy to let you have charge of the body, and I shall have charge of the killer. Are we agreed? Let's go, my lads.'

Mallender and the hunters left us, walking in a close huddle around the black boy. When we had stood for a few moments to watch them go, Etherington turned to me.

'Shall us fashion the hurdle and take the body down now, Mr Cragg?'

'No, do not move it yet. I want Dr Fidelis to look at it *in situ* first. He should be here – ah! There in fact he is.'

Fidelis had appeared walking briskly along the path towards the Bale Stone, carrying his medical bag. His face, as it usually did in the early morning, looked a little creased and drawn. But as soon as he saw the body he began to regain vitality like a drooping buttercup in water.

'Aha! Didn't I tell you this was a matter worth killing over?'

Soon he had vaulted up onto the Stone and knelt beside the dead man. I told Etherington that he could finish constructing the litter now, as I thought we could be on our way in about ten minutes. And so we were.

Fidelis and I walked behind the four men that carried the litter, at sufficient distance to make it impossible for them to hear us. I said:

'Give me your impressions.'

'He still has warmth. He is not yet in the slightest stiff. I think he cannot have died more than five hours ago.'

'What about the wounds? Which of them killed him?'

'I need to open the body to see how far the stick in his chest penetrates. If it reached his heart it would certainly have killed him, providing he were not dead already.'

'So can you tell if the face wounds were done before or after the stick?'

'That is a very good question. And the answer is at the moment I can't. But I will think about it.'

'You saw Mallender dragging away the negro boy?'

'I passed them on the path.'

'He already has him lined up on the scaffold with the noose around his neck. But I doubt he is the killer.'

'He cannot be the killer alone – there must have been *killers*, Titus. Did you not perceive the same?'

'Go on, Luke.'

'The attack did not start on the Bale Stone. Jackson was put there after he had been significantly wounded, if not actually killed. I rather fancy he *was* already dead: there had been no great spillage of fresh blood on the Stone. I could clearly see bloodstains where he was pulled up over the edge and onto the top surface, and also the drag marks made as he was manoeuvred into the position in which he was found, but no large pools as would have formed if he had pumped out his life-blood here.'

'You're right, Luke. One man could not have got the body up there – and certainly not a boy like that poor waif.'

'A boy, you say?'

'Yes.'

'I only caught a short glimpse, but I must place a caution beside that word.'

'A caution?'

'Yes. Of course, the assumption is that it is a boy, because, when one has a black servant, it is of course always a boy, is it not? And your poor waif was indeed dressed as a boy. Yet to my eyes the physical outline was not that of a boy, but female, Titus. Under that shirt I'll warrant you she had the makings of breasts and under those breeches a girl's arse.'

Chapter Eighteen

∞

HEADING FOR THE House of Correction, we came into town by the Friary Bar and immediately made the turn into Marsh Lane. But here Fidelis excused himself,

'I must leave you here,' he said. 'I have a busy round of calls.'

I gestured at the improvised litter and its burden.

'Will you examine him for me, later?'

'With pleasure, but not before afternoon. Shall I meet you at three o'clock?'

The town was shaking itself awake. Already there were children sitting on their doorsteps with slices of bread and dripping larger than their hands, watching their mothers as they sluiced and swept the cobblestones. Men, stumbling towards the market under laden hods or heavy satchels, wove a mazy path to avoid the women's brooms. Boys idled on the way to the Grammar School, stopping in groups to roll marbles, or to tussle and taunt each other.

Every head turned to us as we passed. I had picked up an old sack from the roadside along the way and used it to cover poor Jackson's broken face, but this served only to increase the general curiosity, and soon we had a parade behind us like a disorderly funeral, the mourners calling out questions to the litter bearers, and shouting up to houses along the way for people to come and see. Death is all around us, yet we will never treat it as a commonplace. I suppose it is because we don't know the manner of our own deaths that we are so powerfully drawn to discover how others have died.

We arrived at the House of Correction and asked the porter to send for Arnold Limb, the Keeper of Correction. A minute later he hurried out to the lodge, flapping his hands.

'Bless me, Cragg, what have you brought me now?'

The Keeper had not had time to take breakfast, which would have made a dourer man bad tempered. But the genial Limb's dominant humour was sanguine and, though he was agitated, he retained his bonhomie.

'You are having an eventful morning, Mr Limb?'

'I am. I have already received into my hands a young negro stranger who can't or won't speak, and who Mallender says is a violent murderer. I have to entertain him until he is brought before the Mayor at ten o'clock, and to keep his cell on for him, as Mallender says he is sure to be coming back when the Mayor commits him for the Assizes.'

'Well just for the sake of completeness,' I told him, 'may I present the man that was murdered? I would like to billet him on you, Mr Limb, just as we did Pimbo.'

Limb's conceit was always to speak as though his small prison were an inn, and that his prisoners were there for their own pleasure, and not at that of the law.

'Yes, yes, of course, Cragg. Take our new guest to those same quarters. Mr Pimbo's remains are leaving us this morning, I am glad to say, so they won't have the inconvenience of sharing for long. I have Oatseed boxing him up now to be taken home for his funeral tomorrow. There's just one thing . . . the reckoning has not been paid for Mr Pimbo's time with us.'

I suggested he send the account in to my office, and so we took the body to the same chamber, set apart from the main accommodation, that the goldsmith had been occupying. Pimbo who wore nothing but a simple winding sheet lay beside it in a plain box supported by trestles while the coffin builder added a few refinements – four iron rings through which to lower him into his grave, and an engraved brass plaque for the coffin-lid. When we had placed Tybalt Jackson on the table he had vacated I lifted the sacking from his face and retrieved from the floor the sheet that had covered Pimbo.

'I suppose he will not mind another man's covering sheet,' sighed Arnold Limb, as we left the cell and made our way back towards the porter's lodge. 'Perhaps I should have found him an unsoiled one, but my weekly laundry bill is very burdensome.'

'He won't mind anything earthly now, Mr Limb.'

'I wonder what it is that protrudes from his chest.'

'He was stabbed with a sharpened stick.'

'Oh dear. Should you not pull it out? It would be more comfortable, I think.'

'Dr Fidelis will come this afternoon to attend to that, with your permission.'

'Oh, most willingly. He should have a doctor, even though it is too late. You must find it a great pity that his face is so horribly disfigured. I remember your renowned father telling us when I served as juror in one of his inquests that there's much to learn from the expression of the face in death.'

'Yes, my father wrote notes upon that and they are in his book.'

I had not recently looked at my father's distillations of everything he had learned during a quarter century as a Coroner. He had them printed, before he died, as *Notes on the Appearance of the Human Body upon Death, with Indications Therein of the Means of Expiration, for the Guidance of Coroners* by Samuel Cragg. The chapter on the face, as I remembered, listed all the qualities of death that may be detected through facial expression, such as the surprised death, the resigned death, the desired death, or the just death. Much as I loved and respected my father, I had myself found death always too contrary and misleading to leave such simple signposts; but he like many Coroners of his time believed in these easy facial auguries.

'Well we can learn little from that particular face now,' sighed Limb. 'It has been destroyed.'

'Oh, I don't know that we can't,' I said. 'We shall see what Dr Fidelis has to say on the matter.'

We were passing the door of the main building, and I stopped to listen to the cacophony within. There were shouted conversations between the cells, repeated banging, screams and curses and a good deal of plaintive weeping.

'I know what you are thinking,' laughed Limb ruefully. 'It is like a madhouse. But many of them are troubled souls, we must remember that.'

But I had something else on my mind.

'I wonder if I might take this opportunity to speak with your latest arrival,' I said. 'The African?'

'Oh, yes, if you like. There is nothing against it – and much to be said for it, if you can persuade him to speak. We cannot do so. Ground floor, I think. Warden Rawley will show you the chamber. I myself am heading for my breakfast, at last. Good day, Sir. You will find Rawley inside.'

I ventured in. There were rooms immediately to the right and left of the door, one of which was the punishment room, where whippings were sometimes carried out, and the other was Billy Rawley's personal domain. I eased open the door of the latter and saw the rotund official sprawled in a basket chair, gently snoring.

Shutting the door again I walked along the ground floor passage, looking as I passed through the grilles set in the doors ranged on each side. Two or three centuries ago this building had housed friars, in what may have been some comfort by the standards of the time: I noticed, for instance, that the cells each had a fireplace. But no warming fires burned in those grates now. The place showed in every room the distress of time and, even in June, it felt draughty and damp.

The eighth and last cell on the left contained the prisoner I was looking for, sitting on the bed, back to the wall, legs drawn up, arms wrapped around the knees, head sunk onto the arms. It looked like a case of pure dejection.

'Miss!' I called out.

The head was raised and two huge brown eyes were turned upon me.

'I am Titus Cragg,' I went on. 'I'm Coroner here. It is my duty to investigate the death of Mr Tybalt Jackson. Do you understand?'

But there was no sign of it and after a moment the eyes closed and the head returned to its previous position.

'How can I eat a good breakfast,' I said, 'with that poor wretch sitting hungry and shut up in that terrible place?'

Elizabeth put a dish of cold roast lamb and pickled beetroot in front of me.

'You can, Titus, because as soon as you have done I shall go over there with some bread and soup. What's the boy's name?'

'I don't know. I don't even know if it is a boy or a girl. Fidelis thinks the latter.'

'A girl? What a terrible thing, if so. And all alone.'

'And by the way, it is quite impossible that she – or he – did the murder. Certainly not without help. Oswald Mallender is a fool if he thinks it.'

'Everyone agrees Mallender is a fool.'

'The boy – or girl – must have been near Jackson, though, when he was attacked and probably witnessed his killing. I do need to know what happened, if only she – or he – can find her way to telling me.'

It had chimed eight by the time Elizabeth left on her mission to the House of Correction. I went into the office, and found that Furzey had already arrived.

'We have another body this morning, I hear,' he observed, without looking up from his writing.

'Yes, found on the Moor. I regret it is our surprise Bristolian witness from yesterday's inquest. He's in the House of Correction, badly hacked about the face. We'll inquest him tomorrow – no, on Saturday. There's a lot needs finding out. We'll go back to the Friary Bar Inn for the hearing, I think. Send a notice over to them directly, will you? I must be going. I want to see if Elizabeth has returned and then I'm due at Moot Hall.'

The Mayor's courtroom was an imposing panelled chamber at the heart of Moot Hall and had been used for centuries by the Court Leet, enforcing the rules for everyday life in Preston. Here traders and townspeople aired complaints against their neighbours or the Corporation, pursued cheats and infringers and, if called upon, gave account of and penance for their own misdemeanours. But the courtroom was also that of the magistrates – of whom the chief was the Mayor – and of quarter-sessions, in which the Mayor sat with two of His Majesty's justices. So the room heard criminal as well as civil matters. It dealt directly with minor felonies while remitting more serious cases through the Grand Jury for trial at the Assizes in Lancaster. And looming over all these proceedings was the versatile power of the Mayor.

The room was constructed to reinforce that power. Grimshaw sat highest of all, in a throne-like seat that commanded a view of every upturned face in the well below. The hearing had been called *ex tempore*, so that on this occasion the court was thinly populated. As well as myself, there was Mallender, the prisoner, a couple of clerks and William Biggs, Grimshaw's mayoral predecessor, whom he had brought in to sit with him. Biggs could be relied upon to agree with whatever was proposed.

'Now, Mr Mallender,' intoned Grimshaw, looking down from his perch like an overfed cock bird surveying the dunghill. 'Pray tell us what is the name of this boy standing here before us.'

Mallender had brought the forlorn figure from the House of Correction, still in bare feet, rough trousers and buttoned shirt, though looking perhaps a little less forlorn since hungrily slurping down Elizabeth's soup, as she had described it to me on her return half an hour earlier. Now stationed in the balustraded dock immediately facing Grimshaw's chair, the prisoner's two small hands, one of them wrapped in a bandage, could be seen grasping the rail, on either side of a large and uncomprehending pair of eyes.

Mallender cleared his throat and straightened his back.

'This boy here is or is pretending to be a mute, Sir. No word of a name have we got out of him.'

'Then tell us in clear language please why he has been brought here before us.'

I rose to my feet.

'May I speak, Mayor?'

'Cragg! Why are you in this court?'

'As an observer with a demonstrable interest, Sir. I shall shortly be holding an inquest into one Tybalt Jackson, who has been murdered with great violence on Preston Moor.'

'Yes, murdered by this boy, which is why we're here. So can we please get on?'

'May I suggest that you do not get on, Sir, but adjourn the hearing pending my inquest?'

'Why on earth should I do that, Cragg?'

'I presume it will provide you with more facts—'

'Do not presume, Mr Coroner! What more facts can I possibly

want? I have a dead body, I have a boy caught red-handed for murder.'

'Well, may we examine one of those facts in particular? Is this really a boy?'

'Are you in your right mind? Of course it is!'

'You will find that medical opinion differs from you. Dr Fidelis is sure this is a female.'

Grimshaw, as I was gratified to see, was caught entirely by surprise. With his mouth falling slightly open, he looked the prisoner up and down.

'A female? But, Cragg, the costume. And there are no ... I mean, where are its ... ?'

'She is young, Sir, and underfed.'

Grimshaw glanced uneasily at Biggs, and then turned directly towards the dock.

'Well, will you tell us?' he rasped. 'What are you? Boy, or girl? Out with it!'

In a trice and without self-consciousness the prisoner undid three shirt buttons and pulled the shirt wide open. Her ribcage was painfully evident but so, above it, were two small but undoubted breasts. Grimshaw's eyes near popped from their sockets.

'Good God! Cover yourself in this court! This is an outrageous display. Mallender! Cover her up, man.'

I left the court a few minutes later, in a fair way satisfied. Grimshaw had been so disconcerted by what he had just seen that he had taken a completely different view of the case. He had told Mallender that he was an oaf, and had made a wrongful arrest; he ordered that the girl not be sent back to the House of Correction; and decreed instead that she be taken into domestic custody by some good person of the town.

But I felt some discomfort, too, at his handling of the case, for I had detected in the Mayor's face, and that of his fellow magistrate, not just moral outrage at the sight of a young woman's bare breasts in his courtroom, but the slightest glint, just for a moment, of another emotion altogether.

Chapter Nineteen

∞

THE LANDLORD OF the Lamb and Flag Inn in St John's Court was George Houndsworth, a dirty fellow who kept a dirty house, in a part of town not much frequented by those who lived on the prosperous ridge of Fisher Gate, or could boast proximity to the Earl of Derby's magnificent Patten House on Church Gate. St John's Court had never boasted fine houses. What it had were hovels of various sizes that canted, tottered and stank together like rows of rotten teeth. Here lived families equally various except for one thing: all were uniformly poor and dirty.

The Lamb and Flag was the most decayed in a street of decayed houses, and so old that it had no history. If there had been any days of its glory, they belonged to a past beyond memory or record. I picked my way from the street into a bridged passage, too narrow for a modern coach (even could a coach-driver be persuaded to make the attempt), and into a smelly yard. Around this, precariously supporting each other, stood the worm-eaten, rot-ridden buildings of the inn.

I pressed my handkerchief to my nose and crossed to the largest door I could see. It opened onto a semi-dark hallway where stood a dusty staircase and a greeting-hatch with, on its ledge, a small much tarnished brass bell. This I rang vigorously.

Mr Houndsworth, a man of about fifty, came himself in answer to the summons, and peered at me. He was dressed in a grubby shirt and grubbier breeches, and had the appearance of one who had been rudely woken from sleep. However, he was affable enough.

'Mr Cragg, is it? This is an honour, Sir. What can I offer you? A mug of ale? Or some of our elderflower wine?'

I declined all suggestions for my refreshment and asked merely for a few words in private. The landlord took me through to his own quarters, a square fireless room behind the greeting-hatch where a fat dog lay on the bed alternately snoring and farting, and a skeletal cat sat on watch in the middle of the table. Houndsworth cleared the cat off with a sweep of his arm and invited me to take a chair.

'This must be about the Jackson fellow that was staying here and was found dead,' he said.

The table evidently served for both dining and business, for there were dirty glasses and plates, as well as pen, ink and ledgers on it. I swept crumbs from the seat of the chair with my coat tails and sat down.

'It is,' I said. 'He was your guest. Pray tell me about him.'

Houndsworth settled into the chair opposite and spat accurately across the room into the cold fireplace. For a moment he reminded me of one taking the strain on a hauling rope; then he began speaking effortfully, with brief pauses, as if pulling the words uphill behind him.

'Let me think. They arrived on ... Tuesday, was it? Yes, Tuesday. After dark, about ... nine o'clock. Said he was staying not less than two, I think it was, days.'

'Did he say why he was here?'

'No. He didn't say owt. I don't badger my customers here with questions. I'm just glad of their money, me.'

'What then?'

'I put him in the best room – well, the ... biggest room, as there's no "best" room here, as such. We call it the White Room.'

'Tell me about the young negro with him – his servant.'

Houndsworth brightened, even smiled.

'Right pretty little piccaninny, wasn't it?'

'It was a young woman, Mr Houndsworth. Did you hear her speak?'

Houndsworth frowned, then humorously wrinkled his nose.

'A female, was it? I took it for a boy. Well, well. That would explain—'

'I am curious to know what language was used, Mr Houndsworth.'

'Well, yes, I did hear it chattering away, I did, in a kind of English. Not exactly the English of these parts but I understood some of it.'

'And what did Mr Jackson ask for on the evening he arrived?'

Returning to his earlier gravity, Houndsworth gave this some ponderous thought.

'Oh, I don't know. Not much.'

'Didn't he eat?'

The landlord frowned.

'Oh, yes . . . Asked for drink and bread and cheese for himself and the piccaninny.'

'And then?'

'Went out for a night walk. Came back soon enough and shut himself in his room. I didn't see him until the next morning.'

'How long was his walk?'

He made a shrug.

'Half an hour. Not long.'

'Did he say where he'd been?'

'No. Just good-night.'

'And next morning, what did he do?'

'Ate a crust, then went out. Oh! He'd asked me about the inquest you were holding, such as where it was and when, and

I told him. That's when I got the idea he was in town to attend that inquest, y'see. I was right in supposing that, wasn't I, Mr Cragg?'

As I ignored the question he was forced to go on, his speech gathering speed now as if the cart with his load of words had finally breasted the brow of the hill.

'But there was another thing – that street boy Barty, you know him? He turned up asking questions about strangers at the inn. I told him about Mr Jackson and the piccaninny, and he ran off again. I reckoned that boy was sent by someone else, y'see, who had business with Mr Jackson, but who Jackson preferred to avoid because – I forgot to say – on the night he arrived he asked me expressly not to tell anyone asking questions about him. Expressly.'

'And yet you told the boy Barty?'

Slowly Houndsworth scratched the pate, whose skin was visible through his thinning, greasy hair.

'Oh, aye, I did. But that weren't . . . I mean that were next day. It were on the night *before* that he told me to shut up about him.'

'I see. Let's talk about after the inquest. Did Jackson return here?'

'Aye, he came back. Went to his room, and asked for some more food which I took in to him.'

'What was he doing?'

'He was writing a letter. It looked a long'un.'

'Was his servant there?'

'Yes, curled up on the bed, it were.'

'You didn't see who Jackson was writing to?'

'No. Later he asked for the post office, and went out. He posted the letter, I suppose.'

'When was that?'

'I don't know for sure. Half of four, maybe.'

'Did he come back again?'

'Yes.'

'And did he have any visitors?'

'No.'

'Not even any messages? Think hard, Houndsworth. This is very important.'

'I tell you solemnly, Mr Cragg, I don't know of any message or letter delivered for him that evening. But then, fact is, I weren't here. I left my sister in charge while I went for a few jugs at Cowley's Tavern.'

'I see. Is your sister here? Can I speak to her?'

'She's married, at Kirkham. She just comes here Wednesday nights to help me. I need my weekly respite, Mr Cragg. This place is very hard to keep going when a man's on his own. I can't afford a maid or even a boy, because I'm—'

I cut him off.

'What other guests were there at the inn that night?'

'Oh, er, let me see.' He rubbed his chin. 'We don't get many . . .'

'For God's sake, Houndsworth, this is only last night! Don't you have a register of arrivals and departures?'

'Oh no, we don't bother us heads with one of those. Too much work, and I'm not that handy with a pen, myself.'

'What about your sister?'

'Oh, Betty, she writes with a lovely hand. She is much cleverer than me, like our old mam used to say, she—'

'I mean, did she say anything to you about arrivals or any other events at the inn, when you got back from the tavern?'

'She might have. I were not thinking too straight on account of the ale I'd supped, y'see. I think I remember that she said some sharpish words to me and then she took herself off to her bed, and I to mine.'

'So when was the last time you yourself saw Mr Jackson in person?'

'When he came back from going out – to the post office as I thought.'

'So that would be at about half past four yesterday afternoon?'

'Yes.'

'And when was the last you saw the negro child?'

'I didn't. I mean I'd seen it curled up on the bed in the room at dinner-time. I never saw it after. What's happened to it?'

I ignored the question.

'So this morning there were no guests at the inn, no one to give breakfast to?'

'If there were, Betty saw to them. I didn't waken up till half of eleven, me, and by then she'd shot off back to Kirkham. I were that far gone in the drink, y'see, that I—'

'So there might have been visitors who came last night while you were at Cowley's Tavern, or even guests for the night who left this morning while you slept off your drinking session?'

'Might have.'

'May I see this White Room that Mr Jackson occupied?'

'Yes Sir.'

He led me, with a shambling rheumatic gait, up the stairs and along a dusty corridor. He opened a door about half way along and gestured me to go first inside.

Houndsworth lingered just inside the door, his small eyes watching me as I went to the window, threw it open and looked around. It was an upstairs room and its brownish walls had once, possibly, been white. Otherwise it was a little larger, but no less dingy and fetid, than Houndsworth's apartment downstairs. There was a travelling valise on the floor, open and spilling some linen under-clothes. On a chair by the bed were a candle-holder and two small books, one being, as I could see from the cross on its cover, a pocket New Testament. On the small table were smoking and writing materials, though nothing written. The waste-basket was empty.

The Scrivener

I squatted down to look into the fire-grate. Jackson had not lit himself a substantial fire but, from a heap of black ash, I saw that he had burned some paper. The ash lay in deformed charred sheets, which crumbled to dust as I touched them. Were they a rough draft of the letter he wrote? Who had he been writing to? It was too late to go to the post office tonight, but it would be worth paying a visit to Richard Crick the postmaster in the morning. It was too much to hope that the letter might still be there. But Crick was young and keen: he would remember the letter posted by a stranger less than two days ago, and maybe the person it was sent to.

Next I turned out the valise, but it contained only clothing. I peered under the bed and saw a thick and undisturbed layer of dust. I surveyed the whole of the open floor, but did not see what I was looking for – Jackson's missing shoe.

Next I picked up his Testament and opened it where the ribbon marker indicated – the gospel of Matthew, chapter six, where the famous words were underscored: '*No man can serve two masters for either he will hate the one and love the other; or else he will hold to the one and despise the other. Ye cannot serve God and Mammon.*' I could see how this might apply to Jackson. One of his masters was undoubtedly Mammon, in the shape of the insurance company that had sent him to find out about the voyage of *The Fortunate Isle*. But what was that other Master? What, in his life, was God?

Then I opened the other book at the title page and was astonished to see it was the *Essays* by Montaigne, and that Jackson had evidently been reading 'On Cannibals'. After the passage in which the author lists all the things in our lives which we think necessary to society, such as employment, money, letters and numbers, none of which the cannibals have need for, there were again some underscored lines, that evidently meant much to Jackson himself. In these lines Montaigne says that '*among them the very words that signifie lying, treachery, dissimulation, avarice, envy and detraction were never heard of.'*

At that moment my whole idea of the dead man changed. He was a fellow reader, and he was occupied with the very same author whom I had been so much enjoying. I felt an entirely new kind of sympathy for Tybalt Jackson. When I had first seen his destroyed face I had felt ordinary human pity for him. But I now began to see him, and especially the views he had expressed about slavery the previous day, in a different light. The lines of Montaigne that he had picked out were so admiring. They spoke of cannibals as people that surpassed even the legend of the Golden Age: surely one who underscores those words does not in his heart support the buying and selling of such people into servitude – whatever he may feel obliged to say in public.

I riffled the pages and noted that Jackson had underlined other sentences here and there. Thinking they would be worth more study, I slipped both books into my pocket.

'Thank you, I have seen enough,' I said, slipping out past Houndsworth and heading for the stairs.

'I've just thought,' said Houndsworth as he followed me down to the hallway. 'What about my money for two nights' rent, and his bread and cheese on Tuesday night and his dinner on Wednesday? He owes me for all that, does Mr Jackson. Who's going to give it me?'

'No one, I am afraid,' I said, making haste to pull open the outside door. I had had more than enough of breathing the stale air of George Houndsworth's sorry establishment.

'But I must have my money, Mr Cragg!'

'Death trumps debt, I'm afraid. Now, there is just one more thing I need from you, Mr Houndsworth.'

'Yes Sir?'

'The married name of your sister in Kirkham, if you please.'

Chapter Twenty

∞

'I T ALL PROVES she can hear and understand English,' I said, as Fidelis and I walked back together that afternoon to the House of Correction. I had been telling him of the extraordinary revelation at the Mayor's court in the morning, and how it confirmed his own opinion of the African servant's sex. 'But she still has not spoken, and we know nothing about her.'

'You will need her as a witness, Titus. That will present difficulties if she proves a mute.'

'Elizabeth took her some breakfast this morning and indeed found her mute, but when she drank the soup there was a tongue in her mouth. Besides, George Houndsworth claims he heard her speaking.'

'There is muteness and muteness, Titus. In all probability this negro girl has had the words frightened out of her. They may return at any moment. And it is good that she seems to know English.'

'Yes, but the really good thing,' I said, as we arrived once again at the Porter's Lodge of the House, 'is that she is no longer incarcerated in this Godforsaken place.'

I am usually present when Fidelis examines a body though if there is to be any cutting open I sometimes retire to a distance until he has made his various incisions, separations and removals. He told me he would attend first to the rough piece of wood that still protruded from the body – the 'stake' that the body's discoverers had described.

'You may prefer to look away,' he said, picking up a large butcher's knife and shears of a size roughly between those of scissors and hedge-trimmers. I went for a walk around the yard and when I returned he had opened the chest by cutting through the sternum with the shears, and separated the two sides of the ribcage.

By pulling the ribs apart and peering inside with a lit candle he was able to see how far the stick had penetrated. It was not very far.

'The stick was not the primary method of attack. It went in on the heart's side but did not hit it.'

He pulled the stick out from between the ribs and held it up. It was about eight inches long in all so that three or four inches had penetrated the body.

'In fact, I think this was done *post mortem*. Let's look at the head. There are terrible wounds to the features but I would say the fatal one is here.'

He pointed to a four-inch split in the skull, scabbed along its length with dried blood. With his fingers he carefully took off the scab and felt within the split.

'I would say a metal edge did this. It must have made him unconscious and more than likely killed him outright. Note the position a little below and to the side of the crown.'

'Meaning?'

'Meaning he was hit from behind as well as in front.'

'He was attacked by more than one person, then.'

'Either that, or Jackson turned away to protect himself during the assault.'

'What weapon? A sword?'

'If it was, a very heavy one.'

'The same could have been used to damage the face.'

'Yes. It was a thorough job, but see here? This ear was not sliced through with a sharp blade like a knife. It has been roughly severed by a chopping, blunt blow. I think this is more likely the work of an axe than a sword.'

I looked the length of the body, still clothed, still with one stockinged foot.

'If we can find the missing shoe, we may find the weapon too,' I said. 'But where do we look?'

'Your little black girl might tell us, I fancy.'

'Aye – but how to get it out of her? This is the same blind alley that we face with Adam Thorn in the matter of this treasure, is it not?'

'Not at all the same. The girl's tongue may spring loose by itself. Thorn's silence is buried deeper, and it is bound to his paralysis.'

'Oh dear. I have been hoping Adam's tongue might just spring loose, as you put it.'

'It's possible, but not likely. However there may be other ways of unearthing what he knows.'

'You have a treatment for him?'

'I did not say that.'

'By the way, you should see this,' said Fidelis. 'I received it this morning.'

We had quit the House of Correction and, at my insistence, called at the Friary Bar Inn. I wished to make sure that the same room I had used for the Pimbo inquest would be available on Saturday for the Jackson hearing. The landlord, delighted at the prospect of a second day of prodigious takings, poured out a gift of two bumpers of his best claret. After Fidelis had savoured this liberality, he had taken from his pocket a letter, which he handed to me, adding as if casually 'It is from Mrs Butler in Liverpool.'

I unfolded the paper and read:

'*Dear sweet doctor*',
'Your musical acquaintance is very fond,' I remarked.
Fidelis coloured.
'That is her nature. Please read on.'

I am grateful for yours of 7th inst. You say you are unsure about Mr Canavan's suitability to be my husband and that you wish that I knew him better before entering into marriage. I protest I have done much in that regard. Since he proposed that we marry I have written him a note every day – leaving him I hope in no doubts as to my affection – and he replies most kindly. I have invited him to Edmund Street many times for tea and, on several occasions as you know, he has honoured me by accepting, being on these occasions sweet and charming. His last letter assured me of his own honourable intentions, and that too has much encouraged me. Your fears, dear doctor, do you credit but I am sure they are groundless.

Mr Canavan has never spoken or written to me of the Mr Jackson you enquire about. I have had the opportunity to make mention, as you asked me to, of Mr Moon. Mr Canavan was very curious to know how I had heard the name and I had to tell him of the paper I found. He says he is a business acquaintance who has gone out of Liverpool on business and does not expect to see again in the town for several days. Mr Canavan has not told me where he is gone. Mr Canavan too is being kept very busy.

Please do not distress yourself on my account, dear doctor, and assure yourself that I am your vy affectionate B. Butler.

I lowered the paper.

'Moon is not in Liverpool. That's interesting. Where is he?'

'I have been thinking he could be somewhere hereabouts.'

'Who I wonder is his accomplice?'

'Accomplice?'

'I am sure two men killed Tybalt Jackson.'

I drained my glass and sprang to my feet, suddenly full of energy.

'So shall we walk up to the Stone,' I proposed, 'and see if we can find any trace of these villains and their activities?'

Fidelis looked at his watch.

'I can spare you an hour.'

We found several knots of Prestonians gathered around the Bale Stone, though at a respectful, or wary, distance: apprentices and their girls, schoolboys and servants, but also respectable shop keepers and their wives, and some from our population of middle-aged retired ladies. Murder, violence, blood: these were the reasons they had been drawn to the place, even though there was nothing much for them to see – a few of the smears of blood that we had noted in the morning, perhaps, even though no one dared approach near enough to see them clearly. Gazing at the Stone from twenty feet they passed the most commonplace remarks about it – how heavy it was, how flat on top, and how rough-hewn beneath, and how lonely the place where it stood.

Amongst these I noticed one of my clients Amelia Colley, with her friend Lavinia Bryce.

'Oh, la, Mr Cragg!' Miss Colley called out as she saw me approach. 'Mrs Bryce and I have walked out, as it is such pleasant weather, to see the horrid scene where poor Mr Jackson met his end. Tell us, I beg you, what you found when you came here to the body.'

'It was not a scene fit for your ears, Miss Colley,' I assured her.

'Is it true it was a—'

She lowered her voice.

'A *sacrifice*, by worshippers of Satan and the like?'

'No, I do not think that was the case.'

'But they do say he was stabbed by a— Well, there is no delicate way to say it: by a rough stake of wood, Mr Cragg.'

'Dear Miss Colley,' I said. 'All these matters will be revealed at the inquest, which you are most welcome to attend.'

'Oh, yes – yes indeed! Mrs Bryce and I never miss one of your inquests, Mr Cragg. We shall be there, you may depend upon us. They are always so interesting and well conducted.'

'I am grateful, Miss Colley. Now, the doctor and I do have some business connected with that same inquest. Please would you be kind enough to stand further away?'

The two ladies said they had been here long enough and would set off for home. Luke and I went around all the other groups, chasing them away so that within a few minutes we had the place to ourselves.

During our walk I had devised a plan for our search of the area immediately around the Stone, and this we carried out. We started close to the Stone, circling it in opposite directions. We then continued going round but by taking a couple of steps further away after each turn we gradually widened our area of search. Forty minutes later, when the perimeter of search had reached the other side of the racetrack, and nothing had been found, Fidelis looked again at his watch.

'I must go.'

'Not yet. We are still looking.'

'There is probably nothing to find. Not here. I am more and more sure that Jackson was murdered in another place and merely disposed of on the Stone. Besides, I am due at Adam Thorn's.'

'Oh? To carry out this new treatment of yours?'

He did not answer, but merely strode off towards Peel Hall Lane Cottage with a wave of his hand. Left alone, I returned to the Bale Stone and heaved myself up to sit upon it and think. The time was after five but I felt warm in the sunshine and mopped the sweat off my face with a handkerchief. Facing north, I had my back to the town and could see the trees of the Fulwood to my right, and the roofs of Cadley to my left. If it had not been here that Jackson died, it may have been out there, somewhere around the rim of the Moor. When and why had he gone there?

I jumped down again and restlessly prowled around the Stone. I picked up a stick as I did so, and poked it into the undergrowth that sprouted from beneath the overhanging sections, hoping to strike the missing shoe. The first four or five times that I poked, the end of the stick penetrated just a few inches before butting into the rock. But the next time I tried, in some particularly thick and bushy furze, I felt something different. Kneeling down I thrust my hand into the undergrowth and my fingers closed around something unexpected. I pulled it out: a man's black buckled shoe.

The explanation was not too complicated. This must have been the place at which Jackson was hoisted onto the Stone. The shoe would have fallen off Jackson's foot during the struggle to lift him, and been kicked further beneath the overhang by the feet of the men doing the lifting. I carefully parted the branches of thick furze and stuck my head in cautiously to see just how the shoe had been placed. I was looking at the opening of a rabbit burrow, or even a fox's den, with a spread of sandy earth in front of it. I was about to withdraw my head again when I noticed a string tied to a furze branch, which extended into the hole. Turning my head to the side, and compressing my cheek against the sandy ground, I reached my fingers towards the string until I hooked one of them around it. And so I began to pull.

The other end of the string was tied to something that seemed bulky enough almost to fill the hole, and which clinked as it moved. It snagged here and there on some roots, and needed to be more firmly pulled where the hole narrowed, but at last it came out. It was a full sack made of gunny, the neck tightly tied by the extreme end of the string. I hastened to untie the knot and open the sack. What I found inside made me forget for the time being all about murder and the missing shoe.

The bag was filled with metal objects, somewhat tarnished to be sure, but consisting of table plate and silver – or what I guessed to be silver: a cream jug, caddy spoon, candle-snuffer, a nest of assorted small dishes and two salt cellars – at most twenty items in all. The last of these was a bundle of spoons, held together with a leather thong. I picked them out and counted them. There were eleven, and they looked very much like Adam Thorn's apostle spoon.

On my way through town I stopped at Oldswick's shop. The watchmaker was sitting at his work-bench and peering into the mechanism of a fob watch that lay open before him.

'Mysterious in the extreme, some watches,' he said, rising to his feet as I strolled in. 'Take this one. Everything seems in order, nothing is broken or clogged up or bent out of shape, and yet she won't go. She's like one of your corpses, Titus. Dead for no reason anyone can determine.'

'I find persistence usually pays off, Nick. If I keep looking I find the answer.'

He sighed.

'Aye, that's the only way. So, what can I do for you?'

I slid the gunny-sack from my shoulder and laid it carefully on the seat of a chair.

'Would you put this in your strong cupboard? It contains silver that I fancy the Mayor might try to appropriate for the town's coffer. But I want to investigate it myself first.'

'I think there's room, now Robert Hazelbury's taken back the bits and pieces he lodged with me. It'll just fit.'

The cupboard was set into the wall and had a thick, ironbound oak door secured by a heavy lock. As it swung open I saw it was fitted with shelves a foot apart, on which were laid parcels wrapped in brown paper, and a range of shallow wood trays containing cases and other watch parts in precious metal.

Oldswick took the gunny-sack and shoved it onto a vacant stretch of shelf.

'Will you keep this to yourself, Nick?' I asked.

He merely grunted, but I knew he would do so.

I reached the office, still carrying the shoe I had found. Furzey was on the point of leaving for the day.

'There's a woman in Kirkham, a Mrs Betty Ransom,' I told him. 'I shall be going to see her early tomorrow morning for a statement, so you must get out the summonses for the jurors and for other witnesses yourself – here's a list.'

'As if I don't have enough to do,' he grumbled, looking the list over.

'But even before you do that, you must go to the post office and ask Crick about a letter posted close to four-thirty yesterday afternoon. If the letter itself happens still to be there, seize it. Otherwise get anything Crick can remember about it.'

Furzey raised his eyes from my list of names, suddenly looking a shade happier. There was nothing Furzey liked more than to be sent on business out of the office.

'And by the way,' I added, 'as for that silver, I have an idea of whom to consult. Do you happen to know if Mr Marmaduke Flitcroft, of Kirkham, is still living?'

'Oh, aye, Mr Cragg, I do think so, and I follow your drift exactly. Yes, Mr Flitcroft will suit your purposes admirably, I would say. Quite admirably!'

Over our supper, and unable to keep it to myself, I told Elizabeth of all that I had found at the Bale Stone.

'It does not sound like my idea of Benjamin Peel's treasure,' she said. 'I was thinking that would be an ironbound chest full of Spanish coins and jewels set in precious metal.'

'I am wondering if it is a separate part of a larger hoard, put in the rabbit hole by Adam Thorn for some reason I cannot think of. I think he took that spoon of his from it.'

We turned over various possibilities, none of which convinced us.

'You have had an eventful day, husband,' Elizabeth said at last. 'You started with the discovery of a murder and ended with hidden treasure. How does it go with your investigation into poor Mr Jackson's death?'

'I have been bustling all day long, and getting nowhere,' I said. 'Tybalt Jackson – what do I know about him? He was from Bristol and had little money, though an insurance company employed him. He read the Bible and Montaigne. He had a black girl with him, probably to warm his bed, that he pretended was a boy. And, finally, someone killed him, mutilating his face and driving a stake into his heart.'

'That is quite natural, Titus.'

'What? Mutilating his face? Driving a stake?'

'No, of course not. Turning the girl into a boy, because it attracts less attention.'

'That does seem to have been his special concern – causing as little stir as possible. Which makes it so remarkable that he spoke out at the inquest on Pimbo. What his profession required was that he gather intelligence privately, not make it public.'

'He learned much for himself about Pimbo at the inquest. That will have satisfied him.'

'It may also have killed him, Elizabeth. That's what I am concerned with. Somewhere around here is a pair of killers who did for a witness because he gave evidence in my court. That concerns me personally. I must find them.'

'Surely, my love, they will have gone far away by now.'

'No – I do not believe so. They will not leave until they have the girl. They do not want her blabbing.'

Chapter Twenty-one

∞

ADAM THORN NO longer lay all day in a dark room on his pallet bed, for Amity had obtained an old bath chair. The basketry was loose and ragged, and the wheels wobbled alarmingly, but it meant she could now bring him into the sunshine outside the cottage door, as she had done today, which, she said, would cure him if anything could. This is how Fidelis found his patient after he had parted from me at the Bale Stone: wrapped in a blanket and with an old straw hat on his head, facing the western sun. He was just as silent as before, though with small shivers or quakes running from time to time through his body.

'The chair came from Peel Hall Stables – John Barton,' Amity Thorn told Fidelis, when he asked about it. 'He found it in a corner of his place and brought it over.'

'But how do you get Adam into the chair? Surely not on your own?'

Quietly she drew him into the cottage, where their talk could not reach Adam's ears.

'Barton does it,' she said. 'He comes over and lifts him in. He'll be back tonight to put him to bed.'

'Kind of him. He is a good friend.'

'It's not out of kindness, or friendship. The way that man looks at a woman, folk have another word for. But me, I can't lift Adam so without John Barton we can't use this chair at all. And it means such a lot. The children can see their dad more naturally. I put Honor up on his knee to kiss him. But if I want him to use the chair, see, I've not got the choice. I've to put up with John Barton.'

She bustled around the room, picking up things left on the ground by the youngsters.

'And I've had another visitor,' she said. 'The constable Oswald Mallender's been round. Seems he didn't understand what's happened to Adam. Got vexed when he wouldn't answer his questions about that spoon and where he'd got it.'

'It'll have been the Mayor sent him. There's been new talk in town about that old treasure from Cromwell's time. The Mayor wants to get his hands on it.'

'Well I gave him a piece of my mind for bullying a sick man, and he left. So. What can I give you? A cup of tea?'

Fidelis knew better than to accept tea from a poor household. The poor bought used tea leaves second-hand from the servants of the well-to-do, but even these were hard for them to afford – and in any case made a foul-tasting brew.

'Thank you, no tea. I am here to make an experiment with your husband.'

'An experiment?'

'Yes. I have been thinking about what you said to me, that Adam – the real thinking and feeling Adam – was there all the time inside him, but occluded by his physical paralysis. Well, I have thought of a way in which he might be able to speak to us again.'

'To get Adam to speak is what I dream of. Can you do it, really? Can you waken up his tongue?'

'He won't speak with his tongue.'

'With what, then?'

'You will see. Let's try it. Let's go out again to him.'

Fidelis carried two chairs from around the family table and

placed one on each side of the bath chair, facing towards Adam, who remained with rigid head and fixed expression, as if unaware they were there. Amity settled her children inside the cottage and he sat down, and Fidelis began to address the patient directly.

'Now Adam, the world believes that you can no longer hear or understand anything of what I'm saying. But I consider you can. The trouble is that you are not master of your tongue, or your breath, and so cannot speak. But I think there is one thing – or two things as a matter of fact – that you are master of. So let us try it. Will you blink for me, Adam? Simply shut and open your eyelids. Go on.'

Together they watched Adam's eyes. At first nothing happened, and then suddenly he blinked.

Amity looked at Fidelis across her husband's stricken body.

'Nothing special about that, doctor,' she whispered. 'He does that anyway.'

Fidelis put a finger to his lips while keeping his eyes on his patient's face.

'Adam,' he said in a firm voice, 'have you caught my intention? If so, will you blink for me again, but now I want you to do it three times – three times in a row.'

They waited and at first it seemed nothing would happen. Then Adam blinked, once . . . and again. But immediately one of those periodic spasms passed through him, and it wasn't clear if he had completed the sequence of three blinks.

Fidelis persevered. He asked him the question a second time, and this time added a refinement.

'Give me three blinks if you do understand me, Adam, and just two if you don't – go ahead.'

This time it was unmistakable. Adam's eyes shut and opened again three times in succession. Amity gasped.

'Very good, Adam. So, let us make this into a signalling system.

Three blinks are for the answer yes, and two are for no? I am going to put to you a series of childish questions. You must not mind because eventually they will lead to something a good deal more interesting. Are you ready?'

He paused, watching Adam's eyes. They blinked once, twice and then a third time.

'Good. You are ready. I will speak in a clear voice. Is your name Adam Smith?'

Two blinks – no.

'Is it Adam Thorn?'

Three blinks – yes.

'And is this place Peel Lane Cottage?'

Yes. No.

'Concentrate, Adam. This is not Peel Lane that runs past your house, is it?'

No.

'It is Peel *Hall* Lane, isn't it?'

Yes.

'Good. Now, you have two children, I think.'

No.

'Three?'

Yes.

'Is one of them called Honor?'

Yes.

'Is another of them called Theophrastus?'

No.

And so it went on, with Fidelis probing the limits of Adam's understanding and memory. He established that he was not blind, but could see things placed immediately before his eyes, though if put to one side or the other he became doubtful of them. He also established that Adam could do simple mental arithmetic, and could remember events in his life before the accident.

After about twenty minutes, though, Adam's eyes suddenly drooped and then, without warning, he fell asleep.

Fidelis rose and beckoned Amity into the cottage where the eldest daughter, Honor, came and wrapped her arms in a tight clinch around his legs. The boy was banging a stick on an old pot and the baby in the cot-bed was beginning to cry. But Amity's eyes were shining.

'It's a kind of miracle what you've done, doctor,' she said, picking up the baby and jiggling it up and down. 'I always believed it, me, but a lot of people didn't. He's himself inside there. He's been buried, like, and you've found him, and given him a way of talking – of getting his messages out.'

'Yes. We know now that his cognitive power is more or less intact. You can speak with him – you must ask the right questions, of course, and the yes-and-no method will be tedious and frustrating sometimes, I'm afraid.'

'But it's much, much better than nothing, and nothing's all we've had until now.'

Fidelis gently detached the clinging child's arms from around his knees.

'I must go back to Preston now. I fancy you will receive another visit from the Coroner, my friend Mr Cragg, in due course. He's interested in how Adam's seizure came about. He will use the method to obtain a statement about it. Oh! And one more thing. May I suggest that just for the time being you don't speak of our discovery to others – to John Barton, for instance? And please, if that man gives you any cause for grave concern, if he becomes any sort of danger to you, apply directly to me.'

Fidelis had told Amity Thorn that he was going back to Preston, but he did not do so directly. Instead he turned right along Peel Hall Lane and purposefully covered the mile or so to Barton's stables in less than a quarter of an hour, getting there shortly after six o'clock.

He found John Barton in the middle of his stable yard, unsaddling a horse. The fellow looked shiftily at Fidelis who decided to deal with the horse-coper in the first instance by using a very formal tone, as if carrying out a diplomatic *démarche*.

'Mr Barton, I am Adam Thorn's medical attendant. His doctor.'

Barton's relations with people were generally conducted as grudge fights, and he had his own way of dealing with a relative stranger whom he chose to see in the light of a rival.

'Doctor or medical attendant,' he said in a low, graceless voice, 'why should I mind what you call yourself?'

'Either will do, Sir.'

'What I mean is,' said Barton, 'I'll have the same low opinion of you either way.'

Fidelis chose to ignore the remark, and continued in a pleasant vein.

'I wanted to express how gratified I am by your therapeutic gift of a bath chair to my patient. I expect him to make faster progress towards recovery because of it.'

John Barton's eyes flashed a look at Fidelis.

'Oh aye?' he said. 'You reckon he will recover?'

'He might. He can take the sunshine now, and will benefit greatly.'

Barton heaved off the saddle, dropped it to the ground and led the horse towards its stable. When he came out, his faintly twisted face displayed a gleam of pleasure, and Fidelis realized the fellow was in his bitter way enjoying himself.

'Me, I just did for the Thorns what a neighbour should do.'

He pointed his finger at Fidelis.

'But I know why *you're* forever going in and out of that house. She tells me you don't charge a fee. Of course you don't! You expect your fee to be paid another way, am I not right?'

'Mr Barton, I—'

'You'll deny it of course. My dad told me about doctors. Keep them out of your life, he said, and you'll keep them out of your *wife*. Hah!'

Fidelis was determined to maintain the civilized façade for as long as he could.

'Your attack on me is not new, Sir. I have heard it many times. So have all doctors. It does not provoke me as, it is clear, you would like to.'

'Not new because it's true, nine times out of ten. Like I said, I am only a neighbour. I brought Thorn home when he had his seizure. That's my interest. What's yours? I'll tell you – that of a lecher with a medical bag, a wig, and a silver tongue.'

'You quite fail to grasp what we do, Barton. A doctor promises on oath—'

'Worthless cock! Lying hypocrisy! I know the game you're after – and money is only the half of it.'

No red-blooded man, however much he wants to play diplomat, can finally stand and receive this kind of assault. Fidelis began to smart and grow heated.

'I'll tell you something, and you know very well it is true, Barton. Your slanderous accusation against me is exactly what, in fact, is in your own mind. You turn lustful eyes on Mrs Thorn, not me. You've observed the laying low of her husband and you've seen your opportunity.'

Barton had put a bucket of water in with the horse and slammed shut the door of its box. He now took four or five rapid strides forward and brandished his fist in front of Fidelis's face.

'Listen. Shall you take yourself off, or shall I shut that mouth of yours first?'

Fidelis took a step back.

'Tell me, Barton, just how long is it you've lusted after Amity Thorn? How long is it that—'

The flimsy catch on Barton's anger snapped. With a snarl he made another leap forward and this time delivered a box on Fidelis's ear. The doctor, taller by several inches, immediately caught the man's wrist and used the grip to force him down towards the ground. Barton was almost on his knees but he managed to kick upwards and deliver the doctor a sharp blow in the shins with his ironshod shoe. Less well equipped for a kicking match, Fidelis stepped backwards and bunched his fists.

'So come on! Let's have it out! Don't disappoint me, Barton. I'd hate to miss the opportunity to break your nose.'

Breathing heavily through his mouth, Barton climbed to his feet. He was about to speak when he heard a sound from the stables behind him – a cough from one of the horses perhaps. He half turned and in that movement it seemed that sanity returned to him.

'There'll be no fighting,' was all he said. 'Get yourself off.'

'I'll go with the greatest of pleasure, when I have knocked you senseless.'

'You know something?' sneered the horse-coper. 'I don't care what you do with Amity Thorn. She's naught but a pretty slice of cabbage, and there's a lot of that in the world. Now get off.'

Fidelis seethed with anger all of the way to Preston, and again when he described these dramatic events to me that evening at the Turk's Head Coffee House. He was far from regretting his part in the argument with Barton, for his feelings towards Amity were entirely chivalrous, as he was quite certain Barton's were not. He only wished that he and the horse-coper really had fought, and he had felled the bloody clown. As a knight from Sir Thomas Malory should – but perhaps not a Lancashire medical practitioner – he passionately wanted to have broken Barton's lance.

That evening as I walked into the Turk's Head to meet Fidelis, a group of men that were enjoying a joke together stopped me.

'What d'you reckon Titus? What should they have done with that black slip of a child that Mallender arrested?'

'They should be putting her up with some responsible widow woman,' I said. 'You know she's mute. She's had a lot of bullying and she needs kindness now if she's to get her voice back.'

'That's a shame, then.'

'What do you know?'

'It's all over town. They've placed her all right – but with Billy Biggs.'

Another eruption of laughter followed me as I moved away.

'I fear for the safety of the negro girl,' I told Fidelis, telling him the news.

'You wonder if she will avoid Biggs's wandering hands. Yes, if he thinks he's dealing with a mere slave, he might think anything is allowed.'

'I doubt Mrs Biggs would allow him anything. But you are right. Some men that are not in the habit of denying themselves feel freer than they should in such circumstances. I would not like either Biggs or Grimshaw to be left alone with her.'

'Why Grimshaw?'

I described the scene in the courtroom and Grimshaw's reaction to the sight of her bared breasts in court. Fidelis laughed and I reproved him.

'You laugh – but the possibility is serious.'

'I laugh because such suspicion can get us into fights, Titus. I will tell you about my own adventures this afternoon in that way.'

And so everything I have described above was divulged to me, with Fidelis being scrupulously unsparing of his own feelings or embarrassments. I was incredulous at first about the experiment with Adam Thorn, and then a little taken aback by the *rencontre* with John Barton. Fidelis dismissed this with a wave of his hand, wanting to return to the subject of his discovery at Peel Hall Lane Cottage.

'Adam's mind is working, Titus. That's the wonderful thing. He became tired under my questioning, and I had no opportunity to get the details of what happened to him on that day when he was struck down. I am most eager to know more. But what is certain is that you will be able to get a statement from him.'

'It seems,' I said, 'that you have most cleverly found the mind of Adam Thorn. I congratulate you. But I too have made some finds today.'

I had the shoe in my coat pocket. Now I produced it.

'Good heavens, the shoe!' he exclaimed. 'Where was it?'

'After you left me this afternoon it occurred to me that we had never looked right *under* the Stone, so that was where I searched. This shoe was right there. It must have fallen off Jackson's foot, and been kicked into the bushy undergrowth.'

'Well I'll be damned.'

'That, however, is not all I have found under the Bale Stone today.'

I gave a full account of the bag of silver objects pushed deep into the burrow near where the shoe had been lying. Luke listened intently. I expected he would cap my discovery with observations of his own, but he uttered only one.

'One thing is certain. The silver, unlike the shoe, was deliberately concealed in that hole. The person who put it there intended to go back for it. That satisfies the definition of treasure trove, does it not?'

'It would seem to.'

Fidelis chuckled.

'I wonder how many instances there have been of the Coroner being also the one finding the treasure.'

'I wasn't the first finder, Luke. Someone found it before me, and I believe his name is Adam Thorn.'

'How can you be sure?'

'Because among that silver was a bundle of apostle spoons – eleven of them.'

'Well, well, well!'

He considered the matter briefly, rubbing his chin, then abruptly rose to his feet and reached for his hat.

'Titus, it has been a day of remarkable discoveries indeed. But I am tired and would like my bed.'

Chapter Twenty-two

∞

ON FRIDAY MORNING I rode the few miles to Kirkham in cheerful weather, which promised another hot day ahead. But I was feeling baffled, and wringing my brains to understand what I had just discovered at the House of Correction.

Before leaving town through Friary Bar I had diverted down Marsh Lane, intending to take the chance of reuniting the late Jackson with his errant shoe. The Porter took me straight to the locked cell in which Jackson reposed, turned the key and left me to it. I found that the corpse-washers Mary and Dolly had been in, and now Jackson lay under a plain sheet, awaiting his next appointment – the viewing by tomorrow's inquest jury. The clothes bag lay on the floor nearby and this I emptied until I came to the single shoe, to which the one I had with me was the pair. Except that, when I put them side by side, I saw at once that it wasn't.

The shoes were much alike in style, but the one that had been on Jackson's left foot was a clumsy, much scuffed and dented object, with worn-down heel and thinned sole. The shoe I had found at the Stone was a less exhausted and more refined thing, with some fancy stitching here and there, though it was by no means new. When I tried slipping the corpse's right foot into this unexpected shoe I found that it fitted well enough. Tybalt Jackson's dress had been a little shabby, but not slovenly. Why would he have been wearing odd footwear?

Arriving at Kirkham I found the shop of Joseph Ransom to be a small and hardly prosperous establishment. Instead of a proud position on or beside Kirkham's Market Square, where it might assert itself as the town's prime centre of the cordwainer's art, it kept apart at the bottom of a row of backstreet cottages, a shy business that disdained acclaim.

Yet if this is a true image, Betty Ransom did not fit it very well. She was a forward woman, with flashing eyes and a comfortably upholstered body – a woman who enjoyed inhabiting her own flesh.

'Come in, Mr Cragg,' she said gaily, after I explained that I was gathering information about a man that had been staying at her brother's inn. 'Ransom is at the tannery, fetching leather, so he's not here to object to my entertaining a strange man in my parlour.'

We passed through the shop and into the living quarters. The parlour was as orderly and clean as her brother's was disorderly and foul. She insisted on my waiting while she fetched in some elderflower wine.

'I make it for sale at my brother's inn but the fool only gives it away. Drinks nothing but ale himself, and a lot too much of it.'

I took a sip. I would rather have had Tokay, or even Cyprus wine, but in its way this wasn't bad.

'I have had a conversation yesterday with your brother,' I said, when I had complimented her on the wine. 'He says he went out to the tavern on Wednesday night, leaving you in charge of the inn.'

'He did that. I go over to him every week, Wednesdays. I like it, for a change, though I would wish he'd keep the place cleaner. So who is this man you want to know about?'

'His name is Tybalt Jackson, whom your brother had received at the inn late on Tuesday, lodging him in the largest guest chamber.'

'Him with the blackie boy? What about him?'

'He is dead, I'm afraid. Attacked and found murdered.'

Her eyes widened.

'Murdered? At the inn?'

'I don't know – he wasn't found at the inn and I doubt he was murdered there. But I want to know anything about his activities during the night. Did you see Mr Jackson, or his servant, at any time?'

'No. They kept to their room.'

'You didn't take them any food or go to their room for any reason?'

'No. But you mention "activities", Sir: I did hear them, you know, as I was passing by the door.'

'What did you hear of them?'

Looking downward, she began to blush and her cheeks dimpled.

'Well, I'm not sure I can say, Mr Cragg.'

'You heard talking?'

She looked up at me again, her eyes lit by suppressed merriment. 'Yes, talking they were, in a way. They were saying things . . . intimate things, if you get my meaning there. And making intimate sounds, too, if you get my meaning *there*.'

'I think I can, Mrs Ransom. But just to be clear, you are referring to Mr Jackson and his servant?'

'Exactly, Sir. And if the master were murdered, well, I doubt he was killed by the blackie. That boy sounded like he were properly enjoying his'self.'

She retained a serious face, but somewhere behind her eyes that smile still lay concealed. She did not appear to disapprove of what she had heard through the door, even though she thought Jackson's 'blackie' was a boy.

'What time did you hear this?'

'Eight or nine o'clock, or between the two anyway. It was just dark.'

'Half past eight then?'

'Yes, about.'

'Now this is very important. Did anyone else come to the inn during the evening?'

'It was quiet, it always is, but another gentleman did arrive later on, asking for a room. I said yes, if you have the money beforehand. He paid me sixpence and I showed him up to what's known as the Red Room. There's a lot of old bedrooms at the Lamb, but most of them's unfit. I had a job finding one that was not too bad.'

'What was this man's name?'

'Said it was Moon. I laughed. I thought, that's a made-up name, or sounds like it. The man-in-the-moon! Anyway, it didn't matter, so long as he had the money.'

'Did he say where he had come from?'

'No. I asked if he'd travelled far, you know, out of politeness, but he just said a day's ride.'

'A day's ride from where?'

'For all he told me, it was *from* the moon.'

She laughed, and then as quickly grew serious.

'Is *he* the murderer, Sir? Oh, just to think I spent the night in the house with a murderer.'

'It's much too early to say who was the murderer, Mrs Ransom. But can you describe Mr Moon for me?'

'It were after dark so I only saw him by candlelight, and he did keep his hat on, which was a bit disrespectful – but as I say, so long as they have the money . . .'

'What was his appearance?'

'He was ordinary height, or a little above. Skinny. About thirty years old, maybe a year or two more.'

'His face – was there anything to note about it?'

'No, Sir. Not to notice. Except maybe for what you might call a thin nose. But it was a wide hat and I couldn't rightly see under it.'

'Did he have a beard?'

'No, Sir, his chin were clean shaven.'

'Apart from the hat, how was he dressed?'

'There was nowt special about his clothing. I think he wore a green coat.'

'And his speech?'

'He talked roundly, not exactly as a gentleman but like one that wants to impress you that way, if you understand what I mean.'

'And was he alone?'

'Well, he had a man with him.'

'A servant?'

'I don't know about that. He was just a chap carrying Mr Moon's valise.'

'Can you describe him?'

'Not really. I hardly looked at him and as soon as he dropped Moon's bag he left.'

'So where was the room you showed Moon to in relation to the one occupied by Mr Jackson?'

'Oh nowhere near. Red Room's round on the other side of the yard, though both of them look out on it.'

'They both had windows commanding a view of the courtyard?'

'Yes.'

'And the windows of the two rooms were visible to each other across the space between?'

'That's right. I suppose this new chap could've seen what Jackson was up to if the curtains were not drawn.'

'And were they?'

She shrugged her well-shaped shoulders.

'I never did look, Sir,' she said.

'Did Mr Moon ask for anything – food, drink?'

'Ink. He asked for a bottle of ink. I got him one and left him to it.'

'So there were just three sleeping that night at the inn – or five if we count yourself and Houndsworth?'

'That's it. Three more than usual, you could say.'

'And the newcomer was definitely alone. He had no servant or companion with him.'

'That's right.'

'Did he have a horse?'

'Yes Sir, but I told him we couldn't stable it, as we had no boy at the moment. So he took it up to the livery at the top of the street.'

'What baggage did he have?'

The question was not answered for we were interrupted by noises from the shop, a banged door and a shout. Immediately Mrs Ransom's manner towards me changed, her voice becoming formal and distant.

'That will be my husband, Mr Cragg. I shall go and greet him and, if you wouldn't mind waiting here, you yourself shall meet him in a few moments.'

Hastily she snatched up the jug of wine and glasses and left the room. Moments later the couple's murmuring voices could be heard from the shop, and then Ransom came through to the parlour alone. He had on a pair of steel-rimmed spectacles fitted over icy blue eyes in a lean, narrow face. The set of his mouth looked uncomfortably tight.

'My wife tells me you have come all the way from Preston, Sir.'

'Yes, it is on Coroner's business. One that lodged a night at the Lamb and Flag has died rather suddenly.'

'Of the food, no doubt,' said Ransom drily.

'No, not the food—'

'Then of breathing the air in the place. Fetid. I won't go there, and I won't have my brother-in-law here neither. I don't under-stand my wife's devotion to the wastrel.'

Ransom was hardly one for skylarking, I thought. Self-indulgence was not his ruling passion.

I told him I still had one or two questions for Mrs Ransom and wondered if he would be kind enough to call her to join us. But coming back in and sitting in the shadow of her husband's presence, Betty Ransom became a very different interlocutor. All sense of imparting confidences, of vivid recall, left her. The responses were stiff and as brief as possible.

'I was just asking about Moon's baggage. How much was there?'

'He had only a single valise.'

'And next morning, what happened?'

'I rose at seven and left to come home.'

'Is that what you usually do?'

'Yes. I catch a lift from carrier Johnson's cart, that always leaves for Kirkham at half after seven.'

'Who makes breakfast?'

'My brother.'

'Did you see anyone at the inn that morning, before you left?'

'No one. They must have been all asleep.'

'And in the night – did you hear any activity?'

'My brother coming in. Nothing else. Nothing at all.'

'Do you generally sleep soundly at the inn, Mrs Ransom? I mean, if there is ever any disturbance in the night, do you hear it or sleep through it?'

'I sleep well enough. And I didn't hear owt unusual on Wednesday night. If a man truly was murdered in the dark hours, I didn't hear it.'

There seemed little more to extract from her, so I thanked them both and rose to leave. Ransom showed me back into the shop and he was about to open the street door to shuffle me out when a thought suddenly struck me.

'I wonder if you would look at something for me, Mr Ransom. I will need to fetch it from my saddle bag.'

I went out to the horse, which I had tethered by the door, and returned with the shoe that mistakenly we had thought belonged to Tybalt Jackson. I placed it in the cobbler's hand and, as he turned it over, I was most surprised to see a wiry little smile creep across his lips.

'It's a few year since I set eyes on one of these,' he said.

'Don't tell me you know who wore it.'

'Not who wore it, who made it. See this?'

He pointed inside the shoe to the insole. It was impressed with the mark of a stamp – T.T.

'That's his mark, is that.'

'Who is T.T.?'

'Thomas Truss of Liverpool. I learned my trade for seven years as that man's apprentice. This shoe is typical of him. It's beautifully stitched and made of good leather. I don't get much chance to make shoes like this now. It's mostly boot-work and clogs for the likes of me out here. Primitive.'

'So this is an expensive shoe?'

'Not very: middling. Thomas never asked prices anything like as steep as he could or should have. He were a master shoemaker – and I do mean a *master* – but he always endeavoured to keep the charge low. A fair fit at a fair price: that was his boast, and it's one I still try to live up to here.'

'So what kind of person bought their shoes from Thomas Truss?'

'Not the richest. Not the poorest. Liverpool folk in the middle, with a taste for well-made sturdy footwear. And younger folk rather than older because – well, see this bit here? That fancy stitching wouldn't appeal to everybody, and especially not to those more set in their ways. The more adventurous types of men and girls liked our shoes, though, because they were a little bit different from the general.'

He sighed and gave me back the shoe.

'He's retired two years now. The business on Dale Street was sold, so I heard.'

The last service Joseph Ransom did for me was to direct me to the house of Mr Marmaduke Flitcroft, which was a solid building of the last century, overlooking the market square. Mr Flitcroft was a sleekly tailored old gentleman with a straight back and an equally straight manner. He received me courteously, putting me at my ease with a pinch of snuff and a small glass of port.

'I remember your father well, Sir. Old Sam! Such a character.'

I looked around the spacious room in which he had received me. There were objects set out on all the sills and tables – carved stones, ivories, bronze figures, medals mounted in frames, jars.

'My father spoke of you often, Sir,' I said. 'I believe you helped him in some of his cases.'

'Indeed I did. Let me see. There was the Stoney Gate Hoard, so-called, though in fact it was dug out of Titmouse's Orchard a few yards at the back of Stoney Gate. I gave evidence at your father's inquest that it was old English coin, because there were those who said they were Roman, you know, without bringing a scruple of knowledge to the matter. Not a scruple.'

'And that is your chief antiquarian expertness – old silver coins?'

'Well, perhaps I flatter myself, but I suppose I know as much as any man in the county about them, yes. But it is silver plate that I find most attractive.'

He found a key in his waistcoat and opened the glass front of a cabinet containing eight drawers. He slid one of these fully out and, making room, placed it on a table for my inspection.

'Here is a drawer containing some pieces of old silver. Anglo-Saxon, some of it is.'

The items were polished, none of them more than a few inches in length but they glinted with the singular authority that good silver possesses. I picked up one, that was shaped like a miniature shovel.

'An earwax scoop,' said Flitcroft. 'And this here is a cheekpiece for a soldier's helmet, while this other one is more likely either a buckle or a brooch.'

'Where did you obtain these?'

'Several pieces come from ploughboys. They turn them up in the field, and bring them to me in return for a shilling or two. The rest I received by way of sale or exchange from other interested gentlemen.'

'It would appear you are the very man for me, then. I have to inquest a possible treasure trove and would value your opinion of it.'

'What is it, coinage or plate?'

'Silver objects, and thought to be from before the time of Cromwell's victory at Preston.'

'Oh! Recent indeed! Nevertheless I shall not mind taking a look. The Carolean and Cromwellian periods have some points of interest, and in the case of plate there is a degree of rarity with so much having been melted down to pay for the war.'

I produced the apostle spoon and handed it to him.

'This is from the supposed treasure. We believe it's an apostle spoon. What do you make of it?'

He took the spoon to the window and peered at it through a pair of spectacles.

Then he fetched a powerful magnifying glass, which he screwed into his eye to examine the four indentations along the spoon's shaft. Then he went to a shelf, took down an almanac and leafed through it until he found a table of letters of the alphabet, all in different typefaces. Running his forefinger down one column he found a match for the spoon's letter stamp, and closed the book with a snap.

'Fifteen hundred and ninety six,' he said. 'Reign of Queen Elizabeth. It is a spoon of true silver, of London manufacture, and London assayed it, which is all I can tell you from these marks. And, yes, it is of course an apostle spoon, with I fancy the figure of St John holding the poison cup. It is a fine piece, in its way. Have you any further examples from the hoard?'

'Not on my person, but if you can come to Preston one day next week I will arrange to show you everything.'

'If you can show me more pieces of this quality I shall come with pleasure. And I have some other business in Preston on Monday next. Will that suit you?'

Chapter Twenty-three

∞

IN PRESTON I went directly back to the Lamb and Flag, and demanded that Houndsworth show me the Red Room which Moon had occupied on the previous Wednesday night.

'If you like,' he said. 'I don't know owt about him, mind. Was that his name – Moon?'

'So now you remember that a man did lodge here on Wednesday as well as Jackson?'

Houndsworth led me outside, across the courtyard and through a door into the building on that side.

'I didn't when I spoke to you, Sir. But after your visit, I found a note that Betty wrote me, wrapping some cash. She said it was for the let of the Red Room for one night. I were surprised because I'd not seen a sign of anyone about the place in the morning. I supposed he must have gone off early, before I rose to the surface meself.'

We climbed a bare wooden stair and along a passage with three bedrooms off it. He stopped at the second bedroom, opened the door and indicated with something of a flourish that I go in before him.

'The Red Room, Mr Cragg, Sir.'

The bed hangings, dusty, cobwebbed and moth-eaten, were a rusty red, making it the only possible name for a room otherwise drab and colourless. I saw that someone had slept, or at least lain, on the bed rather than in it. An ancient upholstered chair, the stuffing frothing out at every corner, stood before the window.

'Is that the chair's usual position?'

'No, Sir. Happen the gentleman pulled it across to face the window so he could get the light.'

'The light, Houndsworth? It was pitch dark outside. No, he moved the chair because he wanted to keep watch on the window opposite.'

On the table there was the ink-stand and writing materials, a glass and an empty wine bottle. There was no other sign of occupation.

'Have you been in here since Wednesday? Tidied up?'

'No. There's so much to do I haven't yet put it to rights.'

The curtains were open. I closed them except for a chink in the middle and put my eye to this. I had a clear view, as described by Betty Ransom, of the row of windows on the other side of the yard.

'Which is the White Room?' I asked.

'That's the one right opposite, Mr Cragg.'

Ten minutes later the Lorrises' maid was answering my ring on the door of Fidelis's lodgings, and telling me to go straight up as the doctor was in. I found him weighing chemicals and making notes in a ledger.

'There were only two guests staying at the Lamb on Wednesday,' I announced. 'One was Jackson and the other was spying on him. And guess what name the other went under.'

Fidelis looked up from his work.

'Moon, I suppose,' he said.

Fidelis was a difficult man to surprise.

'How did you know that?'

'If he was spying on Jackson, who else? It's the only name we've got for his murderer.'

'It is corroboration – that's what it is. We are making progress. But here is another more puzzling new fact.'

I passed the shoe to him.

'I have established that it's the work of Thomas Truss, shoe-maker of Liverpool.'

Fidelis now rose from his work table and motioned me to sit by the fire. He offered me his snuffbox and settled into the chair opposite.

'I want to hear all the details,' he said.

I gave him a full account of my discussion over the shoe with Joseph Ransom, and we both sat meditating on the object itself, which Fidelis had placed on the mantel like a sculptural exhibit. After a while Fidelis reached it down.

'Jackson didn't really fit the type Ransom described, did he? He was not a very "adventurous" dresser. Interesting too that the shoe was made in Liverpool while Jackson was from Bristol. How and when would he have bought it? Note, it is not new.'

'It's easy to explain both points, Luke. It wasn't Jackson's shoe.'

He looked at me sharply, a look of doubt but with a scintilla of excitement. Fidelis enjoyed it when an apparent state of affairs was contradicted.

'How could you possibly know it not to be Jackson's, Titus?'

'Because before I went to Kirkham I took this shoe to the House of Correction, thinking I would reunite it with its partner. But there's no match, Luke. It fits the man's foot, but is differently made from the other shoe. I am therefore convinced that this shoe is an irrelevance, and we shall have to begin again our search for Jackson's missing footwear.'

There was another silence while Fidelis minutely examined the shoe, even removing the monogrammed insole, and replacing it when he found nothing beneath.

'It isn't an irrelevance, Titus,' he said at last, handing it back to me.

'Well it cannot be Jackson's. Surely you are not going to tell me he was wearing odd shoes.'

'No, I accept it was not Jackson's.'

'But his shoe is what we want. This one is of no interest.'

'Apart from your discovery that Moon was at Jackson's inn on Wednesday night, this is perhaps the most relevant piece of evidence yet found in the case. It tells us something important about what happened when Jackson died. And it will help us catch Moon, I fancy. Keep it safe, its history is precious to you.'

I was used to these sudden predictions by my friend, though reckoned over time they were as often wrong as they were right.

'Very well,' I said. 'Tell me the story.'

Fidelis leaned forward in his chair, and his voice took on a certain dramatic quality as he began to speak.

'Picture it, then. It was dark, the darkest part of the night under a cloudy sky, and no help from the moon. Jackson is killed and carried somehow to the Stone. It is a struggle to lift him. A shoe falls off Jackson's foot, but one of the killers also loses a shoe, perhaps as he clambers up onto the Stone. Once they have disposed Jackson's body in the way they want, suggesting – I don't know – some kind of ritual killing, they climb down and our man gropes around for his missing shoe – and in the dark picks up Jackson's, which he puts on and walks away. His own shoe has been kicked right under the Stone.'

I was pleased with all this. As well as his professed love of abstract puzzles and mental calculation my friend was a good story-teller too.

'So, if your tale is true,' I said, 'we have only to find the owner of this shoe, and we have one of the killers of Tybalt Jackson.'

'It is true: it must be. Let's consider your next step. Thomas Truss is alive, did you not say?'

'Retired, according to Ransom.'

'Are you thinking of the same next step as I am?'

'I am thinking I should make a trip to Liverpool. Will you come with me?'

'I was afraid you wouldn't ask. It had better be soon.'

'It had better be tomorrow.'

'If so you must delay the hearing.'

'I don't mind that. Furzey always says Saturday inquests come to bad decisions. We shall make new arrangements for Monday.'

We had arranged to travel to the funeral of Phillip Pimbo in the carriage of Burroughs, the cabinet-maker who was a member of the Corporation and our nearest neighbour on Cheapside. The drive to the church at Cadley was slow, as six or seven other carriages were making the journey at the same time. So we processed up Friar Gate and along Fylde Road in a procession, being continually held up by slower traffic – a mule train, a pair of bullock carts, a flock of driven geese.

'Drive on! Drive through 'em!' shouted Lionel Burroughs to his driver after we had crept along for several minutes at the speed of the geese. 'It is maddening that the slow movers do not wait to one side and let the fast traffic go by. Drive, man!'

The carriage lurched forward, scattering the geese to right and left and incurring the wrath of the gooseherd, who cursed and hurled his hat to the ground in fury as we passed. Burroughs put his head out of the window.

'Scoundrel!' he roared.

'Calm, Mr Burroughs, calm,' soothed his wife. 'You know there is time enough for us to arrive at church. The coffin is in no such hurry as you are.'

Minnie Burroughs was an outwardly submissive woman whom Elizabeth assured me exerted powerful control over her hot-tempered husband. She now steered our talk towards a less aggravating matter, though one much debated in gatherings of Prestonians: Ephraim Grimshaw's new scheme to raise funds for the Guild by issuing a bond.

'Mr Burroughs is so relieved that the Guild is not bankrupt and there will be money enough to pay for all,' declared his wife. 'He is of the opinion that the Guild is worth no less than ten thousand pounds in money coming into our town.'

'Yes, we shall profit all right,' said Burroughs himself. 'We shall make Grimshaw's expense twofold, if he spends his money wisely in the first place.'

'Mr Burroughs has heard,' went on Minnie, 'that there will be no less than two masquerades. One will start the Guild and the other will be the Grand Finale. It will be an assembly such as we have never seen. Mr Burroughs expects more than four hundred tickets will be taken out.'

'And *I* have heard,' said Elizabeth, 'that in addition to our own players we are to have a visiting company from Dublin at the theatre. What have you heard, Titus?'

She gave me a nudge. I had heard little about the Guild's programme.

'That there will be a lot of drunkenness and greedy trencher-work, if history is any guide. But Grimshaw is not in the clear just yet. We know little of raising money with bonds. What if the bonds fail to sell?'

Burroughs snorted.

'They've been using them in London for years. They'll do the job.'

'Let us hope so,' I said.

The funeral was well-attended, but the mourning was purely formal, for the deceased had had few close friends and his only relative, his mother, was out of her mind. She called out several times during the service, and on the way to the grave kept asking whose funeral this was, and then claiming it was hers.

'Are all of you going to bury me now? Are you going to put me in the ground?'

Walking straight-backed in support by Mrs Pimbo's side, Ruth Peel allowed the woman to rave, her own face showing the expressionless serenity of classical marble.

Afterwards the Burgesses and other town notables at the funeral were invited to Cadley Place. As the weather continued warm, tables had been set up on the lawn at the rear of the house with wine, tea and cakes served. I was aware that many of the guests in their groups must have been discussing, not Pimbo's dreadful death, but the more recent one of the stranger Tybalt Jackson, who had made such an impression at Pimbo's inquest, and speculating on why he had been killed. I heard the name Zadok Moon pronounced more than once in this connection. Murder and fraud were now inseparably entwined into that name, and these words touched the two fears planted deepest in the Preston Burgesses' heart: for his life, and for his cash.

I noticed Michael Ambler talking with another man at the edge of the crowd. Each held a tray of cakes but instead of passing through the company to offer their wares they were speaking exclusively and vehemently together. Out of his customary setting of the stables, and the Moor, it took me a moment to recognize the other fellow as John Barton, the horse trainer. Surprised, I strolled over to join them, at which they abruptly broke off their conversation.

'Ambler. May I trouble you for a cake?'

I took one and turned to his companion.

'Barton. What brings you here?'

'I am helping.'

He had spoken stiffly, as if it were unnatural to him to admit helpfulness.

'That does you credit.'

'And I have also been looking over Pimbo's horses.'

'To buy them?'

'There's one entire that might make a teaser.'

'A teaser? I'm sorry, you will have to explain.'

'In the stud, to get the mare ready. You bring in the teaser to tickle her up before the big boy comes in and finishes the job.'

He leered at me.

'I find some women got to have that an' all.'

Hearing this Ambler laughed and slapped Barton on the shoulder. I was tempted to ask the horse pacer if he liked to play the part of the teaser himself, but instead I took a step back and said,

'Very interesting, but please, let me not distract you from your voluntary duties.'

Later over our supper table at home I told Elizabeth about my conversation with John Barton after the funeral.

'They were very familiar together. It was striking.'

'I saw Michael Ambler talking to a dark sallow chap,' she said.

'That would be Barton.'

'Thick as thieves they were.'

'A nasty insinuating tongue has Mr Barton.'

I relayed to her the remarks he had made about the coupling of horses.

'A teaser, you say?' she asked when I had finished.

'That is what it is called.'

We had finished eating and she rose with her empty plate and came to pick up mine. She leaned towards me as she did so.

'Happy the woman whose husband is also her teaser,' she murmured in my ear.

Chapter Twenty-four

∞

'REMEMBER, MY LOVE, that Liverpool is a wicked pit of vice and iniquity.'

These were Elizabeth's parting words, spoken with a playful smile, as I rode off beside Fidelis the next morning. Instead of my old cob I had asked the liveryman for a more spirited animal to match Fidelis's latest fine gelding, and so we made very good time on the road, arriving at the Mermaid Inn before noon.

'We must dine at Pinchbeck's,' said Fidelis, 'as you have not seen it yet. And we may run into Canavan there.'

'But first Truss's shop. It's on the way.'

Dale Street was a long street with a string of fine and various shops stretching north from the Town Hall. We enquired at three shoemakers before we found the one that had been Thomas Truss's, now trading under the name of Theophilus Fowler, and Son.

It was the son James Fowler, a man in his middle years, to whom we spoke first. I asked if he could provide some information about his father's predecessor in the shop.

'Dad!' he shouted. 'You're needed out here.'

A bent white-haired old man appeared from the rear, which was apparently the workshop. He was wearing an apron, and had obviously been interrupted in his work.

'Yes, son. What is it?'

'These gentlemen are asking about Truss.'

Old Fowler's face lit up.

'The finest craftsman of upper-stitching, and the finest friend you are ever likely to meet was Thomas Truss,' he said. 'I had the honour of being his partner in business for his last five years.'

'And you took over when he retired?'

'I did that – me and the boy here.'

'Where did he go? Is he still in Liverpool.'

Old Fowler's bright expression faded visibly.

'How I wish he were. No, he's in Childwall, six feet under.'

'He's dead?'

'This time last year, he left us.'

I looked in disappointment at Fidelis. His lips shaped the words 'the shoe', so I took it out and showed it.

'I am very sorry to hear that. But I wonder if you can help us in his stead. Can you tell us anything about this shoe, please? I believe it to have been made by Thomas Truss.'

'Oh yes, this is his work, see? "T.T." stamped on the inside. We use "T.F.". Where did you get this?'

'I am the Coroner of Preston. It is evidence in an inquest and I am interested in knowing more about it.'

'Well, you have come to the right man,' Fowler said. 'I could talk all day about my friend Tommy Truss's shoe work.'

'I hope you won't dad,' said James sharply. 'We have Lord Saunders's order to complete by tonight, remember?'

The old man blinked, scowled and ducked his head in irritation.

'Oh, yes, so we do. So we do.'

'Then I suggest you get back to work at once.' James's voice was brisk. 'Or his young lordship's man will have nothing to take away when he gets here and his young lordship will have nothing to put on his shapely feet at the Assembly tonight.'

Old Fowler smiled bleakly at his visitors and shrugged, then shuffled meekly back towards his workshop.

'I wonder if we might continue the discussion in the morning, then?' Fidelis said.

'Tomorrow is the Sabbath,' said James.

'Let me say,' I put in, 'that though this is a legal enquiry, it is not business as such. There is no money in it. So perhaps a conversation on the matter is permissible on the Sabbath.'

'A shoe is a worldly object, Sir,' replied James stiffly. 'It is one to be bought and sold, and therefore a most doubtful subject for the Sabbath. I am a preacher. Folk might hear of this and say it is unseemly in me.'

'It is not you, but your father we wish to speak to.' I lowered my voice. 'And surely he will take pleasure in talking about his late friend. Can you deny him that?'

James Fowler hesitated, then he said,

'Call here at ten. I shall be at the Meeting, but my father'll be here.'

We walked into a roar of voices at Pinchbeck's ten minutes later, it being full of boastful Saturday trade talk. Having cast his eye around the room, Fidelis immediately went up to a man sitting at a table with a cup of chocolate beside him, as well as pen and ink, abacus, and a low pile of papers that were covered in figures. His lips were moving incessantly as he summed the columns of numbers, flicking the abacus beads along their rails with extraordinary rapidity.

'Good morning,' said Fidelis. 'Do you remember me?'

The question was ignored but there must have been something about the accountant that gave my friend patience, because he took no offence at all. As the relentless counting continued, Fidelis persisted.

'I do not see my acquaintance, Mr Moreton Canavan, here today,' he observed. 'You will remember my asking you to point him out to me in this room on Monday last.'

The eyes and index finger shifted relentlessly down the figures, the other finger was busy on the abacus. The man's concentration was such that I could not believe he had even heard Fidelis's words.

'Has he been here at all in the last few days? Have you seen him?'

The reckoner reached the bottom of the column, and wrote a total down, then cleared the abacus beads back to their starting positions.

'It's Mr Canavan that I'm asking about,' prompted Fidelis. 'Moreton Canavan.'

The man closed his eyes, took a sip of his chocolate and said wearily, without looking up at Fidelis,

'Canavan has not been here recently. I have been here every day. I believe I last saw him on Tuesday.'

He placed his finger at the top of the column that he had to sum next.

'Thank you Sir,' said Fidelis warmly, and took me off to find a table.

While we ate he pointed out Pinchbeck to me. He then indicated the table where Moon had been sitting when they had met, and the door through which Moon had disappeared having taken possession of my letter. I was struck by the unusual dispatch with which Fidelis cleared his plate of chops. As soon as he had done so he summoned the serving man to bring the reckoning.

'We'll find nothing more here,' he said, 'and there's someone I want you to meet. We need to know more about the Guinea Trade before we can fully understand this tangled affair. So come on.'

He led me out to the street and directly down to the dock. As soon as we got there he strode towards an ancient seafarer sitting in a bollard.

'May we fill your pipe for you, Sir, and stand you a tot of rum?'

The greybeard didn't mind if we did. He rose to his feet with sudden sprightliness and led the way to the tavern of his choice. This was very different from Pinchbeck's. Here the roar was not that of prices and profits, but of drink and women and the hardships of the seafaring life.

With a bottle standing on the table between us, Fidelis asked the old man if he remembered their last meeting, and in particular the mention of the ship *The Fortunate Isle*. He did.

'And you thought her poorly fitted out, I think.'

'Yes, she didn't look the shape from dockside. She wasn't Liverpool registered, and I'd not seen her before. I might've bin wrong. I didn't see all of the loading and fitting she had. But if what I saw of her is all she was, then she wasn't good enough for Guinea or the Spanish Main. What I saw of her crew an' all. Skinny old men and skinny boys is all they were, good for goatherds maybe, but not sailing a ship in blue water. I seen that before, and when they set sail for slaves and do it on the cheap it don't come off. Not nine times out of ten, it don't. They end slaughtered, by sickness or swords, it don't matter.'

'And her captain?'

'I saw him, I s'pose. Didn't know him to speak to him.'

'They say he is Edward Doubleday. Have you heard the name?'

'No. Never heard it.'

His answers were not getting us very far. It was no good being told the ship was not fit, unless we knew what she wasn't fit for.

'Tell us more about the Trade,' I said. 'I mean the Guinea Trade. How does it work?'

He turned to me and said nothing but his mouth gaped in a toothless grimace. After this hesitation, he looked away and spoke in a gruff emphatic way.

'Painful it is for me to speak about it, Sir, very painful, for I lost an arm and two brothers in that dangerous business. Dangerous to do and in this town dangerous to speak of, too, if you understand my meaning.'

'I'm afraid I do not.'

'I won't elaborate, Sir, if you'll excuse me. The Baltic, now. I'll tell you about that with pleasure.'

'We are concerned only with Guinea and the West Indies. Where should we go to find out what we want to know?'

The sailor half closed his eyes and spoke almost in a whisper.

'All right, Sir. Come along with me. I know a place not far where folk'll tell you – and tell you better'n I can.'

When we had drunk up, he took us through a maze of streets where the houses had cellars under them, which were entered from the street by sets of stone steps. We arrived at one such stairwell and heard the sound of some sort of celebration in progress. Raucous noises came from the place – whoops and shouts of laughter. Our guide wouldn't go down with us.

'Not a resort for me, kind Sirs. You may be all right. Go down. They will tell you the truth of the Trade, if anyone will.'

Many dark bodies filled the cellar, and someone was pounding a drum, using no stick but just his palms and fingers. A young woman had just begun to dance, shaking her body in a way that was both utterly abandoned and beautiful. I had never seen a dance in any way like it. Finally, as if bringing herself to a pitch of ecstasy, she gave out a wild shriek, and fell to the floor. Fidelis went to her side, knelt and cradled her head as she looked vacantly up into his eyes.

I suddenly knew that we were in danger. All around us dark faces pressed closer, eyes flashing. They were murmuring angrily about what Fidelis was doing. A woman shouted at him to leave her be. A fellow with a ring in his ear touched Fidelis on the shoulder in warning. Just then a burly man pushed through the bystanders and picked the dancer from the ground as easily as you might pick up a house cat.

'Come with me,' he said curtly to Fidelis. 'Bring your friend. Unless you want to be eaten alive.'

He laughed most heartily when he saw our faces, then led us out of the cellar, up the stair and into the afternoon light. The woman was still lying insensibly in his arms.

'My name is Elijah Quick, Sirs, and what I said down there was a figure of speech. Come with me and we shall taste some ale together.'

He jerked his head in the direction of an alehouse across the street, and set off ahead of us still carrying his burden lightly. I looked at Fidelis, who nodded his head and we followed our new acquaintance. Soon we had settled ourselves around a table, with the woman's body now popped up across Elijah Quick's knee, with her head lolling against his shoulder.

'May I look at her?' asked Fidelis. 'I am a doctor.'

'No need. It's only the gin. She has a deadly taste for it.'

Fidelis leaned across and raised the girl's eyelids with his thumb, then placed his fingers against the underside of her wrist. This satisfied him, and he sat back in his chair.

'I am curious: what brought two gentlemen like yourselves into that cellar?' said Quick.

He spoke accurate, educated English. I explained that we were gathering intelligence about the Guinea Trade and had been directed there. Quick's merriment immediately drained away. He said,

'You are interested in the Guinea Trade, you say. Then you are speaking to a product of it.'

'Would you oblige us by telling your story?'

'My story is a long one.'

'Nevertheless. Where are you from?'

'Barbados. I was purchased as a houseboy by a clergyman when I was a young lad, having just made the Middle Passage. I was eager to learn and he easily taught me English and how to read scripture. He was a good man, or at least not a cruel one, but as soon as I became a man myself I ran away from him to freedom.'

'In Liverpool?'

'Of course. No black man can be free in the West Indies. Here I have found work for myself as a schoolmaster for my people, which they sorely need.'

'Will you tell us about the Trade and about how it starts in Africa?'

'There are many lies told about this by white men. I will tell you the truth. The Trade has made our home country evil and violent. War is ceaseless. Armies go about burning villages and taking the innocent people into slavery to sell them for gunpowder and rum at the coast. They march them in long lines chained together, which they call coffles. The slaves eat next to nothing, but their lot does not improve when they reach there. They are haggled over as they struggle to survive or die. The white men's ships sail away loaded with them, our people lying wedged together day after day in the dark. We hated the coffle men but feared the white men. We believed we were being taken across the ocean to be eaten.

'Down below during the Middle Passage there was sickness and misery – endless, hopeless misery. Those that died were thrown to the sharks. Our captors knew we would all die without some fresh air, so we were brought up onto the deck each day and made to dance. Those that would not dance were whipped. The sailors thought it all very diverting.

'When we got near to where we were going they would try to do something about us, to make us look better. They shaved our heads and rubbed our skins with grease. A good price was all they cared about.'

'Are there rebellions against this inhumanity?' I asked.

'Yes, of course, there are uprisings. Always useless, always ending in many deaths.'

'What happens to the slaves when they reach the Indies?'

'Almost all get sold to work on the plantations. The masters tell them that now their troubles are over so long as they work. And they do work, because if not they are whipped and maybe killed. They work every day while it is light. Only when it is dark do they rest. But the masters are always frightened that the slaves will rise up. It is their greatest fear. They prevent this by breaking their spirit. The women, they rape. The men, they simply terrify. The punishment for any black man caught stealing or doing what he shouldn't is terrible. They cut his tongue out, his balls off. If you have never seen a person whipped slowly to death, or hung up in a public cage and starved, you cannot know the slave's life. Living on the plantation, every day is the same. There is no hope, no future, only the same endless now.'

'You were fortunate in your Christian master, that you escaped being sent to the plantation.'

'He did not buy me to save me from slavery; he bought me because he wanted a houseboy. I ran away because, by then, I had grown and was a man, and he was ready to sell me again as a strong and healthy worker. Had I not got away I would be cutting cane now – if I happened to be still alive.'

We stayed with Elijah Quick for some hours, listening intently to what he had to say, questioning him on certain particulars, and finding him intelligent and eloquent. By the end we were much better informed.

'It's an evil Trade, Titus,' said Fidelis, when we had said good-night to Quick and were making our way back to the Inn. 'And it is conducted by evil men. Why is there no outcry?'

'Because people are making money.'

'Tainted money. And why doesn't the Christian religion stand against it?'

I told him of some remarks I had read in Montaigne, that people are more likely to use Christianity to justify their hatreds and cruelties than to endorse their love and moderation.

'So far from rooting out evil, he argues, our religion has become a way of screening, nourishing and inciting evil. I am a little inclined to agree with that idea.'

'It is cynical, though,' said my friend, 'and very contrary and odd. That author of yours will find no friend for his views in either Rome or Geneva.'

'I am sure he wouldn't be perturbed about that.'

And so – as conversation will – our talk strayed from the subject of slavery. But what I had learned that day I have never forgotten. The Guinea Trade continues, and even increases, yet I loathe it and would like to see those who do it stand at the bar of human justice, if there ever happened to be such a thing.

Chapter Twenty-five

∞

THE NEXT MORNING, Old Fowler welcomed us at his shop with a gap-toothed smile.

'The boy's safely out at his meeting,' he told us. 'Very pious he is. Keeps talking about the end time and the rapture of the saints and I don't know what.'

I judged him to be an educated old man for, among the volumes and tracts on his shelf, there were other books on subjects too broad to interest a religious enthusiast such as the son. I handed across the shoe.

'Yesterday I showed you this. Can you tell me a little bit more about it? When it was made, for instance.'

He took it to the light and squinted inside. Then he turned it over and inspected the sole, the stitching.

'It shows a few years of wear. I reckon it was made about five years ago, and some repairs have been made. It might be less if the fellow wore it every day without stint.'

'What sort of a man would wear this shoe?'

'It is not a cheap shoe. He was not a labourer. Let's say it was someone from the middling sort. The fashion of it is what we call in this shop Number 14. Now we always kept and still keep a record of every shoe we make with the number, date, size, price, and name of customer – all the details we might need later.'

'So you can give us the name of the person that wore this shoe?'

'I can tell you the names of men who have ordered such shoes to be made here. But shoes can be sold or given away. Many people wear a shoe that was made for the foot of another.'

'How do you record each shoe?'

He opened a cupboard and a pungent smell wafted out. The lower half was full of rolls of finished hide but the top shelf contained six foolscap-sized ledgers. He took one out and opened it.

'The first column as you see is the date, followed by the shoe's number – the Number 14s beginning with those digits, like here ... and here! D'you see? Then we have the shoe's size and the price received and the signature of the customer to say that he has received the goods.'

'Can we find this shoe amongst all these listed?'

'Every shoe has its own individual number. Let's see, it should be inked under the tongue – it will be of six digits beginning with one and four.

Fidelis had picked the shoe from his hands and was peeling back the tongue.

'I can't see anything,' he said. 'No, what's this?'

He showed the back of the tongue to Fowler.

'Yes, 1455 something-something,' the shoemaker read. 'The last two numbers are rubbed away. But those numbers tell us where to look. All we have to do is find the entry in the book. As we don't know the date, we will have to work within estimates.'

He turned the pages of the ledger until he found the one he wanted to show us.

'Let us start three years back. These are some of the last shoes Thomas made before he went sadly to Childwall in January three year ago.'

He fetched a straight-edge and laid it under the top line of records to make it easier to read.

'I'll write down all the possible shoes for the last six months in which Mr Truss was still shoemaking,' I said. 'May I have writing materials, Mr Fowler?'

These were brought and Fowler ran his finger down the column in which the shoe-numbers were recorded.

'Here is the first!' he said. 'Date 4 September 1739, shoe number 145542, price eight shillings and signed by — I can't read it. What's the name? Lewis Mottram, I think. What's the next one? Here. 15 October 1738, shoe number 145561, signed Jos. Garritty. Oh and another within a week. 19 October, 145564, signed by Martin Carman. Then three weeks later shoe number 145576 signed Chas. Cheeseby. Are you getting this down, Sir?'

He licked his finger and turned the page.

'And there's one more in November, number 145579 signed for by Geo: Galliford. And finally, how many in December? Three it looks like. Number 145585 signed T. Barlow, 145590 signed Ben Philps and 145598 dated 29 December signed Henry Scott.'

I reviewed my list of names: Mottram, Garritty, Carman, Cheeseby, Galliford, Barlow, Philps and Scott. I read them out loud. Fidelis, I noticed, listened with his eyes closed.

'No help for us there,' was all he said.

After a week in which the days had been largely fine and warm our ride back to Preston was wet. So, as riding companionably in the rain is almost impossible, each of us went along with our own thoughts and it wasn't until we stopped for refreshment at Ormskirk, before we had covered twenty miles, that we were able to compare those thoughts.

'We may not have connected Zadok Moon with that shoe,' I said, 'but the evidence against him is still strong, because he was at the inn.'

We were sitting with a jug of hot punch between us. Fidelis took a pull from his glass.

'A clean-shaven, not a bearded man was at the inn, Titus. It is hard to prove that was Moon.'

'It is not difficult to find a barber. The murderer of Jackson wanted to prevent any more revelations, did he not? The testimony given at the inquest was bad for Zadok Moon and could have been even worse.'

'Quite so. We didn't find out what it was that he had done by way of fraud. We can only surmise.'

'So he took part in the murder to prevent any further details being made known.'

Fidelis raised a hand high above his head and snapped his fingers.

'That is the crux, Titus. We still don't know what it was about Zadok Moon that Jackson either already knew, or was still trying to find out. Nor do we know who helped Moon kill him. Was it, perhaps, Moreton Canavan?'

'Only Jackson could tell us, surely.'

Fidelis laughed.

'The same can be said of every murdered man, that he could tell who killed him.'

'We would surely learn something from the letter Jackson wrote from the Lamb and Flag. I have asked Furzey to try to get it. And perhaps his companion could speak for him, if only she *would* speak.'

Fidelis now sat upright, struck by an idea.

'Think of this. With her, we have a not dissimilar problem of communication as we have had with Adam Thorn. So what if we can solve it in the same way?'

'I don't follow you.'

'Difficult matters are easier to hear than to say. But of all words the easiest to say are Yes and No. So let her hear the case stated and let her simply affirm or deny, nod or shake.'

'That's clever, and it might work,' I agreed. 'But it must be someone the girl trusts who puts the questions to her.'

'If there's anybody in Preston to do it, it might be your Elizabeth,' said Fidelis. 'Did you not say she took the girl soup when she was incarcerated in the House of Correction?'

'That is a good idea, but I have a better one – our friend Elijah Quick! He is intelligent, agreeable and best of all his skin is black.'

Luke slapped the table.

'Yes, Titus! And I am sure he will agree. Shall I go back to Liverpool and put it to him?'

I arrived in Preston wet through and chilled to the bone. With hot water ready, Elizabeth banished Matty from the kitchen, poured the water with a handful of pine needles into the bathing tub, and made me sit in it until I was warm through. As I sat there I told her of our adventures in Liverpool, including an account of the Guinea Trade of which I only spared her the very worst details.

Later, as we sat over our supper, the puppy was heard barking in the hall. I went out to him as the door-knocker sounded, and I opened to find Amity Thorn, her face pale and pinched, standing alone at the door.

'Doctor Fidelis was kind enough to say I could apply to him anytime if I was in trouble, and that I am. I can't find him at his lodging, though I left word. Is he with you, Sir? Little Peggy his niece that's been working at Cadley Place is watching the children.'

'What is the trouble, Amity?'

'It's Adam. I haven't been able to rouse him this last five hours. And now he's stopped breathing.'

The rain had cleared away and it was by no means yet dark as we

rode out to Peel Hall Lane Cottage, having left word at the Lorrises'
for Fidelis to follow hard upon us when he returned. Amity sat up
behind me on the horse's rump, her arms strongly enclosing my
waist and her breathing, mixed with a few sobs, falling on my neck.
We jogged along like this for fifteen minutes until we arrived at her
house.

Outwardly the place was quiet and still. The first thing I saw
was the empty bath chair beside the door.

'He was in it when he had his turn,' Amity told me. 'Then me
and Peg dragged him out and into his bed.'

'That must have been difficult.'

'Not really, Mr Cragg. He's that scrawny now, he's as light as
my nose.'

From within came the reedy wail of a sleepy infant, and we
found Peg with the baby in her arms, walking around in front of
the range and rocking it with what – to my inexperienced eye –
seemed an unnaturally vigorous motion. The other two children
were asleep on their straw mattress while, beside the fire, a man sat
at ease, smoking a stubby pipe. It took me a moment to recognize
John Barton, dressed in his best.

'What's he doing here?' asked Amity of Peg, with acid sharpness in her voice.

Barton answered for himself, in a smooth, light tone that
sounded nonchalant in this house of mourning.

'I've only come to offer a neighbour's condolence and services,
if there's any I can do.'

Amity's voice persisted in trying to cut him.

'There's nowt. You can take yourself off.'

Weighing the situation for a moment, he took into account my
presence, then knocked out his pipe and stood.

'Right. You'll send for me if you've need.'

When he had gone we slipped into the inner room. The light

was dim and the air already staled by the corpse on the bed. I approached and touched the forehead: it was marble cold.

'The doctor always said this might happen, with no warning,' I said, picking my words gently. 'His suffering is over, at least we can say that.'

A few minutes later, after Amity had told me again the story of the day's events, I heard the snort and jingle of a horse and suddenly Fidelis came striding in. He had read my message at his lodgings and followed me without pause. Going in to the body, he produced a tinderbox and struck a flame for a candle. This he passed in front of the dead man's face and for the first time I clearly saw the look of surprise locked onto it. My father might have called it the Astonished Death.

Gently Fidelis closed the eyes.

'Perhaps he died dreaming of his treasure, but without letting us know about it. I am at fault. I should have carried my questioning by the eye-blinking method sooner. Now it's too late.'

We left him and returned to his wife, who was sitting in the chair vacated by Barton, her eyes closed. Peg had somehow induced sleep in the baby and all was quiet.

Riding alongside Fidelis on our way back to town I told him about John Barton sitting at ease by Amity's fireside.

'He was like a man taking possession of what he considers rightfully his.'

'She won't allow it. She is too proud.'

'Do you believe he and Adam were friendly, as he claimed when he spoke to me last week?'

'If they were, his wife knew nothing about it.'

'What's his object, finally? The woman, or the treasure?'

'Supposing he knows about the money, it would be both, I'm thinking. But does he?'

'He says the two men were friends. Adam might have confided in Barton: asked his advice.'

'In that case there would have to be trust and some kind of friendship. Adam would've been a fool to confide in Barton otherwise.'

'I never talked with Adam,' I said, 'but my impression is he was anything but a fool. Now, I am anxious to know if you brought Quick from Liverpool. Tell me.'

'Yes. He is at my lodging. You should have seen Dot Lorris's face when she saw him with me.'

It was ten o'clock and dark when we reached town. The day had been an exhausting one for both of us.

'You know me, Titus,' he said before we parted to go to our own homes. 'I need my sleep, and there is a patient I must see in the morning. Forgive me if I do not present Elijah to you until afternoon.'

Fidelis went to his bed but for me the day was not yet over: I found Ephraim Grimshaw waiting impatiently at home, his face glowing not only from the wine that Elizabeth had given him, but also from self-congratulation.

'I have been much puzzled in the matter of the death of this man Tybalt Jackson,' he said, 'as I am sure you have been, Cragg. I mean over why the victim's face was so crushed and battered out of shape. So I am happy to tell you I have come to the answer.'

'I am glad to hear it, Mayor. What is it?'

'It was done deliberately by the murderer in order to make him unrecognizable. There you have it.'

'Why would he want to do that?'

'In order to make his escape. To disappear, who knows where – to Scotland, Ireland, America, or wherever malefactors do go to secrete themselves.'

'Forgive me. I am tired, having ridden today from Liverpool, so perhaps my powers of understanding are weak. Please explain.'

'Well, who have we all been assuming the corpse is?'

'We know it is Tybalt Jackson.'

'Why is that, Sir? It cannot be from his face, which is the usual method of identifying someone.'

'No, it was his clothes.'

'But, unlike a face, clothes may be exchanged with ease. A face cannot be exchanged in that way, but it can be changed – dangerously and with great effort, but changed out of recognition. I therefore submit that this dead body that we have is not that of Tybalt Jackson at all. It has been dressed in Jackson's clothes and its face brutally altered to prevent anyone seeing that it isn't Jackson.'

'Then whose is it, Mayor?'

'Tell me, if you can, who was shadowing Tybalt Jackson, Mr Cragg. Tell me who arrived at the same inn within a few hours of Jackson and spied on him. Tell me who Jackson feared and perhaps, if driven to extremes, he might kill. Tell me the name of that man and you will have told me the name of the murdered man.'

'You mean Zadok Moon?'

'The very person. I do believe we have brought in the elusive Mr Moon, whom we have been seeking with such anxiety this last week. Brought in dead, unfortunately, but nevertheless brought in.'

'And your conclusion as to the murderer's identity?'

'I am convinced, Mr Coroner, that the murderer wished us to believe that he himself was the victim. In short, I believe that the said murderer was Tybalt Jackson.'

Chapter Twenty-six

∽

O N MY BREAKFAST table the next morning was a letter from Ruth
Peel:

Dear Mr Cragg,

*I beg you to pay us a visit as soon as you are able, for we are
out of our wits at Cadley Place, not knowing how to pay our
way and urgently in need of advice from you as executor of
my late employer's Will.*

Ruth Peel.

The letter jarred my conscience. Mr Flitcroft of Kirkham was
due later the same morning to look over the silver hoard but, if I
hurried, I would have time to go to Cadley Place, and return, before
he arrived. I sent for my horse and rode off. The first freshness of the
morning had given way to a growing oppressiveness as smoky clouds
from the west had crept across the Preston sky. The wayside flowers
seemed to hang limply on their stalks and birdsong was infrequent
save for the harsh cry of rooks flapping across the farmland.

On arrival at the house young Peggy told me that the housekeeper was in the orchard across the road and I found Miss Peel

sitting alone on a seat that had been cut into the trunk of a fallen oak. She was staring into the east where the distant fells, still unreached by the massing clouds, formed a clear and sunlit horizon.

'Thank you for coming, Mr Cragg,' she said, rising to her feet as I approached. 'Shall we walk?'

As we strolled under the trees, she explained that, with so many household bills unpaid, she was finding it increasingly hard to obtain credit with tradesmen.

'We are desperate. The dairyman is threatening to stop supplying us. The butcher has already done so. I cannot shop at market without ready money. I am everywhere in debt and to be refused credit is so shaming.'

'I must apologize,' I said. 'I should have anticipated your difficulty. However I can reassure you. Now that the inquest has determined that your employer died as a result of a simple accident, there is no legal impediment to Mrs Pimbo taking possession of her lifetime interest in her son's estate – this house and its contents, and whatever other property he may have had. There remains only the purely formal business of proving the will. So you may assure your creditors that they will be paid.'

'But they may not believe me. How can I convince them?'

'I shall provide you with a letter to that effect, Miss Peel. Show it to your suppliers and they will extend your credit for the time being. So if you live economically, you shall make ends meet.'

'And the shop in Preston, Mr Cragg? Does it still conduct business?'

'No, it is closed and I fear cannot trade. As to the longer future it does not appear that Mr Pimbo's mother can carry the business on herself, so I expect a tenant or a purchaser must be found. I have asked Mr Hazelbury to examine the books and report to me about this. I cannot be sure exactly how but, as you heard at the inquest, it does look as if Mr Pimbo's fallen foul of an embezzler. We do not know the extent of his loss, but it may have been great.'

'And what of my own—'

She gestured to right and left.

'I mean, my legacy.'

'This orchard?'

'Yes.'

'It is safe. It is yours, always provided you abide by Mr Pimbo's curious condition – that you do not marry.'

She closed her eyes for a moment and let out a barely audible laugh.

'I hardly know what I shall do with all this, Mr Cragg.'

'I suggest you cultivate it, Miss Peel. Its fruit and honey will yield you produce and even an income, you know.'

'Yes I suppose so.'

She gave me a faltering look.

'And if I should, at any time . . . I mean, if I should marry – what then?'

'Then I am afraid the orchard would revert to Mrs Pimbo or her direct heirs. You would lose it.'

Miss Peel did not desire to pursue this matter and we discussed instead ways in which the Cadley Place household could make economies, and what should be done about Mrs Pimbo. As her employer's executor I asked her to continue for the time being in her position as housekeeper.

'And if you need to raise money you have my authority to sell items of moveable property, or to make any of the economies we have mentioned. You may submit your accounts to me.'

My watch was now telling me I must hurry my old horse back to town. I therefore said my farewells and left her to contemplate her newly-acquired dominion over apples, pears and plums.

'I am disappointed, Cragg, most grievously.'

It was less than an hour later and Mr Flitcroft was in my

office, surveying, with scepticism, the collection of silver that I had brought from Nick Oldswick's strong cupboard, and had now arranged for his inspection on my desk.

'I am sorry to hear it,' I said. 'Why?'

'I was looking forward to inspecting something that might interest an antiquary, you know. But – oh dear! – this does not appear at all promising.'

Flitcroft took out his eyeglasses to examine more closely the goods spread out before him. He picked up one object – a small jug – and studied it briefly before he put it down with a click of his tongue and picked up another. Having been through half a dozen or so in the same way, he sighed and turned to me.

'These are all such *modern* pieces, Cragg. Have you nothing of any age to show? I do not expect Roman silver – that is exceedingly rare – or even Anglo-Saxon. But nor did I think I should be looking at such recent silverware.'

'I believe I did explain,' I said, 'that the find would be from the time of Cromwell, and King Charles the First.'

Flitcroft barked a laugh, without mirth.

'Most is not even that, Sir, but of the present century – Queen Anne, the first King George, the present monarch, all of these are represented here! This is not a hoard of old metalware, Cragg. It is nothing but the jumbled contents of a middling family's silver cupboard. The oldest and best pieces are the apostle spoons. They have at least something well-bred about them.'

With a sigh he produced from his pocket the almanac with its table of assay dates and asked for a sheet of paper and writing materials.

'However, having ridden all this way, I may as well make a list for you of the objects whose hallmarks are legible. Give me a few minutes.'

I waited out the minutes as patiently as I could while he worked his way through the items, checking each hallmark before adding it to a list. When he had finished, he sat back, handed me the paper and, snapping open a snuffbox that he drew from his waistcoat, took a pinch of snuff.

'The cities named beside each item are not necessarily those of the manufacture,' he explained. 'They are merely the assay-office at which the silver was warranted.'

I looked down the list and read:

Item: 11 Apostle spoons – London – 1596

Item: Candle-holder – York – 1637

Item: Triangular Salt-cellar – Chester – 1630

These, dated before the Battle in which Benjamin Peel lost his life, might have formed part of Peel's hoard. But the next four objects immediately negated that possibility.

Item: Caddy spoon – Chester – 1727

Item: Buckle – Chester – 1676

Item: Little Jug – York – 1712

Item: Marrow spoon – Edinburgh – 1719

So there it was in ink: Flitcroft's scornful assessment was right. Most of these things were not even as old as the century – the caddy spoon had been made only fifteen years ago. Whatever this miscellany of plate was that I had found in the rabbit hole, it had nothing to do with Benjamin Peel's hoard.

Bidding me a disgruntled farewell, Flitcroft was shown out by Furzey, who himself now wandered into my room with the letter I had asked him to draft for Miss Peel to show to her tradesmen. He looked over the silver as I was replacing it in its bag.

'You thought *this* was Benjamin Peel's lost treasure?' he said.

'I thought it might be part of it.'

Furzey's lip curled into a shape that could have been amusement, and could have been scorn.

'If you'd asked me, I would have told you it wasn't. That doesn't look half important enough to be a Corporation's plate, even of a century ago.'

'What *does* it look like?'

'It looks like what you would find in a burglar's satchel. It looks like common and sundry booty.'

When a man comes across lost or hidden items of value, the law requires that he do his best to discover their owner. I therefore sat down at my desk with Flitcroft's list beside me to draw up a notice for insertion into the *Preston Journal* and also as a bill to display at the Moot Hall and post office. I had finished the task, given my work to Furzey and returned to my desk when Robert Hazelbury walked into the office. He was carrying a fat ledger under his arm.

'I need your help, Mr Cragg,' he told me. 'I've been working every day at the shop, going through the books, and this morning I've had Mrs Pauline Owen in. She requires her necklace.'

'I'm sorry, Mr Hazelbury. I don't follow you.'

'She'd pawned a pearl necklace with Mr Pimbo a couple of weeks before he died and now she wants to redeem it to wear at the Guild Ball, she says. But you have told us that the shop is shut and cannot engage in business. How should I proceed? She is threatening to make a great to-do in public over the matter.'

'What? And tell the world she's been to the pawn-shop with her pearls? I doubt that.'

'Well, she is ready to pay the redemption money in full. It seems hard on her not to let her claim the necklace back – and there'll be others, no doubt, who are in the same position but as yet too discreet to come forward.'

'How was Mrs Owen's transaction recorded?'

The cashier slid the ledger from under his arm and, coming round the desk to stand by my side, placed it in front of me.

'I've brought the Pledges Book to show you,' he said, opening it. 'It was kept by Mr Pimbo personally. As you may see, each item is listed against its ticket number and the customer's name, date of transaction, amount loaned and period of loan. Then there are these columns, recording if and when the pledge was redeemed, and the gross amount including interest paid to us for the goods' return. Alternatively they note the expiry of the redemption period, and the amount the item sold for. The final column gives the final profit or loss. You will see that the most recent loans recorded are only a few days before Mr Pimbo's death.'

I picked up the ledger and turned the pages. I soon found Mrs Owen's transaction and saw that the necklace had been pawned on the sixteenth of May for a period of thirty days.

'So that means the period of the loan runs out . . .'

'The day after tomorrow, Mr Cragg. That's the reason for Mrs Owen's anxiety. And here you see the names of some of our other clients who may always have intended to claim their jewellery in time for the Guild.'

'I see. This is a sensitive matter, of course.'

I thought for a moment.

'Very well,' I went on. 'Out of consideration for Mrs Owen, and others, I shall relax the ban on trading to this extent: items still in pawn may be redeemed, and you may advertise the fact. But there are to be no new pawns, Hazelbury. Money in, you see, but no money out.'

I turned the pages backwards, looking idly up and down the lists of pledges. I admit I was diverted by the discovery of my fellow Prestonians furtively pawning their valuables to tide them across a few weeks of shortage, or to pay the unexpected fee of a doctor or a lawyer – Luke Fidelis's perhaps. Or my own. To learn the secrets of others is surely one of the most natural, if not the most fragrant, of our desires.

Then an entry of more than three years ago caught my eye: '*1 hall-marked silver salt in shape of triangle 4 1/2 oz*'. It had been pawned by a Mrs Crossley for the term of a month and deemed worth a seven shillings advance. Running my finger along the line, I saw that the space for redemptions and sales was blank. I said,

'Tell me something, Hazelbury. Here is an object that has not been redeemed, and has not been subsequently sold on in the shop. What happened to it?'

He leaned over to look more closely.

'Oh, aye. Happen it will have taken Mr Pimbo's fancy, will that. There have always been some of those, that he decided not to part with.'

'Have you ever seen this silver salt of Mrs Crossley's yourself?'

'No, I don't recall it. Not that I would. Mr Pimbo always conducted the pawning business himself, you see. For discretion, he said. It were only when a thing came on sale in the shop that I took note of it.'

'And you think this salt cellar was never even offered for sale in the shop?'

'I'm sure it wasn't. It's not written down as sold, and it's not in my stock, or ever been. I would remember a three-sided salt.'

I pushed back my chair and crossed to the cupboard in which I had put the silver I had earlier shown to Flitcroft. A moment later I returned holding the triangular salt that the antiquary listed as having been assayed at York in 1637.

'Could this be the one?' I asked.

Hazelbury took it, turned it over in his hands, and shrugged.

'Like I said, I never saw the thing. And I haven't seen this before either.'

I called out to Furzey in the outer room to bring in the scales, which I set up on the desk. The salt weighed exactly four and a half ounces.

'May I borrow the Pledges Book from you for an hour?' I asked Hazelbury. 'I promise to send it back to you promptly.'

After he had gone I began a systematic search through the ledger for all silver items that had been neither redeemed by their pawners, nor sold in the shop, and one by one I found items of similar description to the things I had pulled out of the rabbit hole on the Moor four days ago – a cream jug, a belt-buckle, a marrow spoon and a caddy spoon. It took me the longest time to find the apostle spoons, and I did not do so until I had gone back in the book thirty-five years, when I found they had been pledged by Mrs Georgina Peel, who had inhabited Peel Hall in its last years of ruin and dereliction. How ironic that what we no longer supposed to be Benjamin Peel's hoard contained at least one thing that really had belonged to Benjamin Peel.

On being weighed each piece was of exactly the same weight as a corresponding object in Pimbo's ledger, pawned with him at some time in the last ten years, and remaining unredeemed and unsold. I sat back, mystified. What I had originally supposed – hoped, even – to be part of the treasure of Benjamin Peel had turned out to have been the property of the late Phillip Pimbo, and now of his estate. To explain by what means it found its way into a rabbit's burrow was quite beyond me.

But there was no time to consider the puzzle now. I summoned Furzey again.

'You may forget about taking that notice to the *Journal*,' I said. 'Will you instead return this ledger to Robert Hazelbury at Pimbo's shop, with my thanks. I must wait here for Dr Fidelis and Mr Quick.'

With his usual show of reluctance when receiving a direct order Furzey picked up the volume and trudged back to his own area in the outdoor office, but almost immediately returned with a letter in his hand. This he casually placed in front of me.

'This almost slipped out of my mind, Mr Cragg.'

I picked up the paper and saw it was addressed to Messrs Willoughby and Pickle, Lloyd's Coffee House, Lombard Street, London.

'What is this?'

'You asked me to get it if I could. I got it.'

I looked at the back and immediately saw the sender's name written there: Tybalt Jackson Esq.

'Furzey! This is wonderful! You found Jackson's letter at the post office.'

'It wasn't difficult. It was to travel as a by-letter with the Duchy mail to London, but the post-boy had been obliged to wait for a packet from the Duchy office that was delayed. Mr Crick dug Mr Jackson's letter out of the pouch when I told him the one that wrote it's been murdered, and his letter is needed in evidence. He said he'd want a written retrospective warrant from you, but he didn't argue. Now, if you'll excuse me, Sir, there's the *very* pressing matter of the return of Mr Hazelbury's book.'

He left me once more and, with some impatience, I broke the seal on Jackson's letter and unfolded it.

The Scrivener

To Messrs Willoughby and Pickle, insurance brokers.

Sirs,

Your business has now brought me to Preston, where I compose this letter in a miserable stinking inn more suited to the accommodation of beasts than men. I have come to this town in the expectation of finding Zadok Moon, though I have not yet done so. There is indeed talk in this town of him being an embezzler, as you in London have long suspected, but of proof there is none. I have met one who tells me he can bring Moon and me together and I hope he will do so this night, after which I hope to have more intelligence of the slaver The Fortunate Isle *and her fate. I am, Sirs, compelled to add that during my long journey from Bristol and stay in Liverpool, I have spoken with many who engage in the business that occupies that ship, and the many other ships you gentlemen transact with. I have concluded it is a vile business and the Devil's work and if I cannot persuade you to leave off dealing with slave-traffickers, which I hardly think I can, then I beg leave to tender my irrevocable resignation from your employ, after my present commission has been discharged. There are others on hand who will judge me and, if I do not resign, I shall not be able to face them out.*

Yours, Tybalt Jackson.

My father used to tell me that a prudent man reads every letter two times, but a lawyer reads it thrice. My first perusal informed me of the facts: Jackson was on the track of Moon; he had met a person – unnamed, alas! – who claimed to know where to find him;

and his mind and purpose had turned so wholly against the Guinea Trade that he meant to leave his employment while it had to do with that. My second reading left me pondering on how that fateful conversion had taken place, while my third allowed some deeper reflections on the state of Jackson's mind. He seemed angry in his righteousness, but he also stated his intention of continuing his commission to the end. Jackson was evidently a man of the strictest probity. Finally I gave some time to thinking about the meaning of his last sentence, referring to 'others on hand who will judge me'.

'What others would those be, that he would not be able to face out?' I mused aloud. Hearing me speak the word 'out' Suez pattered over to my side and looked up with his head cocked and his ears pricked.

Glad for the chance to get some air, and with no sign still of Fidelis and Elijah Quick, I took him for a trot around Market Place. Then I left him in the kitchen to be looked after by Matty, and returned to wait at the office.

Chapter Twenty-seven

∞

IT WAS HALF past one o'clock when they walked into the office –
Fidelis and, close behind him, the imposing and smiling figure of
Elijah Quick who filled the doorway with his great size. I began by
asking Quick if he understood the reason for his coming to Preston.

'The doctor, Sir,' said Quick in his deep mellifluous voice, 'has
told me during our journey that the girl was Jackson's bed-mate. I
understand she has not spoken a word since he died because, having witnessed his murder, the shock has struck her dumb.'

'Temporarily dumb, I would say,' said Fidelis. 'But there is no
knowing how long the effect will last.'

I said:

'Dr Fidelis and I hope that you may be able to win her confidence, and break the spell, Elijah. We know nothing of her history,
which does not help. But someone of her own race—'

Quick interrupted me again, anxious to correct my assumptions.

'There are many races in Africa, Sir. Many nations and many
tongues, so I regret there is a small chance that she and I will be
able to communicate in any of the continent's languages.'

'The girl understands English. We are hoping, however, that she
will be reassured by your appearance.'

'The colour of my skin?'

'Exactly.'

'In that case I hope I can indeed communicate with her.'

'Let us go to her and see, shall we, Mr Quick?'

And so I fetched my hat and we set off to introduce him to the girl.

When we came to the Biggses' door and the maid saw Elijah with us, her eyes grew to the size of billiard balls and she clapped her hand to her mouth. But she recovered sufficiently to show us into the hall and hurry away to fetch Mrs Biggs. The lady herself appeared a few minutes later.

'My husband is not at home,' she stated, her eyes looking Elijah up and down with distaste.

'There is no need to trouble him,' I said. 'I would like to question the girl you have staying with you about the murder of Tybalt Jackson, and I have brought Dr Fidelis and this other gentleman to assist. May we have a few words with her?'

Mrs Biggs's mouth twitched into a mean smile.

'Barbara, as we have been calling her, has continued mute and sulky, Mr Cragg. I warrant you will not be able to extract a sound from her, let alone a word. We have tried.'

Trusting that the Biggses had not been trying to extract sounds too hard, or too painfully, from their guest, I gestured towards Quick.

'I am hoping that she will be willing to speak to Mr Quick here.'

Looking Quick upwards and downwards once more, Mrs Biggs tightened the wings of her nostrils and sniffed.

'He may try it,' she said.

'Then will you bring the girl to us, if you please?'

Jackson's girl, as she now appeared to us, had been restored to her own sex. Coming into the parlour she looked scrubbed and demure in a servant's plain grey dress and linen cap.

'Will you sit?' I asked, indicating one of the four chairs that surrounded a circular table at one end of the parlour. She stood for a moment uncertainly, then made up her mind and sat. Fidelis, Quick and I took the other places at the table while Mrs Biggs sat on a stuffed wing chair by the fire at the other end of the room.

'I hear you go by the name Barbara in this house,' I said. 'But what is your real name?'

Her glance darted to each of the faces that confronted her, but she did not reply. There was more of timidity than sulk in her expression and her silence seemed a way of protecting herself rather than a defiance. She ended with a long look of curiosity at Quick while I addressed her as gently as I could.

'This here is Mr Elijah Quick, from Liverpool. If you truly cannot speak, or prefer not to, he will show you another way in which you can help us.'

With a touch on his arm I invited Quick to enter the conversation.

'Now, missy,' he said, leaning a little towards her and fixing his eyes upon hers, 'these are kind gentlemen who mean you no harm. Will you nod your head, please, if you understand me?'

We waited. Again her eyes did the rounds of our faces before returning their gaze to Elijah. He continued watching her carefully.

'Or if you prefer you could say "no" by shaking your head – like this – if you do not understand me.'

The girl hesitated a moment longer, then seemed to make up her mind that Elijah Quick, at least, was more her friend than her foe. She gave him a slight but distinct nod of the head.

He smiled broadly.

'That's very good, missy.' He grew immediately more grave. 'Now we want to know about your Master, Mr Jackson. You understand what has happened to him? That he has been horridly murdered?'

Another nod, a miserable one.

'Did you see it?'

Yes. Tears flooded her eyes and Quick took out a handkerchief, which he handed to her. His next question was spoken very low, and very seriously.

'And was you a pal of the one that did that murder?'

A dab of the eyes and a vehement head-shake.

'We did not think you was, but must ask. You witnessed a terrible thing happening. Was it just one man that did it – attacked Mr Jackson?'

No.

'Two?'

No again.

'Show me how many there was. Show me with your fingers.'

She held up three fingers.

Three? I looked in surprise at Fidelis but he was leaning forward, and concentrating intently on the girl. I was equally enthralled. It was just the same procedure as Fidelis had devised for communicating with Adam Thorn. It was also like a stalking game. You just had to find the right sequence of questions to ask and, finding it, you gradually crept closer to your quarry. Quick, it appeared, was by instinct very good at it.

'Had you seen any of the three before that night?' went on Quick.

No.

'Do you know the name of any of them?'

This time she did not move and Quick immediately saw her difficulty. The schoolmaster's manner was skilfully attuned to the circumstances: it was gentle and yet had authority.

'Might you know the name, but are not sure?'

Yes.

'And is that name —?'

He looked at me. He must have forgotten the name I'd given him earlier.

'Zadok Moon,' I whispered.

'Zadok Moon,' repeated Quick. 'Yes. Might one of them have been this man, Zadok Moon?'

She had stiffened when she heard the name, and now nodded her head.

'Did Mr Jackson speak to you about this man?'

Yes.

'But you never saw him?'

No.

'Do you think Mr Jackson and Mr Moon were friends?'

She did not.

'Did Mr Jackson believe that Mr Moon meant him harm?'

Yes.

'Did he say why?'

He did.

Fidelis, who had continued to watch the girl as a cat sits over a mouse-hole, suddenly intervened.

'Did he say it was because of what Mr Jackson revealed at the inquest here in Preston?' he asked, sharply.

The girl, still looking steadily at Quick, did not move her head, but her eyes opened a fraction wider. Quick said, more gently,

'Did he, missy? What the doctor said?'

He did.

I murmured in Quick's ear that I would like to ask her some questions myself, as I wanted to know what had happened on the previous Thursday night.

'Will you answer the Coroner's questions, missy? You only need to show him your "yes" or your "no", in the same way as you have shown me.'

She had begun to appear less frightened now and indicated she would answer me. I put my thoughts in order for a moment, and began.

'You and Mr Jackson were staying at the Lamb and Flag Inn, here in Preston?'

Yes, they were.

'And late in the evening Mr Jackson went out of the inn.'

Yes.

'Did you go with him?'

No, she did not.

'And did he tell you where he was going?'

No

'Did he tell you to stay in the room and wait for him?'

He did.

'And did you do that?'

She did not.

'Because you were concerned for his safety – and didn't want to be left alone?'

Two nods: yes to both.

The process continued until we understood that Jackson had met someone that night in Market Place, and that they had walked out of town. She had followed without being seen, as it was a dark night.

'Did you follow them to the wild place where Mr Jackson's body was found? The place with the big Stone?' I asked.

No.

I had seen the dip of the head, but I had also seen her lips move, and heard the faintest sibilance. Fidelis had noticed something too, and he made an impatient gesture of the hand, which meant 'go on'. But now it was Elijah Quick who picked up the thread.

'What was that, Missy?'

Her voice was barely a whisper, but this time I heard – or believed I heard, 'Houses.' So did Quick.

'They went to a place with houses?' he said. 'A village, was it?'

She shook her head vigorously and whispered again.

'Houses . . . houses.'

'I don't understand. Can you tell me what it was like, this place? How many houses?'

She shook her head even more vigorously. Her voice was beginning to gain strength, but it was still the slightest whisper, as she repeated the word twice more. Suddenly, I heard something about the way she had pronounced it, a difference between the word and the repetition.

'I think she is saying "horses",' I broke in. 'Young lady, are you saying horses, or houses?'

'Horses,' she said, more distinctly now.

'They mounted horses?'

She was shaking her head.

'Horses . . . houses.'

I could not be sure which she was saying and Quick was equally uncomprehending. But Fidelis had been listening to the exchange with his head tilted up, and eyes closed.

'Is that where he died?' he interjected, coming awake. 'Somewhere with houses *and* horses?'

Her voice, though still faint, was stronger now.

'Hor-ses in . . . hou-ses.'

'Good God!' exclaimed Fidelis. 'That is it. Horses *in* houses! Where do you find horses living in their own houses, Cragg?'

I shrugged.

'A stable, I suppose.'

'Precisely. And who has a stable at the edge of the Moor and not far from the Bale Stone?'

Then I saw it too.

'I'll be damned! John Barton!'

'Yes. She is speaking of Peel Hall Stables.'

'But what association is there between John Barton and Zadok Moon? We have never suspected such a thing.'

'We do now, Titus!' he said. 'We must go there. We shall ride over at once and this poor girl shall come with us to identify the villains.'

But it was not going to be as easy as that. Mrs Biggs rose from her chair and moved to stand in front of the door. Her face was set in grim determination.

'My Lord Mayor has committed Barbara to be held in this house, Mr Cragg. She cannot leave.'

'Madam, Barbara must come with us.'

'I cannot allow it.'

I adopted a stern but reasonable tone.

'I'll take the responsibility upon myself but, if it will persuade you to stand away from the door, I'll send for Oswald Mallender and the Parkin brothers to accompany us. The girl will be deemed to be in their custody while absent from your house.'

To this plan, and after a little more argument, Mrs Biggs gave her grudging assent and so I sat down to write a note to Mallender requesting that he assemble his forces. Fidelis, meanwhile, went out to collect transport – horses for himself and me, and Peter Wintly's sprung cart for the girl and Elijah, who had agreed to come along in case of need. When I had sent my note by hand of the Biggses' kitchen boy, I asked Barbara to tell me something of her story, and how she had first become acquainted with Tybalt Jackson.

No start in life could ever have been less promising than hers. In a whisper at first, but with increasing confidence, she told how she had been born on a slave ship amidst the horrors of the Middle Passage and was saved from certain death by the ship's surgeon who had taken her mother out of the slave deck when her labour-pains came on and put her into his quarters to give birth. He had had his eye on a profit, however, since when they arrived at Barbados, he had sold the mother and child to a former sea captain who put the mother to whoring. The child had grown almost into a woman when the captain died of a fever, and she and her mother were sold off again. This time her mother had been bought by a planter and taken away to work in his fields. Then she herself was sold to a ship's bosun that wanted a girl for his bed on his next voyage.

That voyage had been to Liverpool. Once on land she ran away and found shelter in one of the cellar-dwellings in the streets around the dock, where many of the negroes and Irish of the port clustered. But she had no money and before long there was nothing for it but to sell herself on the streets. Tybalt Jackson had picked her up one day and, after taking her to bed at an inn – in a most kindly way, she said – he had questioned her earnestly about her former life.

The story had an extraordinary effect on him. Jackson's lust had quickly given way, it seemed, to the fondest feelings for the girl. As he listened to the shame and indignities of her birth and upbringing, he had been filled equally with outrage and pity. He said he had never realized until now that the Trade was such a cruel abomination, and that he would like to save her, and wished that she stay with him as his companion. If she would agree he asked, for the sake of propriety, that she put on a boy's clothing. And that had been the guise in which she had come with Tybalt Jackson to Preston.

At length the horses and the cart arrived. As we were gathering ourselves to go out to them, the negro girl caught hold of my arm.

'Amy,' she said.

'I beg your pardon?'

'It's Amy, Sir. My name that I was given from a baby in Barbados. I like it more than Barbara.'

Her voice, which had become free and clear by now, sounded lilting and musical.

'Very well, Amy,' I replied. 'You shall be Barbara no more.'

The oppression of the day had intensified, and the air felt dense, as if intermixed with some thickening agent. Only insects thoroughly enjoyed it, buzzing and spinning around our horses and ourselves. I noticed Suez, who had somehow escaped the eye of Matty at my house, sniffing around the churchyard as we jogged past on our way towards the northern road. I called him and running joyously towards us he was soon trotting along at my side.

It was a ride of some twenty-five minutes, during which I entertained Fidelis with the complete story of the hoard of silver, Marmaduke Flitcroft's unflattering appraisal of it and my discovery of where it had come from.

'Treasure!' I laughed when I had finished. 'I think the word was invented to make fools of us. The silver was no more than a thief's miscellany.'

But Fidelis did not take the episode as lightly.

'Well, we were interested in the man he stole from. It follows we must be interested in this thief. I wonder who he is?'

And for the rest of the way, I could not get a word out of him.

The first thing we saw on arrival at Barton's stable yard was a horse standing in the open, saddled and seemingly ready to go on a journey, for there were boxes of leather strapped over its rump and withers. The second thing was John Barton, who darted out of what appeared to be one of the box-stalls at the sound of our cavalcade.

'What do you want?' he shouted, giving a kick to Suez who had bounded forward impulsively to greet him. 'Clear off! What the devil are you – sight-seekers? We are conducting business here.'

I dismounted and only then did he recognize me. A moment later he took in the presence of the other horsemen, first Fidelis and, now coming up, the bulky figure in the dirty scarlet coat – Sergeant Mallender astride a sagging palfrey. The black anger on Barton's face paled. He began to look concerned, and then afraid, for now Wintly's cart carrying Elijah and Amy with the Parkin brothers in attendance had rumbled into the yard. Barton backed a short way in the direction of the box from which he had emerged, but quickly thought better of it and commenced a rapid diagonal retreat towards one of the doors on the opposite side of the yard, tracked more cautiously now by Suez.

'Hey!' cried Mallender, descending from his jade as soon as it came to a halt and stumbling after Barton. 'We want to have a talk with you. There is a witness here we want to show you to.'

But Barton had disappeared into a horse box, and Mallender was making urgent gestures to the Parkins to follow him. I myself made directly for the box Barton, it seemed to me, had been trying to divert us from. I entered and saw that it served as a tack room, and that a man was standing there in a cowering attitude. In spite of the heat he was dressed in a big travelling coat and riding boots, evidently ready for the journey on which he would ride, I presumed, the waiting horse outside. At once I jumped forward, seized him by the collar and pulled him out into the yard.

'We have him, Luke! Finally, he stands plain before us. For here I present to you, if I am not very much mistaken, the man we have all been so desirous to meet: Mr Zadok Moon.'

A triumphant feeling had risen inside me, but the mood was not to last. The fellow made no attempt to get away as Fidelis came and stood by my side. His face wore a sly, knowing smile.

'I am afraid, Titus, you *are* very much mistaken. May I on the contrary introduce you to someone else: Mr Moreton Canavan of Liverpool?'

At that moment a rumble of thunder rolled around the sky.

Chapter Twenty-eight

∞

JOHN BARTON, SKULKING in a horse box on the other side of the yard, had given himself no way out, or so Mallender thought. With grim satisfaction the Sergeant planted himself obstructively in front of the box that he'd seen Barton enter, with Suez in attendance at his feet, and waited for the Parkins to come up, whereupon they all went boldly in. After a short interval, they came out again, looking baffled.

'No one in there,' Mallender said, 'not even a horse.'

I had by now conducted Moreton Canavan back to the tack room, telling him he must stay confined in there for the moment. He was trembling and complied with a docility that surprised me. I bolted the door on the outside and beckoned Quick to join me there.

'Guard this door, Elijah,' I said. 'The fellow cannot be allowed his liberty.'

Standing with his legs apart and arms folded, Quick formed an implacable barrier to Canavan's escape, while I turned back to look across the yard.

'Wait! See there!' I shouted, pointing to the dormer-window immediately above Mallender's head, where a dim face had appeared. 'He's at the window. There are lofts above the horse boxes.'

Mallender spotted a ladder propped up against a corner of the yard. He sent the Parkins to fetch it and, while waiting, peered warily through the stable door, then paced with fuming impatience in front of it. The two constables made clumsy work of handling the ladder, letting it fall and tripping over it before finally running it across the yard and erecting it under the window. Jacob put a foot on the lowest rung while Esau cautiously climbed up and peered through.

'Nowt to see, Mr Mallender,' he called.

'Open the window, and get inside!' shouted the Sergeant. 'Be quick about it.'

Esau was far from quick about it: he was reluctant to even try it. But after further urgings and threats from the ground he attempted to prise the window open with his fingers. He found he could get no purchase.

'Can't, Mr Mallender. I'll need a crow.'

'No you won't. Smash it.'

'What with, Mr Mallender?'

Mallender cursed and picked up a loose cobble lying near his feet. This he hurled upward but missed his aim and the stone, instead of hitting the window, cracked against Esau's skull. With a cry of surprise the constable lost his footing and slithered down towards his brother, who was still holding the ladder's foot. Esau bowled Jacob to the ground and the two lay in a heap, Jacob on his backside and winded, while Esau rubbed his injured head.

Meanwhile John Barton was taking his chance. The loft ran along the whole length of the stable building, no doubt with trap-doors in the floor for the dropping of clean hay into the stables below. One such door had enabled Barton to get up to the loft and now another, at the extreme end of the building, let him down again into the one where one of his fastest running-horses was quartered – none other, in fact, than Mayor Grimshaw's pride and joy Molly, The Flanders Mare. It was on this animal, bridled but lacking a saddle, that Barton now exploded into the open. He was bent so far forward that he almost lay on the horse's back, as he kicked her flanks and rode like a madman for the yard gate. In a moment he had gone, with his sallow cheek jammed against the horse's neck, and his lean legs clamped around her sides.

'I'm after him!' said Fidelis, running to his own mare and remounting.

'You'll never keep up,' I called. 'That's a racer he's on.'

'But he's bare-backed,' Fidelis shouted over his shoulder as he turned the horse. 'I'll keep him in sight. You follow on.'

As he kicked on and was away I shouted that I would. Shortly after that a few spots of rain began to fall.

Divided into two hinged sections arranged vertically, the doors of individual stables can swing together, or separately, as desired. In daytime the lower part is bolted and the upper opened wide, so that an animal may stand for hours with his head sticking out, watching the passing show. Several of John Barton's charges were doing so at this moment.

Quick and I unbolted and swung open the upper door of the stable that contained Canavan and called on him to present his face. Mallender and the Parkins joined us as the merchant's face appeared, looking wary and a little bewildered at the turn of events that had unexpectedly made him a prisoner. He placed his hands on the top edge of the half-door and stared out.

I returned to the back of Wintly's cart, handed Amy to the ground and walked her on my arm back towards Canavan. I placed her in front of him, though being careful to keep her out of his reach.

'Amy, do you recognize this man?'

'I do, Sir.'

'When did you see him last?'

'He was one of those with my master's body when they put him on the stone table.'

'One of the three men you saw?'

'Yes, there were three of them.'

'Was this man one of those that had assaulted Mr Jackson before that, and killed him?'

'I don't know. But he was there.'

'Was it him that damaged Mr Jackson's face?'

'I don't know. It happened inside . . . over there.'

She gestured towards Barton's cottage, which stood across the far end of the yard, linking together the two rows of stable boxes.

'That one that rode away just now – do you know him?'

'Yes Sir, he was one of those that took the body up to the wild place.'

'Do you know his name?'

'No.'

'It's John Barton. Did your master ever utter the name to you?'

'No Sir. I've never heard that name before.'

I turned to Canavan.

'This girl states that she saw you taking the body of Tybalt Jackson away from here at dead of night, with John Barton and another. Have you anything to say?'

Canavan glowered. It had been discomfiting to hear himself accused but he had evidently decided that his best course was to keep his counsel.

A skinny youth, with greasy black hair and a face peppered with pockmarks, now wandered into the yard carrying a rake. I recognized Bobby, the boy that I had seen exercising a horse along with Barton just after the body of Jackson was discovered. I strode over to him and took the rake from his hand.

'Bobby is it? Are you stable boy here?'

His mouth twitched and he grunted in a way I took to be yes.

'And what is your full name?'

This time he opened his mouth but another burst of thunder, like a distant cannonade, rendered his reply inaudible.

'What was that, boy?'

''S Robert Roberts.'

'And do you know me, Robert Roberts? Do you know what I do?'

'I reckon so. You find out about the dead people. What happened to them.'

'That's right. Now, I want you to come over here and look at this man. I want you to tell me what you know about him.'

Roberts looked dispassionately towards Canavan.

''S been here since end of last week. Mr Barton's guest, like. 'S all I know 'bout him.'

'Not even his name?'

'No. What's this about?'

'Have there been any other guests here at the same time as him?'

'Yer, other chap went, though. 'S morning.'

'Do you know *his* name?'

'Never heard it. Is this about that body on the Stone?'

I ignored the question.

'Do you know where this other man has gone? Which direction he rode in, for instance?'

'North, he went.'

Robert nodded his head in the direction he meant.

'Up the great road. Left some time this morning, early.'

'What was his horse like?'

'Grey gelding with a braided tail.'

I went across to Barton's cottage to find some writing materials, and there composed a note to James Shuttleworth Esq of Barton Lodge, the nearest county magistrate. I requested that a hue and cry be raised after one Zadok Moon that had headed northward towards Lancaster on a grey gelding and was suspected of murder. However, as there are magistrates who hold the office of Coroner in a degree of contempt, I called in Oswald Mallender to sign the note. One can never play it too safe when dealing with the gentry magistrates, who on the one hand resent Coroners and on the other rarely put themselves to the trouble of acquainting themselves with the minutiae of the law. I heated the sealing wax while the Sergeant applied his name in a cramped, painstaking script, then seized the paper, folded it and dripped the wax.

What, all this time, had been happening to Fidelis?

He had given hot pursuit across the Moor in the direction of Cadley. Barton was an excellent horseman but even he could not keep a horse going at full pace with no saddle or stirrups, and Fidelis had little difficulty in holding him largely in view. But then, like a chased fox, the quarry went to ground.

It happened when a sharp bend in the way ahead had temporarily made Fidelis lose sight of Barton. He kept up a canter along the road, just as it snaked past Cadley Place, and it was another few minutes before, reaching a straight stretch and seeing no horseman, he understood what had happened. He wheeled around and trotted back.

Barton, it would appear, had seen his opportunity at – of all places – the house of the late Pimbo. He had turned in at the gate, ridden up the carriageway and hammered on the front door. They took him into the house willingly enough, knowing Barton and having little reason to think him anything but a friendly visitor. But no sooner was he inside than he frightened the women with loud shouts, and eventually took one of the maids by the throat until she fetched the keys to the gun room and the saddle room.

By now Fidelis had looked in at the gate of Cadley Place and recognized Barton's lathered and tethered horse. He scanned the house, and saw no figure in any of the windows, but he knew Barton must be inside. What, though, was he doing?

Fidelis hesitated. Rain was falling in larger drops now, but the air was otherwise still so that spatters of water on the shrubbery leaves could be individually heard. He was weighing up the advisability of a frontal approach to the house, and deciding against as he would be at a disadvantage if Barton were looking out. It was better, he thought, to remain on watch.

Wintly had cracked his whip and driven his cart out of the yard. Moreton Canavan, Elijah and Amy were aboard with Esau Parkin who was still in attendance on Amy. Meanwhile his brother rode the luggage-laden horse belonging to Canavan, which before our arrival had been on the point of conveying him away, presumably to Liverpool. The brothers were deputed by Mallender to deliver the two prisoners back to town – Amy at the Biggses' and Canavan to be lodged in the cells below Moot Hall, with an appointment to go before the Bench in the morning, as Mallender and I, with Suez careering dangerously around my horse's feet, followed the cart as far as the main road, where I suggested to Elijah that he go back to Fidelis's house and await developments. The Sergeant, however, was not for going back. He was red in the face and breathing excitedly from the knowledge that he was still in the heat of the action, and in pursuit of murderers and desperate men.

'I shall ride with you, Mr Cragg,' he said.

At this meeting of lanes, a faint track across the Moor branched off towards the race course and from fresh hoof prints in the ground I saw that this was the way Barton, followed by Fidelis, had taken. According to my promise, I must take it myself – but not, I preferred, in the company of Mallender. I said:

'Between us, Dr Fidelis and I will comfortably catch him and take him, Sergeant. You may rely on it. Meanwhile hadn't you best join the hue and cry up the north road and make sure in your own person that Zadok Moon is arrested?'

Mallender considered the question, then fell in eagerly with my suggestion. Of course, as the hue and cry had been raised at his own formal request, he certainly ought to be present at any taking up – and receive the credit for it. So he bade me farewell and urged his poor mount into a shambling trot up the road that led to Lancaster. A little relieved I turned my own hack into the branching lane, and set off at a fast trot to catch up with Fidelis. Suez, recovered from his kick and full of alacrity, bounded along in my wake.

We soon joined the racecourse and were heading towards the Bale Stone, when the dog started to bark and shot ahead towards the monument itself. At the course's nearest point to the Stone I pulled the horse up and listened. Suez was barking furiously but beneath his shrill yaps I could hear the calls of a human voice strangely stifled, and not a little desperate. I walked the horse up the bank and across the open ground towards the Stone. From its other side I could hear the noises of a struggle, mixed with oaths. Then, coming to the brambly outgrowth that concealed the place where I had found the sack of Pimbo's silver, I was surprised to see the feet, legs and wriggling rear end of a human being. The forward part of his body was thrust deep into the bush, not in a comfortable way, for he was struggling to get himself out, and signalling his distress with cries and curses. As if to help him out, Suez had now got a mouthful of his breeches and was tugging at them. I immediately dismounted and, pulling the dog away, lightly kicked the calf of the stuck man's leg with my boot. His writhing ceased instantly.

'Who are you?' I asked.

I interpreted the muffled response to be, for God's sake, let me be hauled out. I therefore took hold of his legs and began to pull. At first nothing happened. The fellow was – as I later learned – stuck fast by his coat and waistcoat on thorns and protruding roots.

His head was inside the narrow rabbit burrow and he had thrust his arms further inside, so that he was quite unable to get elbow purchase or bend his arms to push himself out. As Suez danced and yelped around me, I braced my legs, took the strain into my back and heaved. Slowly at first, and bringing most of the bramble bush with him, he came sliding out.

It was a young man, who climbed stiffly to his feet. He had a scratched, blood-streaked face and heavily soiled clothes. I knew him instantly. So indeed did Suez, who wagged his tail and thrust his nose familiarly into the man's crotch, being used to seeing him every day: his late master's craftsman-jeweller.

'Mr Ambler!' I exclaimed as he struggled sheepishly to his feet. 'What a surprise.'

He avoided my gaze, shifting his feet and mumbling something about trapping rabbits.

'Rabbits, is it?' I enquired. 'That's a tasty dish in the hands of a good cook, which I believe your mother is.'

I had already seen the truth, though I did not want Ambler to know that. I told him instead that I was pressed for time and must go on, but there was a matter respecting the goldsmithing business, and the future of Pimbo's shop, that I would like to discuss with him. Would he, I asked, be kind enough to attend me in the morning at my office? He brightened up at this and said he would. Then I sent him on his way.

As Suez and I picked up the trail of Fidelis and Barton, lightning flashed across the sky, followed by a smack of thunder and a rumbling chain of reverberations. The air, which all day had been so heavy, was charged now with energy and excitement. On my part, too, I felt a sense of relief as I kicked my horse to pick up its speed. The collection of silver from Pimbo's strong room that I had found under the Stone – why it was there and what I should do about it – had been weighing a little on the back of my mind all day. Now quite unexpectedly I felt sure of the truth.

I drove the horse as hard as possible along the lane that wound its way across the Moor to Cadley. Coming to the inward gate of Cadley Place, I saw a horse secured to its post: Fidelis's sleek and distinctive animal. I dismounted, attaching my own mount in the same way, and tying Suez similarly by a length of rope from the saddlebag. The gate itself was closed and secured to the post with baling twine in a complicated manner, so I vaulted over it and ventured into the carriageway.

I had advanced no more than a few steps when Fidelis's arm shot out from a thick clump of bushes and hooked me into his hiding place. The rain was falling steadily now, but the storm for the moment held its peace.

'See there?' whispered my friend.

He pointed to Barton's horse, standing close to the front door of the house with its reins tied to a climbing plant. The animal, I noticed, was now furnished with a saddle.

'He's in the house and he's armed,' Fidelis went on. 'I was just on the point of walking up to the house when a maid came out with the saddle. He sent her to put it on the horse while he pointed a gun at her from inside the door. I saw the gun-barrel. He's getting ready to fly.'

'Does he know you're here?'

'He knows someone's here: he was aware of being followed. He's been shouting out, making threats against the women inside and calling on me to show myself. I've shut both gates and tied them with some baling twine that I found. I put in some complicated knots: he will not undo them easily.'

Now the front door of the house opened and two figures edged into sight: they were Barton and a woman that he was pushing before him like a shield. He held a hunting gun in one hand while gripping his hostage tightly above the elbow with the other. The hostage was Ruth Peel. He was aiming to get behind the horse, but she was making it difficult, struggling and giving out cries of indignation. The rain, falling harder now, blurred our vision but it seemed that suddenly the horse-coper clubbed the woman viciously over the head, for she ceased to resist. He lifted and deposited her face down over the crupper, checked the girth straps and swung himself into the saddle.

The horse wheeled and I touched Fidelis's arm in warning: we were not well placed to stop him, having no firearms, and being a little too far from our own horses. In a moment, as we watched helplessly, Barton had ridden towards the out-gate but instead of trying to open it he simply put his horse at it and leapt into the lane. It was an easy jump for such a horse but one which never-theless nearly jolted the girl off. Barton, though he still gripped the musket, managed to haul her back into position across the crupper, and immediately made towards our own horses tethered to the in-gate. Running up, we saw him begin loosening the horses from the gate-post, intending no doubt to take them with him far enough to make a clean escape. He had not, however, reckoned with the temperament of Grimshaw's mare – nor with the tenacity of Suez.

No doubt remembering that earlier kick, the dog was enraged by John Barton's appearance and he let fly a furious volley of growls and barks, leaping on his hind legs at the end of the rope that restrained him. In a couple of seconds the rope came loose and, free to move, he dived at the feet of Barton's high-strung horse, nipping at the fetlocks and hooves so that the animal, who was already unnerved by her proximity to two geldings, spooked and finally kicked out. A crack of thunder added to the confusion and all three horses suddenly bucked and reared, and I saw one of Barton's feet slip from the stirrup, causing him to cant sideways and let go the weapon in his hand. As it clattered to the ground, the woman was also finally dislodged from her place athwart the horse, and landed in an untidy heap on the ground.

We broke from our cover and ran forward. Fidelis got hold of Miss Peel and plucked her from further danger while I seized hold of the gun. Barton was still trying to bring his horse under control.

'Dismount, Sir!' I shouted, 'or I shall blow your damnable brains out.'

I put my finger to the trigger and levelled the weapon until it was pointing to a spot exactly between his eyes. I was shaking furiously but, at that range, I could hardly have missed. Barton, having regained control of his mount, looked down at me, his wormy lips apart, his face muscles drawn tight and his eyes narrowed. There was a moment in which he considered his chances, but it was a very short one. Then he kicked one leg up and over the horse's head and descended to earth.

Chapter Twenty-nine

∞

D AY WAS BECOMING evening as Fidelis and I made our way back across the Moor towards Preston, with a sullen John Barton tightly roped around the wrists and riding between us. Before our departure we had brought Miss Peel into the house and revived her with the help of a smelling-bottle. She was weak and unsteady, though Fidelis found the bodily harm to be superficial. He bandaged her injured head, then settled her at the parlour fireside, with an order to the servants to give her a Jamaica ginger infusion, or a ginger posset with white bread for her shock. He promised to return on the morrow.

The storm clouds cleared as quickly as they had gathered and now warm, watery sunlight made the land glisten. Abreast once more of the Bale Stone, I turned to Barton and said,

'So tell me, Barton: why did you mutilate Jackson's face? And why did you stab him with the wooden stake?'

Barton's habitual expression was sullen, but now it was a good deal sullener.

'I know nothing about it,' he uttered. 'I'll say no more.'

And, for the time being, he didn't. In thirty minutes' time we had come up Friar Gate, crossed Market Place and dismounted at Moot Hall where I asked for the Mayor to be sent for, or any member of the magistrates' Bench that happened to be in the building. A few minutes later Grimshaw himself came hurrying out to us.

'I hope this is not one of your trivialities, Cragg. I have grave matters in hand. I am writing letters to London about the issue of my bond by which we shall finance the Guild.'

'I have brought John Barton to you, Mr Grimshaw.'

'How do, Barton? Good God, man, is that my Molly you're riding? You have her in the devil of a lather.'

The enquiry elicited nothing but a scowl. I said:

'I am delivering this man a prisoner into your hands.'

Grimshaw looked at Barton in surprise, noticing for the first time his bound wrists.

'What on earth? A prisoner? What is this, Cragg?'

'It is murder, Mr Grimshaw. He is suspected of killing Tybalt Jackson.'

'Great heavens! But we have already had a fellow brought in today on that charge. What has John Barton to do with it?'

'A joint enterprise is suspected. He should appear before you tomorrow with Moreton Canavan to answer. There is also a third man.'

'A third man? This is a gang, then?'

'The third is Zadok Moon.'

'Moon! The one Pimbo accused of – what was it? Fraud?'

'Yes, the same. He's fled along the northern road, and is perhaps making for Scotland. I hope by now that Mallender has taken him, and that he too will be brought before you.'

'Well, I look forward to meeting the fellow at last, as he appears to be certainly a villain. But I have no time to discuss this now.'

He looked at the prisoner severely.

'Well, Barton, I am appalled at your treatment of my mare. Do you presume to use her as a mere riding horse?'

The horse-coper would not look at the Mayor, but shuffled his feet with his eyes cast down.

'Very well,' said Grimshaw, 'if you will say nothing in your defence: I mandate your committal to the cells, and order you to appear before the Bench tomorrow morning.'

He jabbed Barton in the chest with his finger.

'You can state your case then, man. And in the meantime I shall take Molly back. You have lost my confidence and I'm damned if you shall have her to train any longer. Bring him in.'

No sooner had the Parkin brothers taken Barton inside than their superior officer Mallender arrived fresh from the hue and cry. His laden horse approached us with whistling breath and staggering legs and, with much to-do and head-shaking, the Sergeant got himself to the ground. He had no one with him.

The hue and cry, Mallender told us, had caught a man at Garstang, which stands on the old Roman road about half way to Lancaster. They were sure it was their quarry. He was at the largest inn, trying to bargain a fresh horse out of the landlord in exchange for the lame one on which he had earlier ridden into town. The landlord was asking for additional money, which this stranger either did not have, or would not pay. On their arrival the pursuers produced old Shuttleworth's warrant, took the man up and asked to see his limping horse, which indeed was a grey with a braided tail, exactly according to the description given on the warrant. It was at this point that Mallender arrived and himself took charge of the prisoner.

'I examined the gentleman in the inn parlour,' Mallender said. 'I was surprised to find him angry, passionately angry, you know. He called me names that I would not care to repeat, and others that I did not even know the meaning of. I said that I suspected him of being Zadok Moon, and a murderer, but he denied it flat. Said he had never heard of Zadok Moon. I challenged him to prove that he was not the man and he brought out letters and documents and a captain's commission, all addressed to or concerning one with a different name, and nothing on him in the slightest degree to do with any Zadok Moon. So I was forced to the conclusion, Mr Cragg, that he was not Moon at all. It was a question of crossing scents, and the hounds picking up the wrong one half way through the hunt, with the mischance that the two men had the same kind of horse.'

'Perhaps,' I said. 'But tell me more about the man you questioned. You said he had a captain's commission. You mean in the militia?'

'No, Sir, a sea captain, he said he was. On his way back to his ship in Lancaster it seems. Well, the more I saw of him, the more he looked like a ship's captain and the more I heard him, the more he sounded like a ship's captain. So I agreed that he was indeed, as I just said, a ship's captain and not Zadok Moon, as named on the warrant. So I was obliged to let him go on his way.'

'I am nevertheless interested in knowing what his name was.'

'Well, I've got it writ down safe. Let me see.'

He searched one coat pocket after another until he brought out a slip of paper. This he unfolded and handed across. I held it up for Fidelis to see and, though written in Mallender's crabbed handwriting, it was quite clear: the name was Edward Doubleday.

Canavan, and now John Barton, were due to appear before the Bench at ten next morning. Thinking to get Canavan's statement taken down before the Mayor could trample over the ground with clumsy questions, I decided to go immediately to him in the gaol below Moot Hall. Fidelis came with me and Suez, sticking to my heels like a shadow, followed us.

We were taken to the cell by Tarlton, the Moot Hall turnkey – a man of few words, and none of them pretty. The cell, though it was gloomy and dank enough, was the largest and best at the town's disposal, as might befit a prisoner of the merchant class. What light there was came from openings in the wall immediately below the ceiling – you would hardly call them windows – which gave onto the outside world at ground-level and were fitted with grilles. Canavan had had Tarlton bring candles and his boxes down to him, and, casting off his travelling clothes, had dressed himself in the trappings of respectability – an embroidered waistcoat, full wig, lace in the collar and cuffs, buckle shoes. It was attired in this way that we found him, sitting on his plain bed of wooden planks.

'I shall need to take your statement for my inquest into the death of Mr Tybalt Jackson,' I told him. 'Will you tell me what happened at the Bale Stone last Thursday night?'

He shook his head slowly.

'I don't know. I wasn't there. You can't prove the assertion.'

'We found you at John Barton's stable less than a mile from the place where the body was found.'

'I was only there to see about my running-horse. Barton is its trainer.'

For a moment Suez distracted us by playing his old trick of worrying at our shoe buckles. Having tried Luke Fidelis's and been pushed away he turned to those of Canavan, who raised his foot to kick the dog. But, as he did so, Suez pulled the shoe clean off his foot and took it into a corner of the room.

'Allow me to get that for you,' said Fidelis, and went to the corner, where Suez was shaking his prize from side to side and growling. At first the dog wanted to play tug of war, but Fidelis eased his mouth open and rescued the shoe, which he carried back to Canavan, but did not hand it over.

'You say we cannot prove you were present at the death of Mr Jackson,' he said. 'Well, I believe I can prove, at the least, that you were there at the Bale Stone when his body was laid out upon it.'

'How?' challenged the prisoner. 'Not from the deceiving black boy that had travelled with him. People now tell me it is really a female. Nobody's going to believe what a black harlot has to say, any road.'

Fidelis showed the shoe first to me and then to Tarlton, who was lingering in the doorway listening with dropping mouth to all we said.

'It is not only the girl – her name is Amy by the way – that says you were there, Canavan,' Fidelis went on. 'This shoe says you were. Just show me the other, if you please.'

He went down on one knee like a pageboy and waited until Canavan, who suddenly looked bemused, raised the foot that was still shod. Fidelis removed the shoe leaving Canavan with his stockinged feet planted on the dirt floor. Fidelis held the two shoes together.

'See? They are very alike, and much of a size, but they are not a pair of shoes. This one—'

He held up the shoe that Suez had pulled off Canavan's foot for closer inspection.

'We can show that it belonged to poor Mr Jackson whom you and your confederates so wickedly murdered, because we have recovered the pair to it from Jackson's corpse. This one came off his foot during the struggle to heave his dead or dying body onto the Stone. In the same struggle one of your own shoes also came off and in the dark you accidentally recovered, and put on, the wrong shoe. The correct one – your own errant shoe – was found by Mr Cragg the next day having been kicked under the Stone. It was made for you I think by the shoemaker Mr Thomas Truss of Liverpool. Now, for a witness of what we have found in your possession this evening, let us enlist Mr Tarlton.'

He now showed both shoes to the turnkey, asking him to take careful note of the differences between them, before handing them over to me.

'I suggest you wear your riding boots to court, Canavan. The shoes will be produced in evidence, and will be enough, I fancy, to see you hanged at Lancaster Castle.'

I sat in the Turk's Head, alone for the moment except for Suez, who lay in an exhausted sleep across my feet. I was waiting for Fidelis and Elijah to join me. My body felt as tired as the dog's, but my brain was working furiously. It was repeating over and over the memory of the moment at which I had stood pointing the gun straight into Barton's twisted, calculating face. Would I have done it – shot him full in the forehead – if I had had to? I could not say, and still cannot. I had never killed a man or even fired a gun and have always detested violence. Yet the question tormented me like an aching tooth.

Fidelis arrived, on the other hand, in excellent humour. Elijah was with him.

'What a stroke of luck that he had put on the shoes, just for us! You've ascertained that one of them was the pair to the shoe we found at Flat Rock?'

'Yes. It has the same "T.T." stamped inside. Odd that Moreton Canavan wasn't to be found in the shoemaker's register.'

'But he was!' exclaimed my friend. 'Remember, one of the customers was, we thought, a Mr Martin Carman? Allow for deaf ears and hasty handwriting, and what might you have?'

'I am with you, Luke. Moreton Canavan! How very stupid we were to miss it. But at any rate we have done good work this afternoon.'

'Yes, but are you not aggravated that the fool Mallender let Doubleday go?'

I had ordered a bottle, glasses and pipes, which now arrived at our table. I made an effort to banish my obsession and attend to the matters of the moment.

'I suppose there is no doubt that Doubleday was another

conspirator in the death of Tybalt Jackson. Amy saw three men, but surely there must have been four of them.'

Fidelis was inclined to think so.

'Doubleday was the captain of *The Fortunate Isle*, the ship Jackson was looking into. I cannot be sure of his connection with John Barton, but he certainly knew Moon and Canavan, as they were both investors in his ship.'

'We don't know that certainly, in Moreton Canavan's case.'

'Why else was he here in Preston? You can't believe the tale that he came to look to his running-horse! He must have travelled here with Moon as criminal conspirators to stop Jackson's mouth and protect their crime.'

'But gents, what was their crime?'

The question was Elijah Quick's, and it was a pertinent one. He went on,

'Now, I have asked folk here and there in the town about this Zadok Moon, and they all say he's been engaged in some fraud, but nobody knows what the fraud is.'

I said, 'We must assume it is to do with *The Fortunate Isle*, as that is the ship Jackson's company was engaged with.'

'We heard the old sailor at the dock tell me she was not a Liverpool ship,' said Fidelis. 'He also said she was unlikely to stand up to a Guinea voyage. Perhaps she never had to, and it was all a game of pretending.'

We were not carrying Quick with us.

'Why pretend to go on the voyage?' he asked. 'These men wanted money, and to get it, must they not trade?'

'The ship was insured, Elijah,' I said. 'As a total loss, with a full cargo, she was worth 15,000 guineas. We heard at the inquest that Doubleday had reported the ship a total loss. But what if, in reality, she wasn't? What if she returned, let us say disguised under a false name and false colours?'

'They would hang for that if discovered,' observed Fidelis. 'And to protect themselves they might murder first.'

'But why did they beat Jackson about the face?' I went on. 'I don't understand that. Was it in the hope he would be unrecognized, so the word would not get back to his employers that he was dead?'

Fidelis shook his head.

'They could hardly hope for that. They left him lying in the clothes he'd been seen wearing in Preston.'

'And there's the wooden peg they drove into his chest. What of that?'

'They did that, Sirs, because they wanted people to accuse Amy.'

This was Elijah, speaking deliberately and with a taint of bitterness in his voice.

'They wanted it to look like witchcraft . . . you know, what an African would do.'

It sounded possible, especially remembering that Amy was then thought to be a boy.

'What will happen to her, Mr Cragg?' Elijah asked me.

'She will be released, now. There is no reason to hold her any longer. She will be required to give her evidence here in Preston about what she saw – at the inquest and the Magistrate's Court – and then, I suppose we must get her back to Liverpool.'

We puffed at our pipes and considered for a few moments. Then Elijah touched my arm.

'Don't worry, Sir. I will take her back, and I will look after her. She saw bad things at that Stone, and she must be treated kindly.'

'That is good of you, Elijah,' I said.

But his mention of the Bale Stone had set my mind on another path – the path Suez had taken on our way across the Moor in the afternoon.

'Luke, I haven't told you what Suez and I found at the Stone today.'

I related how the dog had alerted me to muffled cries, and the sounds of struggle, just as we rode along the part of the racing track that passed the Stone.

'And there I came upon the legs of the man sticking out of the bramble bush, kicking like a swimmer. I simply pulled him, as you pull a cork from a bottle – and who d'you think he was, Luke?'

Fidelis had been leaning towards me, listening intently and without laughter. His reply caught me by surprise.

'I think he was Michael Ambler, Titus.'

Next morning I attended the Magistrates' Court at the early hour of eight. The hearing was preliminary to a session in front of a Grand Jury, at which the men would be committed, or otherwise, for trial. Grimshaw was making a journey to Manchester as a guest at a banquet later in the day and he wanted to arrange matters before he left.

First Barton and Canavan, standing together in the dock, were asked to state their names, after which Grimshaw formally told them that they were held in the matter of the death of Tybalt Jackson, and that they would continue to be held until the Grand Jury here in Preston determined whether they must go to the Assizes in Lancaster.

'I see the Coroner is in court,' he then observed without great enthusiasm. 'Mr Cragg – doubtless you can enlighten us as to the future of your own deliberations on the death of Jackson.'

I told the court that the inquest into the death of Jackson would be held next day.

'All matters about this sad and violent death will be aired,' I said, 'with both of these men required to give evidence. Afterwards, if the indications are towards foul play, I shall forward the inquest papers to the Bench as usual.'

There was little enough that Grimshaw liked about the

Coroner's jurisdiction, since it operated outside his control. But he well knew that, even if he were not going away to Manchester, he could not raise a Grand Jury in time to trump my inquest. He extended the present session by a few minutes with some blustering interrogatory remarks towards the two prisoners, which they refused to answer, and at last, exasperated, he ordered that they be kept in custody pending the inquest and then a Grand Jury meeting later in the week. After that we all, except the prisoners, went to our homes and to breakfast.

Chapter Thirty

∞

NOT AN HOUR later I was sitting in my dining room with the greater part of the meal inside me, when Matty came in.

'If you please, Sir, the young man from the goldsmithy's in the hall asking to see you.'

Michael Ambler! I had forgotten all about our appointment. I rose from the table and hurried out, finding Ambler looking unaccountably pleased to see me. His face and hands still showed signs of the scratches he'd sustained in the briar patch, but he was otherwise washed, with hair scraped into place and wearing what may have been his best suit of clothes.

'Come into the office,' I said, leading the way through the door that stood between the domestic half of the house and the business half. I found Ambler's demeanour disconcerting. It was I that had summoned him, yet he chose from the start to treat the meeting as his own, and one that he was eager for.

'Oh, thank you for seeing me, Sir,' he said. 'I am right glad now that you found me out rabbiting on the Moor yesterday, for it proves to you how badly we are reduced, my mother and me. We are that short at home, we haven't had a penny-piece come in by way of money since Mr Pimbo died.'

'Michael, we are not here to—'

But Ambler was not to be interrupted. He had prepared the

rudiments of a speech and he was set on to delivering it, walking restlessly this way and that in front of my desk.

'What I'm here to ask you, Mr Cragg Sir, is would you kindly reopen the shop as soon as possible? I know that I can manage my part of it, if Mr Hazelbury will do his part. That is all we ask, I know he says the same. I am a good craftsman, me, and the best there is in this town by a mile. And Mr Hazelbury knows the books and that, so with the two of us we can do it – we don't need the boss, or anyone else. We are ready and we can do it.'

I told him, with a touch of impatience, to stop pacing and sit down.

'I am sorry, Michael, but I cannot do as you ask. I have already told Mr Hazelbury that it is out of the question.'

Puzzlement creased his face.

'But I thought you said he could—'

'I have allowed Mr Hazelbury to deal with customers that want to redeem their pledges. But, Michael, you mistook me if you thought that means I am going to continue the business as before. It may never be possible to do that. The estate cannot be finally settled until the will is proven but, even then, I would feel it my duty to dispose of the shop on Mrs Pimbo's behalf to a new owner.'

'A new owner, Sir? Then I shall be that man! I have the ambition, and the—'

'No, Ambler. I am afraid not.'

I had raised my voice, thinking this fantasy must stop at once.

'You see, I am aware of the reason you had your head in that rabbit hole.'

'I know, Sir. I told you.' Ambler was stammering now, and reddening. 'I was setting a snare.'

'You were not, Michael. You were looking for something.'

I went to the side-board in which I had stored the sack of unclaimed silver pledges. I brought these out and plumped them down on the desk with a metallic clank that caused Ambler's eyes to widen in shock.

'You were looking for this sack, I think.'

I pulled it open and began bringing the objects out – the salt, the marrow spoon, the little jug and the buckle.

'How did you get those?' he gasped. 'Who brought them to you?'

'I will only say that they were recovered from the same rabbit hole in which I found you stuck yesterday afternoon. You were trying to recover them, I suppose.'

Ambler's eyes darted to right and left. He knew now he was in a corner. I went on, unrelenting.

'Furthermore, I know the precise origin of these things. Each one is an unredeemed pledge that Mr Pimbo kept in his strong room, to which you somehow gained access, and from which you took them. How long have you been a thief, Ambler? Did you take them piecemeal as and when the occasion arose, or did you rather sweep them up in one haul?'

He swallowed, making the Adam's apple bob up and down in his neck as he struggled to compose himself. When he spoke, his voice was low and full of husks.

'It's a long story, Mr Cragg. And it's all because, and only because, I was there when it happened.'

'When what happened?'

'When Mr Pimbo was shot, Sir.'

I was engaged in picking out a small snuffbox from the sack, but immediately swung round in astonishment.

'Great heavens, Michael! You *saw* Mr Pimbo shot?'

'I didn't say I saw it. I said I was there.'

'I see. Then you had better tell me your long story – and make it the whole truth, mind!'

It came out haltingly at first, but Ambler was cocksure by

nature and gradually as he unfolded the tale his crest began to rise and his tongue grew more valiant. On the fatal morning, he had come early to the shop, being behind with his work on a bespoke golden watch-chain. He let himself in at a little before six o'clock thinking the premises empty, and went directly to his work-bench. Only a few minutes had passed before he jumped at the sound of a gunshot coming from Pimbo's room, and went to the closed door with its pasteboard sign forbidding entrance. He called out and knocked and, getting no response, tried the door, which was unlocked. So Ambler had entered the room and there found his employer sprawled across his desk, with blood in every direction. Ambler stood aghast until thought prevailed over horror, and he concluded that Pimbo had deliberately killed himself – there was no one else in the room but the dog – and so he began looking around for a letter Pimbo may have written to explain this terrible action. He found none, but he did see that the door of the strong room was open, with both keys in place. Curiously – for he had never been allowed to do so before – he went inside.

'It was then that I felt the hand of the Devil on my shoulder, Mr Cragg, truly I did. He was a-whispering in my ear that my master was dead, and what was to stop me now from taking his place as Preston's goldsmith, and becoming a gentleman, which is every man's desire who has a head on his shoulders? Of course I had no money, as yet, to realize my ambition – but what of these silver oddments that people had pawned and never claimed? Mr Pimbo always kept the Pledges Book under his own control and I knew that if these things disappeared no one would ever know what became of them.'

Seizing the Pledges Book he matched the ticketed objects on the shelf with entries in the book, and selected only the things that he thought no one would miss. These he put in a linen bag that he fetched from the shop and, when he had what he considered a sufficient collection of silver, he locked the strong room, returned Hazelbury's key to its place in the drawer under his writing desk and lodged the bag out of sight beneath his work-bench. He had gone back into Mr Pimbo's room one last time to make sure there was no trace of his presence there, when he heard Hazelbury arriving for work. Now his escape was blocked and he had a vision of himself discovered in the fatal room, with his employer's corpse and a discharged gun – circumstances that, combined with the fact that he had stolen from the strong room, would undoubtedly lead to an appointment with the public executioner.

Ambler had spotted the office's key in the lock on the inside of the door. Quickly he locked that door and waited. But as the apprentice came in to work, and then a succession of early customers, he knew that he had missed the chance of a simple escape. He bitterly regretted not having made his presence immediately known to the Chief Cashier, but now it was too late. With just the dog for company he had waited an hour or more in the agony of suspense and then heard the locksmith's first efforts to open the door. Stationing himself against the wall that would be behind the door when it swung open, he waited. And, when at last the crowd came bursting in, he took his chance and contrived to escape unnoticed, in the exact manner that Fidelis had sketched to me when propounding his 'Hidden Man' hypothesis.

'I couldn't believe my good fortune, Mr Cragg,' said Ambler. 'There was so many coming into the room, and all looking in the one direction, that no one took notice of me when I slipped out from behind the door. I was just one of the crowd that was crying ooh, and shoving, and gawking at the dead man, until someone chased them out.'

'When did you take the silver out of the shop and hide it in the rabbit burrow?'

'At dinnertime. No one saw me. I used to go a lot to the Bale Stone as a lad and I knew about the rabbit hole. Unlike most, I was not afraid of it. It was the best place I could think of to hide the silver.'

'How did one of the spoons get into the hands of Adam Thorn? Did you give it to him?'

'I got the spoons before. It was them that gave me the idea to steal the rest, when I had the chance that morning. It was months earlier. I'd been into the strong room for some unworked silver sheet and I saw them and took them. They were the first things I put in the rabbit hole, but I must have dropped one on the Moor, and that were the one Adam found.'

'Why did you do it, Michael? Why, finally, did you steal?'

'I am no hardened thief, Sir. You must believe me. But I needed money for my future plans. I thought with Mr Pimbo dead I must do all I could to make the shop *my* shop.'

'Was that all? You said you had "plans".'

'Must I tell, Sir?'

'You must.'

'I meant to be Miss Ruth Peel's husband too.'

'You wanted to *marry* Miss Peel?'

'Yes, Sir, for is she not a fine woman?'

'I would not dispute that. Did she know of your plan?'

'No Sir. I was biding my time.'

A silence fell between us. The conversation with the love-sick Ambler had made me gloomy. Yes, it had shed light on events in Pimbo's office on the morning of his death. But I was oppressed by doubts about how I should use the revelation. If I passed the information to the magistrates, Michael Ambler would be sent for trial on a charge of larceny against his lawful employer, and would likely be hanged.

He seemed to read my thoughts, for he asked,

'What are you going to do, Sir?'

'I will give it further thought, Ambler. In the meantime do not go chasing after Miss Peel. Confine any chasing you do to rabbits – understood?'

'Yes, Sir.'

'There is one more thing that I would like to know. Why did you not replace Mr Pimbo's key to the strong room, in his pocket, or wherever it was that he kept it?'

'I was afraid of the body, Sir. I had meant to put it into his pocket, but I hesitated and slipped it in my own pocket instead. Then I forgot about it.'

He reached into the pocket of his coat and took out a generously proportioned brass key, which he placed without another word on my desk.

I dined that day with Luke Fidelis, who insisted on treating me at the White Bull Inn on the north side of Market Place, which boasted Preston's grandest kitchen. We ordered a fine meal of spit-roasted eels in their own sauce, then broiled pigeon-squabs and finally a dressed knuckle of veal, with which we drank Bordeaux wine in cork-stopped bottles – part of a consignment imported before the French war broke out and kept in the inn's cellars. As we waited he told me of his visit to Cadley Place in the morning, and that Miss Peel was recovering well.

As we began dinner I was burning to ask one question.

'How did you know in advance that the legs of the fellow I pulled from the bramble bush were those of Michael Ambler?'

'I didn't know. It was a rational guess. I realized you must have run into either the actual thief of the silver, or his accomplice, or a third party who had found out about the silver's hiding place. On the assumption that it was the person who himself stole the silver, I was pretty sure that person was Ambler. No one else, of all the people who might have had access to Pimbo's strong room, would in my judgement have had the courage or the desire to commit such a theft.'

'Not Hazelbury, I agree. He is honest. But what of the apprentice?'

'I think he's too young, and too timid. If it had been money that was stolen I would have considered him but I do not think he would know what to do with plate. Ambler would. He was the smith. And he was confident of himself.'

'Would it surprise you that I know, in advance, that you are right?'

'How?'

'What I tell you is in confidence, Luke, for I don't know yet how to proceed.'

'I'll tell no one.'

So I set out everything that I had just learned from Michael Ambler.

'And that's why I must congratulate you, Luke,' I finished. 'Your "Hidden Man" in the Pimbo case was real, after all. My difficulty is that I find it hard to condemn Michael Ambler to death for this, though he admits he is a thief and, worse, has stolen his master's property.'

'What then is your decision?'

I sighed.

'In confidence?'

'Of course.'

'I shall do nothing.'

Elizabeth shut her book with a sound between a slap and a pop.

'There! I've finished it, Titus. I've finished *Pamela*.'

We were lying in bed, each with candles beside us to light our books. I looked up from mine.

'Are you pleased with the ending, my love?'

'No, indeed I am not, though I never had so much fascination for a book before.'

'That I noticed.'

'Yet now I feel utterly unsatisfied.'

'Why?'

'Because she marries him, the silly chit, so that all is to be happiness for ever and ever, which I cannot believe.'

I took off my spectacles and said,

'Novels, or so I understand, must always have a happy end.'

'Nonsense. It is not a happy end that *I* look for when I read a novel, but a just one; one in which good people are vindicated and villains are punished.'

'Is that not what happens in *Pamela*?'

'Not at all. The second title of the book is *Virtue Rewarded*, but I don't see a reward for Pamela. She marries a man who has proven himself a terrible satyr. In one attempt to seduce her – and I do not exaggerate, Titus – he dresses himself up in the guise of an old serving woman, so that he can slither safely into her bed. If she hadn't locked her thighs together the story would have ended there. And he's supposed to be a fine gentleman! I could never have forgiven that, or respect him after. Yet Pamela does.'

'Mr B is landed and rich I suppose?'

'Of course, vastly.'

'That would explain it. Her reward is to marry money.'

'You are cynical. For real happiness she should have married the Reverend Williams, and that would have been quite just besides.'

'Williams? Who is he?'

'You must read the story. Mr B has a clergyman's living in his gift: Williams holds it, and is in love with Pamela himself. He is a good young man and would have made her a good husband, I think, for he loves her tenderly, and not savagely like Mr B.'

'Well, well!' I said.

I had suddenly remembered my earlier conversation with Michael Ambler, which I had not told her about. 'Didn't you say the other day that the circumstance of Ruth Peel and Phillip Pimbo was just like that of the novel? I have learned today who it was that played the role of the wretched Reverend Mr Williams in this real story. Michael Ambler told me he wanted to marry Ruth Peel.'

I gave her a full account of how Ambler had been in the next room when Phillip Pimbo had died, and seized the chance to steal from the strong room because he would need the capital to carry out his plan to take over the goldsmith's shop.

'It was then that he confided to me his other plan: to marry Ruth Peel. In your story this man Williams wished to marry the woman who resisted the lust of her master, a man who was also *his* master. It is an example of the coincidence of literature and life, is it not?'

'The difference is more instructive than the parallel, Titus. Pimbo died, unsatisfied. Miss Peel received an uncertain and circumscribed inheritance. And Ambler is not good, like Mr Williams, but a thief and a liar. Oh well! However hard we may try, we cannot turn our true lives into moral fables.'

'Characters in novels are the toys of their author, my love, and must stand for whatever that author decrees. We, on the other hand, are the playthings of Fortune, who is morally blind.'

'Blind, and deaf, and a mountebank, or so I think. Consider poor Amity Thorn. She thought her husband had found Benjamin Peel's hoard: all he really had was one stolen spoon.'

My own participation in the matter of Tybalt Jackson's death ended with the inquest, over which I presided at the White Bull Inn in front of as great an audience as I have ever attracted. A verdict of murder by Moreton Canavan, John Barton, Edward Doubleday and Zadok Moon was returned, and so the matter was passed to the magistrates and then, a few weeks later, to the Assizes.

John Barton did not stand trial, for he was quick to turn King's Evidence and testify against the merchant and the sea captain, by which he saved his own miserable skin. He told how he himself had been the mysterious second guest at the Lamb and Flag, and brought Jackson to the stables that fatal night, on the promise that he would meet Canavan and Edward Doubleday and hear from the captain's very lips the story of *The Fortunate Isle*'s sinking. Jackson did indeed meet the two men; he also met his death when the captain, supposedly in a fit of anger, attacked his head with a hatchet.

According to Barton, the disposal of the body on the Moor had been Canavan's idea, which I found implausible. The body had been arranged on the Bale Stone under the pretence of a savage ritual which, so the villains had hoped (and as Elijah Quick had surmised), people would think had been performed by the victim's negro servant. It was Barton, not Canavan, who possessed the knowledge of the Moor and its history; only he would be likely to suggest the Bale Stone as a suitable place for a pretended satanic ritual. But Barton was the Crown's witness, and these considerations counted for nothing.

Doubleday did not stand trial either. Having evaded capture at Garstang, and despite further attempts to run him down, the captain got clean away into Scotland. From there it was thought he travelled to Holland, and beyond the reach of English legal authority. Canavan from the dock tried to follow Barton's example in placing all blame on Doubleday for the killing, but he failed to convince the court. Standing alone in the dock, he was speedily convicted and, a few days later, they hanged him at the gallows on Lancaster Moor. I did not attend: the legal rituals of death do not attract me.

It was not until some time after this that we learned the truth about *The Fortunate Isle*. A ship trading from Ireland had put into Liverpool with the name *Looby* painted on her. An old mariner sitting by the dock loudly said he'd be damned if she weren't *The Fortunate Isle*, that had sailed for Guinea a year before. Captain O'Riordan, who had been in command of the *Looby* a bare two months, claimed to have little knowledge of his vessel's previous history. One of his crew, however, gave a statement to Messrs Willoughby and Pickle of Lombard Street, marine insurers, that he had served on the ship three years continuously and that she had indeed put to sea previously as *The Fortunate Isle*. He also attested that she had never sailed further from Liverpool than the port of Galway on the western coast of Ireland. So it was that we knew the whole of her Guinea voyage, and supposed end in the Spanish Main, had been a sham.

And what of Zadok Moon? He seemed to have disappeared into the air.

Chapter Thirty-one

∞

FOR THOSE OF us who could remember the festivities of twenty years earlier, the Guild Merchant that opened on the penultimate day of August 1742 was composed of all the expected elements. In between the pompous bestowal of freemanships and promulgation of by-laws, the town danced and drank its way through the fort-night. The trade guilds put on their fancy hats and decked their carts with flags, banners, fruits and flowers and rode through the streets singing and posturing as they had always done – except for the goldsmiths, who had had the festive spirit somewhat knocked out of them by the Pimbo scandal. There was also a string of assemblies, masquerades, banquets, concerts and balls for the quality, who came to town from near and far to enjoy themselves, and at the same time court popularity by distributing largesse to the poor.

Yet the grand programme that Grimshaw had hoped to pro-vide contained rather too many disappointments for the Mayor's own comfort. All summer he had barked for the Guild whenever he spoke in public. He had boasted that Mr Thomas Arne would return, with a performance of music from his opera *The Judgement of Paris*; but Arne it seemed had better things to do. Grimshaw then claimed to have engaged a company of players, 'that has lately acted to public acclaim in Dublin, with Mrs Woffington and Mr Garrick', according to the programme he had printed. The town

333

was agog for their appearance on the Preston stage, but the celebrated pair, like Thomas Arne, let us down. Many explanations were bandied around: Arne had made enemies in Preston during his last visit; Garrick was opening a new season in London; Peg Woffington was with child; adverse winds had pinned their ship inside Dublin harbour. The more likely truth was that insufficient fees had been offered, for this was, in truth, a relatively impoverished Guild following the loss of all the money entrusted to Pimbo.

There was further humiliation for the Mayor at the races, when The Flanders Mare came last in the main prize, as well as in his attempt to stage the first bear-baiting to be held in the town for fifty years. He had made a grand announcement that a full-grown animal had been obtained with great difficulty for the purpose, but a committee of ladies was immediately formed against the project and the brown bear was left to sit out the fortnight in a cage in Market Place, a passive object of vulgar curiosity.

'The poor old Bruin!' exclaimed Elizabeth when we had strolled out one morning after breakfast to see him. 'He is so alone. I am glad we put a stop to the baiting. It would have been quite barbarous.'

The bear sat on his haunches, chained by neck and leg, regarding those who had gathered to gawp at him. As his head swung slowly this way and that, I discerned a depth of wary sadness in those eyes. There were patches missing from on his pelt where the fur had moulted. The flies that sported themselves around his nose received from time to time an ineffectual swipe from his paw.

Feeling ashamed that my own kind should so traduce and maltreat such a noble creature, I turned away and immediately noticed a large dark-skinned man in fantastic costume passing among the crowd and giving out hand-bills. His face was painted in stripes and he seemed to be clad mostly in coloured feathers. It was not until he came nearer that I recognized him.

'Look!' I said, turning Elizabeth in his direction. 'It's Elijah Quick.'

We hurried over to him and shook his hand heartily. His smile was as broad and candid as ever.

'What brings you back to Preston, Elijah? And why are you dressed as a bird?'

'I am a living advertisement of tonight's play, Mr Cragg. I am not a bird, you see, but a savage.'

He handed me one of the bills.

To be played at the PRESTON GUILD in the Playhouse, Mr Robert Southerne's excellent Tragedy OROONOKO or THE ROYAL SLAVE, by the Old Ropery Players of Liverpool, being the FIRST TIME IN THE COMPANY'S HISTORY that it has presented this celebrated drama.

'We have tickets,' I told him. 'Shall we expect to see you acting on the stage?'

'No, Sir. I would willingly do so but the actors will not let me, which is very perverse as the play has numerous Africans in it, and I am the only natural black man amongst them all, and the only one that was ever a slave.' He sighed at the contrariness of his fellows. 'But all I do is see to the costumes and direct the negroes when they dance in their black paint.'

I asked after Amy.

'She is here, with me, Sir. We have hardly left each other since we returned to Liverpool.'

'Then you must both come to the play,' exclaimed Elizabeth, 'and we will all sit together.'

I had not seen this famous play before. It told of a noble African prince tricked by a sea captain into slavery and conveyed to

Surinam. At the colony are many slave-owning planters whose wealth attracts young ladies from England in search of husbands, which provides the comic part of the plot. There is nothing comic about Oroonoko, however. He is a modern Othello, a great warrior who leads a slave revolt and is briefly reunited with his beautiful wife, who has also been enslaved. But she has become the object of the Governor's lust and after the revolt's defeat she still resists him. So, though Oroonoko manages to contrive the death of the hated Governor, the pair of noble slaves themselves suffer, in the final scene, their own bloody and terrible deaths.

At several moments during the performance I glanced at Amy and Elijah, and never had I seen two people more enwrapped in a play. They groaned as the slaves were brought ashore in chains, cheered as the flag of revolt was raised, wept as Oroonoko and his wife fell into each other's arms, and cheered again at the thrilling defiance in Oroonoko's words:

'Thou hast roused the lion in his den; he stalks abroad and the wide forest trembles at his roar.'

Yet when the rebels were betrayed and defeated, and Oroonoko was once again loaded with chains and forced to look on as the Governor renewed his attentions towards the lady, I thought mournfully of poor, caged, helpless Bruin. At the last, most of the audience was in tears over the bloody fate of the great black hero and his love, but none sobbed more than Amy and Elijah.

In our party, as well as Elijah and Amy, were Elizabeth's parents. Immediately in front of us sat Luke Fidelis with a handsome companion beside him who had travelled for the occasion from Liverpool – Belinda Butler.

'You know this is the first time our players have done the play,' Mrs Butler had told us as we waited between acts. 'It is thought too strong at Liverpool, you know, with so many Guineamen growing rich with every new completion of a voyage, and not wanting to have their consciences pricked. New men, not true seamen, my late husband called them.'

'He did not engage in the Trade himself, then?' asked my ever curious mother-in-law.

'Oh no, he plied Leghorn and the Levant. He would never consent to trade in human beings. Silk and spices and Italian marbles, that is what he carried.'

Later our conversation turned to admiration of the actors. Oroonoko was splendid even in slavery, and his wife was beautifully woebegone. The fellow playing the evil-hearted, black-bearded Governor gave an especially fine turn, his strutting lasciviousness drawing whistles and cat-calls from the pit whenever he walked on stage. I glanced at my playbill to see his name: Mr Goodenough. He was, I thought, better than his name.

After the third interval I became aware that, whenever the Governor appeared, Luke grew more attentive to the action, leaning forward and watching his performance with singular concentration. Then, at the play's conclusion, while both Elijah and Amy were having their tears mopped by Elizabeth, he stood up and, taking my arm, pulled me to my feet.

'Come, Titus. There is someone I want you to meet.'

He would not explain further as he summarily abandoned his companion and hurried me away, forcing a path against the tide of departing playgoers that filled the aisles and doorways. A few moments later I found myself behind Fidelis at the door of the tiring room which, without ceremony, he pushed open and marched through.

Arranged along the walls were tables, loaded with pots of face-paint, wig-stands, and boxes overflowing with false moustaches and paste jewellery. Each table had a looking glass set above it, and the actors sat in front of these, dabbing some sort of cream on their faces and scrubbing them, as they were fawned over by knots of ladies and gentlemen. Fidelis walked around behind their backs, scrutinizing each mirrored face as he came to it. At last he spied one with no admirers in attendance, which was understandable since this was the one that had played the villain of the piece: Mr Goodenough.

Fidelis approached him.

'May I congratulate you on your acting, Sir?' he said.

'Thank you, I have enjoyed taking the part,' said the actor smoothly, without looking around. 'Most gratifying it was, to hear the cat-calls.'

'You are used to playing the villain, I think.'

'I am, Sir. You have perhaps seen my Iago at Liverpool? My Captain Bluffe? My Dorax, in *Don Sebastian*?'

'No. It was indeed in Liverpool that I saw you, but in another role.'

Goodenough stopped working on his face. There had been something in the doctor's voice that disturbed his complacency.

'When was that?' he asked.

'In the early part of June, I think.'

'There you must be mistaken. We suffered a fire and the theatre was shut for all of the month.'

'It was not in the theatre, Mr Goodenough, but in Pinchbeck's Coffee House that I saw you acting the role.'

Now Goodenough was visibly shaken. He turned and looked hard at Fidelis, and then at me, but did not seem to recognize either of us.

'I do not understand. What role are you talking about?'

'The role, Sir, of Zadok Moon.'

Goodenough's mouth dropped open.

'I . . . I, well . . . What role is that? I do not know it. I haven't—'

'It is the role you played at the behest of Mr Moreton Canavan in the coffee house, at the time of our meeting there. It was a small part, but an important one, in which you were brought across the room in the character of a merchant called Zadok Moon, in order to accept from my hand a letter written to the said Mr Moon by my friend here, Coroner Titus Cragg, of Preston.'

'I know nothing of this letter.'

'I have no doubt that is true, at least to the extent that you did not read it. I recall you scurrying out by a back door when you thought I would not be looking. You met Canavan outside, I suppose, and passed the letter directly to him, according to his instructions. Had you played Zadok Moon before, though? I fancy you had, if only for an audience of one: I mean, Mr Phillip Pimbo of Cadley Place.'

Goodenough sat half twisted around in his chair, with his eyes fixed on Fidelis's face. I understood that he was trying to read it, while wondering how many of the facts he could afford to admit, and how many to omit.

'What are you going to do?' he asked in a low, croaking voice.

Fidelis smiled and, like an indulgent uncle, patted Goodenough on the back of his shoulder, then turned to me.

'What *can* we do, Titus? Should Goodenough pay for the crimes of Zadok Moon? Or is that a case of hanging the horse instead of the highwayman?'

The surprise of my friend's coup of recognition had abated a little, and I tried to take a clear view of the case.

'No,' I said, after a moment's consideration. 'In such a case I think one should continue to pursue Mr Zadok Moon himself, as it would be hard to prove that his impersonator was anything but an unknowing recruit.'

'Oh thank you Sir!' burst out the actor, his manner beginning to regain its previous assurance. 'I was, as you say, an innocent in all this. Poor but pure, you know. We were all out of work with the playhouse closed. One does what one has to at such times.'

Fidelis offered Goodenough his hand.

'Extenuate no more, Sir, lest you make matters worse again. I wish you luck!'

Goodenough shook with Fidelis, but grimaced at his words.

'I beg you, Sir, do not wish me that in here. It is bound to lead to misfortune. Gross, gross misfortune!'

Returning to the theatre, we found it nearly empty.

'Where is Mrs Butler?' said Fidelis. 'I had quite forgot her.'

'Gone with Elizabeth and the others back to Cheapside, I am sure,' I said. 'My wife is charmed by her and we are all to have a bite of supper, which I hope you will join us in.'

He said he would, and we walked directly to Cheapside, where we found Mrs Butler among the party. The dining room's sideboard was dressed with a great steaming ham, that had been boiling all through our excursion to the theatre, a dish piled with buttered potatoes and a big boat of parsley sauce. Elizabeth carved and distributed the ham while I made sure the wine decanter was handed around the table. Then, when everyone was served and we began to eat, I told of the extraordinary thing Fidelis and I had learned about the actor that we had all just witnessed playing the wicked Governor of Surinam.

'He had impersonated none other than Zadok Moon, Phillip Pimbo's cheating business partner,' I told them.

'Does he know this Moon, then?' asked my mother-in-law. 'And can he lead you to him? If so, the last and biggest mystery of all that Pimbo business will be revealed and all the gossip can stop, for which I for one will be grateful.'

I doubted the veracity of the last part of her statement, for Mrs George enjoyed gossip as much as anyone I knew.

'In that case, Mrs G, you will be glad to know there isn't any mystery now about Zadok Moon,' said Fidelis, who was in the process of cutting his sliced ham into small dice.

'Apart from the mystery of where he's hiding himself,' I said.

'Oh, no. That is solved.'

Mrs Butler turned to him and expressed the surprise of us all.

'Solved, Luke? You know where he is to be found? If so, for heaven's sake tell us. We are on tenterhooks.'

Fidelis put down his knife and contemplated his handiwork for a moment. Every little cube of ham on his plate was an identical size.

'Zadok Moon,' he said, 'is to be found nowhere.'

'Is he dead then?' gasped my mother-in-law.

'No, not dead. He does not exist, Mrs G. He never existed. He was imagined. He was a phantom.'

I was again a link or two behind in my friend's chain of thought.

'Imagined? Not imagined by the actor Goodenough, surely!'

'No, he was imagined by the late disgraced Moreton Canavan. That deceitful and devious merchant now emerges, with Captain Doubleday, as the real instigator of the fraud against Pimbo – of the other one, too, for there were two frauds. The attempt to diddle the insurers Willoughby and Pickle out of fifteen thousand guineas was the other. The crimes are linked, of course, because Canavan needed Pimbo's money first to buy a leaky old ship, *The Fortunate Isle*, and then to insure its fictional Guinea voyage, during which it would suffer a pretended slave revolt and be reported sunk far from the land.'

'But why did he invent for himself a business partner?'

'Moon was not supposed to be a business partner. Canavan sought to protect himself, in case the scheme were ever discovered, by making out that he himself was just another innocent investor, like Pimbo, and that the real embezzler, then, would be discovered to be Zadok Moon – a man who could not be arrested and turn King's Evidence against Canavan, or anyone else, since he did not exist. But also, for that very reason, Canavan had to hire someone, when required, to be Zadok Moon. He was lucky enough to find Goodenough at Pinchbeck's Coffee House, an actor used to taking on roles of doubtful honesty.'

'I see it all now!' I burst out. 'Of course! His original, and most important job was to play the role for Pimbo. He made one or two secretive night-time visits to Cadley Place in the guise of Zadok Moon, and did so, naturally, at Canavan's behest. I did not previously understand why they did not meet in Preston, but now I see that Canavan would not risk exposing a mere actor to the people in the real business world. He'd have no difficulty fooling poor gullible Pimbo in his own home, but he might not stand up to scrutiny by members of the Corporation, should he meet any of them.'

'He did not reckon with the insurance company investigator, though.'

'No, Jackson was incalculable. He was altogether too intelligent and determined.'

'I'm right sorry for Mr Jackson,' said Elijah who, until now, had been listening carefully to all that was said. 'To have died just as he saw the light and understood that his whole profession was founded on nothing but injustice and cruelty. He did not have the chance to make amends.'

He spoke his words with all the solemnity of a preacher so that the company, as if in meditation, fell into a few moments' silence. This was broken by Mrs George.

'But what about this actor, Goodenough? Should he not be taken up? Put on trial? Something should be done to him, surely.'

'I fear he will escape punishment,' I said. 'The proof of his part in the affair has been extenuated, by time and circumstance. Pimbo cannot give evidence. Doubleday has gone. Miss Peel saw the man she thought was Moon, but only in the dark of night, and cannot swear to what he looked like. Fidelis here is the only witness who clearly saw Goodenough playing Moon, but in that case he merely took delivery of a letter addressed to someone that did not exist. It is not a crime of much weight.'

There was another pause as the company contemplated the doubtfulness of the legal process. Then, quite unexpectedly, old Charles George, who had seemed throughout to be attending more to his food than the conversation, rose unsteadily to his feet with his glass in his hand.

'Titus,' he said in booming tones, 'it has been a long pull but you've got there, you and your clever friend. As a member of the profession myself, I am glad to say it was also done with the help of shoemakers. But however it was done, you have got to the bottom of the reasons for the death of poor Phillip Pimbo, and I must congratulate you on that. Truth, Sir, that is what counts: more than punishment, more even than retribution. Without truth, and the trial of truth, there is no justice and no advancement. I salute you, son-in-law, with all my heart. You are a credit to this town. You are an apostle of truth!'

It was a strange moment that I had not looked for. Everybody around the table rose, lifted their glasses and drank my health. I felt myself reddening and, as I got up to reply, stammering.

I did not say much – only that Mr George was right, of course. My job was not to find and punish malefactors but the more significant one of asking questions and finding true answers. In this I always relied on the help of others – my darling Elizabeth, my household, the invaluable Furzey – and in this case, even that pest of a dog Suez, of which I had somehow grown increasingly fond.

'But not least of all, I owe rather a lot to my friend who has twice the brains and twice the energy of myself. You all know to whom I refer. May I ask you therefore to join me, now, in drinking his health?'

And we did, turning as one to him, lifting our glasses in the air and saying with one loud voice,

'Luke Fidelis!'

As we called out his name I noticed Mrs Butler looking at our friend, and caught the very faintest gleam in her eye.